Praise for *The First Day*

"Over the years, Marc Levy has seduced millions ~f ~~~~~ What's his secret? He writes about quintessential the~~~~, ~~~~ ~~ ~~~~ ~riendship, and the mysteries of life, in an a~~~~~~~~~

"Marc Levy's latest novel, *The* ~~~~~~~~~~ ~~~~ ~~~~~~ ~~ scope, a page-turning adventure story.'

"A wonderful read." *Le Parisien*

"One of the literary successes of the summer. Against the backdrop of a scientific adventure, *The First Day* is also a love story." *La République*

"From one end of the world to the other, *The First Day* is a poetic and philosophical saga. As always, Marc Levy creates brave, bold characters who dream with the hopes and imagination of youth." *Télé 7 Jours*

"In the vein of his previous books, *The First Day* is a sensitively written novel, full of adventures that will surprise and delight readers." *20 Minutes*

"Marc Levy has found a recipe for success: heartwarming novels that flirt with fantasy, told with simplicity. His books are accessible to all and make for great travel companions – even at home on a bookshelf, their pages are dusted with the sand of a summer beach vacation. This summer, *The First Day* carries on the tradition, weaving a love story through a metaphysical adventure." *Ouest France*

"Marc Levy, a former architect, knows how to successfully craft a story woven through with suspense as the action carries the reader to all four corners of the world. He immediately draws us into the atmosphere of the adventure novels we loved when we were young." *24 Heures*

"*The First Day* leads the reader on a journey in time and space, around the world. From the Omo Valley to Africa and Chile, from the Aegean Sea to Paris and Myanmar, Marc Levy weaves together two destinies: she is an archeologist on a mission to discover the first human being, and he is an astrophysicist trying to unravel the origins of the world. This novel is not just a love story, but it is also a page turner that explores these two fundamental mysteries." *L'Est Républicain*

THE FIRST DAY

A novel

Marc Levy

Translated from the French by Sarah Black

McArthur & Company
Toronto

First published in English in Canada in 2011 by
McArthur & Company
322 King Street West, Suite 402
Toronto, Ontario
M5V 1J2
www.mcarthur-co.com

First published in French as *Le premier jour*
by Éditions Robert Laffont

Library and Archives Canada Cataloguing in Publication

Levy, Marc, 1961-
The first day / Marc Levy ; translated from
the French by Sarah Black.

Translation of: Le premier jour.
ISBN 978-1-55278-904-9

I. Black, Sarah II. Title.

PQ2672.E9488P7313 2011   843'.92   C2011-901327-4

Text design and composition by Szol Design
Cover photographs © Richard Hallman, Joy Tessman
and Mark C. Ross, Getty Images
Author photograph © Denis Lécuyer & Marc Hansel

Printed in Canada by Webcom

10 9 8 7 6 5 4 3 2 1

"We are all made of stardust."
ANDRÉ BRAHIC

For Pauline and Louis

Prologue

"Where does the dawn begin?"

I was a painfully shy ten-year-old the first time I asked that question. Our science teacher turned round, shrugged in a defeated sort of a way, then carried on writing up our homework on the blackboard, as if no one had said anything. I stared at my desk, pretending not to notice my classmates' taunting looks; not that they knew any more than I did. Where does the dawn begin? Where does the day end? The sky is lit up by millions of stars we can't see, whose universes we know nothing about. How did it all begin?

As a child, I would get out of bed as soon as my parents were asleep and tiptoe over to the window where, each night, I peered up at the sky through the slats of my bedroom shades.

My real name is Adrianos but everyone calls me Adrian, except in the Greek village where my mother was born. I'm an astrophysicist and I specialise in stars beyond our solar system. My office is on Gower Street, in the Department of Physics and Astronomy at University College London, but I'm hardly ever there. The Earth is round, space is curved and, if you're trying to get to the bottom of the universe's mysteries, you have to develop a taste for travel: always roaming the planet, visiting the most deserted regions in search of the best observation point and total darkness, far from the big cities. I suppose what drove me for so many years to lead a different life from most people – one with a house, wife and kids – was the hope that one day I'd find an answer to the question that has never stopped haunting my dreams: *where does the dawn begin*?

And it's with another hope in mind that I've decided to write this diary: so that one day, someone might find it and be moved to tell my story.

The humble scientist accepts that nothing is impossible. Today, I realise how far I was from that kind of humility, until the evening I met Keira.

What I've been through these past few months has expanded my field of knowledge far beyond anything I could have dreamed of; and everything I thought I knew about the birth of the world has been turned on its head.

First Notebook

The Omo Valley, Ethiopia

The sun was rising over the easternmost point of Africa. The archaeological site in the Omo Valley should already have been lit up by dawn's orange glimmers, but this particular morning was unlike any other. Sitting on a low wall made of dried mud, Keira was cupping her metal tumbler of coffee as she stared hard at the horizon, which was still dark. A few drops of rain bounced off the dry earth, causing the dust to fly up. A boy ran over to join her.

"You're up already?" asked Keira, ruffling his hair affectionately.

Hari nodded.

"How many times have I told you not to run in the excavation area? If you trip, you could ruin several weeks' work. You might break something that can never be replaced. See those pathways, marked off by ropes? Well, imagine they're a big outdoor china shop, with a Keep Out! sign. I know this isn't a very exciting playground for a boy your age, but it's the best I can do."

"It's not my playground, it's yours! And anyway, your shop's more like an old burial place."

Hari pointed at the cloud mass coming towards them.

"What's that?"

"I don't know, I've never seen a sky like that before, but it doesn't look good."

"I want it to rain!"

"Hari! That'd be a disaster! Go and find Melku – I think we'd better get the dig area covered. This time you really can run. Now scoot!" she ordered, shooing him away.

In the distance, the sky was turning pewter; a gust of wind ripped away the cloth protecting a cairn.

"Just what we need," muttered Keira, getting down from the wall.

She took the path to the camp, meeting Melku the supervisor halfway: "If it's going to rain, we need to cover as many plots as possible. Strengthen the grids, get all our men onto it, and we'll ask for help from the village if we have to."

"That's not rain," sighed Melku, sounding resigned, "and there's nothing we can do about it. The villagers are already fleeing."

A gigantic dust storm whipped up by the Shamal was closing in on them. In normal times, this powerful wind that crosses the Saudi Arabian desert would make for the Gulf of Oman, to the east, but these were not normal times and the devastating wind was on a westerly course.

"I've just heard the warning on the radio," Melku continued, seeing how worried Keira looked, "the storm's already swept through Eritrea, it's crossed the border and is heading straight for us. Nothing can stand up to it. All we can do is run for the hills and find shelter in the caves."

But Keira refused to abandon the dig.

"Keira, those bones you're so fond of have been buried here for thousands of years. We'll dig again, I promise, but we need to be alive to do that. We can't waste another moment, there's not much time left."

"Where's Hari?"

"No idea," answered Melku, looking around, "I haven't seen him this morning."

"Didn't he come to warn you?"

"No, like I said, I heard the news on the radio; then I gave the order to evacuate the camp and headed here to find you."

The sky was black now. A few kilometres away, the cloud of sand was rolling towards them like a giant wave between sky and earth.

Keira dropped her cup of coffee and started running. She veered off the path and raced down the hillside to the riverbank below. By now it was a struggle to keep her eyes open. The dust whipped up by the wind was stinging her face; each time she tried to call out Hari's name, she swallowed a mouthful of sand. But she didn't give up. Groping her way through the thickening grey veil, she managed to locate the tent where Hari came to wake her up every morning; they had a ritual of watching the sunrise together, on top of the hill.

She pushed back the flap to reveal an empty tent. The camp looked like a ghost town: not a living soul in sight. Far off, she could just make out the villagers clambering up the slopes to the hilltop caves. Keira inspected the neighbouring tents, calling out the little boy's name again and again, but the rumble of the storm was her only reply. Melku grabbed hold of her, almost forcibly dragging her with him.

"Too late!" he shouted through the cloth he'd tied over his face, as Keira glanced up to the hilltops. The supervisor had wrapped his arm around Keira and was steering her down towards the riverbank.

"Run, for heaven's sake! Run!"

"Hari!"

"He'll have found shelter somewhere, come on, keep quiet and hold on to me!"

There was a tidal wave of dust close on their heels, gaining ground. Downstream, where the river forced its way between two steep cliffs, Melku spotted a crevice and quickly tucked Keira inside.

"There!" he said, pushing her in deeper.

They only just made it. In a swirl of earth, scree and plant debris, the wave swept over the top of their makeshift shelter. Inside, Keira and Melku huddled together.

The cave was plunged into total darkness as the storm roared over them deafeningly. The sides of the crevice began to shudder and Keira and Melku wondered if they might collapse and bury them alive.

"Perhaps they'll find our bones ten million years' from now: your humerus against my tibia, your clavicle near my scapula," Keira said. "Palaeontologists will declare that we were a couple who lived off the land, or that you were a freshwater fisherman and I was your wife. Of course, the lack of offerings in our burial place means they won't pay us much attention. We'll be classified in the 'schmuck' skeleton category and left to languish forever in a cardboard box on the shelves of some museum or other."

"This is no time for jokes," complained Melku. "And anyway, what *are* schmucks?"

"People like me, who work their socks off to achieve things nobody really cares about; and who have to stand by and watch their efforts being wiped out in a matter of seconds."

"Well, better two living schmucks than two dead ones."

"You can say that again!"

The roaring carried on for what felt like an eternity. Clumps of earth came tumbling down every so often, but their shelter held strong.

Daylight entered the cave again as the storm abated. Melku stood up and held out a helping hand to Keira, who ignored it.

"I'm staying here" she said, "I'm not sure I want to see what's out there." But moments later, Melku heard Keira shouting "Hari!" as she rushed outside.

*

She emerged to total devastation. The shrubs that grew along the embankment had been decapitated; the riverbank, usually ochre, was covered in a layer of brown earth. The river was transporting vast quantities of mud towards the delta, a few kilometres downstream. Not a single tent was left standing in the camp. The village hadn't withstood the assault either: the huts had been blown for tens of metres before smashing against rocks and tree trunks. The villagers on the hilltop were venturing out of their shelters to find out what had happened to their livestock and crops. One woman from the Omo Valley was clinging to her children and sobbing; further off, the members of another tribe were assembling. No sign of Hari. Keira looked all around her: three corpses lay spread-eagled on the riverbank. Her stomach lurched.

"He'll be hidden in a cave. Don't worry, we'll find him," Melku reassured her, forcing her to look away from the carnage.

Keira gripped his arm and together they clambered back up the hill. On the plateau where the excavation site had been, the neatly marked-out squares had vanished and the ground was strewn with debris: the storm had destroyed everything. Keira bent down to pick up a microscope. Her reflex was to dust it off, but the lenses were beyond repair. A bit further off a surveyor's tripod lay overturned, its legs in the air. Suddenly, in the midst of all this wreckage, little Hari's frightened face emerged.

Keira ran over and hugged him, which was out of

character for her – she didn't generally go in for physical gestures of affection. Now, though, she clung to Hari so hard that he was struggling to break free.

"You frightened me to death," she scolded, wiping away the earth stuck to the boy's face.

"I frightened you? All this happens and I'm the one who's scary?"

Keira didn't answer. She looked up and took in what remained of her work: nothing. Even the low mud wall she'd been sitting on that morning had collapsed, battered by the Shamal. In the space of a few minutes she'd lost everything.

"Your shop's gone," said Hari.

"... my china shop," whispered Keira.

Hari slipped his hand into Keira's. He was expecting her to pull away, to take a step back, like she always did, pretending she'd just seen something important, so important in fact that she had to check it out immediately; and then later on, she'd stroke the boy's hair, which was her way of apologising for not being affectionate enough. But this time Keira held on tight, her fingers gripping Hari's.

"It's all over," she said, in a hollow whisper.

"You can dig again, can't you?"

"It wouldn't work now."

"Dig deeper," the boy urged.

"It would be pointless."

"So what's going to happen?"

Keira sat cross-legged on the ravaged ground; Hari copied her, respecting her silence.

"You're going to leave me. You'll go away, won't you?"

"I don't have any work now."

"You could help rebuild the village. Everything's broken. The people from here have helped you."

"Yes, we could do that for a few days, a few weeks at most; but then, you're right, we'd have to leave."

"Why? You're happy here, aren't you?"

"Happier than I've ever been."

"So stay!" pleaded Hari.

They were joined by Melku. Keira shot Hari a meaningful look, indicating he should leave them to talk.

"Stay away from the river!" she called out after him.

"What difference does it make, you're leaving anyway!"

"Hari!" pleaded Keira.

But the boy was already heading in precisely the direction she'd just forbidden.

"Are you abandoning the dig?" asked an astonished Melku.

"I don't think we have any choice."

"Why so negative? It's just a matter of getting back to work. There's no shortage of willing hands."

"Unfortunately it's not just about willing hands, but resources too. We hardly had any money left to pay the men as it was. I was clinging to the hope that we'd make a discovery and fast, so we could get our funding renewed. But now I'm afraid we'll all be laid off."

"And the kid? What are you going to do about him?"

"I don't know," Keira confessed.

"You're the only person he's formed a bond with since his mother died. Why don't you take him with you?"

"I wouldn't get the authorisation. He'd be stopped by immigration officials the moment we touched down in France: they'd hold him in a camp for weeks then send him back here.

"Couldn't you look after him?"

"I'm finding it hard enough to provide for my family as it is, I doubt my wife would agree to feed another mouth. And Hari's a Mursi, he belongs to the Omo Valley tribes – we're Amhara, which makes it very difficult. You're the one who changed his name, Keira, and taught him your language over these last three years; you've as good as adopted him. You're responsible for him. You can't abandon him a second time. He'd never get over it."

"What was I supposed to call him? He had to have a name, and he'd lost the power of speech when I took him in."

"Let's just go find him instead of arguing. Given the look on his face when he ran off just now, I don't think he'll be reappearing any time soon."

Keira's team was gathering around the excavation site. The atmosphere was heavy. Everyone was taking in the scale of the damage. They all turned to Keira, awaiting instructions.

"Don't look at me like that, I'm not your mother!" she fumed.

"We've lost all our belongings," complained one team member.

"People have died in the village, I've seen three corpses down by the river," said Keira, "so your sleeping bag isn't top of my list here."

"We should bury the dead as quickly as possible," someone else suggested. "We don't want a cholera epidemic adding to our problems."

"Any volunteers?" ventured Keira.

Nobody raised a hand.

"We'll all go then," she decided.

"We'd do better to wait for their families to come and collect them; we should respect their traditions."

"The Shamal didn't show any respect, and we need to act before the water gets contaminated," Keira insisted.

So the procession set off.

This grisly task took up the rest of the day. They pulled the bodies out of the river, dug graves a good distance from the bank, and covered each of them with a small pile of stones. Everyone prayed in their own way according to their beliefs, or they remembered those they'd worked alongside for the past three years. At dusk, the archaeologists regrouped around a fire. The nights were chilly and there was nothing left to protect them from the cold. One person stood watch while the others slept close to the embers.

The next day, the dig team went to help the villagers. The children had been herded together; so that the female elders from the tribe could watch over them, whilst the younger women gathered whatever they could to rebuild their dwellings. Everyone was busy and each person knew what needed doing. Some chopped wood, others gathered branches to rebuild the huts, and others were in the fields, doing their best to round up the surviving goats and cattle.

Archaeologists and villagers pulled together, and on the second night after the storm they shared a meagre meal. Despite the sadness and the period of mourning that had scarcely begun, they danced and sang to thank the gods for sparing those still alive.

The days that followed were similar. Two weeks later, nature still bore the scars of the episode, but the village had begun to look normal again.

When the tribal chief had thanked the archaeologists, Keira requested a private audience with him. The villagers' glances betrayed their disapproval at seeing a foreign woman enter his hut, but the chief agreed to the meeting out of gratitude. After listening to his visitor's request, he gave his word that if Hari reappeared he would watch over him until Keira's return; in exchange, she made a promise to come back. The chief signalled that the meeting was over. He smiled. Wherever Hari had hidden himself, he couldn't be far away: these past few nights, while the village was sleeping, a mysterious animal had gotten into the food supplies, and the prowler's footprints looked remarkably like those of a young boy.

On the ninth day after the storm, Keira gathered her team together and announced that it was time to leave the site. The radio had been destroyed, so they had to rely on their own initiative. There were two options. The first involved walking to the small town of Turmi, where, with a bit of luck, they'd find a vehicle that could take them north, to the capital. But getting to Turmi would be dangerous: there was no road to speak of, and they'd have to travel along treacherous mountain paths. The alternative was to head down-river into the low valley; in a few days, they'd reach Lake Turkana. Crossing that would bring them to the Kenyan side at Lodwar, where there was a small airstrip. Makeshift planes regularly did shuttle runs to supply the region; there was bound to be a pilot who'd agree to take them on board.

"Lake Turkana, terrific idea!" said one of the team sarcastically.

"Would you rather climb the mountains?" replied Keira, exasperated.

"Well, there are about fourteen thousand crocodiles lurking in the lake. It's swelteringly hot during the day, and the area suffers the most violent storms on the African continent. Given that we've hardly got any equipment left, we might as well top ourselves now!"

There was no miracle solution. So Keira proposed a show of hands. The lake was the unanimous decision.

Melku would have liked to go with them but he had to make his way back north to his family. Helped by the villagers, they started putting together a few provisions. Their departure was set for the next day at first light.

Keira didn't sleep a wink. She tossed and turned on her makeshift mattress all night. The moment she closed her eyes she saw Hari's face. She thought back to that day when, returning from an excursion about ten kilometres from camp, she'd encountered him for the first time.

Hari had been standing alone in front of a hut, abandoned. No one in sight, just this child staring at her, locked away in his own silence. What was she meant to do? Carry on her way, as if nothing had happened? She'd sat down next to him; he hadn't said anything. Poking her head through the doorway to his pitiful dwelling, she realised that his mother must have recently died. She'd tried asking the little boy a few questions, to find out if he had any family, or somewhere she could take him, but she couldn't get a squeak out of him; just that bright, relentless stare. Keira stayed by his side for hours in silence. Then she got up and set off again. As she walked along, she had a hunch he was following her at a distance and hiding whenever she turned round. Not that there was any sign of him on the path behind her as she drew near the camp. At first, she thought he must have turned back. But the next day, when Melku announced that some food had been stolen, Keira felt a sense of relief.

It was some weeks before they set eyes on each other again. Keira ordered that a meal and something to drink be left out by her tent each night. And, every evening, Melku complained that the food would attract predators. Except that the wild animal Keira wanted to tame looked more like a forlorn and frightened child.

As time went by, Keira became preoccupied by the child's unusual behaviour. At night, inside her tent, she would listen out for the footsteps of the boy she'd already nicknamed 'Hari'. Why that name? She didn't know, except that it had come to her in a dream. Then one evening she decided to wait by the crate where his meal had been left out. This time she'd laid a place for him and the table looked set for dinner for two, in the middle of nowhere.

Hari appeared on the footpath that snaked up from the river. Shoulders relaxed and head held high, he looked proud. As he approached, Keira waved at him and started to eat. He'd hesitated for a moment before sitting down opposite her. And so they shared their first dinner by starlight, and Keira started introducing Hari to his first words in her language. He didn't repeat a single one, but the next day, when mealtime came around again, he recited all the words he'd heard the evening before without making a single mistake.

It wasn't until later on in the month that Hari

showed up in broad daylight. Keira was digging the ground carefully, hoping to make a discovery at last, when he came over to her. Without worrying about whether or not Hari could understand her, Keira explained what she was doing; why it was so important to keep on searching for these tiny fossilised fragments, how each one of them might provide evidence of the way in which human beings had first appeared on the planet.

Hari came back the next day at the same time, and spent all afternoon in the archaeologist's company. He did the same on the days that followed, always turning up with disconcerting punctuality, despite the fact that he didn't own a watch. The weeks went by and, without anybody particularly noticing, the little boy no longer left the camp. When Keira subjected him to vocabulary lessons, at midday and in the evening before mealtimes, he never kicked up a fuss.

Tonight, she longed to hear his footsteps one more time, pacing around her tent, waiting for her to give him permission to enter. She'd have told him an African legend; she knew plenty of those.

How could she leave tomorrow without seeing him again? Leaving without saying goodbye is worse than abandoning someone: silence had always struck her as a form of betrayal. Keira stroked the present Hari had given her one day. A strange object hanging from a leather thong, which never left her neck. It was triangular, smooth and hard as ebony; it was the colour of ebony too, but Keira had no idea if it could really have been carved from wood. The object didn't look like a piece of tribal jewellery. Not even the village chief had been able to determine its origins; when Keira showed it to him, the old man shook his head – he had no idea what it was, and perhaps she'd be well-advised not to wear it. But it was a present from Hari. On being questioned about it, the boy explained to Keira that he'd found it one day on a small island in the middle of Lake Turkana. He and his father had been exploring the crater of an ancient volcano that had been extinct for centuries, when he'd found this treasure.

Keira put it back on her chest and closed her eyes, trying to snatch some elusive sleep.

At dawn, she got her pack ready and woke her team. They had a long journey ahead and, after a frugal breakfast, they set out. The fishermen had given them two dugouts, each big enough for four people. They'd have to go ashore in some places and carry the boats around the falls.

The villagers were all standing on the bank. Just one small person was missing from the roll call. Melku hugged Keira, struggling to hide his emotion. Then the archaeologists clambered aboard the canoes; the children waded into the water to help them push off from the bank, and the current did the rest, carrying them gently along.

For the first few miles, they could see hands

waving from the nearby fields. Keira remained silent, keeping an eye out for the person she still hoped to see. When the river forked, before disappearing between two sheer cliffs, her hopes vanished. They'd already come too far.

"Perhaps it's better this way," whispered Michel, a French colleague Keira got on well with.

She wanted to respond but there was a lump in her throat.

"He'll go back to his life," Michel went on. "Don't beat yourself up about it. Without you, Hari would probably have starved; and the village chief *has* promised to take care of him."

Then, suddenly, as the river wound deeper into the gully, Hari appeared on a tiny strand. Keira jumped up and the small boat nearly capsized. Michel steered it back on course, while his two colleagues complained. But Keira wasn't listening to their protests; she had eyes only for the boy who was squatting down, watching her from a distance.

"I'll be back Hari, I promise!" she called out.

There was no answer from the child. Had he even heard?

"I looked for you everywhere!" she shouted, as loudly as she could. "I didn't want to leave without seeing you again. I'll miss you, little man," she sobbed. "I'll miss you so much. I promise I'll be back, you must believe me, d'you hear? Please Hari, give me a sign, just wave to let me know you can hear me!"

Marc Levy

But the child didn't give her any sign, not even a tiny wave. His silhouette vanished as they turned the bend in the river; so the young archaeologist never saw the boy's hand sketching a tentative farewell.

*

The Atacama, Chile

It's impossible to sleep at night. Every time I'm about to drop off, I get this horrible feeling I'm going to suffocate and I have to sit bolt upright in my bunk. Erwin, my Australian colleague who's used to working at altitude, has given up on sleep since we got here. He practises yoga and seems to cope. I went through a phase of visiting a yoga centre on Sloane Avenue (I was seeing a dancer at the time), but I'm nowhere near good enough to compensate for being up here. When you're five thousand metres above sea level, the oxygen level drops by forty percent. After a few days, you start getting mountain sickness; your blood thickens, your head is heavy, you can't think straight, your writing becomes clumsy and the slightest physical effort burns a disproportionate amount of energy. The people who've been working here longest recommend taking as much glucose as possible. For anyone with a sweet tooth, this would be paradise: there's no risk of putting on weight because the sugar gets metabolised almost as soon as you've swallowed it. The only hitch is that, at five thousand metres above sea level, you lose your appetite. I'm surviving on a diet of chocolate bars.

Time is meaningless in the Atacama Desert. If it weren't so hard to breathe in this vast arid plain, you'd think you were in the middle of any old desert. But we're on one of the rooftops of the world, except that hardly any of that world exists around here: no vegetation, no animal life, just pebbles and dust that happens to be twenty million years old. The air we struggle to inhale is the driest on the planet, fifty times drier than in Death Valley. The peaks surrounding us are over six thousand metres high, but there's no snow on them. Which is precisely why we're working here. Zero humidity makes this the ideal site for the greatest astronomy project the Earth has ever seen. An almost impossible challenge: setting up a giant radio telescope with sixty-four dishes, each one as tall as a ten-storey building, and all of them networked. Once built, they'll be linked to a computer capable of carrying out sixteen billion operations per second. Why? So that we can emerge from the darkness, photograph the farthermost galaxies, discover spaces still invisible to us today, and perhaps capture images of the first moments of the universe.

Three years ago, I joined the European Organisation for Astronomical Research and went to live in Chile.

My office is technically a hundred kilometres from here, at the observatory in La Silla. The region is along one of the largest seismic fault lines on the globe, where two continents meet; two masses of colossal force which, long ago, by pushing up against one another, gave birth to the Andes. More recently, we had an earth tremor here one night. No one was injured but Naco and Sinfoni (all of our telescopes have names) which now need to undergo maintenance work.

The centre's director jumped at this forced period of inactivity to get Erwin and myself to supervise the setting up of the third giant antenna on the Atacama site. Which is why I'm having such difficulty breathing: because of a stupid earthquake I've been sent up here to an altitude of five thousand metres.

Barely fifteen years ago, astronomers were still debating the existence of planets outside our solar system. As I've always said, for a scientist, being humble means accepting that nothing is impossible. A hundred and seventy planets have been discovered in the past decade. All of them were too different, too massive, too near or too far from their suns to be compared with the Earth; or to lend hope to the idea that a recognisable form of life could have developed there... until the discovery made by my colleagues a short while after I arrived in Chile.

Thanks to the Danish telescope installed at La Silla, they saw another 'Earth', located twenty-five thousand light years from our own.

Roughly five times bigger than the Earth, it takes ten years of our time for it to make one complete rotation around its sun. Though who knows whether time there can be divided into minutes and hours like our own? And even if that planet is three times further away from its sun, even if the temperature is colder there, it appears to combine all the necessary conditions for life to exist.

Not that any of this made the headlines: its discovery went almost unnoticed.

Over the past few months, our work had been hindered by various mishaps and breakdowns, and my future was looking uncertain. Without convincing results, my days in Chile were numbered. And yet, despite my problem acclimatising to high altitudes, I had no desire to return to London. I wouldn't have swapped Chile's wide-open spaces and my chocolate bars for the tiny window in my poky office, and the steak and kidney pie with mash served by the pub on the corner of Gower Street, not for anything in the world.

We arrived at the Atacama site three weeks ago, but my body still hasn't become acclimatised to the lack of oxygen. When the centre is up and running the buildings will be pressurised, but in the meantime conditions are gruelling. Erwin thinks I look peaky, he wants me to go back down to base camp. "You'll end up getting really sick," he keeps warning me, "and if you have a stroke, it'll be too late to wish you'd listened to me."

There's some sense in what he says, but giving up now would mean compromising all my chances of taking part in the extraordinary adventure that is unfolding here. Having access to equipment as powerful as this and being part of the team is like a dream come true.

We leave our bungalow at nightfall. It's a half-hour walk to Dish Number 3. Erwin adjusts the settings, I note down the waves we're receiving. These waves, which have travelled through space, come to us from universes so far away that ten years ago we couldn't have begun to imagine they existed. No more than I can picture today the extent of the discoveries we'll make when the sixty-four parabolic dishes are all networked and linked up to the central computer.

"Have you got something?" asks Erwin, perched on a metal walkway that's level with the second deck of the dish.

I answer him, I know I do, but my colleague repeats the question. Perhaps I wasn't speaking loudly enough? The air is dry and sound doesn't travel well here.

"Adrian, are you getting a bloody signal? I'm not hanging around up here for hours."

I'm having a hard time getting my words out, probably because of the cold. It's dreadfully cold; I can barely feel my fingertips and my lips are swollen.

"Adrian? CAN YOU HEAR ME?"

Of course I can hear you Erwin, why can't you hear me? I can hear his footsteps too; he's climbing down from his perch.

"What the hell are you playing at?" he grumbles, walking towards me.

He pulls a strange face, then suddenly drops his

tools and runs over. As he gets close I see him tensing, looking worried.

"Adrian, your nose! It's pouring with blood!"

He lifts me up and helps me to my feet; I hadn't realised I was sitting on the ground. Erwin gets out his walkie-talkie and summons help. I try to stop him, there's no point in bothering the others, I'm a bit tired, that's all. But my hands won't obey me: I've lost all powers of coordination.

"Base, base! This is Erwin at Dish No. 3, answer me, Mayday, Mayday!" he keeps repeating.

I smile: the word "Mayday" is only used in aviation, but this is hardly the time or place for a lesson, especially since I'm giggling uncontrollably.

The more I laugh, the more worried Erwin looks, even though he's the one always complaining I take everything too seriously.

I can hear a familiar voice spluttering from his walkie-talkie, but I can't put a name to it. Erwin explains I'm not feeling well, which isn't true, I've never felt so happy in my life: everything looks beautiful, including Erwin and his craggy face. I don't know if it's because of the moonlight, but he looks almost handsome tonight. Then he doesn't look like anything at all, and his voice, which sounded muffled before, cuts out, as if he's playing that kids' game of moving his lips without actually saying anything. His face goes blurry. Blackout.

*

Erwin stayed by my side, like a brother. He kept on shaking me, to the point where he even managed to wake me up. I felt annoyed at him, seeing as that was the first time I'd managed to get any sleep since coming here. A jeep roared up ten minutes after he put out the call. Some of our colleagues had dressed hurriedly and raced to pick us up. They drove me back to the huts where the doctor gave orders for me to be evacuated immediately. My work in the Atacama was over. A helicopter flew me to the hospital in the valley, at San Pedro. They let me out after three days on an oxygen tank. Erwin came to visit me, accompanied by the director of the research centre, who was sorry to be letting go of "a scientist of your calibre". I accepted his compliment as a consolation prize, a few reassuring words to pack in my suitcase before returning to my dingy university office. I knew that once I was back there, I'd have to ignore the taunts of my London colleagues. We never really shrug off our childhood demons. They stalk us like ghosts, haunting our adult lives, whether we're wearing a suit and tie, a scientist's lab coat, or a clown's costume.

*

There was no question of taking the Bolivian road with its hairpin bends that winds steeply up to four thousand metres. Instead I flew from San Pedro to Argentina, where I boarded the plane for London. As I watched the Andes shrinking through my porthole,

I bitterly resented having to make the journey home. Had I known what lay in store, I might have felt rather differently.

*

London

When I see the drizzle, there's no mistaking which city I'm in. As my taxi heads up the M4, I close my eyes. I can almost smell the old wooden panelling in the college's main entrance, with its polished floorboards, my colleagues' leather briefcases and their dripping trench-coats.

I couldn't find the key to my flat when I was packing my suitcases in Chile, so I can't go straight back home. Hoping I've kept a spare set in my desk drawer, I decide to wait for evening before facing the dust that will have invaded my flat in my absence.

It's after midday by the time I reach the college's offices. A final sigh and I walk into the building where I'll shortly have to resume my old job.

"Adrian! What a pleasant surprise!"

Walter Glencorse, administrator: he must have spotted me from his window. I can just picture him rushing downstairs, then pausing in front of the large mirror on the first floor to re-arrange his thinning blond hair.

"The surprise is all mine, Walter!"

"I'm not the one who scampered off to Peru, old chap, now am I?"

"I was in Chile, Walter."

"Chile, yes of course, what was I thinking? And as for that altitude business... I heard about your little episode, so unfortunate."

Walter is one of those people who can put on a convincing show of sympathy, while inside a little hobgoblin's laughing his head off at your expense.

"Right, I've already put you down for lunch in my diary: this one's on me," he added.

For Walter to splash out meant either it was college business, or he had something important to ask of me. I dropped my suitcase off at the cloakroom (no point in going all the way up to my office to face the shambles there) and stepped back into the street, this time in Walter's company.

We found a table at the pub and Walter put in our order at the bar for two dishes of the day and two glasses of rough house red (so the college *was* footing the bill). Then he leaned towards me, as if concerned our neighbours might overhear what he was about to say.

"You're jolly lucky to have been part of an adventure like that, old chap. Working on the Atacama site must have felt like the chance of a lifetime."

Well, not only had Walter got the country right this time, but he could even remember the name of the place I'd been this time last week. Just hearing him mention it was enough to conjure up the vast Chilean landscape for me, the stately way the moon rose in the middle of the afternoon, those clear nights where the sky was the brightest I'd ever seen.

"Are you listening to me, Adrian?"

I confessed I'd temporarily lost his thread.

"I'm sorry Adrian, I'm being most inconsiderate, I haven't given you any time to catch up after your recent bout of fatigue and that long trip home."

"Look, Walter, let's skip the formalities shall we? Yes, I had a bit of a turn at five thousand metres. I then spent a few days in hospital on an excruciatingly uncomfortable bed, followed by twenty-five hours on a plane with my knees jammed up against my chin, so let's cut to the chase. Have I been demoted? Banned from going into the laboratories? Kicked out of the university, is that it?"

"What are you talking about, Adrian? A turn like that could have happened to any of us. On the contrary, everyone here is full of admiration for the work you've accomplished in the Atacama."

"Stop saying that name every two minutes, please, and tell me what I've done to deserve being treated to this revolting meal."

"We've got a little favour to ask you."

"We?"

"Yes, as in the college, of which you are of course an eminent member, Adrian."

"What kind of favour?"

"The kind that would allow you to go back to Chile in a couple of months."

Walter finally had my undivided attention.

"It's a rather sensitive matter, Adrian, because it concerns money," Walter whispered.

"What money?"

"The money the college needs to continue its work and fund its researchers, as well as pay the rent, not to forget the roof that needs repairing – it's in a sorry state and getting worse. If it carries on raining like this, I'll soon be wearing Wellington boots to work."

"That's the risk you run when you choose an office on the top floor, even if it is the only one to enjoy a bit of light. I'm not heir to any fortune, Walter, nor am I a roofing expert. So what help is my expertise to the college?"

"Ah, well you see it's not so much as a fellow of this venerable institution that you can do us this favour, but rather as an outstanding astrophysicist."

"Who nonetheless works for the college?"

"Quite! But not necessarily in relation to the assignment we'd like to entrust you with."

I abandoned my inedible steak and kidney pie and went over to the bar to order some bread-and-butter pudding and a couple of glasses of decent Bordeaux.

"Walter, hurry up and tell me what you want," I insisted on my return, "or I'll order a double-shot of the finest malt whisky they've got – on your tab."

Walter finally took the plunge. The college accounts were as dry as the air over the Atacama. And, given the current economic climate, there was no hope of a budget increase in the foreseeable future; by the time we'd secured the necessary government funding, Walter would be fishing for trout in his office.

"If word gets out about the poor state of our finances, we run the risk of a brain drain. What we need is a big injection of funding, and fast," he went on.

An organisation called the Walsh Foundation was holding a competition. As it did every year, it would award a substantial grant to the person presenting the most promising research project before its panel of judges.

"And how much is this generous donation worth?" I asked.

"Two million pounds."

"Aha! But I still don't see how I can help..."

"Your research, Adrian! You could present it and win this prize... which you would then, of your own accord, make over to us. The media would portray you as an academic profoundly grateful to the institution that's supported his research for so long. You'd come out of it honourably, as would the college, and the accounts for the Department of Physics and Astronomy might almost balance."

"If you think I'm motivated by money," I said, "a quick visit to my modest one-bedroom abode would rid you of any illusions. However, when you say 'grateful to the institution that's supported his work', I'm intrigued to know exactly what you're referring to. My pitiful office? The stationery and books I ended up paying for out of my own pocket?"

"What about your Chilean expedition? As far as I know we supported that."

"Supported? You *are* talking about the project I could only work on by taking unpaid leave?"

"We supported your candidacy."

"Walter, let's stop being so bloody English about this: you've never believed in my research!"

"Ah, yes, well... Discovering the original star, the mother of all constellations, is somewhat...er... ambitious and risky as a project, wouldn't you say?"

"It's no more risky than presenting that same project to the Walsh Foundation, is it?"

"Necessity knows no law, as Saint Bernard used to say."

"And I suppose you'd like me to wear a cute little keg round my neck too?"

"All right, forget it, Adrian. I told them you wouldn't agree to it. You've always spurned any kind of authority, and a short spell of oxygen deficiency isn't going to change that."

"So you're not alone in coming up with this warped scheme?"

"No, there was a finance meeting and I merely put forward the names of those researchers likely to have a chance of winning the two-million-pound prize."

"Who are the other candidates?"

"I couldn't find any..."

Walter got up to pay.

"This one's on me, Walter. It won't mend the college roof, but at least you'll be able to afford a pair of Wellington boots."

I settled up and we left the pub. It had stopped raining.

"I've got nothing against you Adrian, you do know that."

"And I've got nothing against you, Walter."

"I'm sure that if we both made a bit more of an effort, we could get along rather well together."

"If you say so."

We strolled back to Gower Court in silence; the security guard waved at us from his booth. When we reached the main entrance, I said goodbye to Walter and walked over to the wing where my office was located. Walter turned back on the first step of the great staircase and thanked me for lunch. An hour later, I was still trying to gain entry into the poky room where I worked. The damp had played havoc with the doorframe and no amount of pushing or pulling made any difference. I decided to give up. In what was left of the afternoon, there'd be more clearing up than I could cope with back at home.

*

Paris

Keira opened her eyes and glanced out of the window. The rooftops were glistening after a downpour. She stretched, kicked back the sheets and got out of bed. The kitchen cupboards were empty, apart from one tea bag, which she found in an old metal tin. It was five o'clock in the afternoon by the oven clock, and quarter past eleven in the morning by the clock on the wall. The old alarm clock on her bedside table said two-twenty in the afternoon. She picked up the phone and called her sister.

"What time is it?"

"Hello Keira!"

"Hi Jeanne, what time is it?"

"Nearly two o'clock."

"As late as that?"

"I picked you up from the airport two evenings ago, Keira!"

"I slept for thirty-six hours?"

"That depends on what time you went to bed."

"Are you busy?"

"I'm at my desk, at the museum, and I'm working.

Come and meet me at Quai Branly, I'll take you out for lunch."

"Jeanne?"

Her sister had already hung up.

When Keira had finished in the bathroom, she rummaged around for some clean clothes. There was nothing left from her trip: the Shamal had stolen most of her wardrobe. She dug out a worn pair of jeans that was just about roadworthy, a blue polo shirt that didn't look too bad and a vintage-look old leather jacket. After getting dressed, she blow-dried her hair, hurriedly applied some make-up in front of the hall mirror and slammed the studio door shut behind her. Out in the street, she hopped on a bus and managed to push her way through the passengers and get a place standing by the window. Shop signs, crowds thronging the pavements, traffic snarl-ups...the buzz of the city was quite a high after the long months spent far from civilization. Keira gave up on the bus (too stifling), and strolled along the Seine instead, pausing briefly to watch the river in full flow. They might not be the banks of the Omo, but the bridges of Paris still took her breath away.

Looking up at the Museum of African, Asian, Oceanic and American Arts and Civilisations, Keira was surprised to see its vertical garden. Building works had still been in progress when she'd left Paris, so she hadn't seen the luxuriant vegetation that now covered the museum's façade – it was a real technical feat.

"Fascinating, hey?" said Jeanne.

Keira did a double-take.

"I was on the lookout," said her sister, pointing up at her office window. "Isn't all this greenery great?"

"We had a hard time growing vegetables on the horizontal, where I've been living, so as for growing things up walls – what can I say...?'"

"Nothing. Just follow me."

Jeanne led the way into the museum. At the top of a ramp, which spiralled upwards like a long ribbon, visitors found themselves in a vast expanse that gave a sense of the great geographic spaces where the three thousand five hundred objects and artefacts on display originally came from. A crossroads of civilisations, beliefs, ways of life, and thought systems, the museum allowed you to move between Oceania and Asia, or from the Americas to Africa, in just a few steps. Keira came to a halt in front of a collection of African textiles.

"If you like this place, you can come back and visit me as often as you fancy; I'll get a pass made up for you. But right now, forget about Ethiopia for an hour and come with me," Jeanne urged, tugging at Keira's arm.

They went over to the restaurant and Jeanne ordered two mint teas and some Middle Eastern pastries.

"So, what are your plans? Are you going to stay in Paris for a while?"

"My first major project has been a resounding

failure. After three years we have nothing to show. We lost all of our equipment, and my team was on the brink of exhaustion: it's not a great track record. I doubt I'll be given the opportunity to head up another project for a long time."

"You're hardly to blame for what happened, Keira."

"Maybe not, but my job's all about results. Three years of work without finding anything conclusive... I've made more enemies than friends. The frustrating thing is, I'm sure we were close to our goal. If we'd only had more time..."

Keira went quiet. A woman, probably Somali judging by the patterns and colours on her dress, sat down at a neighbouring table. The little boy clutching his mother's hand noticed Keira staring and winked.

"How much longer are you going to spend digging up piles of earth and sand? Five years, ten years, your whole life?"

"Look, Jeanne, I've missed you a lot, but that doesn't mean I want to listen to a lecture from my big sister," said Keira, unable to take her eyes off the little boy who was slurping an ice-cream.

"Don't you want a kid of your own, one day?"

"Will you stop banging on about the bloody biological clock. Give our ovaries a break!"

"Don't throw one of your fits; I work here, remember," whispered Jeanne. "Do you think you can just ignore the passing of time?"

"Look, I don't give a shit about your pendulum

and its tick-tock, Jeanne, I can't have a kid, okay?"

Keira's sister put her glass of tea down on the table.

"I'm so sorry," she murmured. "Why didn't you tell me? What's wrong with you?"

"Don't worry, it's not hereditary."

"So why can't you have a baby?"

"Because I haven't got a man in my life! That's a good enough reason, isn't it? Now, if you'll excuse me, I've got to get to the shops. My fridge is so empty it echoes."

"Don't worry about that – have supper at my place tonight, and you can stay over too," Jeanne announced.

"Why?"

"Because I haven't got a man in my life either, and I want to see you."

They spent the rest of the afternoon together. Jeanne gave her sister a guided tour of the museum. Knowing how passionate Keira was about Africa, she made a point of introducing her to one of her friends who worked at the Learned Society of Africanists. Ivory looked about seventy. Actually, he was even older than that, over eighty perhaps, but he kept his age a closely guarded secret, no doubt fearing that he'd be forced into retirement against his will.

The ethnologist greeted his visitors in his small office at the end of a corridor. He questioned Keira about her last months in Ethiopia. Suddenly, the old man's gaze was drawn to the pendant around her neck.

"Where did you get such a beautiful stone?" he inquired.

"It was a present."

"Were you told where it comes from?"

"No, it's just a trinket that a little boy found in the ground and gave to me. Why?"

"Would you mind if I looked at your present more closely? My sight isn't what it used to be."

Keira slipped the necklace over her head and held it out.

"How strange, I've never seen anything like it. I couldn't tell you what tribe had the skills to give it this finish. The craftsmanship looks perfect."

"I know, I wondered about that too. To tell you the truth, I think it might just be a piece of wood that got polished by the winds and the river."

"Possibly," murmured Ivory, but he didn't seem convinced. "How about we try to find out a bit more?"

"If you like," Keira hesitated. "I'm not holding my breath for any mind-blowing results, though."

"Who knows? Come back and see me tomorrow," the elderly scholar suggested, returning the necklace to its owner. "We'll try to answer the question of its origins at least. I'm so pleased to have met you. At last, I can put a face to the sister Jeanne has told me so much about. See you tomorrow, then?" he added, showing them to his office door.

*

London

I live in an old mews. It's easy to trip up on the uneven cobblestones, but that's all part of the charm of a place where time has stood still. The house next to mine used to belong to Agatha Christie.

I'd got as far as my front door before remembering I still hadn't found my keys. And then the sky, which had turned menacingly dark, started chucking it down. My neighbour spotted me and waved as she was shutting her windows. I asked if she would mind letting me go through her garden again. Unfortunately this wasn't the first time. She was perfectly pleasant about it, and I jumped over her fence to get to the back of my house. As long as the back door hadn't miraculously been fixed (and I couldn't imagine it had) a sharp yank of the handle would get me inside.

I was exhausted and hadn't yet got my head around being back in England, but the prospect of a quiet night in my own home, reunited with my meagre possessions for which I'd trawled the capital's flea markets, gave me a warm glow.

Not that my quiet night in lasted long: it was interrupted by someone knocking at the door. I still couldn't open up, despite being on the inside now, as the door was still locked and I didn't have the key, so I went upstairs – from where I was treated to a bird's-eye view of Walter, in the street, soaking wet and clearly the worse for drink.

"You can't ditch me like this, Adrian!"

"I didn't know we were an item, Walter!"

"Very funny! My whole career's in your hands!" he roared, even more loudly.

My neighbour opened her window and suggested letting my guest go through her garden. She'd be delighted to assist, she added, if it meant not waking up the entire neighbourhood.

"I'm sorry to thrust myself on you like this, old chap," Walter apologised as he stormed into my living room, "but I've got no choice. I say... this is some one-bedroom gaff!"

"A living room downstairs, a bedroom upstairs!"

"Yes, well let's just say it's not the modest bachelor pad I was expecting. Did you manage to buy this on your salary?"

"You didn't come over at this time of night to evaluate my property, now did you, Walter?"

"No, sorry. But you've got to help me, Adrian."

"If you're here to badger me about that ridiculous scheme of yours involving the Walsh Foundation, you're wasting your time."

"Shall I tell you why nobody's ever supported

your research? Because you're a miserable loner who only ever works for yourself; you're not a team player."

"Thanks for the flattering portrait – I'd say it's pretty much spot on! Would you mind not rummaging through my cupboards? There should be some whisky over by the fireplace, if that's what you're looking for."

It didn't take Walter long to find the bottle; he grabbed two glasses from a shelf and stretched out on the sofa.

"It's ever so cosy here!"

"Would you like a guided tour?"

"Stop trying to be funny, Adrian. Do you think I'd humiliate myself by coming over, if I'd found another solution?"

"What's so humiliating about drinking my finest fifteen-year-old malt whisky?"

"Adrian, you're my only hope, do I have to beg?" continued my uninvited guest, getting down on his knees.

"Please, Walter, just stop it. I don't stand a chance of winning the prize, so why put yourself through all this?"

"You stand every chance, Adrian. Yours is the most inspiring and ambitious project I've read about since I came to work for the college."

"If you think you can win me over with flattery now, you might as well keep the bottle and finish it off at home. I need to get some sleep, Walter."

"I'm not trying to flatter you, I really have read your thesis, Adrian, and it is absolutely brilliant."

My colleague was in a pitiful state. I'd never seen him like this; he was usually so distant, aloof almost. The worst of it was that he seemed sincere. I'd spent the past ten years searching for a planet similar to our own in far-off galaxies, and there weren't many in the college prepared to support my work. Opportunistic it most certainly was, but this about-turn amused me.

"Let's suppose I do get the grant..."

As I uttered these words, Walter put his hands together as if in prayer.

"Reassure me, Walter, you are drunk aren't you?"

"Pissed as a fart, Adrian, but please, do carry on."

"Can you manage a few simple questions?"

"If you keep them brief."

"Let's suppose, for a moment, that I'm in with a flicker of a chance of winning this prize and that, being the perfect gentleman I am, I gallantly make it over to the college straight away. What share of that sum would the finance department allocate to my research?"

Walter coughed.

"Does twenty-five percent sound reasonable? Of course, we would provide you with a new office, a full-time assistant and, if you wished, some of our colleagues could be seconded to your team."

"Don't even think about it!"

"All right then, no colleagues... what about the assistant?"

I poured Walter another glass. The rain was bucketing down and I'd feel churlish sending him out in this weather, especially given his current state.

"Oh well... I'm going to find you a blanket and you can sleep on the sofa."

"I'd hate to impose on you..."

"You already have."

"What about the Foundation?"

"When's this event supposed to take place?"

"In two months' time."

"And when's the submissions deadline?"

"Three weeks."

"I'll have a think about the assistant, but you could start by finding a way to open my office door."

"I'll get onto it first thing in the morning, and you're welcome to use my office any time."

"This is a funny business you're getting me into, Walter."

"Don't say that. The Walsh Foundation has always supported the most original projects; its board members appreciate everything that's – how can I put it? – ahead of its time."

Coming from Walter's lips, I doubted this remark was as generous as it sounded. But his back was up against the wall. And I needed to make up my mind and fast. My chances of winning this prize were slim to none, but I'd do anything to get back to Atacama, the place where I had left my dreams, so what had I got to lose?

"All right, Walter. I'll risk making a complete idiot

of myself in public, but on one condition: if we win, you promise to get me on a plane for Santiago within thirty days."

"I'll come and wave you off at the airport, Adrian, and that's a promise."

"It's a deal!"

Walter leapt up from the sofa, teetered, and immediately sat back down again.

"That's enough booze for this evening. Take this blanket, it'll keep you warm. I'm off to bed."

So much for my quiet evening in.

*

Paris

Keira had fallen asleep in her sister's bed. A good bottle of wine, a TV dinner, chatting all evening, an old black and white movie on one of the cable channels... the last thing she could remember was a tap-dance number starring Gene Kelly. When she was woken by the daylight, her raging hangover suggested that the wine might not have been so good, after all.

"Did we get really sloshed?" asked Keira, going into the kitchen.

"Yes!" Jeanne answered, with a grimace. "I've made you some coffee."

Jeanne sat down at the table and straightened the mirror that was hanging on the wall; the sisters' faces were reflected in it.

"What are you looking at me like that for?"

"No reason."

"You're staring at me in the mirror for no reason, when I'm sitting right in front of you?"

"I'm used to having you on the other side of the world, not next to me. There are photos of you all over this apartment, I've even got one in my desk drawer at the museum. I say 'morning' and 'evening' to you every day; when I'm going through a rough patch I even have long conversations with you, until I realise I'm doing all the talking. Why don't you ever call? If you just made the effort, I wouldn't feel you were so far away. I am your sister, Keira!"

"Stop right there, Jeanne. There aren't any telephone booths in the Omo Valley, and there's no mobile phone network either, just a temperamental satellite link. I called you every time I went to Jimma."

"Meaning every couple of months. Not exactly heart-to-hearts, were they? 'You okay?... It's a terrible line... When are you coming back?...' 'I've got no idea, as late as possible, we're still excavating. What about you, how's the museum, and your man?...' My man is called Jérôme, for your information, and has been for the last three years. You could try to remember! Well, we split up, but I never got a chance to tell you about it – and why bother? You'd have hung up shortly after anyway."

"I'm sorry you've got such a horrid sister, Jeanne. But you must be partly to blame, as you're the eldest and you've always been my role model."

"Cut it out, Keira."

"Too right I will, I'm not playing your game."

"What game?"

"Who gets to blame the other most! I'm sitting here in front of you – not in a photo and not in that mirror, so look at me and talk to me!"

Jeanne stood up but Keira grabbed hold of her wrist and made her sit down again.

"Ouch, that hurts."

"Look, I'm a paleoanthropologist, okay? – I don't work in a museum, and it's been years since I had the time to meet a Pierre or an Antoine or a Jérôme. So no, I don't have a child, but I have had the astonishing good fortune to find a demanding career that I love – I'm not ashamed to follow my heart when it comes to my job. If you're fed up with your life, don't take it out on me; if you miss me, then find a gentler way of letting me know."

"I miss you, Keira," Jeanne mumbled, leaving the kitchen.

Early that afternoon, Keira crossed Quai Branly to meet her sister at the museum; she decided to visit the permanent collection before going up to Jeanne's office. As she was admiring a mask, and trying to guess its provenance, a voice whispered in her ear: "That's Mandinka, from Mali. It's not especially old, but it is rather beautiful."

Startled, Keira recognised Ivory from the previous day.

"I'm afraid your sister's still in a meeting. I tried to find her just a moment ago, but I was led to understand she'd be busy for at least another hour."

"Led to understand?"

"Museums are microcosms of society with their

interdepartmental hierarchies and rivalries. The thing about humans is that we need to live in society, but at the same time we can't help dividing into clans. It probably goes back to our herd instinct. But I must be boring you by rambling on like this. I'm sure you know far more than I do about the subject."

"You're a dark horse, aren't you?" said Keira.

"I suppose I am," Ivory laughed. "Why don't we have a drink whilst you wait for your sister? It's pleasant out, we should make the most of it."

Ivory led the way to the outdoor café. Mid-afternoon, most of the tables were empty. Keira plumped for the one furthest from the large Moai sculpture of a head.

"Did you find anything important along the banks of the Omo?" Ivory quizzed her, picking up the conversation again.

"I found a little ten-year-old boy who had lost his parents. Although archeologically speaking, that doesn't really count."

"I'm sure for the child it was a lot more important than a few bones buried in the ground. So, from what I understand, a terrible storm destroyed your work and drove you from your excavation site."

"Yes, drove me all the way back here..."

"It's unusual for the region. The Shamal never used to blow in a westerly direction."

"How did you find all this out ? I can't imagine it made front page news."

"No, indeed not, your sister told me about your misfortune. I'm naturally curious, so then I typed it into the search engine on my computer. Tell me, what were you really looking for in the Omo Valley?"

"If I tell you that, Ivory, you'll be more likely to laugh in my face – statistically speaking – than show any interest in my work."

"If statistics ruled my life, Keira, I'd have studied maths and not anthropology. Try your luck."

Keira stared at the old man. His eyes drew her in.

"I was looking for the grandparents of Toumaï and of *Ardipithecus Kadabba*. Some days, I even thought I'd be able to find the great-grandparents of their great-grandparents."

"That's it? You want to find the oldest skeleton that bears any resemblance to the human species? Person zero?"

"Isn't that what we're all looking for?"

"And why the Omo Valley?"

"Female intuition, perhaps."

"In a fossil-chaser? I don't think so!"

"Well, look at it this way," Keira conceded. "At the end of the twentieth century, we were convinced that Lucy,* a young woman who died a little over three million years ago, was the mother of humanity. But over the last decade – and I know I'm not telling you anything new here – paleoanthropologists have discovered hominoid bones that go back eight million

---

*Lucy was discovered on 30 November 1974 at Hadar, in the Awash Valley in Ethiopia, by a team of thirty Ethiopian, American and French researchers led by Donald Johanson, Maurice Taieb and Yves Coppens. The skeleton was named Lucy because its finders had all been humming the Beatles song "Lucy in the Sky with Diamonds".

years. Scientists continue to debate, or you could say beat each other up about, the different lineages from which human beings might be descended. I'm not interested in whether our ancestors were bipeds or quadrupeds. I don't think that's the crucial question concerning the origins of the human species. Scientists are obsessed with the mechanics of the skeleton, the way of life, what they ate."

A waitress came over but Ivory waved her away.

"So what does define the human species, according to you?"

"Thought, emotions, reasoning! What distinguishes us from other species isn't whether we're vegetarians or carnivores, or how adept we are at walking. That's like trying to find out where we come from without considering what we are today: highly complex and extraordinarily diverse predators, capable both of loving and killing, of creating and destroying ourselves, of resisting the survival instinct that governs the behaviour of all other animal species. We're extremely intelligent, our knowledge is forever evolving and yet sometimes we can be unbelievably ignorant. But maybe we should order our drinks, that's the second time the waitress has been over."

Ivory ordered two teas and leaned towards Keira.

"You still haven't told me why the Omo Valley, nor what you were really looking for there."

"Whether we're European, Asian or African, and whatever the colour of our skin, we all carry an identical gene. There are billions and billions of us, each distinct from the next person, but we're all descended from one single being. How did that being appear on Earth, and why? That's the being I'm looking for, the first human! And I have reason to believe that he or she is much more than ten or even twenty million years old."

"In the middle of the Palaeogene period? This tea must be stronger than I thought: it's going straight to your head!"

"See, I was right about the statistics, now I'm the one boring you with my stories. So, what about you, Ivory, what research are you engaged in?"

"I've gotten to the age where, frankly, I just go through the motions, and the people around me turn a blind eye. I'm not involved in any new research; at this stage of life, I'd rather tidy up my files than open new ones. Don't make that face, if you knew how old I really was, you'd realise I'm not doing so badly. And don't even think about asking, it's a secret I'll take with me to my grave."

Keira leaned towards Ivory, exposing the pendant she wore on the thong around her neck.

"You look in good shape to me!"

"That's very kind of you! Now, shall we find out a bit more about this strange object?"

"I've told you, it was just a gift from a little boy."

"But yesterday you also told me that you'd be interested to know where it really comes from."

"That's true. Okay, why not?"

"We could start by trying to date it. If it really is a piece of wood, a simple radiocarbon-dating should provide us with the information."

"Provided it's not more than fifty thousand years old."

"Do you think it could be as old as that?"

"Since meeting you, Ivory, I've become wary about questions of age."

"I'll take that as a compliment," said the professor standing up. "Follow me."

"You're not going to tell me there's a particle accelerator hidden in the basement of the museum?"

"Certainly not," smiled Ivory.

"And you haven't got an old friend at Saclay who'll interrupt the atomic energy programme just to study my necklace?"

"Unfortunately not that either."

"So where are we going?"

"To my office, of course."

Keira followed Ivory over to the lifts, preparing to fire more questions his way, but he didn't give her the chance.

"I'd hate you to waste your time with pointless interrogating," he told her. "Let's just wait until we're sitting comfortably, shall we?"

The lift glided up to the third floor.

Ivory settled himself behind his desk and offered Keira the armchair. But she soon jumped up again to see what Ivory was typing on his computer keyboard.

"I'm completely hooked by the Internet! If only you knew how many hours I spend on it! Luckily I'm a widower, otherwise I think this hobby would have killed my wife, or rather she'd have killed me. I just love all the new vocabulary – the web, net, googling – my students taught me that one! – and when I don't know what a term means, I just type it in and hey presto, up it comes. I'm telling you, you can find almost anything, even private laboratories that do radiocarbon-dating. Terrific, isn't it?"

"How old are you really, Ivory?"

"My age varies from day to day, Keira; the important thing is not to let oneself go."

Ivory printed out a list of addresses and proudly waved it before his guest's eyes.

"We just need to make a few phone calls to find out who can handle our request promptly and affordably," he concluded.

Keira looked at her watch.

"Your sister!" Ivory exclaimed. "She must have finished her meeting some time ago now. You go and find her, I'll take care of this."

"No, I'll stay," said Keira, embarrassed, "I can't leave you to do all the hard graft on your own."

"Of course you can, I insist; after all, I'm as keen to find out about the necklace as you are, perhaps even keener. Go and find Jeanne, and come back to see me tomorrow evening. We should know a bit more by then."

Keira thanked the professor.

"Would you mind leaving the necklace with me this evening? I intend to remove the tiniest fragment to be sent off for analysis. I promise to be as nimble-fingered as a surgeon, so you won't notice anything missing."

"Of course, but I've already tried several times and I've never managed to make so much as a scratch."

"Ah, but did you have a diamond-blade scalpel like this?" asked Ivory, proudly taking his cutting tool out of his drawer.

"Didn't I say you were a dark horse, Ivory? No, I didn't have a scalpel like that."

Keira hesitated for a moment before leaving her necklace on the desk. Ivory carefully unknotted the leather thong that held the triangular object in place and gave it back to her.

"See you tomorrow, Keira. Drop by whenever you like, I'll be here."

*

London

"No, no, and no again Adrian! Do you want the selection committee to stage a mass walkout?"

"Excuse me?"

"That was about as dry as the dust in the Atacama!"

"Fine, if what I've got to say is so off-putting,
you'd better find another speaker."

"Who similarly dreams of returning to Chile?
Sorry, haven't got time for that."

I turned the page of my notebook and cleared my
throat, before carrying on reading.

"You'll see," I said to Walter, "the next part is
much more gripping."

But after the third sentence, Walter gave a mock
snore.

"Dull as ditchwater," he declared, opening his
right eye.

"Are you saying I'm a bore?"

"Bull's-eye, this is boring as hell. These stars you
keep telling me are so 'extraordinary' are just figures
and letters that no one can remember. Do you think

70

the judges are going to care about the difference between X321 and ZL254? This isn't an episode of *Star Trek*! As for your far-off galaxies, you're defining those distances in light-years. But who on Earth knows how to count in light years? Your obliging neighbour? Your dentist? Your mother, perhaps? It's just hopeless. Everyone's going to end up with number overload."

"So what the bloody hell *do* you want me to do? Name my constellations after fruit and vegetables so that even your poor mum can understand my research?"

"I know you won't believe this, but actually she has read your work."

"Your mother has read my thesis?"

"Absolutely!"

"I'm very flattered."

"She suffers from terrible insomnia. The pills don't work anymore, so I took her a bound copy of your opus. You've got to get writing again; she's going to run out of reading matter soon!"

"Look, what d'you want from me?"

"I want you to talk about your research in a way that is understandable to ordinary human beings. This obsession with scientific terms is terribly dreary. Take the medical world, for example, why do they have to use such gobbledygook? Isn't being ill enough? Do we need to hear that we've got dysplasia of the hip, when the word 'deformity' would do perfectly well?"

"I'm sorry to hear your bones are playing up, Walter."

"Well don't be, because my dog's the one with 'dysplasia'."

"You've got a dog?"

"Yes. A very lovely Jack Russell. He's at my mother's, and if she's read the last few pages of your thesis to him, they'll both be sound asleep."

I wanted to strangle Walter, but I restrained myself and just stared at him. I found his patience and willingness disconcerting. Without really understanding how or why, the words suddenly started pouring out of me and, for the first time since I was a child, I heard myself asking out loud:

"Where does the dawn begin...?"

Come the small hours, Walter still hadn't dropped off.

*

Paris

Keira was having trouble getting to sleep. She didn't want to wake her sister, so she snuck out of the bedroom and made herself comfortable on the sofa. How many times had she cursed her hard camp bed? But she was missing it now. She stood up and walked over to the window. No chance of a starry night here, just a row of street lights glowing in the deserted metropolis. It was five o'clock in the morning, 5800 kilometres from the Omo Valley where the sun had already risen, and Keira was trying to imagine what Hari might be up to. She shuffled back to the sofa and eventually drifted off.

Mid-morning, a phone call from Professor Ivory interrupted her dreams.

"I've got two pieces of news for you."

"Start with the bad!" said Keira, stretching.

"You were right, I couldn't remove a single fragment from your jewel, not even with the diamond-blade scalpel I'm so proud of."

"I told you. And the good news?"

73

"A laboratory in Germany can handle our request this week."

"Will it be expensive?"

"Don't worry about that for now; consider it my contribution."

"I'm afraid that's out of the question, Ivory, there's no reason why you should pay."

"Oh dear," sighed the old man, "why does there have to be a reason for everything? Isn't the fun of finding out reason enough? If you really want an excuse, then I'll give you one: your mysterious object kept me awake most of the night and, believe me, for an old man who generally yawns all day long, that's worth an awful lot more than the modest sum demanded by this laboratory."

"We'll go halves then, or not at all."

"Halves it is! So you'll let me send them your precious object? You'll have to be separated from it for a few days."

Keira hadn't thought about this and she didn't like the idea of not wearing her pendant, but the professor seemed so enthusiastic, so happy to rise to a fresh challenge, that she didn't have the heart to pull out at this stage.

"I should get it back to you by Wednesday, at the latest. I'll send it registered post. In the meantime, I'm going to dive back into my old books to try and find out what kind of artistic tradition it might have belonged to."

"Are you sure it's worth going to all this trouble?" asked Keira.

"Believe me, it's no trouble at all. In fact, it's doing me the power of good. Right, I'd better go now; thanks to you, I really do have some work to be getting on with."

"Thank you, Ivory," smiled Keira, and hung up.

During that week, Keira got back in touch with colleagues and friends she hadn't seen for a very long time. Every evening was spent socialising, either dining out in small restaurants or else round at her sister's apartment. Keira felt alienated by the repetitive topics of conversation, and quickly got bored. Jeanne had a go at her, as they were leaving a particularly gossipy dinner.

"Don't bother coming to any more of these dinner parties – they're clearly not your thing."

"Who said they're *not* my thing?"

Honestly, Keira, you should have seen yourself at the table: you looked about as animated as one of those fossilised bones you excavate."

"How do you put up with all that mindless chit-chat?"

"It's called having a social life."

"You call that a social life?" snorted Keira, hailing a taxi. "That guy regurgitating interminable trivia on the financial crisis? His neighbour who feeds off sports results like a scavenging hyena? The wannabe psychologist with her clichés about infidelity? The lawyer ranting about the rise of urban crime, just because someone nicked his scooter? Three hours of people being cynical, that's what it was. A load of bullshit about the mess the human race is in, according to them. I'm sorry, but I just can't listen to that stuff."

"No one's good enough for you, that's your problem, Keira," Jeanne admonished, as the taxi dropped them off at her apartment.

Their argument continued long into the night. But the next day, Keira went with her sister to another dinner party. Perhaps because the loneliness she'd recently experienced went deeper than she cared to admit.

That weekend, Keira was walking through the Tuileries Gardens under a sky that threatened to open, when she bumped into Max. They'd both run down the main avenue in a bid to reach the gate on Rue de Castiglione, before the shower broke. Max was out of breath, and had paused in front of the steps at the foot of the plinth where two bronze lions were attacking a rhinoceros; on the other side of the steps, Keira was leaning against the plinth where two lionesses were tearing apart a dying wild boar.

"Max? Is that you?"

For all his good looks, Max was as short-sighted as ever; everything appeared foggy behind his steamed up glasses, but he would have recognised Keira's voice anywhere.

"You're in Paris?" he gasped, taken aback as he wiped his glasses.

"As you can see."

"Now I can!" he agreed, pushing his glasses back up his nose. "How long have you been here?"

"In the park? About half an hour."

Max stared at her.

"I've been in Paris for a few days," a flustered Keira finally admitted.

A rumbling overhead prompted both of them to seek shelter under the arcades of Rue de Rivoli. The rain came sluicing down.

"You weren't going to call, then?" said Max.

"Of course I was."

"So why didn't you? Sorry, I'm bombarding you with stupid questions. If you'd wanted us to see each other, you'd have phoned."

"I..., I didn't really know how I felt about it."

"Well, you did the right thing, waiting for providence to throw us together..."

"It's nice to see you," Keira interrupted him.

"It's nice to see you too."

Max suggested they have a drink at the bar in the Hôtel Meurice.

"How long are you here for? Ouch, there I go again with my questions."

"It's fine," said Keira. "I've just been to six dinner parties back to back where all people talked about were politics, strikes, business and celebrity gossip. Nobody seems interested in anyone else anymore; I ended up thinking I must be invisible. I'd have had to strangle myself with my table napkin for someone to ask me how I was doing, and even then I'm not sure they'd have bothered listening to my answer."

"How *are* you doing?"

"I feel like a caged lion."

"Are you staying?"

Keira told Max about her Ethiopian travels and the reason for her hasty departure. She didn't rate her chances of securing funding for a new expedition. At eight o'clock, she disappeared to call Jeanne and warn her that she'd be home late. She and Max had dinner at the Meurice; they each talked about what they'd been up to over the past three years. After their split and Keira leaving the country, Max had resigned from his archaeology teaching post at the Sorbonne to take charge of the printing works that had belonged to his father, who'd died of cancer a year earlier.

"So you're a printer now?"

"The right thing to say would've been: 'I'm sorry to hear about your father'," retorted Max with a smile.

"You know what I'm like, Max, I never say the right thing. But I am sorry to hear about your father; though from what I recall, you didn't get on too well?"

"We patched things up in the end… at the hospital in Villejuif."

"But why did you leave lecturing? You loved your job."

"I loved the excuses it gave me."

"What excuses? You were a great teacher."

"I never had that real fire, like the passion that drives you when you're out in the field."

"And is printing any better?"

"At least I'm prepared to face up to the truth now. I'm not waiting on some project that's going to lead to the discovery of the century. Let's face it, I was a lecture-theatre archaeologist, my only real talent was for seducing students."

"Poor little innocents like me?" Keira teased him.

"You were the real deal, and you know it. Now I'm just looking for excitement in the suburbs, but at least I'm clear about that. What about you, did you find what you were looking for over there?"

"If you're talking about my excavations, no, just a few sediments that convinced me I was on the right track. But what I really discovered was a way of life that suits me."

"So you're going to head off again…"

"Let's be honest with each other here: I'd like to spend the night with you Max, and maybe tomorrow night as well. But come Monday I'll want to be on my own again, and the days that follow too. If I get a chance to go back, I'll jump at it. When? I don't know. I've got to find some work between now and then."

"Before suggesting I sleep with you, you could at least ask if there's someone else in my life."

"If there were, you'd have called them – it's gone midnight."

"If there were, I wouldn't have had dinner with you. So, have you got any leads to help you find a job?"

"Not for the time being, I don't have many friends in the profession."

"It'd take me two minutes to scribble a list of researchers on this tablecloth who'd be thrilled to have someone like you on their team."

"Thank you, but I don't just want to help out with someone else's discovery. I've done my years of assisting, I want my own project now."

"Fancy lending me a hand at the printing works while you're waiting?"

"I've got happy memories of my time by your side at the Sorbonne, but I was twenty-two, Max. Rotary presses aren't my thing. And I really don't think it'd be a good idea," Keira flashed a smile. "Thanks for the offer, though."

Jeanne got home in the small hours to find the living-room sofa empty. She glanced at her mobile: her sister hadn't left a message.

*

London

The dreaded Walsh Foundation deadline was drawing closer. The presentation would take place in a few weeks. I was spending my mornings at home, in touch with my colleagues around the globe and answering e-mails, giving priority to those that trickled through from my fellow researchers in the Atacama. Walter would come and dig me out around midday and we'd head for the pub, where I'd report on any progress with my application. Afternoons were taken up in the library consulting books I'd already read several times, while Walter ran his eye over my notes. In the evenings I'd stroll towards Primrose Hill, and I spent my weekends rootling around Camden market. Each day, I rediscovered more of a taste for my life in London, for the different areas of my city. I was even getting on better with Walter.

*

Paris

On Wednesday, Ivory received the results from the laboratory near Dortmund. He noted down the analysis report, as dictated to him over the phone, and then requested the object be sent on to another laboratory, on the outskirts of Los Angeles. After hanging up he seemed to be deliberating before making another call, this time from his mobile.

"It's been a while!"

"There was no reason for us to speak again," said Ivory. "I've just sent you an e-mail, take a look at it as soon as you can, I don't think you'll want to waste any time in getting back to me."

Ivory hung up and looked at his watch. The call had lasted less than forty seconds. He left his office, locked the door and made his way down to the ground floor. A group of students was mobbing the main museum entrance and he slipped away unnoticed.

Walking back up Quai Branly he crossed the Seine, opened up his mobile, took out the SIM card and threw it in the river. Then he disappeared into the

Alma Brasserie, headed downstairs to the basement, went into a booth and waited for the phone to ring.

"How did this object end up in your hands?"

"The greatest discoveries often happen by chance; some call it destiny, others luck."

"Who gave it to you?"

"It doesn't matter and I'd rather keep it secret."

"Ivory, you're opening a file that has been closed for a very long time, and the link you're suggesting doesn't prove a great deal."

"You didn't have to call me back so quickly."

"What do you want?"

"I've had it sent on to California for a series of additional tests, but these analyses need to be invoiced to you directly. They're beyond my means."

"And does the object's owner know what's going on?"

"No idea, and naturally I don't intend to say anything."

"When do you think you'll know more?"

"I should get the preliminary results through in a few days."

"Contact us again if you think it's worthwhile and send me the invoice, we'll settle it. Goodbye, Ivory."

The professor replaced the handset and lingered in the booth for a moment or two, wondering if he'd made the right decision. Then he paid for his drink and headed back to the museum.

*

Keira knocked at the office door. When there was no reply she went back down to the information desk. The receptionist confirmed that yes, she had seen the professor. Perhaps he was in the cafeteria? Keira scanned the garden. Her sister, who was eating lunch with a colleague, got up from her table and came over.

"You could've called."

"You're right, I could have. Have you seen Ivory? I can't find him."

"I had a chat with him this morning, but I'm not his keeper, and the museum's a big place. Where have you disappeared off to these last couple of days?"

"Jeanne, you're keeping your lunch date waiting – why don't you save the grilling for later?"

"I was worried, that's all."

"As you can see, I'm perfectly fine, so stop fretting."

"Are we having supper together tonight?"

"I don't know, it's only midday. Right now I need to find Ivory. He left a message asking me to drop by but he's not there."

"Like I said, the museum's a big place. What's the panic?"

"I think your friend has moved on to dessert."

Jeanne glanced over at her colleague who was waiting patiently, leafing through a magazine. When she turned back, her sister had vanished.

Keira explored the first and second floors before retracing her steps to Ivory's office. This time the door was open and the professor was sitting in his armchair. He looked up.

"There you are, thank you for coming."

"I popped by just now, I've been looking for you everywhere."

"I hope you didn't try the men's toilet?"

"Ah, no."

"Well that explains it, then. Take a seat, I've got some news for you... The radiocarbon analysis didn't reveal anything: so either your gift is more than fifty thousand years old or else the object is inorganic and therefore not made of ebony."

"When will we get it back?" asked Keira.

"The laboratory's sending it back tomorrow, so you'll be able to wear it around your neck again no later than in two days' time."

"Please tell me what I owe you for my half, we agreed on that if you remember."

"The laboratory hasn't billed us because the results were inconclusive. The special delivery charges amount to a hundred Euros."

Keira put fifty Euros on the professor's desk.

"So it remains a mystery. It might just be a simple piece of volcanic rock, after all?" she inquired.

"As smooth and satiny as that? I doubt it, fossilised lava tends to be crumbly."

"Well, let's just say it's a pendant and leave it at that."

"That sounds eminently sensible. I'll call you as soon as it's back in my possession."

Keira said goodbye to Ivory and went to find her sister.

"Why didn't you tell me you've been seeing Max?" fired Jeanne, the moment Keira walked into her office.

"Clearly you already know, so why bother?"

"Are you getting back together with him?"

"We spent an evening together and then I went back to sleep at my place, okay?"

"And did you spend Sunday on your own in your studio too?"

"Look, I ran into him by chance, so we went for dinner. How come you're so up to speed on all this? Did he call you?"

"Max call me? You must be kidding. I haven't heard a squeak from him since you split up; I think he even went out of his way to avoid all the parties he thought I might be at."

"So how do you know?"

"A friend of mine saw you at the Hôtel Meurice; apparently you were cooing at each other like love-birds."

"Paris is such a village! Well no, we're not lovers; just two old friends having a catch-up. I don't know who this gossipy friend of yours is, but I don't like her."

"It's Max's cousin, and she doesn't like you either."

"Just give it a break Jeanne."

"Fine, I won't bore you with the news that some flowers arrived for you this morning. The card's in my bag, in case you're interested."

Keira snatched the small envelope, ripped it open and gently pulled out the card. She smiled and slipped it into her pocket.

"I won't be eating with you this evening, I'll leave you to your well- intentioned friends."

"Keira, go easy with Max, it took him months to get over you. Don't open up old wounds if you're only going away again; that's what you plan on doing, isn't it?"

"Great, the million-dollar question with a lecture thrown in! Talk about overdoing the big sister act. Max is fifteen years older than me – don't you think he can look after himself by now?"

"Why are you so angry at me?"

"Because you're always judging people!"

"Fine. Do what you want Keira, I've got work to do. Just try not to leave him in pieces this time. Aside from being cruel, it won't do anything for your reputation."

"I've got a reputation now?"

"There were a lot of wagging tongues after you left, and they weren't exactly singing your praises."

"Luckily I was too far away to hear them."

"But I wasn't, and I had to stick up for you."

"Who are these so-called friends who do nothing but gossip and bitch?"

"The ones who had to cheer Max up, I guess. Oh,

and one last thing, in case it ever crosses your mind to wonder whether you were a pain in the neck for your sister when you were growing up, the answer's YES."

Keira slammed the door of Jeanne's office. A few moments later, she was walking up Quai Branly towards Pont de l'Alma. As she crossed the river, she leaned over the parapet and watched a barge gliding towards the Debilly footbridge. She got out her mobile and called Jeanne.

"Let's not argue every time we see each other. I'll come and meet you tomorrow, we can have lunch together, just the two of us. I'll tell you all about my Ethiopian adventure, although there's not much left to tell; and you can fill me in on everything that's been going on in your life for the past three years. You can even give me the lowdown on why you and Jérôme split up. It was Jérôme, wasn't it?"

*

London

Walter didn't say anything, but I could see he was getting increasingly depressed. Explaining my research was like trying to teach him Chinese in a matter of days. Astronomy and cosmology involve the study of spaces so vast, that the units we use to measure time, speed and distance on Earth are no use. We've had to invent other units, multiples of multiples, never-ending equations. Our science is built on probabilities and uncertainties; we're feeling our way as we go; it's impossible for us to imagine the real limits of this universe we are a part of.

In the past two weeks, I hadn't written a single sentence without Walter pulling a face over a term he didn't understand, or a line of reasoning that escaped him.

"Look Walter, for the last time – is the universe flat or round?"

"Round, probably. If I've followed what you're saying here, the universe is constantly moving and it expands like a piece of cloth being stretched, taking with it all the galaxies attached to its fibres."

"I guess that's one way of explaining the theory of the expanding universe."

Walter put his head in his hands. At this time of evening, the great library was almost deserted. Our two tables were the only ones still lit up.

"Adrian, I may just be an administrator, but I spend my working days in the faculty. So why can't I understand a word you're saying to me?"

I noticed a journal left out on a table, which a reader must have forgotten to put away. Its cover featured the rolling Devon countryside.

"I think I've just had an idea that might make things clearer for you," I told Walter.

"I'm all ears."

"You've listened enough. It's time to make the leap from theory of the cosmos into practice. Follow me."

We tiptoed out of the library. Once we were out in the street, I flagged down a cab and asked the driver to drop us off at my place, double quick. I marched past my front door and made straight for a small adjacent lock-up, Walter in tow.

"Have you got a secret gambling den hidden behind those metal shutters?" Walter teased me.

"Sorry to disappoint you, it's just a garage."

Walter let out a whistle as I opened up. My 1960s MG often got this kind of reaction.

"Are we taking it out for a ride?" Walter was keen to know.

"If she's in the mood to start up," I said, turning the key in the ignition.

A few touches on the accelerator and the engine almost kicked in first time. "Climb in and don't bother looking for a safety belt, there isn't one!"

Half an hour later, we turned off the North Circular.

"Where are we going?" asked Walter, trying to smooth the only remaining lock of hair on his forehead.

"To the seaside, we'll be there in three hours."

As we sped along under a beautiful starry sky, I thought about the Atacama and how I never stopped dreaming about it. And at the same time, I realised how much I'd missed England while I was over there.

"How come this little beauty's in such good nick when it's been languishing in your garage for three years?"

"I left it with a mechanic while I was away and I've only just picked it up."

"He looked after it well enough," said Walter. "I say old chap, you wouldn't have a pair of scissors in the glove compartment, would you?"

"No, why?"

"Oh nothing!" muttered Walter, running his hand over his head.

By midnight we'd passed Cambridge and two hours later we arrived at our destination. I parked the MG at Sheringham Beach and asked Walter to follow me to the shore, where we sat down on the sand.

"We've come all this way to make sandcastles?"

"If that's what you want to do, I have no objection, but it's not why we're here."

"That's a pity!"

"What can you see, Walter?"

"Sand!"

"Look up and tell me what you can see."

"The sea, what do you expect at the seaside?"

"On the horizon, what can you see?"

"Nothing at all, it's pitch black."

"You can't see the light from the lighthouse at the entrance to the port of Kristiansand?"

"Is there an island out there? I don't remember that."

"Kristiansand is in Norway, Walter."

"Don't be ridiculous, Adrian, I've got good eye-sight, but seeing the Norwegian coast from here, I mean really! Why don't I tell you what colour the pom-pom is on the lighthouse keeper's woolly hat, while we're at it!"

"Kristiansand is only 700 kilometres away. It's the middle of the night, light travels at 299,792 kilometres per second, so the light from the lighthouse should only take two and a half thousandths of a second to reach us."

"Thank goodness you didn't forget that half – it makes all the difference."

"But can't you see the light from the lighthouse at Kristiansand?"

"Can *you*?" demanded a perplexed Walter.

"No, nobody can see it. But it's right there, in front

of us, hidden by the Earth's curve, behind an invisible hill, as it were."

"Adrian, are you telling me that we've just driven three hundred kilometres to demonstrate that I couldn't spot the lighthouse at Kristiansand in Norway from the coast of East Anglia? Because if that's the case, I promise I'd have taken your word for it back in the library."

"You asked me why understanding that the universe is round matters, and the answer is in front of you Walter. If miles and miles of reflective objects were floating on the sea, you'd see them all lit up by the light from the lighthouse at Kristiansand, while never actually seeing the lighthouse itself; but, with a lot of patience and some careful calculations, you'd be able to guess that it existed and you'd end up working out its exact location."

Walter looked at me as if I was completely bonkers, but he did gaze up at the stars at last.

"Okay," he conceded after a long moment of contemplation. "If I've got this right, the stars we can see above us are still on this side of the hill. But the one you're looking for is on the other side of the slope."

"There's nothing that says there's only one hill, Walter."

"So you're suggesting that not only is your universe curved but it also concertinas?"

"Or it's like an ocean with some very high waves."

Walter put his hands behind his neck and was quiet for a minute or two.

"How many stars are there out there?" he asked.

"With a clear sky like this, you can see the five thousand closest to us."

"As many as that?" said Walter dreamily.

"There are many, many more; but our eyes can't see further than a thousand light years from here."

"I didn't realise my sight was so good! The lighthouse keeper's girlfriend better not parade around in front of the window in her underwear."

"It's not about how sharp-sighted you are, Walter. There's a cloud of cosmic dust hiding most of the hundreds of billions of stars in our galaxy from us."

"There are hundreds of billions of stars above us?"

"Here's a really dizzying thought: there are several hundreds of billions of galaxies in our universe. Our Milky Way is just one of them, and each one is made up of hundreds of billions of stars."

"That's impossible to even imagine."

"Well, picture us counting up all the grains of sand on our planet, and we might be getting somewhere close to the probable number of stars in the universe."

Walter stood up, grabbed a fistful of sand and let the grains trickle through his fingers. In a silence interrupted only by the crash of the surf, we considered the sky, like two kids overawed by its vastness.

"Do you think there is life out there somewhere?" Walter asked, in earnest now.

"A hundred billion galaxies each containing a hundred billion stars and nearly as many solar systems?

The likelihood of us being the only ones is almost nil. Not that I believe in little green men. Life most probably does exist, but in what forms? From simple bacteria to beings that might be even more highly evolved than we are. Who knows?"

"I envy you, Adrian."

"You envy me? Is this starry sky suddenly making you want to take a trip to the Atacama?"

"No, I envy your dreams. My life consists of figures, of making small cost-savings, trimming budgets. But you get to manipulate numbers that would make my desk calculator explode; and these infinite numbers keep your childhood dreams alive. That's why I envy you. I'm glad we came here. Whether we win the prize or not, I've learned a lot tonight. Why don't you find a nice weekend spot for my next astronomy lesson?"

We lay on the sand of Sheringham Beach with our arms folded behind our heads until sunrise.

*

Paris

Keira and Jeanne had patched things up over a long lunch that stretched into a good part of the afternoon. Jeanne talked about her split with Jérôme. Her eyes had been opened when she noticed how interested he was in the woman sitting next to him at a dinner party. On the way home, she'd muttered the dreaded words: "we need to talk".

Jérôme had flatly denied showing any interest in the woman; he couldn't even remember her name. That wasn't the point: Jeanne had wanted to be the woman he'd flirted with that evening, but Jérôme hadn't even glanced her way across the dinner table. They'd argued about it all night and gone their separate ways in the small hours. A month later, Jeanne found out that Jérôme had moved in with the woman from the dinner party. Since then, Jeanne wondered whether we foretell our own destiny or whether, sometimes, we provoke it.

She asked Keira what her plans were with Max, but her sister replied that she didn't have any.

After three years in Ethiopia, Keira liked the idea

of letting life just take its course. She'd fallen in love with freedom, and she wasn't ready to trade it in yet.

During their meal, her telephone had vibrated several times. Perhaps it was Max trying to get hold of her? Keira eventually picked up.

"I hope I'm not bothering you?"

"Not at all," she reassured Ivory.

"The German laboratory made a mistake with the address when it sent your pendant back. Don't worry, the package hasn't gone astray, it's been returned to them. They're going to send it to us again without delay. I'm very embarrassed, but I'm afraid you won't get your precious object back until Monday; I do hope you won't hold this against me?"

"Of course not, it's hardly your fault, Ivory. I'm the one who should be sorry for all the time I've made you waste."

"Don't be, I've had fun, even if our efforts have come to nothing. I should get it back some time on Monday morning, so do come and find me in my office. I'll take you out to lunch by way of an apology."

*

As soon as the call was over, Ivory folded the report that had been e-mailed to him an hour earlier by the Los Angeles laboratory. He slipped it inside his jacket pocket.

Sitting in the back of a taxi bound for the esplanade of the Eiffel Tower, the elderly professor examined the liver spots on his hands and sighed.

"Why are you still getting involved in this kind of thing at your age? You won't be around to find out what happens in the end. So what's the point?"

"I beg your pardon, sir?" said the driver, glancing at his passenger in the rear-view mirror.

"Sorry, I was just talking to myself."

"Oh, don't apologise, I often do the same thing. In the good old days we used to have a proper chinwag with passengers, but now our customers prefer to be left in peace. So we put the radio on; it keeps us company."

"Well, do switch the radio on; if you like," said Ivory, smiling at the driver.

There were only twenty or so visitors in the queue for the lift.

Ivory arrived at the restaurant on the first floor. He scanned the room, indicated to the hostess on reception that his guest was already there, and went to sit at a table where a man in a dark blue suit was waiting for him.

"Why didn't you have the results sent directly to Chicago?"

"I didn't want to alert the Americans."

"So why alert us?"

"Because the French were more restrained – or they used to be in my dealings with them thirty years ago; and anyway I've known you for a long time, Paris, you're a man of discretion."

"I'm listening," the man stated curtly.

"Since the radiocarbon-testing didn't bring anything up, I've proceeded to an optical analysis test. I'll spare you the details, it's horribly technical and wouldn't mean much to you – but the results are rather surprising."

"What did you get?"

"Nothing."

"You've obtained no result whatsoever and you call this meeting? Have you lost your mind?"

"I prefer direct contact to the telephone; and you would do well to listen to what I've got to say. For this object *not* to react to the dating method is the first mystery; that it leads us to suppose it must be at least four hundred thousand years old is an even bigger one."

"Is it comparable to the one we already know about?"

"It's not identical in form, and I can't make any guarantees about its composition – since we were never able to determine the composition of the object already in our possession."

"But you think it belongs to the same family?"

"Two is a small number to call a family, but they could be related."

"We all believed our one was unique."

"Not me, I never thought that, which is why you sidelined me three decades ago. Perhaps now you can appreciate why I suggested we meet."

"Aren't there any other test procedures that would help us find out more?"

"Uranium dating, but it's too late for that."

"Ivory, do you really think these two objects could be linked, or is this about some old chip on your shoulder? We all know this discovery meant a lot to you and that the withholding of your budget wasn't entirely unconnected from your decision to leave us."

"I outgrew those kinds of games a long time ago; and you won't find anybody who could confirm such accusations against me."

"If I've understood correctly, the only similarity between the two objects is the lack of any reaction whatsoever to the lab tests."

Ivory pushed his chair back, ready to walk away from the table.

"Over to you to establish the connection as you see fit. I've done my bit. The moment I got wind of a possible second example, I used a great deal of cunning to procure it, carry out the tests I deemed useful and alert you. Now it's up to you to decide on the next move; as you've so rightly reminded me, I retired a long time ago."

"Sit down, Ivory, this conversation isn't over yet. When can we get hold of this object?"

"There's no question of your getting hold of it. On Monday, I'm giving it back to the young lady who owns it."

"I thought it was a man who'd handed it over to you?"

"I never said that. Anyway, what does it matter?"

"I don't think our office would view this

favourably. Do you realise how much that object is worth if your gut feeling turns out to be right? It's absolute madness to leave it in circulation."

"Psychology hasn't always been our organisation's strength, has it? For the time being, the stone's owner has no idea, and there's no reason for that to change. She wears it around her neck; it's hard to imagine a safer or more anonymous place. We don't want to draw anybody's attention to it and above all we need to avoid a battle between our offices over who, out of Geneva, Madrid, Frankfurt and goodness knows who else, will try to get their hands on this second example. While waiting to find out if it is indeed a second example – and it's much too early to be able to tell – this object will be swiftly returned to its young owner."

"And what if she loses it?"

"Do you really think it would be any safer with us?"

"*Fair enough*, as our English colleagues would say. We'll consider this woman's neck as a sort of neutral territory."

"I'm sure she'd be flattered to hear that!"

The man in the blue suit, code-named Paris, looked out of the window. The rooftops of the French capital stretched as far as the eye could see.

"But how are we going to find out more if this pendant isn't in our possession?"

"Sometimes I really do wonder if I retired too early. Haven't you understood any of what I've just been explaining? If the stone really is cousin to the one we already have, the tests won't reveal anything further."

"There's been a great deal of progress on the technological front these last few years."

"The only progress made has been in a better understanding of the context we're concerned with."

"Stop lecturing me! We've known each other too long for this. What have you really got in mind?"

"The owner is an archaeologist and a very good one at that. A bit feisty, I'll grant you, strong-headed and fearless. She's got no time for hierarchy, she's convinced she's more talented than her peers and she does exactly what she wants. Why not let her work for us?"

"You seriously expect us to recruit her with a profile like that?"

"Did I say that? She's just spent three years in Ethiopia excavating in difficult conditions, and I'm ready to bet that if a severe storm hadn't destroyed her work she might even have found what she was looking for."

"What makes you think she'd have achieved her goal?"

"She's got one crucial asset."

"What?"

"Luck! The object just came to her: she was given it as a present."

"That's hardly a testimony to her skills. And I don't see how she stands a better chance of solving a mystery that's eluded us for all this time, despite the considerable resources at our disposal."

"It's not about resources but passion. We simply have to give her a good reason to be interested in the object she wears round her neck."

"You're suggesting we try to remote-control a free radical?"

"If we remote-control her, your radical will be free in appearance only."

"And who will be pressing the buttons? You?"

"No, you know full well the committee would never agree to that. But I could set things in motion, arouse our subject's curiosity, whet her appetite. As to the rest, you'd take over."

"It's an interesting approach. I know some people will be very reluctant but I could defend it to a select committee; after all, it wouldn't make undue demands on resources."

"I would, however, insist on one non-negotiable rule, and you can tell your select committee I'll be keeping an eye on things to make sure nobody breaks it: *at no time is the safety of this young woman to be put at risk*. There has to be unanimous agreement on this, and I mean from *all* the bureau chiefs."

"If you could see your face, Ivory: anyone would think you were an old spy! Read the newspapers, the Cold War's come and gone! We're all friends now. Who do you take us for? We're talking about a stone here, albeit one with a very intriguing past, but a stone nonetheless."

"Look, if any of us thought we were dealing with an ordinary pebble, then neither you nor I would be sitting here playing at old spies, as you put it. Don't write me off as more senile than I am."

"Okay, okay. Supposing I do my best to convince them this is the right line to pursue, how can I prove to them that your protégée will be able to make any further discoveries when our own efforts have been in vain?"

Ivory realised that to win Paris over, he'd have to reveal rather more information than he'd intended.

"You all believed that the object in your possession was a one-off. A second suddenly appears. If they're from the same 'family', as you just put it, then why would there only be two of them?"

"Are you suggesting that –"

"– The family might be bigger? That's what I've always believed. And I also think that the more open we are to the possibility of finding other specimens, the better chance we have of understanding what this is all about. What you have in your safe-box is just a fragment; bring the missing pieces together and you'll see that, in reality, the whole is far greater than anything you could ever imagine."

"And you're suggesting that this kind of responsibility should rest on the shoulders of a young woman who is, in your own words, uncontrollable?"

"Let's not blow things out of proportion here. What we need is her knowledge and her talent."

"I don't like this, Ivory, the file's been closed for

years and it should stay that way. We've already spent a lot of money on it for nothing."

"That's not true! We spent a lot of money on hushing the matter up. How long do you think you'll be able to keep that object secret if you're no longer the only ones who suspect its significance?"

"As long as other people hit a dead end too!"

"Are you ready to take that risk?"

"I don't know, Ivory. I'll re-establish contact, they'll decide, and I'll be back in touch over the next few days."

"You have until Monday."

Ivory shook hands with Paris and stood up. Just before leaving the table he whispered in his ear:

"Say hello from me. Tell them this is the last favour I'll ever do for them, and please give my worst regards to you-know-who."

"Consider it done."

*

Norfolk

"Adrian, I've got a confession to make."

"It's late, Walter, and you're sloshed!"

"That's why it's now or never."

"I'm giving you fair warning here, whatever you're planning to tell me, *don't*. You're in such a state, you'll regret it tomorrow."

"No I won't, now be quiet and listen up: I need to get this off my chest. Here goes..."

Deafening silence, followed by:

"...I'm in love."

"That's fantastic news! So why the glum face?"

"Because the woman in question has no idea."

"Yes, that does rather complicate matters. Am I allowed to ask who it is?"

"I'd rather not say."

"Your call."

"Well, er... it's... Miss Jenkins."

"The admissions secretary?"

"That's right, I've been crazy about her for four years now."

"And she hasn't twigged?"

"Well, I suppose she may have her suspicions, you know, female intuition, that kind of thing. But I hide my game rather well. Or well enough to walk past her desk every morning without turning beetroot, at any rate."

"Four years, Walter?"

"Forty-eight months, all told. I marked the anniversary a few days before you got back from Chile. Don't worry, you didn't miss a party."

"But why haven't you told her?"

"Because I'm a coward," spluttered Walter. "A frightful coward. And do you want to hear the most pathetic thing of all?"

"I'm not sure I do!"

"I've been completely faithful to her throughout."

"Well I never!"

"Do you realise how ridiculous that is? Married men, lucky enough to live with the woman they love, still cheat on them, but I'm faithful to a woman who doesn't even know I'm crazy about her."

"Why don't you just tell her? What have you got to lose, after all this time?"

"And risk ending our romance? Are you out of your mind? If she rejects me, I won't be able to think of her in the same way ever again, or cast furtive glances in her direction. Why are you looking at me like that, Adrian?"

"Nothing, I'm just wondering whether tomorrow, when you've sobered up a bit – and judging by the amount you've knocked back this evening, that's not going to be before mid-afternoon – you'll still be telling me this same story."

"It's true, Adrian, I swear, I'm head over heels in love with Miss Jenkins; but the distance separating us is like your universe, with its funny hills that stop you from seeing the other side. Miss Jenkins is in the lighthouse at Kristiansand," wailed Walter, pointing towards the east, "and I'm washed up on the English coast!" He pummelled his fist into the sand.

"But the distance between your desk and Miss Jenkins' can be measured in flights of stairs, not light-years."

"And what about the theory of relativity? I suppose you think your friend Einstein has the monopoly on that? Each of those stairs seems as far away to me as one of your galaxies!"

"I think we should see if we can find a hotel near here, Walter. Here's hoping there's somewhere local that's still open at this hour, or we could be in for a long wait until breakfast."

"No, the night's not over yet, nor are your explanations. I probably won't remember anything tomorrow, but who cares."

There could have been something hilarious about fuddy-duddy old Walter declaring his love for Miss Jenkins in this way but I really felt for him. And here I was thinking I'd known solitude in the Atacama. Could any exile be more excruciating than spending your days three floors above the woman you love, without having the courage to tell her?

"Walter, would you like me to organise a cosy dinner party with you and Miss Jenkins on the guest-list?"

"No, after all this time I don't think I'd dare speak to her. I mean... On second thoughts, would you mind repeating your kind invitation tomorrow – in the late afternoon?"

*

Paris

Keira was running late. She tugged on a pair of jeans and wriggled into a sweater; no time to tackle her hair, she just needed to find her keys and go. She hadn't slept much over the weekend and the wan daylight had failed to wake her. Flagging down a taxi on a Paris morning is always hellish. So she ended up walking as far as Boulevard de Sébastopol before turning down towards the Seine. Glancing at her wrist at every crossroads didn't help – she'd forgotten to put her watch on. A car shot into the bus lane and pulled up right by her. The driver leaned over and wound down the passenger window, calling out her name.

"D'you want me to drop you off somewhere?"

"Max?"

"I wasn't expecting to see you here!"

"I'm not stalking you, honest. But there are lots of printing works in this area, and mine happens to be in the street behind you."

"I don't want to make you go out of your way, if you're nearly at work."

"How do you know I'm not just leaving? Come on,

get in, there's a bus behind me and I'm going to get hooted at."

Keira didn't need much persuading, she opened the passenger door and clambered in next to Max.

"Quai Branly, the Museum of Arts and Civilisations please; and step on it, I'm horribly late."

"Do I at least get a kiss?"

Just as Max had predicted, a blaring horn caught them both off-guard: the bus was right up against their bumper. Max put the car into first gear and pulled rapidly out of the bus lane. The traffic was heavy and Keira felt jittery, constantly checking the clock on the dashboard.

"You're in a hurry."

"I had a lunch appointment… quarter of an hour ago."

"If it's a man, I'm sure he'll wait."

"Yes it is a man and don't even go there, he's twice your age."

"You've always liked your men mature."

"If that were true, we'd never have gone out together!"

"*Touché*! Who is he?"

"A professor."

"What's his subject?"

"You know what, it never occurred to me to ask him," admitted Keira.

"I know it's none of my business, but you're crossing Paris in the rain to have lunch with a professor, and you don't even know what he teaches?"

"It doesn't really matter, he's retired."

"So why are you having lunch with him?"

"It's a long story, just concentrate on the road and get us out of this bottleneck, please. It's about my pendant, a stone that Hari gave me. I've always wondered where it came from. This professor thinks it's very old indeed. We tried to determine its origins but drew a complete blank."

"Hari?"

"Max, *basta* with the questions, Hari's a quarter of your age! And he lives in Ethiopia."

"A bit young to be a serious contender then. So, are you going to show me this ancient stone?"

"No, I don't have it with me; I'm going to pick it up now."

"I've got a friend who's an expert on ancient stones. I could ask him to take a look at it, if you like."

"I'm sure it's not worth troubling your friend. From what I can make out the old professor's bored, and this is just giving him something to do."

"Well, let me know if you change your mind. The traffic's clearing, we'll be there in ten minutes. So where did young Hari find this stone?"

"On a tiny volcanic island in the middle of Lake Turkana."

"It could be volcanic scoria?"

"No, it's infrangible. I couldn't even make a hole in it, I had to fasten a leather thong over it to wear it round my neck. And it's been polished to perfection."

"Now I'm intrigued. Here's an idea: we'll have dinner tonight, just the two of us, and I'll take a look at your mysterious pendant. I might have given up teaching, but I still know a thing or two."

"Nice try, Max, but I'm seeing my sister this evening. We've got so much to catch up on; I keep losing my rag with her since I've been back. I've said a few things I need to apologise for... well, quite a lot of things actually."

"My offer stands for every evening this week. Here's your museum. You're barely late at all: the clock on my dashboard is fifteen minutes fast..."

Keira gave Max a peck on the forehead and got out in a hurry. He wanted to tell her to call him that afternoon, but she was already running towards the museum entrance.

"I'm so sorry to have kept you waiting," Keira panted as she pushed open the door, "Ivory?"

The office was empty. Keira's gaze was drawn to a sheet of paper under the desk lamp. Lines of handwriting had been crossed out but she could make out a series of numbers, as well as "Lake Turkana" and her own name. At the bottom of the sheet was a more than passable sketch of her pendant. Keira shouldn't have gone round to the other side of the desk, still less sat in the professor's chair and opened the drawer in front of her. But it wasn't locked and archaeologists are nosey by nature. Inside, she found an old leather notebook with a cracked cover. She put it on the desk and saw, on the first page, another drawing, not as recent as the one on the sheet, of an object resembling the one she normally wore round her neck. A noise startled her. She hurriedly tidied everything away and just had time to hide under the desk before someone walked in. Curled up like a naughty child, Keira held her breath. A man was standing just a few centimetres away, the fabric of his trousers brushed against her. He switched off the desk lamp and left the room. Keira heard the sound of the key in the lock, then silence.

It took several minutes for Keira to pull herself together. She emerged from her hiding place, went over to the door and turned the handle. Luckily it could be unlocked from the inside. Relieved, she rushed into the corridor, ran down the ramp that led to the ground floor, tripped and fell headlong. A helping hand stretched out towards her. Keira looked up and let out a loud shriek when she saw Ivory.

"Are you badly hurt?" asked the professor, kneeling down.

"No! I just got a fright."

The visitors who had stopped to offer assistance soon dispersed. End of incident.

"I'm not surprised, with a fall like that! You could have broken something. Why were you running? You're a bit late, but that's no reason to risk life and limb."

"Sorry," mumbled Keira, standing up.

"Where were you, anyway? I'd left instructions at

reception for you to join me in the garden restaurant."

"Oh, I went straight up to your office, but the door was locked and then I had the not-so-clever idea of sprinting to find you down here."

"More haste, less speed, young lady. Follow me, I'm ravenous and at my age I'm afraid I need to stick to regular mealtimes."

For the second time that day Keira felt like a disobedient child.

They sat at the same table as before. Ivory, who was clearly annoyed, buried his face in the menu.

"I do think they could vary the menu here once in a while," grumbled Ivory. "I recommend the lamb by the way, it's what they do best. Two lamb shanks," he ordered, turning to the waitress.

The professor unfolded his napkin and gave Keira a long hard stare.

"Before I forget," he said, taking the pendant out of his jacket pocket, "let me give this back to you."

Keira held the pendant and looked intently at it. She removed the leather thong from her neck and wrapped it around the stone, crossing it over twice in front and once behind, exactly as Hari had taught her to do.

"Well, it's certainly set off to its best advantage there!" Ivory remarked, finally breaking into a smile.

"Thank you," murmured Keira, a little embarrassed.

"I trust you're not blushing because of me...? So why were you late?"

Marc Levy

"I could make up all sorts of excuses Professor, but the truth is I just overslept. It's as stupid as that."

"I'm very jealous," Ivory chuckled, "I haven't managed a lie-in for at least twenty years. Getting old is no fun and, as if that weren't bad enough, the days seem to grow longer; but I won't bore you with my sleeping problems. I like people who tell the truth, though: this time you're forgiven. I'll stop pretending to be angry, since it's clearly making you uncomfortable."

"You were doing it on purpose?"

"Of course!"

"I'm guessing the results were inconclusive, then?" asked Keira, toying with her pendant.

"I'm afraid so."

"So you don't have any idea how old this object is?"

"No..." said the professor, avoiding Keira's gaze.

"Can I ask you a question?"

"You just have, but fire away with the one you really wanted to ask."

"What were you professor of?"

"Of religious studies. Though probably not in the way you're thinking. I've devoted my life to trying to understand at what point in the evolutionary process humans began to believe in a superior force and to call it 'God'. Did you know that about a hundred thousand years ago, near Nazareth, and probably for the first-time in the history of humanity, *homo sapiens* buried the remains of a twenty-year-old

116

woman. At her feet lay those of a six-year-old child.
The people who discovered this grave also found a
certain amount of red ochre around the two skeletons.
On a site not far from there, another team of archaeologists unearthed thirty similar graves. All the
corpses were laid out in the foetal position, they were
covered with ochre and each grave was decorated
with ritual objects. These are perhaps the oldest ves-
tiges of a religious ritual. Had the urge to honour the
dead come out of the pain of losing someone close?
Was it at that moment that a belief in another world,
one where the deceased continue to exist, came into
being?

"There are so many different theories on the subject that we'll probably never know at what point our
forebears really began to believe in a supreme being.
Fascinated and terrified by their environment, they
started to deify an external force. People needed to
give meaning to the mystery of dawn and dusk, and
to the inexplicable appearance of the stars at night,
to the magic of the changing seasons and the meta-
morphosis of landscapes, as well as the transforma-
tions in their own bodies over the course of their
lives. It's interesting to note the similarities found in
cave and tomb drawings in one hundred and sixty or
so different countries. The omnipresence of the
colour red, for example, is a definite symbol of contact with worlds beyond the grave. Why, no matter
where they lived, were all the human figures depicted
praying, their arms raised to the sky, frozen in the

same position? So you see, Keira, my research wasn't so far removed from your own. I share your point of view. I like the approach you take to your work. Were the first humans really the ones who stood up and walked upright? Were they the ones who began whittling away at wood and chipping stone to make tools? Or the first to cry when someone close to them died, in the realisation that their own end was inescapable? The first to believe in a superior force, or perhaps the first to express their feelings? With what words, what gestures, what offerings did the first humans express love? And who were they addressed to: their parents, their mate, their offspring, or a god?"

Keira stopped fiddling with the pendant, put her hands on the table and looked long and hard at Ivory.

"We'll probably never know the answer," she concluded.

"How can you be so sure? It's just a question of patience, determination and open-mindedness. Sometimes all we need to do is look closely at something we might miss from a distance."

"Why are you telling me this?"

"You've spent three years of your life digging the ground in search of a few fossilised bones that will allow you to uncover the mystery of the origins of humanity. But it wasn't until we met and I stirred your interest that you started looking more closely at the unusual object you wear around your neck."

"What kind of comparison's that? It's not as if there's any connection between this stone and…"

"It's not made of rock and it's not made of wood, in fact we can't say what it's made of, but its perfection leads us to doubt that nature could have shaped it that way. Do you still find my comparison so odd?"

"What are you trying to tell me?" asked Keira, fingering her necklace again.

"How about if what you've been looking for all these years was already hanging around your neck? Since you've been back in France, you haven't stopped dreaming about returning to the Omo Valley have you?"

"Is it as obvious as that?"

"You're wearing the Omo Valley around your neck, young lady. Or at least, perhaps one of its greatest mysteries."

Keira hesitated for a moment then let out a peal of laughter.

"Ivory, you nearly had me there! You were so convincing I had goose-bumps. In your eyes, I may just be a young archaeologist who shows up late, but still! There's nothing to suggest this object has any real scientific value."

"Let me put my question to you again. This object is much older than anything we could ever imagine, no modern technology has been able to remove even the tiniest fragment, or date it with any certainty, so how do you explain the remarkable way in which it's been polished?"

"It's intriguing, I'll give you that."

"I'm glad you're pondering this question, my dear

Keira, just as I'm thrilled we're getting to know each other. As I'm sure you'll agree, the odds were stacked against me making one last discovery from my little office upstairs. But thanks to you, I've defeated those odds."

"In that case, I'm delighted," said Keira.

"I'm not talking about the object – that's up to you to identify."

"So what discovery are you talking about?"

"Meeting an extraordinary woman, of course!"

Ivory stood up and left the table. Keira watched him walk away, and he turned to give his new friend a wave.

*

London

We had just over one week left to submit our application. The project was taking up all my time. Each day, in the late afternoon, Walter and I would meet up in the library where I'd give him a summary of my day's work; after reading out what I'd written (which often led to an argument), we'd grab some dinner at a nearby Indian restaurant where they did a mean chicken tikka masala. Afterwards, we'd stroll down to the Thames and walk along the river, still mulling over the best strategy for presenting my project. We never missed out on our nocturnal rambles, not even when it rained.

But on this particular evening I had a surprise in store for Walter. My MG had been a bit temperamental since our trip to Norfolk the previous weekend, so a taxi dropped us off at Euston station. We were late and rather than answering Walter's umpteenth "where on earth...?", I led him in a frantic sprint to the platform where our train was about to depart. As the doors were closing, I pushed Walter into the last carriage and just managed to squeeze in behind him when the whistle blew. The London suburbs gave way to the countryside, which in turn vanished as the suburbs of Manchester came into view.

"Manchester? What are we doing in Manchester at ten o'clock at night?" badgered an indignant Walter.

"Who said we'd reached our destination?"

"You heard the driver: *Last stop, everybody leave the train!*"

"Did it ever occur to you we might be changing trains, Walter? Come on, grab your bag and follow me, we've only got ten minutes."

We sprinted through the underpass until we were both safely aboard a local train, this time heading south.

We were the only passengers to alight at the small station of Holmes Chapel. Once despatched by the stationmaster, the train we'd just stepped off was swallowed up by the night. I checked my watch, on the lookout for our pick-up car. The person I was expecting was obviously running late.

"Right, well it's now half past ten, all I've had for dinner was that disgusting cucumber and turkey sandwich you so generously splashed out on, and now we're in some godforsaken hole. Are you or are you not going to tell me what the hell we're doing here?"

"No!"

Seeing Walter work himself up into a lather was quite amusing. Finally a 1957 Hillman Minx estate, which I immediately recognised, turned into the station approach, and about time too. I'd been beginning to wonder whether Martin had forgotten about the arrangement we'd made over the phone the previous evening.

"Sorry," blurted my old friend and colleague, emerging from the rear door. "I know I'm horribly late, but we were all caught up in the excitement and I simply couldn't get away any earlier. Get in quickly if you don't want to miss the big moment! I'm afraid that's the only way in," he added, pointing at the rear door. "Those bloody doors have been jammed ever since the handles fell off, and it's impossible to find parts these days."

The car was a heap of rusty metal with a cracked windscreen. Walter enquired in a high-pitched squeak if we were going far. After brief introductions had been made, Martin vaulted over the back seat. Once he was safely back behind the steering wheel, he asked if Walter would be kind enough to pull the rear door hard, but not too hard. We set off from the little station and rattled along the pot-holed roads of Macclesfield at terrifying speed.

Walter had to let go of the passenger wrist-strap because the last rivet holding it in place had just popped out. I noticed him hesitate for a moment before stuffing it in his pocket.

"Whoa, slow down," he urged, as the Hillman swerved round another bend, "or there'll be spewed turkey and cucumber all over your car."

"Sorry I'm driving so fast, but we simply can't

afford to miss this. Hold on tight, we'll be there soon."

"What, precisely, would you suggest I hold on to?" shouted Walter, waving the strap. "And where are we going anyway?"

Martin shot me a surprised glance, but I signalled to him to keep quiet. Walter glared daggers at me every time we pulled out of a bend; he only stopped moaning when the gigantic radio telescope at the Jodrell Bank Observatory suddenly rose up before us.

"Crikey!" whistled Walter, "I've never seen one close up."

Jodrell Bank Observatory is part of the Astronomy and Astrophysics Department at the University of Manchester. It's also where I'd spent a few months in the course of my studies, and in so doing made friends with Martin; he went on to pursue his career at Manchester, having married one Eleanor Atwell while still at university.. Heiress to the regional dairies of the same name, Eleanor had left Martin after five years of what, from the outside, appeared to be the perfect relationship. She ran off to live in London with Martin's best friend, himself heir to a fortune in the finance sector which, back in those days, was considered a better bet than dairies. Of course, Martin and I never mentioned this sensitive subject.

Jodrell Bank Observatory is unique. It houses a huge satellite dish measuring seventy-six metres in diameter. Supported by a metal cradle seventy-seven metres above the ground, this radio telescope is the third largest in the world. There are three other smaller telescopes. Jodrell runs a complex network of satellite dishes located across England, all inter-connected to cross-check vast amounts of data from space. The network is called Merlin which, as an acronym made from a group of scientists' names, has little to do with wizardry. The astronomers working at Jodrell are tasked with tracking meteorites, quasars, pulsars, gravitational lenses and, in the far reaches of galaxies, detecting the black holes that were formed when the universe was born. "Are we going to see a black hole?" Walter wanted to know, sounding enthusiastic all of a sudden.

Martin smiled but refrained from giving an answer.

"How did it go in the Atacama?" he asked, as Walter struggled to extract himself from the car.

"Very inspiring, and an amazing team," I replied, with more than a hint of wistfulness, which my former colleague immediately picked up on.

"Why don't you come and join us here? We're not in the same league, resources-wise, but this team has a lot of talent."

"I'm sure it has, Martin, and I'm not implying that my colleagues in the Atacama are in any way superior to yours at Jodrell. But it's the Chilean air I miss, the solitude of the high plateau, those clear nights. Anyway, right now we're here, and I'm very grateful to you for that."

"Come on then," grumbled Walter, who was waiting on the grass, "are we going to see this black hole or not?"

"Sort of," I said, clambering out of the Hillman, and Martin couldn't resist a chuckle.

Martin's colleagues greeted us and quickly got back to work. Walter was hoping to squint through a giant lens, and was disappointed when I pointed out he'd have to make do with the images on the bank of computer screens around us. The excitement was palpable. All the scientists had their eyes glued to their consoles. From time to time, in the distance, we could hear the squeaking of the satellite dish as it pivoted a few millimetres on its giant metal axis. Then silence would settle again and each person would tune in to those signals coming to us from the beginning of time.

Walter kept badgering Martin's colleagues with questions, so I decided to give them a break by taking him outside the building.

"What are they all so worked up about?" he whispered.

"You can talk normally now, you don't need to worry about disturbing them out here. This evening they're hoping to see the birth of a black hole, which is a rare event in the life of a radio astronomer."

"Are you going to talk about black holes in front of the Walsh Foundation?"

"Of course."

"Go on then, I'm all ears."

"The black hole represents the ultimate unknown for an astronomer, not even light can escape from it."

"So how do you know they exist?"

"They're formed after the final implosion of a massive star, bigger than our sun even. The debris from that star is so heavy that nothing in nature can prevent it from collapsing under its own weight. When this matter approaches a black hole, it resonates with it and rings like a bell. The sound that reaches us is a B flat, fifty-seven octaves below middle C. Did you ever imagine listening to music from the depths of the universe?"

"That's incredible," murmured Walter.

"Time and space warp around the black hole, and the passage of time actually slows down. A man who could travel to the edge of a black hole without being swallowed up by it would return to earth a lot younger than the people he left behind when he set off."

By the time we went back into the room where my fellow astronomers were keyed up for this eagerly awaited phenomenon, Walter had undergone a dramatic change. He stared hard at those screens filled with tiny dots, witnesses of long-ago eras when human life didn't yet exist. At 3.07am, a great cheer went up that was loud enough to make the walls shudder. Martin, usually so phlegmatic, gave such a jump he nearly fell over backwards. The proof posted on their screens was irrefutable; tomorrow, the community of astronomers around the world would rejoice in my English colleagues' discovery, and perhaps my friends in the Atacama would spare a thought for us.

Walter was fascinated by what I'd told him about time warps. The next morning, as Martin was driving us back to the little station at Holmes Chapel, he explained to Walter that his greatest dream was to identify a wormhole one day. Having only just recovered from finding out about black holes, Walter thought Martin was pulling his leg at first. Since Martin was having a hard time steering a straight course with the Hillman, I took over. I explained to Walter that wormholes were shortcuts in space-time (like the doors between two points in the universe) and that if we managed to prove their existence one day, we could be taking the first steps towards travelling through space faster than the speed of light.

Walter gave Martin a big hug on the platform and even came over slightly misty-eyed telling him what a wonderful job he had. Then he took the strap out of his pocket and solemnly returned it to its owner.

On the train back, as Manchester disappeared behind us, Walter informed me that in his view, if the Walsh Foundation didn't select our project, there was no justice in this world.

*

Paris

Keira spent her evenings that week enjoying some quality time at her sister's place, as she'd told Max she would.

"Do you think about Dad often?"

Keira poked her head round the kitchen door and saw Jeanne staring at a china cup.

"He used to drink his coffee out of this every morning," said Jeanne, pouring some herbal tea and handing the cup to Keira. "It's silly, but every time I see it in the cupboard it makes me feel down."

Keira looked at her sister in silence.

"And every time I use it, I feel as if he's right there in front of me, smiling. Crazy, hey?"

"Not at all. Okay, confession: I've kept one of his shirts which I wear sometimes, and it has exactly the same effect. As soon as I slip it on, it's as if he's spending the day with me."

"Do you think he'd be proud of us?"

"Two daughters in their thirties who haven't got a long-term partner or a child between them? He's probably turning in his grave!"

"I can't tell you how much I miss Dad, Keira – and Mum too."

"Can we change the subject."

"Do you really want to go back to Ethiopia?"

"I don't know. I don't even know what I'm going to be doing next week. In fact, I need to find something and fast, or you'll end up having to keep me."

"You'll think what I'm about to say sounds selfish, but I'd so love you to stay. We miss Mum and Dad, that's normal, and anyway I like to imagine they've got back together again up there; but we're alive, and with you so far away it feels like we're missing out."

"I know Jeanne, but sooner or later you'll meet another Jérôme, except he'll be the right one this time. You'll have kids, and Auntie Keira'll come and visit when she's back from the field with lots of stories to tell. You're still my sister, and I think about you even when I'm deep in the Omo Valley. I promise if I go away again, I'll call more often and not just for small-talk."

"You're right; that was unfair of me. Let's talk about something else. I want you to live where you're happiest. Right, what do you need to get back to your beloved Omo Valley?"

"A team, equipment, and enough money to pay for both: small change, really!"

"Like how much?"

"A lot more, darling big sister, than you've got in your piggy bank."

"Why don't you try to get sponsorship from the private sector?"

"Because archaeologists don't tend to dance around in front of TV cameras wearing T-shirts that promote washing powder or fizzy drinks, or the friendly face of banks. With the result that sponsors are thin on the ground, if they exist at all. Then again, we could always try organising a fund-raising party. A sort of sack race with trowels. The first to dig up a bone wins a year's subscription to *Archaeology Today.*"

"Don't pooh-pooh everything! Why does your knee-jerk reaction always have to be: 'No way!'? If you presented your project to various trusts and foundations, there may well be some opportunities out there for you."

"Nobody cares about my research, Jeanne. Who'd sponsor me, even to the tune of a Euro?"

"You should have more faith in your own work. You've just spent three years in the field; you've written all sorts of reports. I've read your doctorate and, if I had the money, I'd jump at the chance to fund your next expedition."

"Yes, but that's because you're my sister! It's sweet of you Jeanne, really, but I'm not sure it'll stand scrutiny. Thanks anyway, though."

"Instead of frittering your days away, why don't you undertake a spot of Internet research into which French and European organisations might be receptive to what you do?"

"Why waste my time?"

"So what d'you call what you've been getting up

to with Ivory at the museum these past few days?"

"He's an odd fish, isn't he? He's obsessed by my pendant, and I've got to admit that even I'm curious now. We've tried dating it, without any success. He's still convinced it's very ancient indeed, and there's nothing to prove whether he's right or wrong."

"His gut instinct?"

"I've got a lot of respect for him, but I'm afraid that's not enough."

"It's certainly a very unusual object. I've got a friend who's a gemologist, shall I ask him to take a look at it?"

"It's not actually a stone, and it's not fossilised wood either."

"So what is it?"

"We don't know."

"Let's see!" said Jeanne, suddenly sounding excited. Keira took the necklace off and held it out to her sister.

"What if it were a fragment from a meteorite?"

"Have you ever heard of a meteorite that was smooth as a baby's skin?"

"I'm no expert, but I'm guessing we're a long way off discovering everything that's reached earth from outer space."

"Well, it's one hypothesis," said Keira, putting on her archaeological hat again. "I remember reading somewhere that nearly fifty thousand meteorites fall to Earth every year."

"Why don't you ask an expert?"

"What kind of expert?"

"The local butcher, stupid! I don't know, someone who deals in this kind of stuff, an astronomer or an astrophysicist, I guess."

"Let me just get out my diary and open up the page headed 'astronomer friends'. Now, which one should I call first?"

Jeanne bit her tongue, went over to the little desk in the hall and sat down at her computer.

"What are you doing?" asked Keira.

"I'm working on your behalf! I'll start on it this evening, and then tomorrow you're not budging from here; or the next day or the next. The only thing you're allowed to look at is this screen. When I come back, I expect to find a list of all the organisations that support research into archaeology, palaeontology and geology, including those that promote sustainable development in Africa – and that's an order!"

*

Zurich

One office was still lit up on the top floor of the Credit Suisse building. An elegantly dressed man was checking the last of the e-mails that had come in while he'd been away. He'd arrived that morning from Milan, and there'd been no let-up all day. Meetings followed by more meetings; files and then more files to be read. He glanced at his watch: if he hurried up he'd make it home in time to enjoy what was left of his evening. He swivelled his chair, pressed one of the buttons on his telephone and waited for his driver to answer.

"Bring the car round, I'll be down in five minutes."

He tightened his tie and was tidying his desk when he spotted a coloured icon on his computer screen, notifying him that he'd missed an e-mail. He read it and immediately deleted it. Then he took out a small black notebook from the inside pocket of his jacket, leafed through the pages, readjusted his glasses to read the number he was looking for and picked up the phone.

"I just read your message, who else knows about this?"

"Paris, New York, and you, sir."

"When did this meeting take place?"

"The day before yesterday."

"Meet me in half an hour on the esplanade of the École Polytechnique."

"That could be difficult, I'm just going into the Opera House."

"What's playing this evening?"

"Puccini, *Madame Butterfly*."

"Well, she can wait. See you shortly."

The man called his driver, cancelled his instructions and gave him the night off. It turned out he had more work than he'd realised, so he'd be staying late in the office after all. No point picking him up from home tomorrow, he'd probably sleep in town. As soon as he'd hung up, he went over to the window and parted the slats of the blinds to view the street below. When he saw his vehicle pull out of the car park and cross Paradeplatz, he left his observation post, grabbed his overcoat from the coat-stand and walked out of the office, locking the door behind him.

There was only one lift working at that late hour. Down in the lobby, the security guard greeted him and pressed the button to unlock the revolving door.

Once outside, the man made his way through the crowd thronging Zurich's main square. He walked towards Bahnhofstrasse and caught the first passing tram. He sat down at the back, but gave up his place at the next stop to an elderly lady.

Groaning and creaking, the tram turned off the main commercial drag to cross the bridge over the river. Once they'd reached the opposite bank, the man stepped off the tram and started walking towards the funicular station.

The bright red funicular railway is like something out of toy town; magically scaling the outside of a building, it climbs a steep slope and then cuts through the foliage of the chestnut trees to reappear on the crest of the hill. The man didn't pause to take in the spectacular view from the terrace of the École Poly-technique, which overlooked the city. He crossed that expanse of concrete without slowing his pace, walked around the domed Institute of Science, and took the steps leading down to the colonnades. The person he'd arranged to meet was already there.

"Sorry to ruin your evening, but this couldn't wait until tomorrow."

"I understand."

"Let's take a stroll, the air will do me good; I spent all day shut up in an office. Why was Paris tipped off before we were?"

"Ivory contacted him directly."

"Did a meeting really take place?"

The man nodded and added that it had been held on the first floor of the Eiffel Tower.

"Do you have a photo?"

"Of the lunch?" the man asked, in surprise.

"No, of the object, of course."

"Ivory hasn't sent us anything and the item we're interested in had left the laboratory in Los Angeles before we could intervene."

"Ivory believes this object is related to the one we already have?"

"He's always been convinced there were several of them; but as you know, he's the only one to think so."

"Or the only one to have the nerve to say it out loud. Ivory can be an old fool sometimes, but he's also extremely intelligent and cunning. This could be just another of his harebrained ideas, or a stunt to make us look like idiots."

"Why would he do that?"

"Delayed revenge... he's a tricky character."

"And if it is the genuine article?"

"In that case, certain measures are called for. And we need to get our hands on that object at all costs."

"According to Paris, Ivory has returned it to its owner."

"Do we know who this woman is?"

"Not yet, he refused to reveal her identity."

He's even crazier than I thought, but that makes me think he's probably in earnest. I expect he'll engineer it so that, in a few days, we all find out who she is at exactly the same time."

"What makes you think that?"

"Because he's forcing us to reactivate the cell and come together. Look, I've made you late enough as it is, get back to your opera, I'll take care of the next steps in this irksome business."

"The second act doesn't start for half an hour, so why don't you tell me how you plan to proceed?"

"I'm going to drive out this evening and meet him at dawn to convince him to stop his little game."

"You're going to drive across the border in the middle of the night? That's likely to attract attention."

"Ivory is one step ahead of us. I refuse to let him call the shots. I've got to make him see reason."

"Are you in a fit state to drive for seven hours?"

"No, probably not," answered the man, running a hand over his tired face.

"My car's parked two streets away from here, let me come with you, we'll share the driving."

"I appreciate your offer but, as you've pointed out, one diplomatic passport is already likely to attract attention at the border; two would be playing with fire. That said, if you wouldn't mind lending me your car keys, it would save me precious time. I sent my driver home for the evening."

His colleague's sports coupé wasn't far at all. Jörg Gerlstein slid behind the driving wheel, adjusted the seat for more leg-room and switched on the ignition.

Leaning on the door, the car's owner suggested that Jörg open the glove compartment.

"If you start feeling sleepy, you'll find a few CDs in there. They're my sixteen-year-old daughter's and, take it from me, the music she listens to would wake the dead."

At 9.10pm the coupé turned into Universität-Strasse, heading north.

The motorway traffic had cleared. Jörg Gerlstein should have cut across into the left-hand lane in order to take the slip road for Mulhouse, but he preferred to continue northwards. The journey would be longer via Germany, but it would enable Gerlstein to enter France without having to show his papers. Paris wouldn't know anything about his visit.

He reached the suburb of Karlsruhe at midnight, and took the exit for Baden-Baden half an hour later. If his calculations were right, he'd get to Thionville at half past two in the morning and make it to the centre of Paris at around six o'clock.

The headlights picked out the hairpin bends on the road ahead; the engine was purring, responsive to the gentlest touch of the accelerator. At 1.40am the car swerved slightly to the right. Gerlstein quickly regained control of the vehicle and lowered the window. The fresh air stung his face, dispelling the fatigue that made his head feel heavy. He leaned over to open the glove compartment and grope around for the CDs belonging to his colleague's daughter. But he never got a chance to hear the first track. The front right tire hit the hard shoulder then sank into a hole, the coupé skidded and spun off the motorway. Moments later, it rebounded off a rock and ended its journey by crashing into an ancient pine tree. The rapid deceleration from fifty to zero mph in under a second propelled Gerlstein's brain forwards, so that the impact as it smashed into his skull was comparable to that of a three-tonne object. His heart suffered the same fate inside his thorax, and his veins and arteries ruptured.

The alarm was raised at 5am by a lorry driver who'd spotted the wreckage in his headlights. The police found Gerlstein's body lying in a pool of blood. The officer in charge didn't need to wait for the forensic scientist's opinion to pronounce the driver dead: he was too cold and pale for there to be any doubt.

At 10am, an AFP wire announced the death of a Swiss diplomat, a director of Credit Suisse, victim of a road accident in the middle of the night in eastern France. Tests showed no traces of alcohol in the blood and the tragedy was probably due to the man falling asleep at the wheel. The incident was briefly picked up by round-the-clock news websites. Ivory found out about it from his computer at around midday, just as he was getting ready to go out to lunch. In a foul temper he gave up on that plan, transferred the contents of his drawers into his bag and vacated his office, deliberately leaving the door open. He walked out of the museum and made for one of the few remaining telephone booths on the Right Bank.

From there, he immediately called Keira and asked if they could meet up in an hour.

"You sound strange, Ivory."

"I've just lost a very dear friend."

"I'm so sorry to hear that… but what has this got to do with me?"

"Nothing. I'm going to take a holiday; my friend's death has reminded me how precarious life is. I've had enough of stagnating in the museum, I'll end up becoming part of their collection if I don't watch out. It's time for me to make the journey I've been dreaming of for many years."

"Where to?"

"Why don't we have a chat about that over a nice cup of hot chocolate? Angelina, Rue de Rivoli – how soon can you get there?"

Keira was on her way to the Hôtel Meurice, where she had a late-lunch date with Max. She checked her watch and promised the professor she'd join him in a quarter of an hour.

*

Jeanne hadn't been able to stop thinking about an idea she'd had over coffee with Ivory the previous day, and she was using her break to set things in motion. Even as a child, her little sister always used to say to her: "When I grow up, I want to dig for treasure." Unlike her, Keira had always known what she wanted to do with her life. Even if Jeanne hated the distance that Keira's job put between them, she'd do everything in her power to help her sister get back to Ethiopia.

*

Ivory was sitting at a table at the back of the café. He waved at Keira who came over to join him.

"I took the liberty of ordering two slices of the delicious chestnut cake they serve here. I hope you like chestnuts?"

"I do," Keira confirmed, "but I haven't eaten lunch yet and I'm keeping someone waiting."

Ivory looked crestfallen.

"You didn't ask me here just to try cake?"

"No, no. I wanted to see you before I go."

"Why the rush?"

"Because of this friend who's died – I think I mentioned that?"

"How did he...?"

"A car accident. It seems he fell asleep at the wheel, but the awful thing is I have a hunch he was on his way to visit me."

"Without letting you know?"

"That's generally how surprises work."

"Were you very close?"

"I had a lot of respect for him but I wasn't terribly fond of him; he could be rather supercilious at times."

"I don't understand, Ivory, you said he was your friend."

"Knowing who your friends are is one of the hardest things in life."

"Ivory, what exactly can I do for you?" Keira pressed him, checking her watch.

"Cancel your lunch, or at least make it a bit later, I really need to talk to you."

"About what?"

"I have every reason to believe the man who got himself killed last night took to the road because of your pendant. You can choose to forget everything I'm about to tell you, Keira. Write me off as a mad, bored old man who's trying to spice up his life with absurd fabrications if you like. But the thing is, I didn't tell you everything about your necklace."

"What didn't you tell me?"

The waitress put two generous slices of cake, piled high with cream, on the table. Ivory waited for her to move away before carrying on with the conversation.

"There's another one."

"Another what?"

"Another fragment, as perfectly sculpted as yours is. And even if its shape is marginally different, no examination or test was capable of dating it either."

"Have you seen it?"

"Yes, and I've even held it, but a very long time ago, when I was your age."

"And where is this sister fragment?"

Ivory didn't answer, attacking his cake instead.

"Why is this stone so important to you?" Keira persisted.

"I've already told you it's not a stone, it's probably a metal alloy. Not that it matters: stone or not, that isn't what's at stake here. Are you familiar with the legend of Tikkun Olam?"

143

"Never heard of it."

"Strictly speaking, it's not a legend but a story from the Old Testament. The most interesting thing about sacred writings is generally not what they tell us, since their interpretations are subjective and often get distorted over time, but why they were written in the first place —what event prompted them?"

"And in the case of Tikkun Olam?"

"The scripture tells us that a long, long time ago, the world was broken up into several pieces and that it would be the task of every person to find those pieces in order to bring them back together again. Only when this task had been completed would the world be perfect."

"What's this got to do with my necklace?"

"It all depends on what we take the word 'world' to mean. But imagine, for a moment, that your pendant was one of the fragments of this world?"

Keira stared at the professor.

"This friend, who died last night, was on his way to instruct me not to reveal anything to you, and he was probably also looking for a way to separate you from your pendant."

"Are you suggesting he was murdered?"

"Keira, whether or not you decide this object is important, please keep a very careful eye on it. It is highly likely that someone will try to take it from you."

"What do you mean by 'someone'?"

"It doesn't matter. Just concentrate on what I'm telling you."

"But I've got no idea what you're going on about, Ivory! I've had this stone – or pendant, if you prefer – for two years, and nobody's shown any interest in it. So why now?"

"Because my pride led me to do something fool-hardy, in order to prove that I was right."

"Right about what?"

"I've told you that another one almost identical to yours exists, and I'm convinced it's not the only one. Nobody ever believed me, so when your pendant appeared on the scene it provided the perfect opportunity for me, old man that I am, to prove I was right."

"Supposing several objects like mine do exist, and that they're linked in some way to your improbable legend, what then?"

"That's up to you. You're young, perhaps you'll have enough time to find out."

"Find out what?"

"In your view, what would a perfect world look like?"

"I don't know – a free world?"

"An excellent answer, my dear Keira. Find out what prevents humans from being free, find out the cause of all wars, and ultimately you might understand."

The professor stood up, leaving some money on the table.

"Are you going already?" asked a stunned Keira.

"Your lunch date is waiting and I've told you everything I know. I need to pack my suitcase; I've got a plane to catch this evening. I really am so glad we had a chance to get to know one another. You're far more talented than you think. I hope you have a long and fruitful journey ahead; above all, I hope that you are happy. After all, isn't happiness what we're all chasing after without fully realising it?"

Ivory left the café and waved at Keira for the last time.

The waitress picked up the bill which the professor had paid.

"This must be yours," she said, holding out a note from the saucer.

Startled, Keira unfolded the piece of paper.

I know you will not give up. I would like to have joined you on this adventure; with time I could have proved myself a friend. I will be watching over you. Yours sincerely, Ivory.

Stepping out onto Rue de Rivoli, Keira didn't notice the powerful motorbike parked in front of the railings of the Tuileries Gardens opposite the tearoom, nor did she see the rider pointing a lens at her; she was too far away to hear the camera clicking as he took shot after shot. Fifty metres further along, Ivory was sitting in the back of a taxi; he smiled and told the driver he could move off now.

*

London

We had addressed our application to the Board of the Walsh Foundation. I'd sealed the envelope which Walter, no doubt worried I'd change my mind at the last minute, had all but ripped out of my hands, insisting he'd rather post it himself.

If we were shortlisted (and we were expecting a reply any day now) then my presentation would take place in a month's time. Ever since he'd sent the application by registered post, Walter had been permanently on the lookout through his window.

"You're not going to accost the postman, are you?"

"Maybe?" he muttered nervously.

"May I remind you, Walter, that I'm the one who's got to speak in public, so why don't you just leave the stress to me?"

"You? Stressed? I'd like to see that!"

Now that the die was cast, my evenings with Walter petered out. Our lives returned to their usual routines, and I found myself missing his company. I spent my afternoons at the university, attending to various work projects to fill my time, waiting for someone to assign me a class for September. After a tedious day of non-stop rain, I'd dragged Walter over to South Kensington: I was looking for a book by one of my eminent French colleagues, Jean-Pierre Luminet, which was only available in a bookshop I was fond of on Bute Street.

Leaving the French Bookshop, Walter insisted that we go to a brasserie which, according to him, served the best oysters in London. That was fine by me and we found ourselves at a table not far from two very attractive girls. Walter didn't give them a second glance, but the same couldn't be said of me.

"Stop being such a letch, Adrian!"

"Sorry?"

"Do you think I haven't noticed? You're being so obvious the staff have already started laying bets."

"On what?"

"The likelihood of those two girls telling you to take a flying leap – you're about as subtle as a brick."

"I've got no idea what you're talking about, Walter."

"And a hypocrite to boot! Have you ever really been in love, Adrian?"

"That's a very personal question."

"I've confided a few secrets to you, now it's your turn."

It's true that no friendship is cemented without the exchange of secrets; I confessed to Walter I'd been very taken with a girl I'd gone out with one summer, a long time ago when I'd only just finished my studies.

"What made you split up?"

"She did!"

"Why?"

"Look Walter, what's this got to do with you?"

"I want to get to know you better. I'd like to think we're striking up a proper friendship, and finding out about this kind of thing matters. We can't talk about astrophysics all the time; or the weather, come to that. You're the one who told me not to be so up-tight."

"What d'you want to know?"

"Why did she break up with you?"

"I guess we were too young."

"Nonsense! I might have known you'd come out with a feeble excuse like that."

"And what do you know about it? You weren't there!"

"Why can't you tell me the real reason for breaking up with...?"

"This girl"

"That's a pretty name!"

"She was a pretty girl!"

"Well?"

"Well what, Walter?" I exploded.

"I'd like you to tell me everything! How you met, how you broke up, and what happened in between!"

"She had an English father and a French mother. She'd always lived in Paris, where her parents had settled when her older sister was born. After they got divorced, her father returned to England. She'd come over to visit him while on a university exchange scheme, which meant spending a term in London. At the time I was working as a supervisor there, to help make ends meet over the holidays and to finance my PhD."

"A supervisor hitting on a female student... that's original."

"Fine, let's stop right there!"

"Only joking, I'm riveted, go on!"

"We first set eyes on each other in an exam hall where I was invigilating and she was sitting an exam, along with at least a hundred other students. She had an aisle desk and I was pacing up and down that aisle when I saw her unfolding a crib sheet."

"She was cheating?"

"No idea, I never got a chance to read what was written on the piece of paper."

"You didn't confiscate it?"

"Didn't have time!"

"Why not?"

"Realising I'd spotted her, she looked me straight in the eye and, cool as a cucumber, put it in her mouth, chewed it and swallowed it."

"I don't believe you!"

"Well, that's what happened. Anyway, I don't know what came over me, I should have confiscated her exam paper and made her leave the hall, but I started laughing and in the end, I was the one who had to leave the room."

"And then what?"

"Whenever she ran into me in the library or in a corridor, she stared and openly flaunted my authority. One day, I pulled her away from her group of friends and asked her why she laughed whenever she saw me. She said that if I didn't ask her out to lunch, she'd never tell me. So I asked her out to lunch."

"And what happened?"

"After lunch we went for a walk and then, at the end of the afternoon, she left abruptly. No news until a week later, while I was working on my PhD in the library, a girl sat down opposite me. I didn't pay any attention until a chewing noise really started grating on my nerves; I looked up to ask the person in question to make less noise with their gum and it was her, busy swallowing a third sheet of paper. I was genuinely taken aback: I hadn't been expecting to see her again. She told me that if I didn't realise she was there for me, she might as well leave straightaway, and for good this time."

"I'm liking this girl more and more!"

"We spent that evening and most of the summer together. It was an unforgettable summer."

"So why did you split up?"

"That's a story for another evening, Walter."

"Was that your only relationship?"

"Of course not, there was Tara, the Dutch student doing a PhD in astrophysics, whom I lived with for nearly a year. We got on really well, but she got a kitten. I'm allergic to cats and told her it was either the kitten or me. She chose the kitten. Then there was

151

Jane the lovely doctor; she came from a very old Scottish family and was obsessed with making our relationship "official". The day she introduced me to her parents, I had no choice but to end things: I wasn't ready to settle down. After Jane came Sarah Appleton, who worked in a bakery; fabulous cleavage, hips straight out of Botticelli, but impossible working hours. She'd get up when I was going to bed, and vice versa. And then, two years later, I married a colleague, Elizabeth Atkins, but that didn't work out either."

"You were married?"

"Yes, for sixteen days! My ex-wife and I separated as soon as we got back from a disastrous honeymoon. I'm telling you, if people went on honeymoon before they got married, the courts would have a lot less paperwork to push through."

This time I really had shut Walter up; he seemed to have lost his appetite for finding out any more about my love life. Not that there was much more to tell, other than that my professional life had taken over and I'd spent the past fifteen years travelling the world, without really thinking about settling down anywhere; still less about meeting someone special. Having a relationship was not a priority right now.

"And you never saw each other again?"

"I've run into Elizabeth at a couple of cocktail parties at the Royal Society. My ex-wife was with her new husband. Did I mention that her new husband was also my ex–best friend?"

"No, you didn't. But I wasn't talking about her, I meant your young student, the first of your Casanova conquests?"

"Why her?"

"I just wondered!"

"We never saw each other again."

"Adrian, tell me why she left you and I'll pick up the tab!"

I ordered a dozen more oysters from the waiter who was just passing our table.

"At the end of that exchange term, she went back to finish her studies in France. Distance often nips promising relationships in the bud. A month after she left, she came back to see her father; she was worn out after a ten-hour journey that involved a bus, a ferry and finally a train. The last Sunday we spent together was less than idyllic. That evening, when I saw her off at the station, she told me we'd better call it a day. That way we'd just have the happy memories. I could see in her eyes there was no point in arguing: the spark had already fizzled out. She'd already moved on, and not just geographically. There you go Walter, now you know everything. What's with the silly grin on your face?"

"Oh, nothing," he said airily.

"Here I am, baring my soul, confiding in you about the time I was unceremoniously dumped and you find that funny?"

"You've just told me about a relationship that's clearly had a lasting impact on you and, if I hadn't pushed for details, you'd have sworn on your life that it was all in the past, wouldn't you?"

"Of course! I don't even know if I'd recognise her now. It was fifteen years ago, Walter, and it only lasted two months."

"So answer me this: why, if it's such an innocuous story that's been water under the bridge for fifteen years, have you not once been able to say her name? Ever since I confessed to you about my unreciprocated love for Miss Jenkins, I've felt a bit, how can I put it, well, stupid. But not anymore!"

The two women at the next table had got up and left without our noticing. That evening, I remember Walter and I stayed until closing time, and we drank enough wine for me to refuse his offer and to end up paying half the bill instead.

The next day, when we both turned up at work with crushing hangovers, there was a letter informing us that our application had been shortlisted.

Walter was feeling so wretched that his shriek of joy came out as more of a plaintive squawk.

*

Paris

Keira turned the key as slowly as possible, but the lock still made a resounding clunk on the final twist. Carefully closing the apartment door behind her, she tiptoed down the corridor. The dawn glow was already spreading over her sister's desk. An envelope with a British stamp, addressed to Keira, was laid out on a tray. Intrigued, she opened it to find a letter inside informing her that, despite her late submission, the selection committee was considering her application. Keira was expected in London on the twenty-eighth of the month, to present her research before the judging panel of the Walsh Foundation.

"What's all this about?" she whispered to herself, putting the letter back into its envelope.

Jeanne appeared in a nightdress, her hair tousled; she yawned and had a stretch.

"How's Max?"

"Go back to bed, Jeanne, it's hideously early!"

"Or hideously late, depending which way you look at it. Did you have a fun evening?"

"Not really."

"So why did you spend the night with him?"

"Because I was cold."

"Winter's a bummer, hey?"

"Cut it out, Jeanne, I'm off to bed."

"I've got a present for you."

"A present?"

Jeanne held out an envelope.

"What's that?"

"Open it and you'll see."

Keira found a Eurostar ticket inside, as well as a pre-paid voucher for two nights at the Regency Inn.

"It's not exactly four-star, but Jérôme took me there and it's a really sweet little place."

"And is this present connected with the letter I just found in the hall?"

"Kind of, but I've extended your stay so you get a chance to enjoy London too. You can't miss the Natural History Museum, the Tate Modern will blow you away and you've got to squeeze in brunch at Amoul's, on Formosa Street. I fell in love with that place; they do delicious cakes and salads, and as for their lemon chicken..."

"Jeanne, it's six o'clock in the morning, I can't face even the idea of lemon chicken right now..."

"Are you going to say thank you at any point, or am I going to have to make you swallow that train ticket?"

"Before I do, I think you'd better explain the contents of this letter and what you're up to, or you're the one who'll be eating this ticket!"

"Make me a cup of tea and some toast with honey
and I'll see you in the kitchen in five minutes; I'm
going to wash my face. Beat it!"

Keira had picked up her invitation from the Walsh
Foundation and put it where her sister couldn't miss
it, in front of the steaming cup and the plate of toast.

"At least *one* of us has to believe in you!" said
Jeanne, shuffling into the kitchen. "I did what you
should have done by rights, if only you'd give yourself more credit. I searched on the Internet and made
a list of all the organisations that might conceivably
finance your archaeological research. Admittedly,
there aren't many of them out there. Not even in
Brussels. Unless you fancy spending two years filling
out stacks of forms."

"You wrote to the European Parliament on your
little sister's behalf?"

"I wrote to everybody! And then yesterday, this
letter came for you. I don't know if it's a yes or a no,
but at least they've bothered to reply."

"Jeanne?"

"Okay, so I opened the envelope but I sealed it
straight up again. Given all the trouble I've gone to,
I reckoned I had a right to know."

"So this foundation has decided to accept my application on the basis of what documentary evidence?"

"You'll go ballistic when I tell you, but I'm beyond caring. I sent out your thesis each time. It was
on my computer so I decided that was fair enough.

After all, it's already published, isn't it?"

"Let me see if I've got this right: you passed yourself off as me, sent my work to a bunch of organisations we know nothing about and..."

"And now you're in with a chance of making it back to your beloved Omo Valley! Any more complaints?"

Keira stood up and gave Jeanne a hug.

"I love you, you're a pain in the neck and you can be stubborn as a mule, but you're my sister and I wouldn't swap you for anything in the world!"

"Are you feeling all right?" asked Jeanne, looking closely at Keira.

"Couldn't be better!"

Keira sat back down at the kitchen table and re-read the letter for the third time.

"Oh my god, I've got to give a presentation about my research, what am I going to tell them!"

"So here's the deal: there's not much time left, you need to write up your project and learn it off by heart. You have to be able to look the judges in the eye; it won't work if you're reading from a script. You'll be brilliant, I know it."

Keira jumped up and began pacing around the kitchen.

"If you like, I'll pretend to be a judge when I get home from work every evening, and you can rehearse in front of me."

"Please, come to London with me, I'll never be able to do it on my own."

"I can't, I've got too much work."

"Pleeeze, Jeanne."

"I can't afford to, Keira, I'm flat broke after coughing up for your train ticket and the hotel."

"There's no reason for you to pay for my trip, I'll find a way."

"Let's not argue about it, just thank me by bringing back the prize."

"How much is it worth?"

"Two million pounds."

"What's that in Euros?" asked Keira, wide-eyed.

"Enough to pay the wages of an entire international team plus everyone's travel expenses, as well as buying and shipping state-of-the-art equipment so that you can turn over every last clod of earth in the Omo Valley."

"I'll never win!"

"Go and get a few hours' sleep, have a nice shower when you wake up and get down to work. Oh, and remember to tell that Max you won't be seeing him for a while. You're not setting foot outside this apartment until you're word-perfect. Don't look at me like that: I haven't set all this up to keep you two apart. Whatever you may think, I don't have a hidden agenda."

"The thought hadn't crossed my mind."

"Yeah, right. Off you go."

In the days that followed, Keira shut herself away in her sister's apartment, spending most of her time in front of the computer, honing her theories and

documenting them with articles published by archaeologist colleagues from around the world.

And, just as she'd promised, Jeanne put her sister
through her paces every evening when she got back
from the museum. If Keira didn't sound convincing
enough, if she stammered or got stuck or ventured explanations that were too technical for Jeanne's taste,
she would make her start again from scratch. Those
first few evenings were fraught with arguments.

Keira was quick to learn her presentation; now she
just had to pitch it right and win over her audience.

As soon as Jeanne left the apartment in the morning, Keira started practising out loud. The concierge
came by one morning to drop off a book Keira had
ordered, and was promptly made to sit down and listen. Comfortably settled on the sofa with a cup of tea
in hand, Madame Hereira was subjected to the complete history of our planet, from the Precambrian era
to the Cretaceous period – which saw the first flow-
ering plants appear, a whole generation of insects,
new species of fish, ammonites, sponges and all sorts
of dinosaurs which evolved on land from then on.
Madame Hereira was thrilled to learn that sharks resembling those alive today first appeared during this
period. But most gripping of all was the emergence
of the first mammals whose offspring developed in
placental sacks, just as humans would do much later
on.

Madame Hereira dozed off in the middle of the
Tertiary period, somewhere between the Palaeocene

and the Eocene. When she opened her eyes she wondered sheepishly if she'd been asleep for long. Keira assured her she'd only missed thirty million years. That evening, she was careful not to mention the visit or the reaction of her first audience to Jeanne.

The following Wednesday, Jeanne said she was sorry but there was a dinner she couldn't get out of. Keira was exhausted and secretly relieved at the prospect of skipping a rehearsal. She told Jeanne not to worry and promised to rehearse her speech, just as if her sister were there. But no sooner had Keira seen Jeanne get into her taxi, than she prepared herself a plate of cheese, flopped onto the sofa and switched on the television. There was a storm on the way, the Paris sky had turned leaden and Keira pulled a blanket round her shoulders.

The first thunderclap was so violent it made her jump. The second rumble was followed by a power-cut. Keira hunted for a lighter in the gloom, but without success. She stood up and went over to the window. The lightning struck the conductor of a building a few blocks away. As an archaeologist out in the field, Keira had got to know a great deal about thunderstorms and how dangerous they could be: this one was unusually intense. She should have moved well away from the window, but only took one step backwards before instinctively reaching for her necklace. If the pendant was indeed a metal alloy, as Ivory thought, then she shouldn't tempt fate by keeping it around her neck. Just as she was taking it off, a streak of lightning tore through the sky. It lit up the living room and, all of a sudden, millions of tiny luminous dots appeared on the wall, projected by the pendant she was holding. This arresting sight only lasted for a few seconds, before it was gone. Keira was trembling as she knelt down to pick up the necklace, which had slipped from her hand; she grabbed the leather thong and stood up to look out of the window again. The pane was cracked. Several more claps of thunder followed before the storm finally receded. The sky was still lit up by the odd flash in the distance, and a heavy rain started falling.

Keira crouched on the sofa, struggling to get a grip on herself. Her hand wouldn't stop trembling. She kept telling herself it must just have been an optical illusion, but it made no sense and she felt uneasy. The lights came back on. Keira looked carefully at her pendant, she stroked its surface and found that it was warm. Holding it under a light bulb revealed no hole, however tiny, that was visible to the naked eye.

She snuggled under the blanket and tried to get her head around the strange phenomenon that had just taken place. An hour later, she heard the key in the lock. Jeanne was back.

"Aren't you asleep yet? Did you see the storm? It was crazy out there! My feet are soaked. I'm going to make myself a camomile tea, would you like one? What's with the silence? Are you okay?"

"Yes, I think so," said Keira.

"Don't tell me the mighty archaeologist was scared of the storm?"

"Of course not."

"So how come you're white as a sheet?"

"I'm just tired, that's all, I was waiting up for you."

Keira gave Jeanne a kiss and wandered off towards the bedroom, but her sister called her back.

"I don't know if I should tell you this, but... Max was at the dinner tonight."

"No, you didn't need to tell me; see you tomorrow, Jeanne."

Alone in the bedroom, Keira walked over to the window. The electricity had come back on in the buildings but the streets were still plunged in darkness. The clouds had disappeared and the stars looked more dazzling than ever. Keira scoured the sky for the Great Bear. When she was a little girl, her father used to enjoy helping her to recognise the different stars and constellations; Cassiopeia, Antares and Cepheus were her favourites. Keira could identify Cygnus the Swan, Lyra and Hercules, and it was while she was gazing towards the Corona Borealis, in search of Boötes the Herdsman, that her eyes nearly popped out of her head for the second time that evening.

"That's impossible," she whispered, her face glued to the glass.

Hurriedly she opened the window, went out onto

the balcony and craned her neck as if those few extra centimetres could bring her closer to the stars.

"No, it can't be, that would be ridiculous! I must be going mad."

"They say that talking to yourself is the first sign of madness."

Keira swivelled round. Jeanne was standing right next to her, leaning on the guardrail and lighting a cigarette.

"I didn't know you smoked these days?"

"Sometimes. I'm sorry about just now, I should have kept quiet. But it annoyed me so much seeing him trying to get in with everybody. Are you listening to me?"

"Yes, yes..." Keira replied, absently.

"So is it true that all Neanderthal men were bisexual?"

"Maybe," said Keira, carrying on staring up at the stars.

"And that they mainly lived on dinosaur milk?"

"Probably..."

"Keira!"

Keira jumped.

"What?"

"You're not listening to a word I'm saying. What's come over you?"

"Nothing, really, let's go back inside, it's cold."

The two sisters climbed into Jeanne's double bed.

"You weren't serious about Neanderthal men?" asked Jeanne.

"What about Neanderthal men?"

"Nothing, forget it. Let's try and get some sleep," sighed Jeanne, turning over.

"Well, stop tossing and turning then!"

There was a brief silence, followed by Keira turning over in bed.

"Jeanne?"

"What is it now?"

"Thanks for everything you're doing."

"Are you saying that to make me feel even more guilty about Max?"

"Maybe."

The next day, as soon as Jeanne had left the apartment, Keira rushed over to the computer; but that morning her research took her away from her usual line of work. She started looking for maps of the sky on the web. While she was busy searching, every word she typed was simultaneously posted up on a computer screen hundreds of kilometres away; every search term, every site she visited was recorded. By the end of the week, an operator sitting behind his desk in Amsterdam had printed out a file on her work. He re-read the last page to emerge from his printer and dialled a number.

"Sir, I think you'll be interested in the report I've just finished."

"About what?" queried the person on the other end of the line.

"The French archaeologist."

"Meet me in my office straightaway," came the instruction, and the line went dead.

*

London

"How are you feeling?"

"Better than you, Walter."

It was the eve of the big day. The presentation would take place in Docklands, and Walter had taken the executive decision to book us into a hotel the night before. We spent the evening in a local pub. He banned me from drinking any alcohol: I felt like a teenager all over again. By ten o'clock we were back in our respective rooms, and Walter even had the cheek to phone me with instructions not to stay up too late watching TV.

The next morning, we awoke feeling reasonably refreshed (no chance of a hangover!) and with a full day ahead to enjoy a change of scene, before crossing the street to appear before the Walsh Foundation. The event was due to take place in a conference room at the top of a tower located at 1 Cabot Square.

As chance would have it, we weren't far from Greenwich and its Observatory. But on this side of the Thames the district reclaimed from the river was the essence of modernism: concrete blocks and buildings of glass and steel vying to outdo each other in the height stakes. Towards late afternoon, I managed to convince my friend to go for a walk around the Isle of Dogs. We entered the glass dome over the entrance to the Greenwich foot tunnel and crossed the Thames, fifteen metres below the river, to re-surface opposite the charred hull of the *Cutty Sark*. The last survivor of the nineteenth-century commercial fleet looked forlorn, having been gutted by fire a few months earlier. Before us stretched Greenwich Park with its Maritime Museum, the Queen's House and, on top of the hill, the Observatory towards which I led Walter.

"This was the first building in England constructed exclusively to house scientific instruments," I told Walter.

I could tell that his mind was elsewhere: he was feeling anxious and my efforts to distract him were in vain. Still, it was too early to give up. We walked inside the dome, where I re-discovered my sense of wonder at the old astronomical instruments with which John Flamsteed had established his famous star-catalogue in the seventeenth century.

I knew that Walter was fascinated by anything to do with time, so I promptly pointed out the great steel line set in the ground in front of him.

"This is the longitudinal starting point, as determined in 1851 and adopted at an international conference in 1884. And if we were to wait for nightfall, you'd see a powerful green laser rising up in the sky:

it's the only modern touch introduced here in nearly two centuries."

"So that's the big beam I see over the city every evening?" asked Walter, who finally seemed to be showing some interest in what I was saying.

"Exactly, it symbolises the original meridian, even if scientists have moved it by a hundred metres since then. It's also where universal time is situated – Greenwich Mean Time – which serves as the point of reference to calculate time anywhere on the planet. When we travel fifteen degrees to the west we go back an hour; and heading east by the same amount we advance an hour. All time zones start from here."

"Adrian, this is all very interesting but please, when you give your presentation, stick to the subject, won't you?" begged Walter.

I gave up on the explanations and took my friend to the park instead. It was mild out and the fresh air would do him good.

*

Paris

Keira fastened her small suitcase and Jeanne, who'd taken the morning off work specially, insisted on seeing her off at the Gare du Nord. The two sisters left the apartment and caught a bus.

"Promise you'll call me to let me know you've arrived safely?"

"Jeanne, I'm only crossing the Channel and I've never called you from anywhere to tell you I'd arrived safely!"

"Well, this time I'm asking you to. You can tell me about the journey, what you make of the hotel, whether you like your room, what's new in town..."

"Do you want me to account for my two and a quarter hours on the train as well, while we're at it? You're more nervous about this than I am, aren't you? Come on, 'fess up, you're terrified by the prospect of my ordeal this evening!"

"I feel like I'm the one who's got to give the presentation. I didn't sleep a wink last night."

"You do realise we probably don't stand any chance of winning this prize?"

"Stop being negative, you've got to have faith in yourself!"

"If you say so. I should've organised to spend an extra day in England and gone on to visit Dad."

"Cornwall's a long way; we'll go together one day."

"If I win, I'll make the detour and I'll tell him you couldn't come because you had too much work on."

"Bitch!" Jeanne fired back, poking her sister playfully with her elbow.

The bus slowed down and stopped in front of the station. Keira grabbed her suitcase and gave Jeanne a kiss.

"I promise I'll call before I give my presentation."

Keira stepped out onto the pavement and waited for the bus to drive off; Jeanne had her face pressed against the window.

The Gare du Nord wasn't very busy that morning. The rush hour was long since over and there were only a few trains on the platforms. Those passengers travelling to the UK took the escalator up to the Eurostar check-in. Keira went through passport control and security and barely had time to sit down before the departure gates opened.

She slept for most of the journey. When she woke up, the voice coming through the loudspeaker was already announcing the imminent arrival into St Pancras International.

A black cab drove her across London to the hotel.

Captivated by the city, this time it was she who had her face pressed to the window.

Her room was just as Jeanne had described it, small but full of charm. She left her suitcase at the foot of the bed, glanced at the clock on the bedside table to see how she was doing and decided she still had enough time for a quick walk around the neigh-bourhood.

Heading up the Old Brompton Road, she turned into Bute Street and couldn't resist the lure of the French Bookshop.

She spent a while browsing, eventually bought a book on Ethiopia which she was surprised to find there, and sat down on the terrace of a small Italian delicatessen opposite. Re-energised by a cup of strong coffee, she decided to make her way back to the hotel. The presentation was due to start at six o'clock sharp and the taxi driver who'd driven her from St Pancras had warned her that it would take a good hour to get to the Docklands.

She reached 1 Cabot Square with thirty minutes to spare. Several people were already entering the main lobby, their smart outfits a clue that they were all headed for the same place. Keira's casual attitude to the whole affair, which she'd managed to maintain until now, suddenly deserted her – she had butterflies in her stomach. Two men in dark suits were crossing the square. Keira frowned, one of them looked vaguely familiar. She was distracted by her mobile phone ringing. She fished it out of a pocket and saw Jeanne's name flashing on the screen.

"I swear I was about to call you, I was just dialling your number."

"Liar!"

"I'm in front of the building and, to be honest, all I want to do is get the hell out. Public speaking has never been my thing."

"You're going to go through with this, after all we've put into it. You'll be brilliant! And what's the worst that could happen, you don't win? It's hardly the end of the world."

"You're right, but I'm scared rigid, Jeanne; I don't know why, I haven't felt like this since..."

"Don't think about it, you never suffered from stage fright before!"

"Your voice sounds weird."

"I probably shouldn't tell you this now, but I've been burgled."

"When?" Keira said, panicked.

"This morning, while I was on my way to the station with you. Don't worry, nothing was stolen, or at least I don't think so; but the apartment's in a right state, and so is Madame Hereira."

"Don't stay on your own this evening, come and join me, hop on a train!"

"I can't, I'm waiting for the locksmith; plus, they didn't steal anything, so why would they run the risk of coming back?"

"Perhaps they were disturbed?"

"Trust me, given the state of the living room and the bedroom, they took all the time they needed, and I'll need more than tonight to get things ship-shape here again."

"I'm really sorry, Jeanne," said Keira, checking her watch, "but I'm going to have to go. I'll call you back as soon as..."

"Hang up and go right now, or you'll be late. Have you hung up?"

"No!"

"What are you waiting for? Go girl!"

Keira switched off her phone and walked into the lobby. A security guard showed her to the lifts and directed her to the top floor where the Walsh Foundation was meeting. It was six o'clock. The lift doors opened and a receptionist led Keira down a long corridor to a room, which was already full, and much bigger than she'd expected.

About a hundred chairs formed a semi-circle around a large platform. The judges were sitting in the front row, each with a table in front of them, and listening attentively to the person who was already speaking into a microphone to present their project. Keira's heart was racing; she spotted a free chair in the fourth row and worked her way over to it. The first man up was presenting a biogenetics research project. His talk lasted the requisite fifteen minutes and was met with a round of applause. The second candidate presented a piece of prototype equipment that would facilitate low-cost aquifer drilling, as well as a solar-powered salt-water purification system. Water would be the blue gold of the twenty-first century, the world's most precious resource; in many places on the planet, survival would depend on it. Lack of drinking water would be the cause of wars to come, and of whole populations being displaced. Ultimately, the talk was more political than technical.

The third candidate gave a brilliant presentation on alternative energy. A bit too brilliant for the tastes of the head judge, who made a remark to her neighbour while he was still speaking. The brief exchange gave Adrian hope that she wasn't as impressed as the audience seemed to be.

*

"Our turn soon," Walter whispered to me. "You'll bowl them over."

"We haven't got a chance."

"If you impress the judges as much as you seem to have impressed that young woman, it's in the bag."

"Which young woman?"

"The one who's been staring at you ever since she walked into the auditorium. Over there," he went on, nodding his head in her direction, "in the fourth row, to our left. But don't turn around now!"

I already had of course, but I didn't notice anyone looking at me.

"You're seeing things, Walter."

"I'm telling you, she was practically devouring

you with her eyes. And now you've blown it and she's retreated into her shell, like a hermit crab."

I glanced around again, but all that stood out in the fourth row was an empty seat.

"You're doing it on purpose!" Walter scolded me. "You'll come across as desperate."

"Walter, stop being such an idiot!"

Someone called my name out: it was my turn.

"I was just trying to take your mind off things, you know, relieve some of the stress. And I'd say I've rather succeeded. Off you go, all I ask of you is to be perfect."

I gathered my notes and stood up, while Walter whispered into my ear:

"As for the girl, I wasn't making it up. Good luck my friend!" he encouraged me, with a warm pat on the shoulder.

What happened next remains one of the most excruciating moments of my life. The microphone packed up. A technician clambered onto the platform to try to mend it, but nothing doing. They were going to install another, but no one was sure where the key for the equipment store was. I wanted to get my talk over as quickly as possible and decided to do without the microphone; the judges were sitting in the front row and my voice would carry far enough for them to be able to hear me. Walter had second-guessed my impatience and was signalling that this wasn't a good idea, but I ignored his frantic gestures and kicked off.

My presentation felt hard going. I was trying to explain to the audience that the future of humanity didn't just depend on us understanding our planet and its oceans, but also on what we could learn from space. Like those first navigators who sailed around the world when everybody believed the Earth to be flat, we now needed to set off in search of distant galaxies. How could we consider our future without understanding how it had all begun? We're faced with two questions that push knowledge to the limits, two questions that even the greatest scholars can't answer. Firstly, what are the infinitely small and the infinitely big? And secondly, what is the zero moment, from which everything begins? No one who has tackled these two questions has even come up with the beginnings of a theory.

When people thought the Earth was flat, they couldn't imagine their world beyond the visible horizon. They were afraid that if they sailed on the high seas they would disappear into the void. But when they finally ventured forth, they found it was the horizon that receded; and the further people travelled, the better they understood the vastness of the world to which they belonged.

Now it's our turn to explore the universe, to interpret the barrage of information coming at us from remote space and time, far beyond those galaxies we know about. In a few months, the Americans will launch the most powerful space telescope that has ever existed. It might enable us to see, hear and learn how the universe was formed, and whether other life forms have evolved on planets comparable to our own.

Perhaps Walter was right, after all: a young woman in the fourth row was looking at me intently. Her face rang a bell. At least someone in the audience appeared to be mesmerised by my words. But now was no time for flirting and, after a brief pause, I brought my presentation to its conclusion.

The light from the first day is travelling towards us from the depths of the universe. Will we ever be able to capture and interpret it? Will we at last discover how it all began?

A deathly hush. Nobody moved. I was a snowman melting slowly in the sun, until Walter started clapping. As I gathered my notes, the chair of the judges stood up and applauded, then the members of the committee joined in and the rest of the audience followed suit; I thanked everybody and left the platform.

Walter gave me a big hug.

"You were..."

"Pathetic or appalling? It's up to you. I told you we didn't stand a chance."

"Will you be quiet? Before you so rudely interrupted me, I was trying to tell you that you were terrific, old chap. The audience was transfixed, not so much as a hint of a cough."

"What d'you expect, they were all asleep after five minutes!"

As I sat down I noticed the young woman in row four stand up and make her way over to the platform. So that's why she'd been staring at me: we were in direct competition and she'd just witnessed a prime example of how not to give a presentation.

The microphone still wasn't working but her clear voice reached all the way to the back of the room. When she looked up, her focus seemed to extend beyond the room, as if she were seeing a far-off country. She talked to us of Africa, of its ochre soil, which her hands excavated relentlessly. She explained that as humans we'll never be free to go where we want until we've found out where we came from. In some ways, her project was the most ambitious of all: it wasn't about science or about specific technology, but about realising her dream.

"Who were our ancestors?" were her first words. And to think I'd been dreaming of discovering where the dawn first began.

Right from the very beginning of her presentation, she had the audience eating out of her hand. But presentation is the wrong word; what she was doing – and brilliantly so – was telling a story. Walter was completely won over, along with the judges and everyone else in the room. She spoke about the Omo Valley; I could never have described the Andes as beautifully as she conjured up before our eyes the banks of the Ethiopian river. I could almost hear the splashing water, feel the searing heat and the wind as it whipped up the dust. In the time it took her to tell her tale, I was ready to give up my own career for hers; I wanted to be part of her team, to dig the arid soil by her side. She took a strange object out of her pocket and placed it in her palm before holding it out so everyone could see.

"This is a fragment of skull. I found it fifteen metres underground, deep in a cave. It is fifteen million years old. This is a miniscule fragment of humanity. If I could dig deeper, further, longer, I might be able to stand in front of you again, and finally tell you who the first human being was."

This time, the auditorium didn't need any encouragement from Walter to break into applause at the end of the presentation.

There were still ten more presentations to go, and I was thankful not to be among those who had to follow on directly after.

At 9.30pm, the judges retired to deliberate. The room emptied and Walter seemed disconcertingly calm. I suspected he'd given up all hope as far as we were concerned.

"We deserve a decent pint of beer after that," he said, steering me towards the door.

My stomach had tied itself into too many knots to go drinking; I'd got sucked into the game by this point, and I was counting down the minutes, unable to relax.

"Come on Adrian, think of all you've ever taught me on the relativity of time? The next hour is going to feel horribly long. Let's go and get some fresh air and find something else to think about!"

Out in the freezing square, a few candidates who looked as worried as we did were having a smoke, warming themselves up by jumping up and down on the spot. There was no sign of the woman from the fourth row. Walter was right, time had stopped and the wait seemed to last an eternity. Sitting at a table in the Marriott, I couldn't stop checking my watch. At last it was time to head back to the auditorium where the judges would announce their verdict.

The mystery woman from the fourth row was back in her place, but she didn't so much as glance my way. The chair of the judging panel walked in, followed by the judges; she mounted the steps and congratulated all the candidates for the excellent quality of their proposals. She told us that it had been a difficult decision, and that they had gone to several rounds of voting. A special mention was given to the man who had presented the water-purification project, but the prize would go to the first speaker for his biogenetic research. Walter didn't flinch. He patted me and went to great lengths to assure me we had no reason to reproach ourselves, we'd done our best.

The chair of the judges interrupted the applause. As she had already explained, the panel had found it very difficult to reach its decision. This year, exceptionally, the grant would be shared between two candidates: a man and a woman. My alleged admirer in the fourth row was the only female candidate. She stood up, reeling from the shock, as the chair smiled at her, and in the thunderous applause I didn't get to hear her name.

Various congratulations and shaking of hands took place up on the platform and then the candidates started leaving, together with those who'd come along to support them.

"Would you buy me that pair of wellies anyway?" asked Walter.

"A promise is a promise. I'm sorry I let you down."

"Our project had the distinction of being short-listed... Not only did you deserve this prize, but I've also felt very proud to be part of this venture over the past few weeks."

We were interrupted by the chair of the judges, who shook my hand.

"Julia Walsh. I'm delighted to meet you."

A big heavy-set man standing beside her was introduced as a German colleague called Thomas.

"Your project is utterly fascinating," continued the heiress to the Walsh Foundation, "it also happened to be my personal favourite. The decision came down to one casting vote. I would have so loved you to win the prize. Please resubmit in a year's time, there'll be a new panel of judges, and I'm sure you'd be in with a very good chance. The light from the first day can wait another year, can't it?"

She said a polite goodbye and set off again, escorted by Thomas.

"Bloody brilliant!" spluttered Walter. "That makes me feel *so* much better!"

There wasn't much I could say.

"Why did she have to come and tell us that?" grumbled Walter who was already pummelling his fist into the other hand. "*It was down to one vote* – that's just unbearable. I'd rather she told us we were completely out of the running. But a single vote away! Do you realise how heartless that is? I'm going to spend the next years of my life working in a pond thanks to one vote! I'd like to know who cast it, so I could wring their neck."

My colleague's face turned puce and he became breathless.

"Pull yourself together Walter, you'll make yourself ill if you carry on like that."

"How can you tell somebody that their fate was determined by a single vote? Is this just a game to them? How dare she just let it slip out like that!" he thundered.

"I think she was trying to sympathise and to encourage us to apply again."

"In a year's time? Splendid! I'm going back home, Adrian. I'm sorry to walk out on you like this, but I'd be atrocious company this evening. Let's meet back at the department tomorrow; if I've managed to sober up by then."

Walter turned on his heel and stomped off. Alone

in the middle of the auditorium, I looked for the exit.

I could hear the lift pinging at the end of the corridor, and rushed to make it before the doors closed again. Inside, the prize-winner shot me a devastating smile.

She was holding her file. I expected to see her face flushed with victory. But she just kept staring at me, smiling faintly. I could hear Walter's voice in my head; if he'd been there, he'd doubtless have told me I was subtle as a flying brick, no matter how I tried introducing myself.

"Congratulations!" I stammered, modestly.

No reaction.

"Have I changed as much as that?" she asked eventually.

Seeing as I couldn't find a suitable response, she opened her file, took out a sheet of paper, popped it in her mouth and started chewing it calmly, while still smiling at me provocatively.

Suddenly, the memory of an exam room came back to me, along with thousands of flashes from an unforgettable summer, fifteen years ago.

The woman spat out the ball of paper into her hand and sighed.

"Now d'you recognise me?"

The lift doors opened onto the lobby, but I stayed right where I was, feeling helpless; the lift headed up again to the top floor.

"It took you long enough, I'd hoped I'd made a bit more of an impression than that, or else I really have grown old..."

"No, of course not, but your hair colour..."

"I was twenty, I often changed it at the time, it was a phase I was going through. You haven't altered, a few wrinkles perhaps, but you still have that absent look, as if you're lost in space."

"I'd never have expected to run into you here... after all these years."

"Certainly not in a lift. Are we heading up to the top floor again, or are you going to take me out to dinner?"

And without waiting for the answer, Keira dropped her file, flung herself into my arms and kissed me. It was a kiss that tasted of *papier mâché*. First kisses take your breath away, the second kiss too, even if fifteen years have gone by in between.

Every time the lift doors opened onto the lobby, one of us pressed the button and held the other even more tightly. On the sixth trip the security guard was waiting for us, arms folded. His lift wasn't a hotel bedroom, he informed us, hence the camera inside it; we were requested to leave the premises. I led Keira by the hand and we found ourselves in the deserted square, both feeling awkward and embarrassed.

"I'm sorry, I wasn't thinking... it must be the high of winning."

"Or the low of losing, in my case."

"I'm sorry, Adrian, I didn't mean to put my foot in it."

"If Walter were here, he'd say we've got at least

one thing in common. How about we try again?"

"What?"

"My tactlessness? Your victory? My defeat? It's up to you."

Keira brushed my lips with a kiss, then said she wanted to get out of that creepy place.

"Let's walk a bit," I suggested, "there's a wonderful park on the other side of the Thames..."

"I'm too hungry to walk, I could eat a horse. I haven't had a bite to eat since this morning, let's find a pub that's still serving food."

I remembered a restaurant the two of us had often frequented at the time; I didn't know if it still existed, but gave the address to the cab driver.

As we were driving along the Embankment, Keira took my hand. I hadn't experienced anything approaching tenderness in a long time. In that moment, I forgot all about losing out, and the distance between London, where I would be living from now on, and the Atacama, where my dreams had remained.

*

Amsterdam

The man who alighted from the tram to walk back up the Singel Canal could have been an ordinary commuter heading home after work. He managed to look anonymous despite the late hour, the chain attaching his briefcase to his wrist, and the pistol in its holster beneath his jacket. When he reached Magna Square, he stopped at the traffic lights to make sure nobody was following him. As soon as the lights turned green, he set off again. Ignoring the blaring horns, he ducked between a bus and lorry, forcing two cars to jam on their brakes, and narrowly avoiding a motorcyclist who let rip a torrent of insults. He walked hurriedly to Dam Square, where he crossed the esplanade and entered the New Church (an interesting choice of name for a majestic edifice built in the fifteenth century) through a side door. With no time to admire the sumptuous nave, the man carried on to the transept, passing the tomb of Admiral de Ruyter and turning off at that of Commodore Jan Van Galen. Then he made for the absidiole. He took a key out of his pocket, released the latch of the small door at the back of the chapel and descended the hidden staircase behind it.

Fifty steps below he found himself at one end of a long corridor stretching out before him. Someone who knew the way could use this underground passage beneath Dam Square to get from the New Church to the Royal Palace. The man was in a hurry: he always found the narrow passageway oppressive, and the echo of his footsteps only made matters worse. The further he advanced, the thinner the light became, until just the two ends of the corridor had any light to speak of. The man could feel his loafers becoming soaked from the stagnant water that covered the ground. When he reached the halfway point, he was in pitch darkness; from there, he knew he had to take fifty steps in a straight line, with the central gutter serving as his guide.

At last he reached the far end, where another staircase appeared before him. The steps were slippery and he had to cling onto the hemp rope attached to the wall. At the top of a flight of steps, the man was confronted with a first wooden door reinforced with heavy cast-iron bars. It had two round handles, one on top of the other; unlocking it involved working a mechanism that was three hundred years old. The man turned the upper handle ninety degrees to the right, pivoted the lower handle ninety degrees to the left and pulled them both towards him. One click, and the door opened. He emerged in an antechamber on the ground floor of the Royal Palace, built by Jacob

Van Campen in the mid-seventeenth century, when it was officially the town hall. Amsterdamers considered it to be the eighth wonder of the world. A statue of Atlas dominates the Burgerzaal, the state room of the palace, while on the floor are three gigantic marble maps representing respectively the western hemisphere, the eastern hemisphere and the celestial chart.

Jack Vackeers would soon be celebrating his seventy-sixth birthday, but he looked at least ten years younger. He entered the state room, trod on the Milky Way, walked over Oceania, leaped nimbly across the Atlantic and continued towards another antechamber where his contact was already waiting for him.

"What's the news?" he asked, entering.

"It's rather surprising, sir. Our Frenchwoman has dual nationality. Her father was English, a botanist who spent a large chunk of his life in France. Returning to his native Cornwall after his divorce, he died there of a heart attack in 1997. The death certificate and the burial authorisation appear in the file."

"And her mother?"

"She's also dead. She taught human sciences at the University of Aix-en-Provence. She was killed in June 2002, in a car accident. The driver who hit her had 1.6 g of alcohol in his blood."

"You can spare me the sordid details," said Jan Vackeers.

"She's got a sister, who's two years older and works in a Paris museum."

"A French civil servant?"

"Of a kind."

"We'll need to take that into account. Let's get back to the young archaeologist, please."

"She went to London to appear before the selection committee of the Walsh Foundation."

"And, in accordance with our wishes, she won the prize, didn't she?"

"Not exactly, sir, the judge who works for us did his level best, but the chair wouldn't be influenced. Your protégée is sharing her prize with another candidate."

"Will that be enough for her to return to Ethiopia?"

"One million pounds should be plenty for her to continue with her research."

"Perfect. Do you have anything else to tell me?"

"She became friendly with a man she met at the presentation ceremony. They continued their evening in a little restaurant and, given how late it was, both of them…"

"That's none of our business," Vackeers interrupted. "Unless you're about to tell me it was love at first sight, and that she's giving up on her travel plans for good, how she spends her nights is up to her."

"The thing is, sir, we've done our research and the man in question is an astrophysicist who belongs to the Royal Society."

Vackeers went over to the window to look out onto the square below. He found it even more stunning by night than during the day. Amsterdam was his city and he prized it above any other. He knew each little street, each canal, each building.

"That's the kind of unforeseen detail I'm less keen on," he continued. "An astrophysicist, did you say?"

"There's nothing to indicate she's spoken to him about the matter that concerns us."

"No, but it's a possibility we can't ignore. I suspect we'd better keep an eye on the scientist as well."

"It'll be difficult to keep tabs on him without attracting the attention of our English friends – as I mentioned, he is a member of the Royal Society."

"Do your best, but don't run any risks. The last thing we want is to arouse any suspicion over there. Anything else I need to know?"

"Everything can be found in the file you asked me to compile."

The man opened his briefcase and handed a large brown envelope to Vackeers, who opened it. Photos of Keira taken in Paris, in front of Jeanne's apartment block, in the Tuileries Gardens, a few snaps as she was shopping in Rue des Lions-Saint-Paul; and finally a series taken after her arrival into St Pancras International, on the terrace of an Italian delicatessen in Bute Street and through a restaurant window in Primrose Hill, where she could be seen having dinner with Adrian.

"Those were the last photographs to reach us before I left my desk."

Vackeers skimmed the first lines of the report and closed the file.

"Thank you, you can go now. We'll see each other tomorrow."

The assistant said goodbye to Vackeers and left the palace antechamber. As soon as he'd gone, another door opened and a second man entered the room, smiling at Vackeers.

"This chance encounter with the astrophysicist may be to our advantage," he said, walking over.

"I thought you wanted everything to remain as confidential as possible. Two errant knights is rather a lot on one chessboard, don't you think?"

"What matters is that she starts searching, without suspecting we're giving her a helping hand."

"Ivory, you do realise that if somebody found out what we were up to, the consequences for both of us would be..."

"Awkward. Is that the word you're looking for?"

"No, I was going to say disastrous."

"Jan, we both believe in the same thing, and have done for years. Imagine the consequences if we're really onto something here!"

"I know, Ivory, I know. That's why I'm prepared to take so many risks, even at my age."

"Admit you're enjoying it too. After all, we never hoped to become active again; and the idea of being the puppet-masters appeals to us both."

"Agreed," sighed Vackeers as he sat down behind a grand mahogany desk. "What do you see happening next?"

"Let's allow things to take their course. If she

manages to get this astrophysicist interested, she's even smarter than I imagined."

"How long do you reckon before London, Madrid, Berlin, and Beijing realise what's going on?"

"Oh, they'll all be in on the game very quickly. The Americans have already put in an appearance. The apartment belonging to our archaeologist's sister received a visit this morning."

"What idiots!"

"It's their way of leaving a message."

"For us?"

"For me. They're furious I allowed the object out of my hands, and even angrier that I had the nerve to get it tested on their patch."

"It *was* quite mischievous on your part, but please, Ivory, let's be clear that now is no time for provocation. We don't know where we're heading; don't let your resentment against those who sidelined you sway your judgement. I'm with you on this hare-brained adventure, but don't lay us open to unnecessary risks."

"It's nearly midnight, time to say goodnight Jan, let's meet back here in three days, at the same time: we'll take stock then."

The two friends went their separate ways. Vackeers was the first to leave the antechamber. He crossed the state room again and went down into the basement.

The entrails of the Royal Palace, Amsterdam, are a complete labyrinth. Some 13,659 wooden struts prop up the building. Vackeers edged his way through this strange forest of beams, to re-surface ten minutes later via a small door that opened onto the courtyard of a large town house three hundred metres away. Ivory, who left five minutes after him, had taken a different route.

*

London

It turned out the restaurant only existed in my memories. But I'd found somewhere that was just as intimate and Keira swore she recognised the place where I used to take her all those years ago. Over dinner, she tried telling me what had happened in her life since; but how can you cover fifteen years in a few hours? Memory is both lazy and selective, recalling only the best times and the worst times, the powerful experiences; it never logs the day-to-day, no, that gets deleted. The more I listened to Keira, the more I rediscovered the clear voice that had so captivated me, those lively eyes in which I could lose myself of an evening, the smile that came close to making me abandon all my plans; and yet, as I listened to her, I found it hard to recollect the period when she'd gone back to live in France.

Keira had always known what she wanted to do. As soon as she'd finished her studies, she went to Somalia on a work placement. She'd then spent two years in Venezuela, working for a leading light in her field who also happened to be a bit of a despot. After being reprimanded once too often, Keira had told him what she thought of him and was duly fired. Two years of piecemeal excavation work had followed in France, where the construction of a high-speed rail link had unearthed an important paleontological site. The high-speed route had been altered accordingly and Keira had joined the team of archaeologists, assuming more and more responsibilities as the months went by. The high quality of her work attracted attention and she was awarded a grant to travel to the Omo Valley in Ethiopia. She worked there as assistant to the research director; but the latter fell ill, so Keira took charge of the operations and moved the site by fifty kilometres.

When she spoke to me about her time in Africa, I could tell how happy she'd been there. I was rash enough to ask what had made her come back. Her face darkened and she told me about the storm that had laid waste to her efforts and destroyed all her work, without which I'd probably never have seen her again. I would have never dared admit how eternally grateful I was to that meteorological disaster.

When Keira asked me what I'd done with my life, I couldn't really tell her. I tried to describe the Chilean landscape as best I could, attempting to match the eloquent beauty with which she had illuminated her presentation to the Walsh Foundation; I told her about the people I'd worked with for so many years, the camaraderie, and, to spare her asking me why I'd come back to London, I cut straight to the unfortunate incident that had resulted from me wanting to climb too high in the mountains.

"You see, we shouldn't have any regrets," she pointed out. "I excavate the earth and you observe the stars – we really weren't meant for each other, were we?"

"Or you could argue that it's the other way round," I countered. "After all, we're both chasing the same thing."

She looked at me bemusedly.

"You're trying to trace the origins of humanity; meanwhile, I'm excavating the depths of the galaxies to find out how the universe was born, what made life begin and whether it might exist elsewhere, in other forms we know nothing about. Our approaches, like our intentions, aren't so far removed from each other. Maybe the answers to our questions even overlap?"

"That's one way of seeing things. One day, perhaps, thanks to you, I'll climb aboard a space shuttle, arrive on an unknown planet and set off in search of the skeletons of the first little green men!"

"I see you still enjoy poking fun at me!"

"Don't be cross, I wasn't trying to undermine your work. What tickles me is your desire to find connections between what we do, no matter what."

"You may be surprised to learn that some of your colleagues have used the stars to date archaeological sites. And if you don't know about astronomical dating, I can make you up a crib sheet!"

Keira looked at me quizzically; I could see in her eyes that she was scheming.

"Who says I cheated?"

"Sorry?"

"That day we met in the exam hall, the sheet of paper I swallowed might have been blank. Did it ever occur to you that I was simply doing it in order to get your attention?"

"You were prepared to risk being disqualified, just to attract my attention? You expect me to believe that?"

"I wasn't risking anything; I'd already sat my exams the day before."

"Liar!"

"I'd spotted you in the faculty corridors, and I liked the look of you. That day, I was with a girl-friend who really was sitting her end of year exams. She was in a right old state about it, and while I was trying to psych her up by the main exam room doors, I spotted your irresistible invigilator's face and your baggy jacket. I went and sat in a free seat in the row where you were invigilating, and the rest, as they say..."

"You went to all those lengths just to meet me?"

"Quite an ego-trip for you, hey?" said Keira, while playing footsie with me under the table. I was embarrassed but didn't want to let on.

"Did you cheat or didn't you?" I challenged.

"I'm not going to tell you. Both scenarios are perfectly feasible. Your choice: either you doubt my honesty and paint me as a tease, or you prefer the crib-sheet version and write me off as a dreadful cheat. I'll give you the rest of the evening to decide. Now tell me about this astronomical dating."

By studying the position of the sun over time, Sir Norman Lockyer had succeeded in dating Stonehenge and its mysterious dolmens. The position of the sun at its zenith varies from millennium to millennium. At midday, the sun is a few degrees to the east of the position it occupied in prehistoric times.

At Stonehenge, the zenith was marked by a median walkway and the standing stones had been positioned at regular intervals along this axis. The rest could be worked out by mathematical calculation. I was expecting to lose Keira before I'd reached the end, but once again she surprised me.

"You're still making fun of me. You're not the slightest bit interested in any of this, are you?"

"I most certainly am! And if I go to Stonehenge one day, I'll definitely see things differently."

The restaurant was closing, we were the last customers, and when the waiter switched off the lights at the back we took the hint. We walked through the streets of Primrose Hill for a good hour, recalling some of the highlights of a distant summer. I offered to see Keira back to her hotel, but when we climbed into a taxi she suggested we get dropped off at my place.

Keira was checking out the downstairs: "I'm not saying I don't like it," she said, "but you can tell it's a bachelor pad."

"What's wrong with my house?"

"Where's the bedroom in this babe-magnet?"

"On the first floor."

"How predictable," taunted Keira, climbing the stairs.

When I walked in, she was waiting for me on the bed.

We didn't make love that evening. The chemistry was there but there are nights when something even stronger than desire takes hold. Fear of messing up, fear of being caught out by your emotions, fear of the following day and of the days to come.

We talked all night long. Head nuzzling against head, hand in hand, like two students with their whole lives ahead of them. But we had grown up, and eventually Keira fell asleep by my side.

Dawn hadn't broken yet. I heard a footfall, almost as soft as that of an animal. I opened my eyes but Keira's voice begged me to close them again. She was gazing at me from the doorway and I realised she was leaving.

"You're not going to call me, are you?"

"We haven't exchanged numbers, just memories, maybe it's better that way," she whispered.

"Why?"

"I'm going back to Ethiopia, you're dreaming of the Andes, that's a hell of a distance, don't you think?"

"Fifteen years ago, I should have believed you instead of holding it against you; you were right, what we have are those good memories."

"So try not to hold it against me this time."

"I'll do my best. But if..."

"No, don't say another word, it was a wonderful evening, Adrian. I don't know whether the best thing that happened to me yesterday was winning the prize or seeing you again, and I don't want to find out. I've scribbled you a note on the bedside table; read it when you wake up. Go back to sleep and don't listen out for the front door closing."

"You look stunning in this light."

"You've got to let me go, Adrian."

"Promise me something?"

"Anything."

"If our paths cross again, promise me you won't kiss me."

"I promise," she said.

"Look after yourself. I'd be lying if I said I won't miss you."

"Well don't say it, then. You look after yourself too."

I heard the creak of every single step as she made her way downstairs, the squeaking hinges when she closed my front door behind her and, through my half-open bedroom window, the sound of her footsteps along the street. Much later, I found out that she'd stopped a few metres further off and sat on a wall; that she'd watched the sunrise and nearly turned back a hundred times; that she had decided to come back to the bedroom where I was trying in vain to get back to sleep, when a taxi came along.

*

I forced myself to stay in bed as long as possible, without opening my eyes or listening to the noises around me. And I told myself a story; a story in which Keira had gone down to the kitchen to make a cup of tea. We'd eat breakfast together, debating what to do with the rest of the day. London would be ours. I'd wear my tourist gear and play at rediscovering my own city, enjoying the brightly coloured houses contrasting with the grey sky.

Together, we revisit all our old haunts, as if for the first time. The next day, we'd continue our walk, but at a leisurely Sunday pace, our hands entwined. And in this version it wouldn't matter if Keira was leaving at the end of the weekend: each single moment we'd experienced together would have made it worthwhile.

*

The scent of her skin clung to my sheets. In the living room, the sofa still showed the imprint of where she'd been sitting. Something inside me had died a little when she left and now the house felt empty.

Except for those two words I found from Keira on my bedside table: *Thank You.*

At midday I called Walter:

"Can a fifteen-year-old wound really open again as quickly as a torn seam? Don't the scars of dead love affairs ever disappear?"

"I'm not sure that I'm the person best qualified to deal with your first question; after all, you're asking this of an idiot who's hopelessly in love with a woman but has never plucked up the courage to tell her so. And as for the second, I can hardly criticise you for not finding the right words to persuade her to stay. The least we can say is that when you decide to ruin your weekend you don't go in for half measures. What with the prize that was almost within our grasp *and* your chance reunion, you've certainly had one hell of a twenty-four hours!"

"Thanks, Walter."

Still, he knocked at my door half an hour later.

"Sorry to be the harbinger of more bad news but they say it's going to rain. You should think about getting dressed by the way, those pyjamas are beyond the pale and the sight of your calves is doing nothing to improve my day."

While I made myself a cup of coffee, Walter wandered upstairs only to re-appear a few moments later, looking chuffed about something.

"I've got some good news for you at last, although time will tell just how good it is."

He held out the pendant that Keira had been wearing the evening before.

"Don't say a word," he went on, "if you can't recognise an *acte manqué* at your age, then your case is even more hopeless than mine. A woman who leaves her jewellery behind at a man's house can only have two intentions; the first is that another woman finds it and uses it as ammunition for a domestic row – but being the subtle flying brick you are, you'll have told her at least ten times there wasn't anyone else in your life..."

"And the second?"

"That she's planning to return to the scene of the crime!"

"Doesn't the idea that she just forgot it seem a simpler explanation?" I asked, taking the pendant from him.

"Absolutely not! An earring maybe, a ring perhaps, but a pendant that size... Unless you've singularly failed to inform me that your friend is as short-sighted as a mole, which would go some way to explaining how you seduced her in the first place."

Walter snatched the pendant back and weighed it in his hands.

"Don't tell me she didn't notice she was missing half a pound from around her neck; this thing is heavy enough to prevent anyone leaving it behind by accident."

I knew it was ridiculous, that I was too old to be behaving like an infatuated young Romeo, but Walter's words did me the power of good.

"Adrian, I do declare, you're getting a bit of colour back in those cheeks of yours. Right, I'm ravenous and I know a place nearby that does the best brunches in town. Get some clothes on, for goodness' sake!"

*

St Mawes, Cornwall

The train set off down the single track and the hand-ful of passengers who'd got off at Falmouth had left the station already. Keira walked across the mar-shalling yard where two goods-wagons were rusting away. She reached the harbour area and walked over to the dock where her ferry was about to leave. She'd set out from London five hours earlier and the capital already seemed a distant memory. A foghorn made her hurry her step: a sailor was cranking a handle on the quayside, and the footbridge was starting to rise; Keira waved, calling out for them to wait for her; the handle turned the other way and Keira grabbed the arm of the ship's boy who hauled her aboard. By the time she was in the prow, the ferry was sailing past a big crane and tacking against the current. The St Mawes estuary was even more stunning than in her dreams. She could already make out the fortified cas-tle with its unusual cloverleaf shape; further off was a tangle of small blue and white cottages, each jostling for their place on the hill. Keira held onto the guardrail that was eroded by sea-spray and took a

long, deep breath to fill her lungs: the salty tang
mingled with the windborne scent of freshly mown
grass. The captain sounded his horn and the
lighthouse keeper waved. The ferry slowed down, the
moorings were cast and the starboard side of the boat
shunted up against the stone quayside.

Keira took the coastal path to the village; she
climbed up the steep street in the direction of the
church, looking up to admire the flower-filled
window boxes adorning every house. She pushed
open the door of the Victory to find the pub empty,
went over to the bar and ordered a pastie and a pint.

"We don't get many tourists at this time of year;
you're not local, are you?" asked the publican,
pulling Keira's beer.

"I'm not from here, no, but I'm not a total stranger
either: my father is buried behind the church."

"And who was your father?"

"A wonderful man called William Perkins."

"I'm afraid I don't remember him," said the publican. "What did he do for a living?"

"He was a botanist."

"Do you still have family in the village?"

"No, just Dad's grave."

"And where have you come from with that slight
accent of yours?"

"From London and France."

"You've made this long trip to pay him a visit?"

"Sort of, yes."

"Well, this one's on me, in memory of William

Perkins, botanist and fine man," said the publican, putting a plate in front of Keira.

"To the memory of my father," she replied, raising her pint.

Once she'd eaten lunch, Keira thanked the publican and carried on her way to the top of the hill. At last she reached the church; she walked around it and opened the wrought iron gates.

There were barely a hundred souls residing in the small graveyard of St Mawes. William Perkins' tombstone was at the end of a row, propped up against the graveyard wall. Purple wisteria clambered up the old stones, providing a little shade under its foliage. Keira sat down on the grave and brushed her fingers over the carved words. The gold lettering had all but disappeared, and green moss was growing on the stone slab.

"I know, Dad, I haven't visited for ages, but I don't need to be here to think of you. You told me that, with time, the pain of loss gives way to happy memories. So when will I stop missing you so badly? I want our discussions to pick up where they left off, to carry on asking you a thousand questions, to listen to all those answers you used to give me, even when you made them up. I want to feel my hand in yours again, to walk by your side and watch the tide going out.

"I had an argument with Jeanne this morning. It was my fault, as usual; she was furious I hadn't called her last night to tell her my good news. You'd have been proud of me yesterday evening, Dad, proud of your daughter. I presented my research to a foundation and I won; well, I tied for first prize, but you'd have been proud all the same, and you believed in sharing, didn't you? I want you to come back, to give me a hug and we'll head out on foot together for the port. I want to hear the sound of your voice, and gaze into your eyes so I can feel safe again, like in the old days."

Keira was crying now.

"If you knew how guilty I feel for not coming to visit you more often when you were alive, if you knew how sorry I am about that. But I didn't, and I can hear your voice saying I had to get on and live my life, Dad.

"I didn't want you to be annoyed, so I've made it up with Jeanne. I've followed your advice to the letter: I called her twice to say how sorry I was. And then we went and had another row when I told her I was coming to see you, even if I can't *actually* see you. She wanted to be here too. We both miss you so much.

"I'll be able to set off for Ethiopia again, now that I've got this prize. I came to let you know, in case you wanted to drop in on me: I'll be in the Omo Valley. I won't tell you the way, I'm sure you'll be able to find it from here. Come with the wind, just don't let it blow too hard, please, but do come.

"I've got a career I love, the one you encouraged me to study for and succeed in, but I'm on my own and I miss you. Have you and Mum sorted out your differences up there?"

Keira leaned over to kiss the stone; then she stood up and left the graveyard, her shoulders bowed. As she walked back down to the small port of St Mawes, she called Jeanne and burst into tears; her sister talked to her for a long time, comforting her.

*

Back in Paris, the two sisters celebrated Keira's success by painting the town red. Their second night of partying came to an abrupt halt at five o'clock in the morning, when an emergency services crew cautioned Jeanne; she was very drunk and was hell bent on moving in with a down-and-out in the doorway of a shop on the Champs Elysées. Keira's enduring memory of the celebrations was of the forty-eight-hour hangover that followed.

*

That Saturday morning, Jeanne's concierge had delivered three letters addressed to Keira. Archaeology is an academic discipline in which everybody contributes from their area of knowledge to the much-hoped-for discovery. Success on the ground depends on everybody pooling their expertise; it is the result of teamwork. When Keira found out that the three colleagues she'd approached were only too ready to set off for Ethiopia with her, she danced jubilantly around the apartment.

That morning while Jeanne was strolling through a street market, one of the fruit sellers told her she was beautiful; and that morning, she headed home with a basket piled ridiculously high and a huge grin pasted on her face.

At midday, Jan Vackeers and Ivory were eating lunch in a small canalside restaurant in Amsterdam. Ivory's sole was cooked to perfection and Jan was enjoying seeing his companion's gourmet tastes well indulged. Barges chugged past, and the terrace where the two friends were sitting was bathed in sunlight. They were revisiting happy memories and the laughter flowed easily.

At one o'clock, Walter was taking a walk in Hyde Park. A Bernese mountain dog was sitting at the foot of a tall oak tree staring up at a squirrel that leapt from branch to branch. Walter went over to the dog and stroked its head. When the animal's owner called for him, Walter couldn't believe his eyes. Miss Jenkins was as taken aback as Walter by this unexpected encounter, but it was she who initiated the conversation. She didn't know he liked dogs; Walter told her that he was a dog-owner too, even if his pet spent most of its time round at his mother's. They walked together for a hundred metres or so before politely saying goodbye in front of the park gates. Walter spent the rest of the afternoon sitting on a park bench, staring at a rose.

At two o'clock, I was heading home. I'd found an old camera at Camden Lock and was looking forward to spending my evening taking it apart and cleaning it up. A postcard awaited me on the doormat. The photo was of the little fishing port at Hydra, the island where my mother lives. She'd posted it six days earlier. My mother hates the telephone, she doesn't write often and, when she does pick up a pen, she's not exactly effusive. Her message was short and to the point: '*When are you coming to see me?*' Two hours later, I emerged from the local travel agent's with a plane ticket in my pocket for the end of the month.

That Saturday evening, Keira cancelled her dinner with Max because she was too busy getting ready for her trip.

After staring at herself long and hard in the bathroom mirror, Jeanne decided to throw away those last letters from Jérôme.

Walter, who had popped round to his local bookshop, was leafing through a dog encyclopaedia and learning the page about the Bernese mountain dog by heart.

Jan Vackeers agreed to another game of chess, so that Ivory could have his revenge.

As for me, after meticulously cleaning up the camera I'd bought that morning, I sat down at my desk, with a cold beer and a rather tasty home-made sandwich. I started writing a letter to my mother, warning her of my imminent arrival, before putting my pen down again and deciding to make it a surprise visit.

Some days are made up of these tiny moments, days you remember long afterwards, without really knowing why.

*

I had told Walter about my forthcoming trip. My seminars weren't due to start until term began, and nobody in college would notice my absence. I bought biscuits, tea and the English mustard my mother loved, fastened my suitcase, locked the front door, and flagged down a taxi to the airport. I would arrive into Athens mid-afternoon, in time to make it to the port of Piraeus and catch the ferry that docks at Hydra an hour later.

Heathrow was shambolic, as usual. But when you've flown to the furthest reaches of South America, you learn to take the rough with the smooth when travelling. Happily, my flight left on time. We were flying over Paris now, it was a clear sky and those passengers who, like me, were sitting on the right side of the cabin, got a great view of the capital; we could even see the Eiffel Tower.

*

Paris

Keira pleaded with Jeanne to help her do up her suit-case.

"I don't want you to go."

"I'll miss my plane – please Jeanne, hurry up, now's not the time!"

It was a hasty departure. Jeanne didn't say a word in the taxi as they drove to Orly Airport.

"Are you going to sulk until I've gone?"

"I'm not sulking, I'm just sad," Jeanne muttered.

"I promise I'll phone you regularly."

"Let's face it, once you're over there, nothing will exist for you outside of your work. And anyway, you've explained the set-up often enough, no phone booths, no network..."

"Jeanne, the last two months have been amazing and nothing that's happening to me would have come about without you. I owe this trip to you, you're..."

"I know, the sister you wouldn't change for any-one in the world, but you'd still rather spend your days in the company of your skeletons in the Omo Valley. Look at me – I can't believe I'm getting all worked up like this! I really am hopeless; yesterday I went through all the upbeat things I was going to say to you."

Jeanne stared at Keira.

"What's the matter?"

"Nothing, I'm just committing your beautiful features to memory because it'll be a long time before I see them again."

"Stop it, Jeanne, that's just creepy. You can always come out and visit me!"

"I'm already struggling to make ends meet, so my bank manager'll be over the moon if I start talking about a little trip to Ethiopia. What's happened to your necklace?"

Keira stroked her neck.

"It's a long story."

"Fire away."

"I ran into an old friend in London, by chance."

"And you gave away the pendant you were so attached to?"

"Like I said, Jeanne, it's a long story."

"What's his name?"

"Adrian."

"Did you take him with you to see Dad?"

"Of course not."

"Mind you, if this mysterious Adrian can take your mind off Max, good for him."

"What have you got against Max?"

"Nothing!"

Keira looked closely at her sister.

216

"Nothing at all? Or: Nothing, because you've got a thing for him?"

Jeanne didn't answer.

"I'm such a galumphing idiot...," breathed Keira. *"We haven't spoken since you split up; Max took months to get over you, don't open up old wounds if you're only going away again; I don't know if I should tell you this, but... Max was at the dinner tonight –* you're in love with him!"

"That's rubbish!"

"Look me in the eye, Jeanne!"

"What am I meant to say? That I felt so lonely I became infatuated with my little sister's ex? I don't even know any more if it was him or the idea of you two as a couple that I fell in love with; or just the idea of being with someone, full stop."

"Max is all yours, Jeanne, but don't say I didn't warn you, it's a bad move!"

Jeanne walked with her sister as far as the check-in. Once Keira's luggage had been swallowed up by the conveyer belt, they went for a farewell coffee together. Jeanne had too much of a lump in her throat to say much, and Keira was no better. They held hands, each lost in thought. They said their goodbyes at passport control. Jeanne hugged Keira and burst into tears.

"I'll call you every week," sobbed Keira.

"No you won't, but I'll write to you and you can write back. You can tell me about your days and I'll tell you about mine; your letters will go on for pages and mine will only be a few lines, because there won't be much to report. You'll send me photos of your beautiful river, I'll send you postcards of the Métro. I love you, little sis, look after yourself and, most of all, come back quickly."

Keira started walking backwards; she held out her passport and her boarding card to the officer behind the glass. Once she was through security, she turned round to wave goodbye to her sister one more time, but Jeanne had already gone.

*

Athens

The port of Piraeus in the late afternoon buzzes like a hive. Passengers pour off interminable buses, minibuses and cabs and rush across the quay. The moorings slap about with the wind, beating out the rhythm for the dance of the boats berthed alongside. The ferry to Hydra was well on its way, and the crossing was going to be rough. Sitting up on top deck, I tried fixing my gaze on the horizon; despite my Greek origins, I'd never had good sea legs.

Hydra is an island that time has passed by. There are only two ways of getting around: on foot or on a donkey's back. Up in the village that overhangs the little fishing port, the houses cling to the mountainside; you reach them by going up a series of steep, twisting streets. Out of season, everyone knows each other here, it's impossible to step off the boat without a familiar face smiling at you, or someone throwing their arms around you and shouting out to whomever wants to hear that you're back. My challenge was to reach my childhood home before rumours of my arrival had made their way up the hill ahead of me. I don't know why I was so keen on surprising my mother like this. Perhaps because I'd sensed not so much a reproach as a summons.

Old Kalibanos, who has a business hiring out donkeys, was only too happy to lend me one of his best-looking beasts. There are two sorts of donkeys on Hydra, the ones that move very slowly and those that trot along nicely. The latter cost twice as much and mounting them is a lot more difficult than you might think. A donkey goes his own sweet way, and if you want him to obey, he has to accept you first.

"Don't give him any rest," Kalibanos instructed, "he's fast but he's lazy; when you're turning the bend, just before your mother's house, pull on the left rein, otherwise he'll chomp his way through the flowers on my cousin's wall and I'll never hear the end of it."

I promised I'd do my best. Kalibanos told me to leave my luggage with him: he'd make sure it was delivered later. He tapped his watch, giving me fifteen minutes or less to get up there, otherwise my mother would already have heard the news.

"You're lucky your aunt's telephone is out of order!"

Aunt Elena has a little shop selling postcards and souvenirs down by the port, and she can talk for Greece; most of the time she's not saying anything of consequence, but her laugh is infectious, and she's always chuckling.

As soon as I set off, my childhood reflexes resurfaced. I didn't exactly look dignified with my donkey swaying its hindquarters, but I was going at a reasonable lick; the beauty of the place struck me as it did every time I came back. I didn't grow up here, I was born in London and I've always lived there, but we spent every holiday at my mother's family home, before she settled here for good after the death of my father. Here, everyone calls me Adrianos.

*

Addis Ababa

The plane had just landed at Bole Airport, and was about to unload its cargo at the brand new terminal of which the city was so proud. Keira and her team had to wait several long hours before their equipment was finally cleared at customs. There were three minibuses waiting for them. The coordinator, contacted by Keira at the beginning of the week, had kept his promise. The drivers loaded up the boxes, tents and luggage into the first two vehicles, and the team boarded the third; engines coughed and clutches squealed, signalling the start of their adventure. They passed the roundabout commemorating Ethio-Chinese friendship: there was even a sculpture on the pediment of the central railway station in Addis Ababa, depicting the Chinese flag with its stars. The convoy took the main avenue that bisects the capital from east to west. The traffic was heavy and the exhausted crew soon nodded off, oblivious to the chaos all around; not even the jolting as a wheel got stuck in a rut woke them.

The Omo Valley is five hundred kilometres from

the capital, as the crow flies; and three times that distance by road, with the tarmac petering out half way to become a mud road that narrows to a dirt track. The convoy drove out of Addis, then past Tefki and Tulu Bolo, stopping at Giyon as dusk fell. They unloaded the equipment and transferred it to two long multi-terrain vehicles. Keira was relieved that everything seemed to be going smoothly; her team-members looked happy, despite their growing fatigue.

At Welkite, the drivers declared they couldn't go any further; they'd spend the night here. A family took them in and the team gamely ate the meal they were given: a steaming bowl of *wat* stew, after which they gratefully lay down to sleep on the mats laid out in the main room.

Keira was the first up. She surveyed her surroundings from the steps of their overnight residence; a village mostly made up of white houses with corrugated iron roofs. The rooftops of Paris were far away now, but she missed Jeanne, and she suddenly found herself wondering why she'd set out on this adventure. The voice of Eric, one of her colleagues, interrupted her thoughts.

"A far cry from Paris, hey?"

"I was just thinking the same thing. But if this feels like the arse end of nowhere, just wait, because we've still got another five hundred kilometres to go," Keira replied.

"I can't wait to arrive and get going."

"Firstly we're going to have to make sure the villagers accept us."

"Are you worried about that?"

"We left rather hurriedly after the storm – like thieves."

"But you didn't steal anything, so there's no need to feel bad," said Eric, before turning on his heels.

Eric's dry pragmatism caught Keira off-guard, but she shrugged off his remark and made her way over to the vehicles to check the kit was properly secured.

By seven o'clock that morning, the convoy was on the road again. Once they were outside Welkite, the houses gave way to huts with pointy straw roofs. The landscape changed dramatically an hour later, as Keira and her team descended into the Gibe Valley.

Their first contact with the river involved crossing Duke's Bridge, which straddled the majestic waters Keira so loved. At her request, the jeeps stopped.

"When will we reach camp?" inquired one of her co-workers.

"We could have gone down there," said Eric, staring at the water at the bottom of the precipice.

"Yes, we could. But it'd take us twenty days, or longer if the hippopotamuses didn't want to let us pass; and we'd probably lose half our kit in the current," Keira pointed out. "We could also have taken a small plane as far as Jimma, but that was too expensive given that it only saved us a day's travelling."

Eric got back into the vehicle with no further comment. Far below, the river snaked across the savannah then disappeared into the jungle again.

The convoy was back on its way, raising a thick cloud of dust in its wake. The road grew increasingly winding, and the gorges they crossed were more vertiginous each time. At midday, they passed Abelti and began their descent towards Asendako. The journey dragged on and on, and Keira was the only passenger who seemed to be holding up. At last the cars arrived at Jimma; they spent their second night there. Tomorrow, Keira would be back in her beloved Omo Valley.

*

Hydra

"Are you trying to give me a heart attack? It's lucky your aunt called me from the grocer's to warn me you were at the port."

These were my mother's first words when I walked into her house. They were her way of welcoming me, and reproaching me for the long months of absence.

"Your aunt's still got sharp eyesight; I'm not sure I'd have recognised you if I'd seen you in town! Stand in the light so I can get a proper look – you're so skinny and you look pasty!"

I knew there'd be a few more remarks of that ilk before she gave me a hug.

"I've heard you're travelling light, so I take it you're only staying for a few days?"

When I told her I intended to spend several weeks on the island, my mother finally relaxed and kissed me affectionately. I swore she didn't look a day older and she pinched my cheeks and called me a liar, but accepted the compliment. She immediately started bustling about in the kitchen, doing a stock-check on all the flour, sugar, milk, eggs, meat and vegetables she had left.

"What are you doing?"

"My son turns up out of the blue, after more than two years without paying his poor mother a single visit and he's timed his arrival so late in the day that I've only got an hour left to rustle up a feast for half the island."

"I want us to have supper together, just the two of us; I'd like to take you out for a meal down by the port."

"And I'd like to be thirty years younger and cured of my rheumatism!"

My mother clicked her fingers and rubbed her lower back.

"No, it didn't work! It looks like our wishes won't be granted today, so I'll cook up a feast in true family tradition. You don't think your arrival on the island has gone unnoticed?"

It was pointless arguing with her about this, or anything else for that matter. Everybody in the village would have understood that we wanted to spend the evening together, by ourselves, but it meant a lot to my mother to celebrate my arrival more publicly, and I wasn't going to deprive her of that pleasure.

The neighbours brought wine, cheese and olives, the women laid the table, the men tuned their musical instruments. We drank, danced and sang until late into the night. I had a little word in private with my aunt to thank her for her indiscretion; she swore blind she didn't know what I was talking about.

When I woke the next day, my mother had already been up for some time. Everything had been cleared away and the house was back to normal.

"What are you planning to do here for weeks on end?" my mother wanted to know, as she poured me a cup of coffee.

"Not be waited on hand and foot – that'd be a good start. I came here to look after you, not the other way round."

"Look after me? What are you talking about? I've been fending for myself for years now. Apart from Elena who comes to hang out the washing in return for my help in the shop, I don't need anyone."

Without Aunt Elena, my mother would have felt much lonelier. While I was eating my breakfast, I could hear her unpacking my suitcase and tidying my belongings away.

"I can hear you tut-tutting!" she called from the bedroom window.

I spent the first day of the holidays astride Kalibanos's donkey, reacquainting myself with the island. I stopped at a deserted cove and dove into the sea, only to come out again just as quickly, shivering with cold. I ate lunch with my mother and aunt at the port and listened to them telling family stories, memories that one or the other tirelessly reprised. Is that what growing old means? When today we can only speak of yesterday and the present is filled with nostalgia which we try to laugh off?

"What are you looking at us like that for?" asked my aunt, wiping her eyes.

"When I've gone back to London, will the two of you eat lunch at this very same table and recall our meal today as a happy memory?"

"Of course! Why d'you ask such a silly question?" demanded Elena.

"Because I'm wondering why you don't enjoy this beautiful sunny day right now, instead of waiting until after I've gone!"

"Your son hasn't seen the sun for much too long," Elena told my mother. "I don't understand a word he says anymore."

"I do," smiled my mother, "and I take his point. Let's stop with these old stories and talk about the future. What are your plans for this year, Elena?"

My aunt gazed from my mother to myself in turn.

"I'm going to put a fresh coat of paint on the shop wall at the end of the month, before the start of the season," she announced solemnly. "The blue's faded, wouldn't you say?"

"I was just thinking the same thing myself. Now there's something Adrianos could get really enthusiastic about," my mother added, winking at me.

This time, Elena asked if we were making fun of her, but I assured her we were doing nothing of the kind. For two hours, we discussed which blue she should choose for her shop front. Mother woke the napping hardware store owner to get some colour

charts from him; as we held them against the wall to
see which one would work best, I could see a healthy
glow returning to my mother's face.

Two weeks went by, during which we lived by the
sun that I'd missed so badly; the heat grew more intense every day. June rolled slowly past and we saw
the first trickle of tourists arrive on the ferry.

I can remember that Friday morning as if it were yes-
terday. Mother had come into the bedroom where I
was reading and enjoying the cool preserved by the
shutters. I had to put my book down because she was
standing in front of me, arms folded. She stared at me
without saying anything, and with a very strange ex-
pression on her face.
"What's the matter?"
"Nothing," she said.
"So you've just come to watch me reading?"
"I've brought your clean laundry."
"But your hands are empty!"
"I must have forgotten it."
"Mother?"
"Adrian, since when did you start wearing neck-
laces...?"
Whenever my mother calls me Adrian instead of
using the Greek version of my name, I know some-
thing serious is up.
"Don't feign innocence!" she added.
"I've got no idea what you're talking about."

My mother glowered in the direction of my bed-side table.

"I'm talking about the necklace I found in your suitcase and put away in that drawer."

I opened the drawer and found the pendant Keira had left behind in London. Why had I brought it with me? I didn't know myself.

"It was a present!"

"So, people are giving you necklaces now? And not any old necklace either: it's certainly an original present. Who was so generous, might I ask?"

"A friend. Look, I've been here for two weeks now; why the interest in this necklace all of a sudden?"

"You can start by telling me about this friend of yours who gives jewellery to men, and then perhaps I'll show less interest in your necklace."

"It wasn't exactly a present – she left it behind in my house."

"Oh, so it's a she? Why did you say it was a present if it was just a mistake? Is there anything else you've forgotten to tell me?"

"Mother, what are you getting at?"

"Kindly explain to me who the lunatic is who's just stepped off the Athens ferry and is currently doing the rounds of all the shops at the port, asking after you?"

"What lunatic?"

"Are you going to answer every question with another one?"

"I don't know who you're talking about!"

"You don't know who the necklace belongs to, you can't describe the woman who gave it to you, no, sorry, make that the woman who left it at your flat, and now you don't know who this Sherlock-Holmes-in-shorts down by the port is either. He's already on his fifth beer and asking every passerby if they know you. The whole town's talking about him, and my phone hasn't stopped ringing. And I don't know what to say either!"

"Sherlock-Holmes-in-shorts?"

"Flannel shorts, a short-sleeved shirt and a checked cap: all he's missing is a pipe!"

"Walter!"

"So you do know him!"

I pulled on a shirt and rushed over to the door, praying my donkey hadn't chewed through the rope tethering him to the tree in front of the house. He'd developed this nasty habit at the start of the week, ambling off into the neighbour's field to woo a lady donkey who was none too impressed by his advances.

"Walter is a work colleague, I had no idea he was planning to pay us a visit."

"Us? Don't get me mixed up in this, please, Adrian!"

I couldn't understand why my mother, who was normally so welcoming, should be so on edge. Nor the remark she made as I closed the front door: "Your ex-wife was a colleague too!"

Sure enough, it was Walter who had stepped off

the boat an hour earlier and was now sitting on the terrace of the restaurant next to Aunt Elena's shop.

"Adrian!" he yelled, on spotting me.

"What are you doing here, Walter?"

"As I said to the charming owner of this establishment, the college just isn't the same without you. I missed you, my friend!"

"You told the restaurant owner that you missed me?"

"Absolutely, and that's the truth."

I burst out laughing, which was a mistake because Walter took this as a sign that I was happy to see him; fuelled by five or six beers, he stood up and gave me a soppy hug. Over his shoulder, I saw Aunt Elena calling my mother again.

"Walter, I wasn't expecting to see you here..."

"And I didn't expect to be here either. But it just kept on raining and raining – it hasn't stopped since you left; I'd had enough of the grey, and I needed your advice on something, but we'll talk about that later. So anyway, I said to myself: "Why not go and spend a few days in the sun? Why does everybody else always go on holiday and never me? And I actually did something about it for once, I pounced on a special offer in a travel agent's window and here I am!"

"For how long?"

"Just a week, but don't worry I have no intention of imposing on you, I've made my own arrangements. The special offer included a room in a delightful little hotel, somewhere around here, I'm not quite sure where," he trailed off breathlessly, flapping his room reservation.

I accompanied Walter across the narrow streets of the old town, kicking myself for being rash enough to have mentioned Hydra to him.

"Yours is a beautiful country, Adrian, it's just magical. The white walls and blue shutters, the sea, even the donkeys are terrific!"

"It's siesta time, Walter, would you mind lowering your voice a little: these streets are terribly noisy."

"Of course, old chap," he whispered, "of course."

"And might I suggest you change your outfit?"

Walter looked himself up and down, astonished.

"Is something wrong?"

"Let's drop your suitcase off and take care of this."

I hadn't noticed that while I was helping Walter find something more muted to wear in the general store on the port, Aunt Elena had called my mother back to tell her I was shopping with my friend.

Greeks are naturally hospitable, and I had no intention of tarnishing their reputation, so I invited Walter to have supper with me in town. I remembered Walter wanted to ask my advice about something and out on the restaurant terrace I asked him how I could be of help.

"Do you know about dogs?" he enquired.

And he told me about his fleeting walk with Miss Jenkins, a few weeks' earlier in Hyde Park.

"That chance encounter has changed a lot of

things: now, when we greet each other, I ask her about Oscar (the name of her Bernese mountain dog) and each time she assures me that he's well. But as far as our relationship goes, we haven't moved on at all."

"Why don't you invite her to a concert or a musical? You're spoilt for choice in the West End." Walter sighed and stared at the sea for a while.

"Just go for it, invite her, she'll be very touched, believe me."

Walter sighed again.

"What if she says no?"

Aunt Elena appeared and planted herself right in front of us, waiting for me to make the introductions. Walter invited her to sit at our table. She didn't need asking twice and had sat down before I'd even got up to pull a chair out for her. When my mother wasn't around, Elena had a wicked sense of humour that took you by surprise. Once she started talking, nothing could stop her: she was regaling Walter with pretty much her entire life. We were the last ones to leave the restaurant. I showed my friend back to his hotel, and then made it back to the house by donkey. Mother was waiting up for me on the patio, polishing the silver at one o'clock in the morning!

The next day, the telephone rang at four o'clock. Mother came out to find me on the terrace and announced, sounding very suspicious, that my friend wanted to speak to me.

Walter suggested we go for a walk in the late

afternoon; I wanted to finish my book and invited him to join us for the evening instead. I went down to do a spot of shopping in the village and arranged for Kalibanos to pick Walter up from his hotel at around nine o'clock and bring him up to our place. My mother maintained a steely silence; she satisfied herself by laying the table and inviting my aunt to join us for the dinner she clearly felt so put out by.

"What's wrong?" I asked as I helped her with the table.

My mother put down the plates and folded her arms, which never augured well.

"You've been away for two whole years, Adrianos, hardly ever even giving a sign of life, and now the only person you want to introduce to your mother is this Sherlock Holmes character? When are you ever going to lead a normal life?"

"I guess that depends on what you mean by normal, Mother."

"I'd like it if the only thing I had to worry about was … making sure my grandchildren didn't run off and hurt themselves on the rocks."

My mother had never said anything like that to me before. I pulled up a chair for her and poured a glass of ouzo, the way she likes it, no water and just one ice cube. I looked at her affectionately, thinking hard about what I was going to say.

"So now you want grandchildren? You always used to say the opposite, that raising me was enough for you; you insisted you'd never turn into one of those women who, once their offspring fly the nest, play out the same role but as a granny."

"And what if I *have* turned into one of those women? Only fools never change their minds, isn't that what they say? Life rushes by so quickly Adrianos, you've had plenty of time to enjoy yourself with your friends. You shouldn't be dreaming about tomorrow anymore. At your age, tomorrow is today; and at mine, as you've noticed, today has become yesterday."

"But I've got my whole life ahead of me!" I protested.

"No one sells wilted lettuces!"

"I don't know why you're getting so worked up, I'm sure I'll meet my ideal woman one day."

"Do I look like an ideal woman? And yet your father and I spent forty very happy years together. It's not the woman or the man that needs to be ideal, but rather what they want to share together. True love is what happens when two people meet and are prepared to give themselves fully to each other. Have you ever encountered something like that?"

I confessed I hadn't. Mother stroked my cheek and smiled at me.

"Have you even looked for it?"

She stood up, her glass untouched, and went back into the kitchen, leaving me alone on the terrace.

*

The Omo Valley

The pale morning light of the Omo Valley revealed a landscape of marshes and savannah, cut off from the world by the high mountain ridges. All traces of the storm had disappeared. The villagers had rebuilt what the wind had destroyed. Colobus monkeys swung from tree to tree so nimbly that the branches barely dipped.

The archaeologists passed a village belonging to the Qwegu tribe, and further downhill they finally reached the village of the Mursis.

Warriors and children were playing by the banks of the river.

"Have you ever seen such a handsome-looking people as those of the Omo?" Keira inquired of one of her travelling companions.

On their tanned reddish skin were paintings worthy of a master. The Mursis managed to achieve instinctively what some great painters spent a lifetime trying to accomplish. Using their fingertips or a sharpened reed, they applied the red ochre, or whatever pigment the volcanic earth offered them, so that they could decorate themselves with different colours: green, yellow, ash grey. A little girl straight out of a Gauguin painting was laughing with a young warrior designed by Rothko.

Awed by all this splendour, Keira's colleagues remained silent.

If humanity really does have a cradle, the people of the Omo still appeared to be living there.

The villagers started running to meet the team of archaeologists. In the midst of all those dancing to display their joy, Keira was searching for one very special face. She'd have recognised it among hundreds of others, she'd even have recognised his features under an ochre clay mask, but Hari hadn't come to welcome her.

*

Hydra

At 9pm on the dot, I heard a donkey braying on the path. My mother opened our front door and greeted Walter. From the state of his clothes, he looked as though he'd been dragged through a few olive groves backwards.

"He fell off three times!" Kalibanos sighed, "even though I put him on my most docile animal." And with that he set off again, grumpy at not having carried out his mission more efficiently.

"Say what you like," complained Walter, "but these are hardly the Queen's horses. No control round corners, and no discipline."

As Aunt Elena muttered something about Walter not appreciating Greek donkeys, my mother steered us out onto the terrace.

Walter gushed a thousand compliments about the decor; he had never, he swore, seen anything so beautiful. He admired the pebble floor. At table, Elena kept pestering him with questions about his job at the college, and how we'd got to know each other. I hadn't been aware of my colleague's diplomatic skills until that day. Throughout the dinner, he made complimentary remarks about all the food he was served. When the dessert came around, he asked my mother how she'd met my father. Mother is unstoppable on the subject. The coolness of the evening was making Aunt Elena shiver, so we left the terrace to move into the living room where we drank the milky coffees Mother had poured. On the little table over by the window, I was surprised to see Keira's necklace which had mysteriously travelled from my bedside table drawer. Walter followed my gaze and happily burst out:

"I recognise that necklace!"

"I thought as much!" said my mother, triumphantly offering him the box of chocolates.

Walter didn't understand why my mother seemed so pleased, nor did I.

Aunt Elena was tired; it was too late for her to go back down to the village and, as she often did, she went off to tuck herself up in the guest room. Mother decided to go to bed too, saying goodnight to Walter and suggesting that, once we'd finished our drinks, I made sure he got safely back down to the port. She was worried he'd lose his way, but Walter insisted it really wasn't necessary. And the weather, it turned out, had other plans.

I'm constantly amazed by the sequence of tiny events that determines the course of our lives. Nobody can see the jigsaw pieces coming together that will lead to everything changing forever.

Walter and I had been deep in conversation for a good hour when a storm rolled up from the sea, more intense than anything I'd experienced in a long time. Walter helped me to bolt the doors and windows and we calmly picked up the thread of our conversation while the thunder rolled outside.

There was no question of letting my friend go back down to his hotel in this weather. Aunt Elena was in the guest room, so I offered him the sitting-room sofa and a blanket for the night. After making sure he was comfortable, I said goodnight and retired to my own room, ready to drop off as soon as my head hit the pillow. But the storm was stronger now and the lightning struck with such ferocity that, even with my eyelids closed, I could still see the flashes lighting up the room.

Walter appeared in my bedroom in his boxer shorts, fizzing with uncharacteristic excitement. He shook me, urging me to get up and follow him. At first, I thought he'd seen a snake, although we'd never had one in the house before. I had to take hold of him by the shoulders, to get him to make any sense.

"You've got to come with me, you won't believe your eyes."

I had no choice but to follow him. The sitting room was in darkness, and Walter led me over to the window. I quickly understood why he was so blown away: each time a flash of lightning streaked across the sky, the sea was lit up like a vast mirror.

"I'm glad you got me out of bed, it's a beautiful spectacle, really it is."

"What spectacle?" Walter wanted to know.

"The one that's right in front of us, isn't that why you woke me up?"

"You're not telling me you were asleep with this racket going on, old chap? People say London's noisy but it's got nothing on Hydra in the rain. No, that's not why I got you up."

Lightning flickered across the sky and I didn't think it was a good idea to stay close to the window, but Walter was adamant I shouldn't move. He took the necklace my mother had left on the small table and held it up in front of the window, touching it only with his fingertips.

"Now see what happens," he urged, feverishly.

The thunder started growling and, when a new streak of lightning ripped through the sky, the bright light of the storm pierced the necklace. Millions of tiny dots flashed up on the living room wall, so dazzlingly intense that it took a few seconds for what we saw to fade from our retinas.

"Isn't that mind-boggling? I couldn't sleep," Walter continued, "So I went over to the window, and I've got no idea why I decided to fiddle with that necklace, but I did. While I was inspecting it more closely, the phenomenon you've just witnessed took place."

I switched on a lamp, but no matter how closely I examined the pendant there was no hole visible to the naked eye.

"So what do you think it is?"

"I have no idea," I admitted.

What I didn't realise was that my mother, who'd come downstairs to find out what all the kerfuffle in her living room was about, had tiptoed back up to her bedroom again, after seeing Walter and me, in our boxer shorts, in front of the window overlooking the sea, passing Keira's necklace back and forth between us, by the light of the stars.

The next day, Mother asked Walter for his views on cults and sects; and before either of us had even opened our mouths to respond, she stood up and went to clear up the kitchen.

Sitting on our terrace overlooking the bay of Hydra, I shared a few childhood memories connected to this house with Walter. Come the evening, the sky was transparent, the stars crystal clear.

"I don't want to say something that will make me sound like a blundering idiot here," Walter declared, tilting his head back, "but what I see up there looks a lot like..."

"Cassiopeia," I interrupted him, "and, just next to it is the galaxy of Andromeda. The Milky Way, of which our planet is a part, is hopelessly attracted to Andromeda, and there's nothing we can do about it. The two will probably collide in a few million years."

"In the meantime, while we're waiting for the world to end, I was going to say..."

"And a bit further off to the right is Perseus, and then of course the North Star, and I trust you can spot the handsome nebula..."

"Will you stop interrupting me? If I could get two words in edgeways here without you giving me your A to Z of stars, I might be able to explain that what all this really reminds me of are the dots we saw on the wall last night, during the storm."

We stared at each other, both completely taken aback. It seemed impossible, but now that I thought about it, the phenomenal number of dots the lightning had projected through the pendant were indeed dead ringers for the stars twinkling above our heads.

How could we set about reproducing the phenomenon? No matter how close I held the pendant to a light bulb, nothing happened.

"The light from a single lamp is inadequate," stated Walter, who had suddenly become more of a scientist than I was.

"And where do you think you're going to find a light source that's as powerful as a streak of lightning?"

"The lighthouse down at the port?" Walter suggested.

"The beam's too wide – we wouldn't be able to focus it on one wall."

After a day spent doing very little, I didn't fancy going to bed, so I offered to ride with Walter back to his hotel; a bit of exercise would do me good and anyway I wanted to carry on our conversation.

"Let's be methodical about this," I suggested to Walter, whose donkey was trotting along a few metres behind me. "What light sources are powerful enough to be useful to us, and where can we find them?"

"Do you remember telling me about that green beam rising up in the sky from Greenwich: that was pretty powerful wasn't it?"

"A laser! That's exactly what we need!"

"So why not ask your mother if she happens to have a laser in her cellar?"

I responded to my friend's sarcasm by giving my beast a kick and picking up the pace.

"And touchy to boot!" shouted Walter as I increased my lead on him.

I waited for him at the next bend.

"There's a laser in the spectroscopy department at the university," Walter panted as he caught up with me. "But it's a very old model."

"We don't want a ruby laser, I'm not sure a red beam would work. We need a much more powerful piece of equipment."

"Well, all that's in London anyway and I have no intention of cutting short my vacation here, not even to solve the mystery of your pendant; in fact, not for anything in the world. Let's think about this a bit more. Who uses lasers these days?"

"Researchers in molecular physics, plus doctors and ophthalmologists."

"You don't happen to have an optician friend in Athens?"

"Not that I can think of."

Walter scratched his head and volunteered to make a few calls from his hotel. With all his inter-departmental connections, he should be able to find someone to give us a steer. These resolutions made, we went our separate ways.

The next morning, Walter phoned and asked me to join him as quickly as possible down at the port. I found him out on the terrace of one of the cafés, deep in conversation with Aunt Elena; he didn't even acknowledge me when I sat down at their table.

While my aunt carried on telling him a story from her childhood, Walter casually held out a piece of paper to me. I unfolded it and read:

INSTITUTE OF ELECTRONIC STRUCTURE
AND LASER,
FOUNDATION FOR RESEARCH AND
TECHNOLOGY - HELLAS,
GR-711 10 HERAKLION, GREECE.
CONTACT DR MAGDALENA KARI.

"How did you manage it?"

"It's a walk in the park for a Sherlock Holmes, wouldn't you say? And don't play the innocent with me: your aunt's just spilled the beans. I took the liberty of contacting Magdalena, having been put in touch with her by one of our colleagues who said we could use his name as a reference," Walter announced triumphantly. "She's expecting us this evening or tomorrow and assures me she'll do her best to help us out. She also happens to speak perfect English."

It's a two hundred and thirty kilometre trip to Heraklion, and unless we wanted to embark on a ten-hour boat journey, the simplest way of getting there would be to head back to Athens and catch a small plane on to Crete. If we left immediately, we could be there by early evening.

Walter said his goodbyes to Aunt Elena. I just had time to go back up to the house, let my mother know I'd be away for twenty-four hours, and pack a bag before catching the ferry.

Mother didn't ask any questions, she just wished me a safe trip in a slightly pinched sort of a way. She called out to me just as I was leaving and held out a basket with lunch in it for the journey.

"Your aunt warned me you were off again, and your old mother might as well be of some use to you. Off you go, if that's what you need to do!"

Walter was waiting for me on the quayside. The ferry left from the port of Hydra and made for Athens. After quarter of an hour at sea, I decided to leave the saloon area and go outside to get some air. Walter looked at me with a smirk.

"Don't tell me you get seasick?"

"Fine, I won't!" I replied, getting up from my chair.

"I trust you don't mind if I finish your mother's sandwiches? They're delicious, and it would be criminal to leave them!"

From Piraeus, a taxi drove us to the airport. This time it was Walter who felt queasy as our driver wove in and out of the motorway traffic. Luckily, there was still room on the light plane which meant we could make the connection through to Crete. At 6pm, we landed on the tarmac at Heraklion. As he set foot on the island, Walter marvelled:

"How can you be from this country but live in exile in England? Are you that fond of the rain?"

"May I just remind you that I've spent the last few years in the Chilean desert; I'm a man who can make himself at home anywhere, each country has its own attractions."

Walter was still shaking his head as he hailed a taxi, signalling for me to climb in first and give the address to the driver.

*

Dr Magdalena Kari greeted us from behind the Institute's metal gates, where the guard had asked us to wait.

"I'm afraid these security measures aren't much fun," said Magdalena, signalling to the guard to let us through, "but we do have to take all the necessary precautions because the equipment here is classed as sensitive."

Magdalena led us across a park surrounding an imposing concrete building. Once inside, we had to comply with further security checks. We exchanged our passports for two visitor badges, then Magdalena signed a day book and showed us into her office. I started talking first; some instinct prompted me not to tell her everything, and to downplay our reason for wanting to carry out the experiment. Magdalena listened attentively to my sketchy explanation. Walter was lost in his thoughts, which might have had something to do with the striking resemblance between our hostess and Miss Jenkins; even I was struck by it.

"We have several lasers," she confirmed. "Unfortunately, it's impossible for me to make one available to you without first obtaining the proper authorisation, and that may take some time."

"We've travelled a long way to be here and we have to leave tomorrow," chivvied Walter, emerging from his daydream.

"I'll see what I can do, but I can't make any promises," Magdalena said, before asking us to wait.

She left us in her office, insisting that under no circumstances were we to wander about the premises on our own.

We waited for a good fifteen minutes. Magdalena returned accompanied by Professor Dimitris Mikalas, who introduced himself as the Director of the Research Centre. He sat in Magdalena's chair and politely requested that we outline what we wanted from him. This time, it was Walter who spoke, and I've rarely heard him be so unforthcoming. Was his gut instinct the same as mine? He seemed content to cite the names of several university colleagues as our referees, each with a very impressive title, although I hadn't heard of most of them.

"We have excellent relations with your institution, and I'd be embarrassed if we couldn't respond favourably to the request of two of its eminent members. Especially when they have such impressive recommendations. I'll have to do a few of the customary checks, but as soon as your identities have been confirmed I'll be happy to give you access to one of our lasers, so that you can conduct your experiment. We've got one that's just been returned from servicing. It won't be back in normal use until tomorrow, so it could be at your disposal all night. Magdalena will stay with you to ensure that everything runs smoothly.

We thanked the professor warmly for his generous welcome, and Magdalena for agreeing to give up her evening for us. They left us alone while they went off to carry out the final checks.

"Let's cross our fingers they don't look up all the names I've given them," Walter whispered in my ear, "half the list is made up."

Magdalena returned a short while later and showed us to the laser room.

Never, in my wildest dreams, had I imagined using an instrument as sophisticated as the one housed in that basement. I could tell how proud Magdalena was to be operating the laser from the almost maternal expression on her face. She sat down at the control desk and pressed several switches.

"Right," she said, "let's drop the formalities and you can tell me what you really want from this miracle of technology. I didn't believe your garbled explanations back there in my office for one second. I'm surprised Prof Mikalas didn't send you packing: he must have a lot on his mind right now."

"I don't know exactly what we're looking for," I said, "except that we're trying to replicate an unusual effect we witnessed. How powerful is this baby?" I asked Magdalena.

"It's 2.2 megawatts," came the smug response.

"That's some bulb! Nearly thirty-seven thousand times more powerful than the ones in your mother's living room," Walter whispered in my ear, chuffed at his speedy mental arithmetic.

Magdalena paced up and down. Passing in front of the control panel, she pushed another button and the equipment started to hum. The energy emitted by the electrons in the current began stimulating the gas atoms in the glass tube. It wouldn't be long now before the photons were resonating between the two mirrors at either end, amplifying the process; in a few moments, the beam would be powerful enough to shine through the semi-transparent surface of the mirror. "It's almost ready, so put the object you want to analyse in front of the beam and let me make the final adjustments," she said. "We'll discuss the result afterwards."

I took the pendant out of my pocket, placed it on a small stand and waited.

Having kept the instrument in check until now, Magdalena directed the beam onto the pendant, but it ricocheted off as if the surface were completely impenetrable. While she was busy checking the parameters on her control screen, I turned the adjusting screw to intensify the laser. Magdalena shot me a furious look.

"Who gave you permission to do that?" she asked, pushing my hand away.

But I caught her arm and begged her to let me carry on. As the beam intensified, I saw the look of sheer amazement on Magdalena's face. There, projected on the wall, was the same bizarre pattern of dots as we'd seen during the storm.

"What on earth is that?" whispered Magdalena.

Walter turned off the lights and the dots on the wall started twinkling.

"They look just like stars," he said excitedly.

Like us, Magdalena was incredulous. Walter fished a small digital camera out of his pocket.

"The advantages of being a tourist!" he joked, clicking away. He took at least a dozen photos. Magdalena shut off the beam and turned to me.

"What is this thing?"

Before I could give her any sort of explanation, Walter had turned the lights back on.

"You know as much as we do. We observed this phenomenon and wanted to replicate it, that's all."

Walter had discreetly popped his digital camera back into his pocket. Just then Professor Dimitris

Mikalas walked into the room, closing the door behind him.

"Astounding!" he smiled at me.

He headed over to the stand and removed the pendant.

"We have an observation platform," he added, pointing up at some glass panels I'd failed to notice overlooking the basement. "I couldn't help seeing what you were up to."

The professor turned the pendant over in the palm of his hand, raising it to his eye in an attempt to squint through it. He looked at me again.

"You don't mind if I examine this peculiar object tonight, do you? Naturally, I'll return it to you first thing in the morning."

Was it the unexpected arrival of a security guard, or Professor Mikalas's tone of voice, that made Walter react the way he did? My companion suddenly lunged at the professor and dealt him a staggering right-hook. As Dimitris Mikalas went crashing down, it was up to me to deal with the guard who had his baton raised above Walter. Magdalena screamed, Walter bent over Mikalas, who was writhing in agony on the floor, and recovered the pendant. Meanwhile, unfazed by my uppercut, the guard had wrestled me to the ground and we were rolling around like two squabbling kids. Walter put an end to our fight, grabbing the guard by the ear and raising him up with a show of strength I would never have suspected. The guard howled and let go. Walter glared at me.

"Make yourself useful, old chap, put those handcuffs on him – the ones hanging from his belt – only I don't want to rip off his earlobe!"

I obeyed orders.

"You have no idea what you're doing," groaned the professor.

"Quite. As I've already said, we haven't got the foggiest," snorted Walter, before turning to Magdalena: "How do we get out of here? And don't make me use force: I'd hate to raise my hand against a woman."

Magdalena stared at him, refusing to answer. Convinced that Walter was about to hit her, I tried to step in. But Walter shook his head and ordered me to follow him instead. He wrenched the telephone off the desk, ripping it out of its socket. Then, opening the basement door, he glanced around and dragged me through. The corridor was empty. Walter locked the door behind us, calculating that we had barely five minutes before the alarm would be raised.

"What on earth came over you?"

"Let's talk about that later," he said, breaking into a run.

The staircase ahead led up to the ground floor. Walter stopped to catch his breath on the landing, before pushing open the door into the lobby. He checked out with the security guard who returned our passports when we handed our badges in. Just as we were walking towards the exit, a walkie-talkie started crackling. Walter looked at me.

"Didn't you take the guard's radio?"

"I didn't even know he had one."

"Well then, RUN!"

We sprinted across the park, aiming for the railings and praying that nobody would block our way. The guard at the gate didn't get a chance to react. When he came out of his booth, Walter dealt him a blow with his elbow that sent him flying into the bushes. My accomplice pressed the button that controlled the gate and we sped off like bats out of hell.

"What on earth's got into you, Walter?"

"Not now!" he roared, as we tore down a flight of stairs that brought us to the seedy part of town.

We shot down the road ahead, but Walter's pace didn't let up. Another steeply sloping street, a sharp turn and we reached a main avenue, narrowly avoiding a motorbike that swept by. I'd never visited Crete at this speed before.

"This way," Walter called out as a police car headed for us, siren blaring.

By an old arched entrance, I paused briefly to draw breath before Walter made me pick up the crazy chase.

"The port, which way's the port?" he asked.

"That way," I responded, pointing to a tiny street on our left.

Walter grabbed my arm and the great escape was under way again.

The port came into view, Walter slowed down; over on the pavement, two police officers didn't seem to be taking any particular notice of us. There was a ferry bound for Athens at the quayside, and cars were driving on as passengers queuing behind a ticket kiosk waited to embark.

"Go and buy us two tickets," Walter ordered. "I'll keep an eye out."

"You want to go back to Hydra by sea?"

"You'd rather be frisked by airport security? I thought not, so go and get those tickets instead of wittering."

I was back in no time; the ferry would be at sea for most of the night and I'd managed to get a cabin with two bunks. Walter, meanwhile, had bought a cap from a street vendor, as well as a funny-looking hat that he held out to me.

"We'd better not go aboard at the same time, allow at least ten passengers in between us; if the police are on our tail, they'll be looking for two men travelling together. And put that silly hat on, you'll look ever so dashing in it! Let's meet up on the top deck, after we've set sail."

I carried out Walter's instructions to the letter and met up with him an hour later, as agreed.

"I've got to hand it to you, Walter, you're a dark horse all right. That blinding punch and the chase across town – it's the last thing I'd have expected from you! Perhaps you'd like to tell me what in heaven's name possessed you to knock out that professor?"

"Look, from the moment we went into Magdalena's office, I knew something was up. My colleague who'd put us in touch with her had gone to university with her decades ago, but the Magdalena he'd studied with was due to retire in two months' time, whereas this woman was barely thirty-five. And in Hydra, I'd looked up the Institute in the telephone book and the director is definitely not the professor we met who was going by that title. Odd, wouldn't you say?"

"Yes, but there's still quite a leap from there to smashing his jawbone!"

"It was more a case of *my fingers* taking a hammering – my hand is killing me!"

"Where did you learn to fight like that anyway?"

"You didn't go to boarding school, did you? So I suppose you were spared the horrors of initiation rites, corporal punishment and fagging?"

I confessed that I had parents who wouldn't have been separated from their son for anything in the world.

"But why did you react so violently? Couldn't we simply have left?"

"Adrian, when Dimitris asked you if he could borrow the pendant, he'd already got it in his pocket. I strongly doubt you'd have seen your precious object again in a hurry and I don't think the arrival of the security guard would have left you with much choice. One final detail, and it's not an insignificant one, the professor I knocked over seemed distinctly less shocked than us by the results of our experiment.

Perhaps I over-reacted a bit, but I'm quite sure I'm right about that."

"So here we are like two fugitives, and who knows what the repercussions will be?"

"I'm sure we'll find out, just as soon as we get off the boat."

*

Athens

"How's the professor?" inquired the voice in the receiver.

"A fractured lower jaw, a sprained neck, but no trauma to the skull," answered the woman.

"I wasn't expecting them to react like that. I'm afraid things are going to get complicated from now on."

"We couldn't have foreseen any of this, sir."

"And the object has slipped through our fingers, which is highly regrettable. Do we have any idea as to the whereabouts of the two fugitives?"

"They caught a ferry from Heraklion to Athens, which gets in tomorrow morning."

"Have we got someone on board?"

"Yes, chance was on our side on that front. One of our men spotted them at the port; he didn't tackle them without orders, but he had the presence of mind to get on board. I got a message just as the boat was setting off. What else would you like from me?"

"You've done what was needed. Just make sure this incident goes unnoticed: *the professor had a nasty fall down the stairs,* understood? Order the head of security to ensure that no mention of this unfortunate incident be recorded in the day book by anyone at the Institute; when he returns from holiday, the director mustn't get wind of it."

"You can count on me, sir."

"And perhaps we should change the name on your office door. Magdalena died six months ago and it's starting to be in very bad taste."

"As you wish, but it was very handy for us today!"

"Judging from the results, I'm not so sure," the caller retorted, hanging up.

*

Amsterdam

Jan Vackeers wandered over to the window to think for a moment or two. The situation rankled with him far more than he cared to admit. He picked up the receiver and dialled a London number.

"I wanted to thank you for your call yesterday, Sir Ashley; unfortunately, the operation in Heraklion failed."

Vackeers gave a detailed report of the events that had taken place a few hours earlier.

"We insisted on complete discretion."

"I know, I really am terribly sorry about this," replied Vackeers.

"Do you have reason to believe that we've been compromised?" asked Sir Ashley.

"No, I don't see how any link could be established. That would be crediting them with too much intelligence."

"You asked me to tap the phones of two affiliates of the Royal Society, both employed by University College London. I complied and relayed this information to Athens, thereby breaking with normal procedures. I informed you that one of the men prevailed on a colleague to gain privileged access to the research institute in Heraklion. I made sure that his request was met and, when you asked for it, gave you full powers to bring the operation to a successful conclusion. The next day, a fight breaks out in the basement and our two rogues make their getaway. Has it not crossed your mind that they might be asking themselves a question or two?"

"We couldn't have dreamt up a better opportunity to regain possession of the object; it's hardly my fault if Athens botched the job. Paris, New York and our new man in Zurich are now on the alert; I think it's time for us to call a meeting and decide collectively what we do next. If we carry on like this, we'll end up provoking precisely the kind of scenario we're trying to avoid."

"I would recommend precisely the opposite course of action, and much more discretion, Vackeers. It won't be long before news of this rumour leaks out. Do whatever it takes to ensure that doesn't happen. Or I won't be answerable."

"What do you mean by that?"

"You know perfectly well, Vackeers."

Someone knocked at his office door and Vackeers brought the conversation to an end.

"I hope I'm not interrupting anything?" inquired Ivory, walking into the room.

"Not in the slightest."

"I thought I heard you talking."

"I was dictating a letter to my assistant."

"Is everything all right? You look a bit peaky."

"That ulcer of mine is giving me grief."

"I'm sorry to hear it. Still on for chess this evening?"

"I'm afraid I may have to forego the pleasure, I need to take it easy."

"Of course. Another time perhaps?"

"Tomorrow, if you like."

"'Til tomorrow then, dear friend." Ivory closed the door behind him and set off down the corridor towards the exit, before executing an about-turn and pausing in front of the office belonging to Vackeers' assistant. Pushing the door ajar, he saw that the room was empty – not that this was altogether surprising, given that it was 9pm.

*

The Aegean

The ferry was making good headway over a calm sea, and I was sleeping deeply on the top bunk of our cabin when Walter woke me. I blinked, day hadn't yet broken.

"What d'you want, Walter?"

"Which coast are we heading for?"

"How am I supposed to know? I don't have special 'see in the dark' powers!"

"You're the one with the local knowledge, aren't you?"

Reluctantly, I clambered down from my bunk and went over to the porthole. In the gloom, it wasn't hard to recognise the crescent shape of the island of Milos; to make quite sure, I'd need to go up on deck and check that Anti-Milos, an uninhabited island, was on the port side.

"Is the boat going to stop here?" Walter badgered me.

"I don't know the ferry routes by heart, but given that land is fast approaching I expect that yes, we're about to stop off at Adamas."

"Is it a big town?"

"More of a large village, I'd say."

"Out of bed then, we're getting off here!"

"What are we going to do in Milos?"

"We're going to avoid Athens for a bit longer, that's what."

"Walter, do you honestly believe there are people expecting us in Piraeus? We don't even know if that police car was on our tail or just passing by. I think you're making far too much out of this whole sorry business."

"In that case, perhaps you'd like to explain why someone tried not once but twice to enter the cabin while you were sleeping."

"Please don't tell me you battered them to death?"

"I merely opened the door, but there was no one there: the intruder had already slipped away."

"Or else he went into the next-door cabin after realising his mistake!"

"Twice? Permit me to have my doubts. Get dressed and we'll disembark, preferably unnoticed, as soon as the boat docks. We'll wait by the port and take the next boat for Athens."

"Even if it doesn't leave until tonight?"

"Look, we were expecting to spend a night in Heraklion anyway. If you're worried about your mother, we'll call her as soon as it gets light."

I couldn't decide whether Walter's jitteriness was justified, or whether he was just revelling in the previous day's adventure and trying to eke it out a bit longer. That said, as the ramp was pulled up, I got a

266

good view of a man who was staring at us from the top deck. I'm not sure that giving him the finger as the ferry pulled away was the smartest move my companion could have made.

We pulled up two chairs on the terrace of a fisherman's bar, which opened up as soon as the first ferry sloped into port. It was six o'clock in the morning and the sun was rising behind the hill. A light aircraft rose through the sky, changing course above the port before heading out towards the open sea.

"Is there an airport around here?" Walter asked.

"There's an airstrip, yes, if I'm not mistaken, but I think it's only used by the postal planes and some private aircraft."

"Good, let's get going! If we're lucky enough to inveigle our way on board one or the other, we'll have shaken off our pursuers for good."

"You're being completely paranoid, Walter; I don't think for a moment there's anyone following us."

"Frankly, Adrian, fond of you as I am, your naïveté is beginning to get annoying!"

Once Walter had paid for our coffees, there was nothing for it but to show him the road that led to the small aerodrome.

Which is how Walter and I ended up on the verge, trying to hitch a lift. Nothing happened for the first half hour, except for the white stones glinting in the sunlight and the heat growing more intense.

A group of youths was clearly having fun at our

expense. We must have looked like two stray tourists, so they were surprised when I asked in Greek for their help. The oldest kid wanted to be paid but Walter, who'd quickly got the measure of the situation, managed to swing it so that two scooter seats were offered to us, as if by magic.

We set off, clinging to our respective pilots – this being the most accurate description of our drivers who raced along the twisting roads at breakneck speed, swerving low into the bends. A large salt marsh spread out before us; beyond it, a deserted tarmac runway stretched from east to west. The ringleader informed us that the plane that delivered the post every two days had already left: we must have just missed it.

"I guess that was the plane we saw back at the bar," I sighed.

"There's always the flying doctor, if you're really in a rush," the youngest kid pointed out.

"Come again?"

"There's a doctor who flies in, when someone's seriously ill. The phone's in that hut over there, but it's for emergencies only. When my cousin had appendicitis, the doctor was here within half an hour."

"I think I can feel a crippling stomach ache coming on," proclaimed Walter, the moment I'd translated the conversation for him.

"You're not really going to bother a doctor and divert their plane just to get back to Athens?"

"If I die of peritonitis, you'll blame yourself for

the rest of your life!" groaned Walter, falling to his knees.

The kids started laughing, Walter's clowning was irresistible.

The tallest youth led me to the old handset on the wall of what served as the control tower office: a wooden hut, with a chair, a table and a VHF radio that must have dated from the war. He refused to make the call himself: if our hoax was rumbled, he'd never hear the end of it and he didn't fancy a thrashing from his dad. Walter got up to offer him some cash, enough to convince our new friend that getting a hiding wouldn't be as bad as all that.

"You're corrupting minors now!"

"I was going to ask you to go halves on this one; but if you own up to the fact that you're enjoying this as much as I am, I'll pay the whole thing myself!"

I really wasn't enjoying our current predicament, so I promptly took out my wallet to share in the cost of our scam. The boy picked up the receiver, turned the handle and explained to the doctor that help was needed as quickly as possible: a tourist was writhing in pain, he'd been driven to the airstrip and needed to be flown to the mainland urgently.

Half an hour later, we heard the drone of an approaching engine. Suddenly, Walter no longer needed to fake a bellyache in order to throw himself to the ground; the small Piper Cub had just hedge-hopped over us. The plane swerved on one wing then aligned itself with the axis of the runway, where it bounced three times before juddering to a halt.

"I can see why they call these things 'old crates'," sighed Walter.

The plane taxied towards us. Once it was level, the pilot switched off the engine; the propeller carried on turning for a few seconds more, the pistons spluttered and quiet was restored. Eager to witness the scene that was about to play out, the kids kept very quiet.

The pilot emerged from the plane, removing leather helmet and goggles, before greeting us. Dr Sophie Schwarz, who was seventy if she was a day, looked like an elegant Amelia Earhart. In near-perfect English, with just a hint of a German accent, she inquired which one of us was ill.

"He is!" Walter declared, pointing at me.

"You don't look in terrible pain to me, young man. What's the matter?"

I was caught off-guard, and decided it was pointless keeping up Walter's lie. I owned up to our situation, with the doctor interrupting me only for the time it took to light her cigarette.

"If I've understood you correctly," she told me, "you have just diverted an emergency plane because you're in need of private transport to Athens? What a nerve!"

"It was my idea," mumbled Walter.

"That doesn't alter the fact that this is highly irresponsible, young man!" she retorted, stamping out her cigarette butt on the tarmac.

"Please accept my sincerest apologies," offered Walter.

The boys, who were watching the scene without understanding much of what was being said, seemed to be enjoying the show.

"Are the police after you?"

"No," insisted Walter, "we're two scientists from London University who find ourselves in a most awkward situation. We're not sick, that's true, but we really do need your help," he implored her.

The doctor visibly relaxed.

"England, God how I love that country! I was a great admirer of Lady Diana – what a terrible tragedy..."

I saw Walter crossing himself and I wondered if there were any limits to his thespian talents.

"The problem," the doctor went on, "is that my plane only has two seats, including mine."

"So how do you evacuate people when they're injured?" asked Walter.

"I'm a flying doctor, not an ambulance. If you don't mind a tight squeeze, I should think, on balance, that we'll be able to take off."

"Why 'on balance'?" asked Walter, sounding worried.

"Because we'll be a bit over the maximum recommended weight, but that runway isn't as short as it looks. If we take off full throttle and open up the brakes we'll probably pick up enough speed to take off.

"And if we don't?" I grunted.

"Splash!"

In perfect, accentless Greek, the doctor ordered the children to move back, and then invited us to follow her. As she made a tour of the plane to carry out her pre-flight inspection, she took the opportunity to tell us a little about herself. Her father was German-Jewish, her mother Italian. During the war, they set up a home on a small Greek island, where the villagers hid them. After the armistice, they no longer had any desire to leave.

"We've always lived here; it never occurred to me to live anywhere else. Do you know anywhere in the world more beautiful than these islands? My father was a pilot, and my mother a nurse, which might explain why I became a flying doctor!

"Your turn now, what are you really fleeing? Not that it's any of my business, of course, and not that either of you look like proper baddies. Anyway, they're going to take away my licence soon, so I'm making the most of my last chances to fly. All I ask is that you pay for the fuel."

"Why are they taking away your licence?" Walter wanted to know.

The doctor carried on with her inspection of the plane.

"Each year, pilots have to undergo a medical check-up and an eye test. Up until now, I had a very accommodating old friend who conducted this, and who kindly turned a blind eye to my knowing the sight test card by heart, including the last line where the letters have become much too small for me to read. But he's retired now and I won't be able to dupe my colleagues for much longer. Don't worry, I could

272

still fly this old Piper even with my eyes closed!" the doctor insisted, letting out a great guffaw.

Sophie Schwarz explained that she'd rather not touch down in Athens. Landing at an international airport involves radio authorisation followed by a police check on arrival; there'd be endless forms to fill out. She did, however, know a small abandoned airstrip at Porto Éli, where the runway was still usable. From there, all we needed to do was hop on a taxi-boat to Hydra.

Walter got in first, and I perched as best I could on his lap; the seat belt wasn't long enough to go around the two of us. The engine spluttered, and the propeller started turning slowly before accelerating in a burst of smoke. In the midst of all this din, Sophie Schwarz tapped on the cabin to signal we'd shortly be taking off. The machine taxied back up the runway, swivelled to face the wind and then the engine revved hard. The plane was juddering so much I almost expected it to fall apart before take-off. Our pilot released the brakes and the tarmac started to speed by beneath the wheels. We'd almost got to the end of the runway when the nose of the plane finally rose and we left the ground. Down on the tarmac, the kids were waving goodbye. I shouted at Walter to do the same, as a token of thanks, but he roared back that he'd probably need a monkey wrench on landing – to prise away his fingers, which were currently glued to the door-fitting.

I'd never before seen the island of Milos as I saw it that morning; flying over the sea at a few hundred

metres' altitude, looking out the glassless windows
of the plane, the wind blowing in between the wing
struts. I felt truly free.

*

Amsterdam

It took a moment or two for Vackeers to get used to the gloom of the basement; a few years ago his eyes used to adjust instantly, but he had aged since then. When he sensed he could see clearly enough to navigate the maze of strut that supported the building, he began making his way cautiously along the wooden walkways positioned twenty or so centimetres above the water; he didn't take any notice of the cold and damp given off by the underground canal. Vackeers knew his way around and was now directly under the state room; as he stood beneath the marble maps, he pressed down on a retaining plate in the wall and waited for the mechanism to swing into action. Two planks pivoted, to reveal a passage leading to the back wall. A door, previously invisible in the darkness, now stood out against the uniform brickwork. Vackeers locked up behind him and switched on the light.

A metal table and an armchair were the only furniture in the room; and the equipment was limited to a flat screen and a computer. Vackeers sat down at the keyboard and looked at his watch. An acoustic signal informed him that the conference had just begun.

"Good day, gentlemen," Vackeers typed in. "You all know why today's meeting has been called."

MADRID: I thought this file had been closed for years?

AMSTERDAM: That's what we all thought, but recent events have made it necessary for the cell to re-form. This time, it would be best if nobody attempted to defy the others.

ROME: This is a different era.

AMSTERDAM: It's good to hear you say that, Lorenzo.

BERLIN: What do you want from us?

AMSTERDAM: A pooling of our resources, and for each of us to act on any joint decisions.

PARIS: From reading your report, it would seem that Ivory was right thirty years ago – is that correct? Shouldn't we invite him to join us?

AMSTERDAM: This discovery does indeed appear to corroborate Ivory's theories but I believe it's better to keep him at a distance. His behaviour can be unpredictable in relation to the matter that brings us together today.

LONDON: So there really is a second object, identical in every respect to ours?

ATHENS: Its shape is different but it is now certain that they belong together. Last night's episode was unfortunate; however, it did provide us with ir-refutable proof. It has also revealed a property we knew nothing about. One of our members witnessed it for himself.

ROME: The one who ended up with a broken jaw?

AMSTERDAM: Indeed.

PARIS: Do you think there might be other objects?

AMSTERDAM: Ivory is convinced of this, but the truth is we have no idea. What concerns us right now is getting hold of the object that has just appeared, rather than finding out whether or not others exist.

BOSTON: Are you sure about this? As you pointed out, we were wrong not to believe Ivory's warnings. I'm happy for us to free up funds and human resources to capture this object, but I'd prefer to know what we're getting into here. I doubt we'll still be around in thirty years' time!

AMSTERDAM: This discovery was purely acci-dental.

BERLIN: Which means that other 'accidents' might also occur.

MADRID: On reflection, I don't believe that it is in our best interests to try anything right now. Amsterdam, your first attempt ended in failure, a sec-ond botched effort would attract attention. Nothing indicates that the man or woman currently in posses-sion of this object has any idea of what it is. Nor are we sure yet ourselves. Let's not fan flames we can't put out immediately.

ISTANBUL: Madrid and Amsterdam have expressed two different points of view. I'm with Madrid on this, and suggest we don't do anything other than observe them, at least for the time being. We can meet again if the situation develops.

PARIS: I agree with Madrid.

AMSTERDAM: I believe that's a mistake. If we could bring the two objects together, we could perhaps find out more.

NEW DELHI: But that's precisely the point, Amsterdam, we don't want to find out more. If there's one thing we've all been able to agree on for the last thirty years, it's that!

CAIRO: New Delhi is spot on.

LONDON: We should confiscate this object and close the file as swiftly as possible.

AMSTERDAM: London's right. The person who currently has it in his possession is an eminent astrophysicist, and it so happens that it was given to him by an archaeologist, so – given their respective areas of expertise – how long do you think it'll take them to find out the true nature of what they hold in their hands?

TOKYO: That all depends on whether they're putting their minds together on this. Are they still in contact with each other?

AMSTERDAM: No, not right now.

TEL-AVIV: Well then, I agree with Cairo, let's wait.

BERLIN: I'm with you, Tel-Aviv.

TOKYO: Likewise.

ATHENS: You therefore wish us to leave them to move freely?

BOSTON: Let's call it "freedom under surveillance".

Since there was nothing else on the agenda, the meeting was closed. Vackeers turned off his screen, in a foul mood. This wasn't the result he'd been hoping for, but since he was the first to insist his allies stand united, he would respect the majority decision.

*

Hydra

The taxi-boat dropped us off towards midday. Judging from the expression on my aunt's face, Walter and I must have been a sorry sight. She got up out of her folding chair and rushed over from her shop to greet us.

"Have you had an accident?"

"Why do you ask?" said Walter, trying to smooth his straggly hair.

"Have you seen what you look like?"

"Let's just say the trip was rather more eventful than we expected, but it was all good fun in the end," Walter piped up jovially. "That said, I could murder a cup of coffee right now. That and two aspirins for the cramp in my legs – you've no idea how heavy your nephew is."

"What's my nephew's weight got to do with your legs, Walter?"

"Nothing, until he sat on my lap for an hour."

"And why was Adrianos sitting on your lap?"

"Because there was only one passenger seat on the cosy little plane that got us off Milos! Right, are you going to join us for coffee?"

280

My aunt declined the invitation, muttering as she backed away that she had customers to attend to. Walter and I glanced at each other in astonishment, her shop was emptier than ever.

"We're certainly a ragged-looking pair," I conceded.

I raised my hand to attract the waiter's attention, took the pendant out of my pocket and put it down on the table.

"If I'd realised, even for a second, how much trouble this would cause us..."

"What do you think its purpose really is?" Walter asked.

I told him I didn't have the faintest idea, which was true; what on earth was the meaning of all those dots that appeared when the pendant was brought close to a powerful light source?

"And not just any old dots, either," Walter added, "they twinkle!"

Yes, the dots did twinkle, but from there to drawing hasty conclusions was a leap that no scientist worth their salt would make. The phenomenon we had witnessed might also be accidental.

"This porous quality it has, which is invisible to the naked eye, is so infinitesimal that it takes an extremely powerful light source to penetrate whatever it's made of. It's like a dam wall that ceases to be water-resistant when the pressure becomes too great."

"Didn't you tell me that your archaeologist friend

was unable to find out anything about how old the object is, or indeed where it comes from? You've got to admit, all this is frankly rather odd."

I didn't recollect Keira being as intrigued by it as we were.

"Look, that young lady *just happens* to leave behind a necklace with the curious properties we now know about! People try to steal her pendant from us, we're forced to flee as if the devil himself were on our heels, and you still think it can all be put down to chance? Is this what they call scientific rigour? Could you at least take a closer look at the photos I had the foresight to take at Heraklion, and tell me if they remind you of anything other than a close-up of a piece of Swiss cheese?"

Walter put his digital camera on the table where we were eating brunch. I scanned the pictures: they were far too small for me to form a serious opinion. No matter how hard I concentrated, and even with the best will in the world, all I could see were dots; there was nothing that would allow me to confirm them as stars; either a constellation, or some kind of star cluster.

"I'm sorry, but these photographs don't prove anything."

"Well, in that case, it's goodbye to my holidays – let's head back to London! I want to have a clear conscience about this," Walter declared. "Once we're back at the university, we'll download these photos onto a computer and you'll be able to study them in decent conditions."

282

I had no desire to leave Hydra, but Walter was so excited by this enigma that I couldn't let him down. He'd been incredibly generous and invested so much in helping me with my presentation to the Walsh Foundation that I'd never have forgiven myself if I'd left him to fly home alone. There was just the small matter of going back up to the house and informing my mother of my imminent departure.

Mother stared at me, noted the state of my clothes, the scratches on my forearms, and let her shoulders droop, as if the world had just come crashing down on them.

I explained to her why Walter and I had to return to London, and promised I'd be back before the end of the week.

"If I've understood this correctly," she said, "you're insisting on flying back to London in order to copy onto your computer the holiday snaps you took with your friend? Why don't you just pop over to your aunt's shop? She sells disposable cameras, so if the photos aren't any good you can bin them straightaway!"

"Walter and I may have discovered something rather important, and we want to put our minds at rest."

"And what about putting my mind at rest by coming clean about you and Walter?"

"What on earth are you talking about?"

"Okay, just keep taking me for a fool!"

"I need to be in my office, I haven't got the right equipment here and I really don't understand why you're so annoyed."

"Because I'd like you to feel you could confide in me. Do you think I'd love you any less if you told me the truth? Even if you confessed your undying love for that donkey at the end of the garden, you'd still be my son Adrianos!"

"Mother, are you sure you're feeling all right?"

"Never better, it's you I'm worried about. Go back to London if it's so important to you. I may still be alive and kicking when you return, who knows..."

When my mother went into tragic Greek heroine mode, it meant something was seriously troubling her. But I chose not to dwell on why she was in such a dudgeon bad mood, since the only reason I could think of was completely ludicrous.

I packed my suitcase and went down to the port to meet up with Walter. My mother insisted on keeping us company. Aunt Elena joined her on the quayside, and the two of them waved frantically as the ferry headed out to sea. Much later, I was to find out that my mother had inquired of my aunt whether she thought I was going to make this journey on Walter's lap as well.

*

Amsterdam

Jan Vackeers glanced at his watch: Ivory still hadn't turned up and it was beginning to worry him. Being late like this was out of character for his assiduously punctual chess partner. The Dutchman went over to the trolley and checked on the food he'd ordered. He was snacking on the dried fruit that garnished the cheese plate when someone rang the bell of his hotel suite. The game could begin at last.

"This has just arrived for you, sir."

Vackeers withdrew to read the contents of the envelope he'd just been handed. On a visiting card, a few words had been handwritten in ink:

Apologies for leaving you in the lurch like this, but a last minute call of duty means I have to leave Amsterdam – I shall be back soon.

Best wishes,

Ivory

PS: Check and stalemate! The game is merely postponed.

Vackeers re-read the postscript three times, wondering what Ivory meant; coming from him, it was bound to be significant. He didn't know where his friend was bound for, and it was too late now to have him watched. As for asking his allies to take up the baton... He was the one who'd insisted on keeping Ivory out of it, so how could he explain that the latter might be one step ahead?

Check and stalemate, just as Ivory had written. Vackeers smiled, slipping the visiting card into his pocket.

*

Schiphol Airport, Amsterdam. At this late hour, only a few planes linking Europe's capitals were still operating.

Ivory held out his boarding card to the stewardess and boarded the plane to take up his seat in the first row. He fastened his safety belt and looked out of the porthole. In an hour and a half he would touch down at City Airport, London, where a car would be waiting for him. His room was already booked at the Dorchester: everything was in order. By now, Vackeers would have received his note; just thinking about it made him smile.

Ivory closed his eyes, he had a long night ahead and needed to snatch whatever sleep he could.

*

Eleftherios Venizelos Airport, Athens

Walter was hell-bent on taking a souvenir from Greece back for Miss Jenkins. At duty free he bought a bottle of ouzo, a second bottle in case the first got broken, as he put it, and a third as a present. At last call, both our names came booming through the loudspeakers; the voice didn't sound very friendly and I noticed the accusing looks from our fellow passengers as we boarded. Following a crazy sprint down a series of corridors, we'd arrived just in time for the hand wipes being handed out by the steward, as well as a few tut-tuttings when we strolled up the gangway towards the only two spare seats, in the back row. The time difference with England gave us an extra hour: we were due to land at Heathrow at midnight. Walter wolfed down the in-flight meal and mine too, which I was glad to be rid of. Once the trays had been cleared away, the stewardess dimmed the cabin lights. I glued my face to the porthole and took in the sights. Viewing the sky at an altitude of ten thousand metres is a wonderful experience for an astronomer. The North Star was glimmering in front of me, I saw

Cassiopeia, and I could make out Cepheus to the right of it. I turned back to Walter who was dozing.

"Have you got your camera on you?"

"If it's to take a holiday snap of me, old chap, the answer is strictly no. Given everything I've just eaten and the uncomfortable reality of being squashed up in these seats, I must look like a pregnant whale – in a tin."

"No, Walter, it's not to take a photograph of you."

"In that case, if you can manage to reach into my pocket, it's yours; I can't move."

We were indeed squeezed in like sardines, and getting hold of the camera was no mean feat. As soon as I'd got it in my hands, I took another look at the series of photos taken in Heraklion. A thought crossed my mind, but it was completely absurd, and I felt altogether baffled as I gazed out of my porthole once more.

"I think we did the right thing returning to London," I told Walter, slipping the camera into my pocket.

"Wait till you're eating steak and kidney pie tomorrow morning on the rainy pavement in front of some pub, and we'll see if you still feel the same way."

"You'll always be welcome back in Hydra."

"Are you going to let me get some shuteye? I suppose you think I can't see what a kick you're getting out of disturbing me?"

*

London

I dropped Walter off by taxi and then, the moment I got home, rushed to switch on my computer. After uploading the photos, I studied them carefully and decided to get in touch with an old friend who lived a few thousand kilometres away. I wrote him an e-mail, attaching Walter's photos, and asking him what they looked like to him. He got straight back: Erwin was thrilled to hear from me. He promised he'd study the pictures I'd just sent over and that he'd give me an answer as soon as possible. But another radio telescope in the Atacama was out of order, so he had a lot on his plate right now.

I heard back from him seventy-two hours later, in the middle of the night. Not by e-mail this time, but on the telephone, and Erwin's voice sounded strangely excited.

"How did you pull off a coup like that?" he demanded, without even saying hello.

That threw me and then Erwin fired another question, which took me even more by surprise.

"If you're dreaming of the Nobel Prize, you're in

with a cracking chance this year. I've got no idea how you went about engineering that kind of computer modelling, but it's a stroke of genius. If you sent me these images to wow me, all I can say is bravo! You've succeeded!"

"What did you see, Erwin, tell me!"

"You know perfectly well what I saw, don't go fishing for compliments. Now, can you please tell me how you pulled off this master stroke, or are you going to keep stringing me along? Am I allowed to share these images with our friends here?"

"Absolutely not!"

"Got you," Erwin sighed, "I feel very privileged you gave me a sneak preview before you write your official press release. When are you going public? Of course, it's your dream ticket to join us again, although naturally you'll be spoilt for choice; every astrophysics team out there will want a piece of you now."

"Erwin, please, describe what you saw!"

"What is this? You're tired of telling yourself, so you want to hear me say it? Well, my friend, I suppose I'd be just as excited in your shoes. But let's make this a fair exchange. First of all, you've got to tell me how you did it."

"How I did what?"

"Don't even think about telling me you landed on it by chance."

"Erwin, you go first, please."

"It took me three days to work out where you were

taking me. I quickly recognised the constellations of Cygnus, Pegasus and Cepheus; even though their magnitudes weren't accurate, the angles were false and the distances absurd. If you thought you could trick me as easily as that, you were mistaken. I wondered what game you were playing, why you'd brought all those stars closer together and using those equations. I tried to find out what would have made you position them like that, and that's what got me thinking. I'll confess I cheated a bit: I took full advantage of our computers, submitting them to two days of intense calculations, but when the results finally came through, I had no qualms about having used our resources for that purpose. I was on the right track, of course, except I could never have guessed what was in the middle of these extraordinary images."

"And what did you see, Erwin?"

"The Pelican Nebula."

"And why is that so exciting?"

"Because it is depicted just as one would have seen it from the Earth, four hundred million years ago!"

My heart was pounding fit to burst and I could feel my knees giving way; none of this made any sense. What Erwin had just revealed to me was insane. That an object, however mysterious, could project a fragment of the sky was already difficult enough to get my head around; that the sky appeared as it would have been seen from the Earth nearly half a billion years ago was simply unimaginable.

"Right Adrian, now it's your turn to tell me how you achieved such a perfect piece of computer modelling?"

"I know I was your training partner for several weeks and I should probably be able to remember everything you taught me. But since our failed bid in the Docklands, the weeks have been so eventful that I really don't feel guilty about forgetting a few details."

"A nebula is a cradle of stars, a diffuse cloud, made up of gas and dust, located in the space between two galaxies," I summarised tersely for Walter. "It's where the stars come to life."

But my mind was elsewhere, my thoughts were thousands of kilometres away from London, towards the eastern point of Africa, with the woman who had left her strange pendant at my place. The question that still haunted me was whether or not she really had forgotten it. When I put this question to Walter, he shook his head as if I were born yesterday.

Two days later, on my way into the university, I had an unusual encounter. I wanted to grab a coffee in one of those chains that had invaded the capital while I'd been away in Chile. It doesn't matter what area or street of London you're in, the decor is always the same, as is the range of cakes and biscuits, plus you need a degree in café-babble what with all the different combinations of teas and coffees and their strange names.

A man approached me as I was waiting at the counter for my "skinny cap with wings", whatever that would turn out to be. He insisted on paying for my drink and asked if I wouldn't mind sparing a couple of minutes; he wanted to discuss a subject which, according to him, would greatly interest me. He led me over to the seated area and we grabbed a couple of badly made imitation leather armchairs, though they were at least reasonably comfortable. The man stared at me for a long time before starting to talk.

"You work at University College London and you're a member of the Royal Society, is that right?"

"Er... yes. And who, may I ask, are you?"

"I often see you here in the mornings. London may be a vast capital but each area is like a village – it's all part of the city's charm, wouldn't you say?"

I didn't recall ever having seen this person now before me, but I'm absent-minded by nature and didn't see any reason to doubt him.

"I'd be lying if I said this was altogether a chance meeting," he went on. "I've been wanting to talk to you for a while."

"Well, you've succeeded, so what can I do for you?"

"Do you believe in destiny, Adrian?"

Now, perhaps it's just me being paranoid, but when a complete stranger addresses me by my first name, my anxiety levels immediately shoot up.

"Please call me Ivory, seeing as I've taken the liberty of calling you Adrian. I hope I'm not abusing the privilege of age."

"What is it that you want?"

"We have two things in common. First, I'm a scientist, just like you, although you have the advantage of being young with many long years ahead of you to explore your passion. I'm just an old professor who re-reads dusty books to pass the time."

"What did you teach?"

"Astrophysics, which I believe is your own discipline, is it not?"

I nodded.

"Your research in Chile must have been fascinating, I'm only sorry you had to come back. You must miss working on the Atacama site dreadfully."

This man knew rather too much about me for my liking, and his calm veneer did nothing to allay my concerns.

"Don't be suspicious. If I know a bit about you, it's because I was there, in a manner of speaking, when you presented your research to the jury of the Walsh Foundation."

"In a manner of speaking?"

"Let's say that while I wasn't a judge myself, I was part of the selection committee. I read your application very carefully. If it had been down to me, you'd have won the prize; in my view, your research was the most deserving of our support."

I thanked him for the compliment and asked him how I could be useful to him.

"You're not the one who can be useful to me, Adrian, as you'll see, it is quite the reverse. The young lady you left with that evening, and who won the prize..."

This time I felt thoroughly uncomfortable and began to lose my cool.

"You know Keira?"

"Yes, of course," the stranger replied, sipping his coffee. "Why aren't you in touch anymore?"

"I think that's a private matter," I retorted, no longer trying to hide the fact that I didn't appreciate this conversation.

"I'm sorry, I didn't mean to pry, please accept my apologies if my question offended you in any way."

"You said we had two points in common, what's the second?"

The professor took a photograph out of his pocket and slid it across the table. It was an old Polaroid, as attested to by its faded colours.

"I'd be prepared to wager this doesn't look completely unfamiliar to you," he said.

I examined the photo closely: it featured an object that was almost rectangular shaped.

"And the most intriguing thing about this object? We can't date it. State-of-the-art methods have nothing to say on the subject. I've been asking myself how old it is for thirty years, and the idea of leaving this world without knowing the answer still haunts me. It may sound stupid, but I'm obsessed by it. No matter how much I try to be reasonable about it, telling myself that when I'm dead it won't matter anyway, I just can't help it. I think about it, day and night."

"And something makes you believe I could help you?"

"You're not paying attention, Adrian, I've already told you I'm the one who's going to help you, not the other way round. It's important that you concentrate on what I'm about to tell you. Sooner or later, this mystery will monopolise your thoughts. When you decide to apply yourself properly, the doors to an extraordinary journey will open up before you, and you'll find yourself travelling further than you could ever have imagined. I'm perfectly aware that right now I must seem like a mad old man to you, but you'll change your mind. Those crazy enough to realise their dreams are rare, and society often makes them pay for their eccentricity. Society is fearful and jealous, Adrian, but is that reason enough to hold back? Isn't upturning entrenched beliefs and questioning what is taken for granted the real reason for living? Isn't that the essence of the scientific mind?"

"Have you taken risks that society has made you pay for, Professor?"

"Please, do just call me Ivory. Allow me to share with you a piece of information which I'm sure you'll find intriguing. The object in that photograph has another property, every bit as original as its first. You see, when it is subjected to a powerful light source, it projects a strange pattern of dots. Does that remind you of anything?"

The shock must have registered clearly on my face; the professor watched me and smiled.

"You see, I wasn't lying when I said I was the one who'd be useful to you."

"Where did you find it?"

"It's a long story. What matters is that you know of its existence – this will come in handy later on."

"Why?"

"Because you won't need to waste huge amounts of time asking yourself whether the object in your possession is just a freak of nature. It will also protect you from the blindness humans are capable of when faced with terrifying reality. Einstein used to say that only two things were infinite: the Universe and human stupidity, and that there could be no doubt about the second."

"What have you learned about the example in your possession?" I asked.

"It's not in my possession, I've merely studied it. Unfortunately I know very little about it; and what I do know I certainly don't want to tell you. Not that I don't trust you, or I wouldn't be here. But chance isn't enough; in the best-case scenario, it does little more than arouse the curiosity of the scientific mind. Only ingenuity, method and nerve lead to discovery. I don't want to steer your future research; I'd rather leave you free and open-minded."

"What future research?" I said, conscious that this man's presumptions were starting to bug me.

"May I ask you one final question, Adrian? What future awaits you at your prestigious university? A professorship? A class of brilliant students, each convinced of the superiority of their own intellect? A passionate affair with the prettiest junior lecturer? I've experienced all of that, and I can't remember a single face. But I'm talking too much and not allowing you to answer my question. So, your future?"

"Teaching is just one phase of my life; I'll be going back to the Atacama sooner or later."

I remember uttering those words like a kid who's both proud of having learnt his lines and furious at being confronted with his own ignorance.

"I made a very silly mistake in my life, Adrian. I never really realised it, but just talking to you about it already makes me feel a lot better. You see, I thought I could do it all by myself. How arrogant of me and what a waste of time!"

"What's this got to do with me? And who *are* you?"

"I'm the mirror image of the man you're in danger of becoming. And if I could rescue you from that fate, I'd feel as if I'd been useful. It's an odd experience, you know, contemplating oneself in the mirror time gone by. Before leaving you, I'd like to communicate one other piece of information, which is perhaps even more interesting than the photograph I just showed you. Keira is working on a dig a hundred and twenty kilometres north-east of Lake Turkana. You're wondering why I'm telling you this? Because when you decide to go and find her in Ethiopia, that information will save you a lot of time. Time is precious, Adrian, terribly precious. It's been a real pleasure meeting you."

I was surprised by his handshake: honest and affectionate, almost avuncular. Ivory turned round in the doorway and took a few steps towards me again.

"There is one favour I'd like to ask of you," he said, "when you see Keira, please don't mention our little meeting, it wouldn't help matters. Keira is someone for whom I have the greatest respect, but she's not an easy character. If I were forty years younger, I would already be sitting on that plane."

The conversation had rattled me. I felt frustrated at not having asked all the questions that sprang to mind only afterwards; I'd have had to make a list of them, there were so many.

Walter appeared in the café window, waved, pushed open the door and came over to join me.

"What's with the long face?" he asked, sitting down in the armchair vacated by Ivory. "By the way, I had a good think last night," he went on, "so it's just as well I've found you here – we really need to talk."

"I'm listening."

"You're looking for an excuse to see your lady friend again, aren't you? Yes you are, don't argue! You definitely want to find a way to see her again! Well, I think you could do worse, old chap, than ask her the real reason why she left that pendant on your bedside table. There are some things you just can't put down to chance!"

What had I done to deserve this double attack? And

why was everyone so determined to hook me up with Keira?

"Of course I'd love to be going with you to Ethiopia," Walter was saying, "but I won't!"

"Did I say I was going to Ethiopia?"

"No, but you are."

"Not without you."

"That's out of the question, Hydra gobbled up my savings."

"If that's what it's about, I'll buy your ticket."

"Absolutely not. Thanks for being so generous, but I'd rather you didn't put me in an embarrassing situation on your account."

"It's not about me being generous: do I have to remind you what would have happened to me in Heraklion, without you?"

"Don't tell me you want to hire me as your bodyguard, I'd take that very badly. I'm not just brawn, you know, I'm a qualified chartered accountant and human resources manager!"

"Walter, don't make me beg, just come with me!"

"It's a terrible idea, for all sorts of reasons."

"Give me just one and I'll leave you in peace!"

"Well, picture the following scenario. Landscape: Omo Valley. Time: dawn or the middle of the day, your choice. Considering what you've already told me about it, the landscape is spectacular. The scene: an archaeological excavation site. Principal characters: Adrian and the archaeologist in charge of the project.

Now, tune in to the dialogue. Our hero, Adrian, arrives in a jeep; he's looking dusty but rather dashing. The archaeologist hears the car, lays down her trowel and small hammer, takes off her glasses..."

"I don't think she wears any!"

" ... Doesn't take off her glasses but stands up to discover that the unexpected visitor is none other than the man she reluctantly left behind in London. The emotion is writ large on her face."

"I've got the picture, what are you driving at?"

"Be quiet and let me finish! The archaeologist and her visitor walk towards each other, neither of them knows what they're going to say. And then – *TA-DA!* – nobody's been paying any attention to what's going on in the background. Over by the jeep, good old Walter, in his flannel shorts and checked cap – who's just about had it up to here with being baked in the sun while the two lovebirds kiss in slow motion – demands of whoever's prepared to listen what to do with the luggage. Now, be brutally honest here, wouldn't you agree that he ruins the scene? So, are you now resolved to go it alone, or would you like me to paint you another picture?"

In the end, Walter managed to persuade me to make the trip, although I like to think I'd already made up my mind.

Having secured a visa and organised my arrival, I turned up at Heathrow and landed ten hours later in Addis Ababa.

The same day, Ivory, who wasn't unaware of this trip, returned to Paris.

*

Fellow Cell Members:

Our subject flew out today, destination Addis Ababa. No need to spell out what this means. Without involving our Chinese friends, who retain a number of interests in Ethiopia, it will be difficult for us to continue our surveillance.

I suggest we meet no later than tomorrow.

Sincerely,
Amsterdam

Jan Vackeers pushed away his computer keyboard and went back to the file that had been handed to him by one of his staff. He stared at the photo of a coffee shop window in London for the umpteenth time. Ivory could be seen taking breakfast with Adrian.

Vackeers pressed down on his lighter, placed the photograph in an ashtray and set fire to the evidence. When it was all burnt out, he closed the file and muttered:

"I don't know how long I'll be able to keep our colleagues from finding out that you've decided to go it alone, my friend."

*

Ivory was waiting patiently in the taxi queue at Orly Airport.

When it came to his turn, he got into the back of the cab and gave the driver a slip of paper. This had on it the address of a print works not far from Boulevard de Sébastopol. The traffic was moving freely and he would be there in half an hour.

*

In his Rome office, Lorenzo read Vackeers' e-mail, picked up his handset and asked his secretary to come in and see him.

"Have we still got active contacts in Ethiopia?"

"Yes, sir, I know we've got two people out there because I've just updated the Ethiopian file for our meeting with the Foreign Office next week."

Lorenzo held out a photograph to his secretary, together with a timetable scribbled on a sheet of paper.

"Get in touch with them. They need to inform me about the movements, meetings and conversations of this man, who will land in Addis Ababa on a flight from London tomorrow morning. He's a British subject, discretion is in order. Tell our men they should on no account run the risk of being spotted. This request is off the record: I want it to remain as confidential as possible, for the time being, at least."

The secretary scooped up the documents that Lorenzo handed over to her and left.

*

Ethiopia

The stop-off at Addis Ababa Airport had only lasted an hour. Time enough to get my passport stamped and to pick up my luggage, before boarding a light aircraft headed for the aerodrome of Jinka.

The wings of this decrepit plane were so rusty it was a wonder it could still get airborne. The glass in the cockpit was oil-stained. And, apart from the compass with its jiggling needle, none of the dials on the instrument panel showed any sign of life. Not that the pilot seemed unduly worried: when the engine spluttered alarmingly, he was happy to pull lightly on the throttle lever or to push it back in again, depending on what worked best. His most high-tech instruments were his eyes and his ears.

Then again, under the battered wings of this old crate – and amid a terrifying din – some of the most beautiful landscapes in Africa were unfurling.

The wheels bounced on the baked earth landing strip as we shuddered to a halt in a thick cloud of dust. Children came rushing over and I was worried one of them would get hit by the propeller. The pilot leaned over me to open the door, threw my bag out and I got the message that our paths separated here.

I'd hardly set foot on terra firma when his plane turned round; I just had time to glimpse it flying off above the tops of the eucalyptus trees.

Stuck in the middle of nowhere, I bitterly regretted not convincing Walter to join me. Sitting on an old oil drum, my bag at my feet, I surveyed the surrounding wilderness; the sun was sinking and I realised I didn't have the faintest idea where I was going to spend the night.

A man in a string vest came over to greet me and offer his help, or so I understood. It was no mean feat of creative communication, explaining to him that I was looking for an archaeologist who was working nearby. I remembered the game of charades we used to play as a family, where you had to mime a situation or a word which the others had to guess. I'd never been very good at it, and yet here I was pretending to dig the ground, to get over-excited about an ordinary stick of wood as if I'd just discovered a piece of treasure; my audience seemed so bewildered that I gave up in the end. He shrugged and walked away.

But he reappeared ten minutes later, with a young boy in tow who spoke to me first in French, then in English, and finally talking in a mix of both languages. He informed me that there were three teams of archaeologists in the area. One team was working seventy kilometres to the north of where I was, a second in the Rift Valley in Kenya, and a third, which had only recently arrived, had set up camp again nearly a hundred kilometres north-east of Lake Turkana – at last I'd located Keira. All I needed to do now was to find a way of joining her.

The boy suggested I follow him. The man who'd greeted me in the first place wanted to put me up for the night. I followed, feeling incredibly grateful and not quite sure how to thank him, while admitting to myself that if an Ethiopian, lost in the streets of London as I was lost out here this evening, had asked me the way, I probably wouldn't have been warm-hearted enough to offer him a bed under my own roof. Whether this was a cultural difference or a prejudice, it made me feel very small.

My host shared his meal with me, and the boy stayed with us. He kept staring at me. I'd put my jacket down on a stool and he unashamedly proceeded to go through my pockets. Inside, he found Keira's pendant which he immediately put back. I suddenly had the sense that he was no longer pleased to see me, and he left the hut without saying another word.

I slept on a mat and woke at dawn. After drinking one of the best coffees of my life, I went for a stroll near to the little airstrip, looking for a way to continue my journey. It wasn't a bad spot, but I had no intention of lingering there. I heard an engine in the distance. A cloud of dust enveloped a big jeep that was heading my way. The 4x4 pulled up by the airstrip and two men got out. They were both Italian and chance was smiling on me: they spoke reasonable English and were amiable enough. Neither of them seemed especially surprised to see me there; they asked me where I was trying to get to. I pointed to my destination on the map they'd unfolded on the car hood, and they immediately offered to drive me in that direction.

Their presence, even more than mine, seemed to trouble the boy. Did they remind him of the period his elders would have told him about, when Ethiopia was an Italian colony? I couldn't tell, but he clearly disapproved of these two heaven-sent guides.

After warmly thanking my host, I clambered into the jeep. In the course of the journey, the Italians asked me hundreds of questions: about my job, life in the Atacama and London, as well as the reasons for my trip to Ethiopia. I wasn't forthcoming on the latter topic; I simply told them I was here to be with a woman, which, for two hot-blooded Latins, was reason enough to travel to the ends of the Earth. And then it was my turn to ask the questions. It turned out they were textile exporters, with their own company based in Addis Ababa, and since both of them loved Ethiopia, they enjoyed exploring the country whenever they had the chance.

It was difficult to locate the exact spot I wanted to get to, and in any case there were no guarantees we'd be able to reach it by road. The driver suggested dropping me off at a fishing village on the banks of the Omo, from where it would be easy to buy a passage on a boat heading downriver. This would give me the best chance of finding the archaeological camp I was looking for. They seemed to be very familiar with the region, so I put myself in their hands and followed their advice. The man in the passenger seat offered his services as an interpreter. Since being here, he'd acquired the rudiments of some of the Ethiopian languages and was confident he'd be able to find a fisherman who'd be prepared to take me aboard his dugout.

By mid-afternoon, I was saying goodbye to my fellow adventurers. The flimsy boat I'd just climbed into drifted away from the shore, and we were carried along by the current.

Finding Keira wasn't as straightforward as my Italian friends had led me to believe. Each time the canoe turned into a more navigable stretch of river, it became clear that the Omo River divided into numerous tributaries and I worried about us passing the camp without ever spotting it.

I'd like to have taken in the full splendour of the scenery that rose up with every bend in the river, but I was too preoccupied trying to think of what to say to Keira if I found her.

The river flowed towards mud-coloured cliffs that left no room for navigational error. The boatman was concentrating on keeping us mid-stream. Another valley opened up before us and at last, on top of a small hill, I spied the camp I'd pinned all my hopes on finding.

We drew alongside a muddy sandbank. I collected my bag, said goodbye to the fisherman who'd taken me this far and started to make my way up a narrow path through the tall grass. I met a Frenchman who seemed astonished to see me; when I asked him if a woman called Keira was working there, he pointed northwards and carried on with his business.

A little higher up, I passed a tent village before reaching the entrance to the archaeological site.

The ground had been dug into squares, with stakes and cords demarcating the edge of each hole. The first two holes were empty, but I spotted two men working on a third. Further away, there were people carefully brushing the ground. From where I was standing, it looked as if they were painting it. Nobody took any notice of me and I continued walking along the rampart formed by the banks between each excavation, or at least I did so until a volley of abuse made me stop. Someone inquired loudly, and in perfect English, who was that bloody idiot walking in the middle of the excavations? A quick scan of the horizon confirmed the bloody idiot could only be me.

It was difficult to imagine a worse prelude to a reunion I was already dreading. Still, I guess not everyone has the distinction of being called a moron in the back-of-beyond. A dozen heads popped up out of holes, like a tribe of meerkats emerging from their den when danger's in the air. A stout man ordered me, in German this time, to clear off immediately.

I've never really mastered German, but I didn't need much vocabulary to understand he wasn't joking. And then suddenly, in the middle of all those accusing faces, I spotted Keira's as she stood up.

Things did not pan out as Walter had predicted.

"Adrian?" she said, sounding alarmed.

For the second time in Ethiopia, I felt totally alone. And when Keira asked me what on earth I was doing there – her surprise over-riding any pleasure at seeing me again – the prospect of responding in such hostile company left me at a loss for words. I stood, rooted to the spot, as if I'd just stumbled into a mine-field.

"Don't move, whatever you do!" ordered Keira, coming over to me.

She guided me to the edge of the excavation area.

"You have no idea what you've just done! You turn up out of nowhere in your great clodhoppers, you could have trodden on bones of unimaginable importance."

"Tell me I haven't," I stammered.

"No, but you could have, which amounts to the same thing. How would you feel if I went charging round your observatory, fiddling with all the telescope controls?"

"I think I've got the message. You're angry."

"I'm not angry, you're thoughtless – it's not the same."

310

"Hello, Keira."

On reflection, I could have said something more original, but those were the only two words that came into my head.

She looked me up and down. I was waiting for her to relax, if only for a second.

"What are you doing here, Adrian?"

"It's a long story, and I've been on an even longer journey. If you can spare me a few minutes, I'll explain everything."

"Yes, but not now, as you can see, I'm really busy."

"Well, I didn't have your number in Ethiopia, or your assistant's number to make an appointment. So I'll just head back to the river and wait by a coconut tree. Drop by when you've got a second."

Without giving her time to reply, I turned on my heels and stalked off in the direction I'd come from. I still had my pride.

"There aren't any coconut trees around here, or any banana trees, you ignoramus!"

I glanced round to see Keira coming towards me.

"All right, so it wasn't such a great welcome, I'm sorry."

"Are you free for lunch?"

I had a real knack for asking stupid questions that day. At least this time it made Keira laugh. She took my arm and steered me back towards the camp; there, she invited me into her tent, opened up a cool box, produced two bottles of beer and held one out to me.

"It's not very chilled, so drink up, it'll be warm in five minutes. Are you here for long?"

Being alone together in her tent felt awkward, so we went for a walk by the river instead. As I was strolling along the bank, I realized how hard it must have been for Keira to tear herself away from a place like this.

"I'm touched you've come all this way, Adrian, really. It was a wonderful weekend in London, wonderful but..."

I'd come all this way, desperate to see her again, to hear her voice, to catch that look in her eyes, even if it was hostile. But of course I didn't say this. Call it stupidity, or ill-placed male pride, but the truth is I couldn't bear to be rejected a second time.

"I'm not here with any romantic intentions, Keira," I muttered. "There's something I've got to talk to you about."

"It must be very serious for you to have come all this way."

Only a few minutes earlier, Keira had appeared deeply irritated at the idea of my undertaking this journey to find her; but now that I was assuring her this wasn't the case, she seemed to be equally angry. Compared to mysteries like these, calculating the depths of the universe is a simple mathematical equation.

"I'm listening!" she said, hands on hips. "And be quick about it, I need to get back to my team."

"It can wait until this evening, if you like. I'm not

here to make a nuisance of myself; in any case, I can't leave today, there are only two flights a week from Addis Ababa to London and the next one leaves in three days' time."

"Stay as long as you like, this place is open to anyone, apart from my excavation site, which I'd rather you didn't wander around without a guide."

I promised her I'd stay away and left her to get on with her work. We agreed to meet up again in a few hours, when we'd have the whole evening to talk.

"Make yourself at home in my tent," she called out, climbing back up the path. "Don't look at me like that, we're not fifteen any more. If you spend the night outside, you'll be eaten alive by trap-door spiders. You could always sleep with the boys, if you like, but I'm warning you, their snoring's worse than a spider's bite."

We ate supper with the team. The archaeologists had stopped being so hostile towards me, now that I was no longer blundering through their dig; in fact they were positively welcoming during the meal. I think they were happy to see a fresh face bringing news that was still hot off the press from Europe; I'd kept a newspaper in my bag that I'd found on the plane, and it caused great excitement. They were all arguing over it and the person holding it had to read out loud to the others. It's hard to appreciate how everyday snippets of news suddenly become so important for those far from home.

Once the group was gathered around the fire, Keira took me to one side.

"They'll be exhausted tomorrow and it'll be your fault," she complained, staring at them as they listened to the newspaper being read. "The days here are very hard, every minute of work counts. We live by the sun, and on a normal evening the team would be sleeping by now."

"So I guess this isn't a normal evening."

A moment of silence. Each of us looked the other way.

"I need to tell you that nothing's felt normal in my life for several weeks now," I went on. "And this succession of abnormal events has a lot to do with why I'm here."

I removed the pendant from my pocket and held it out to her.

"You left this on my bedside table; I came here to give it back."

Keira held her necklace, staring at it for a long time, with a beautiful smile on her face.

"He hasn't come back," she told me.

"Who?"

"The person who gave it to me."

"Do you miss him so badly?"

"Not a day goes by without me thinking about him and I still feel guilty for abandoning him."

I hadn't seen this coming and was really struggling to find something to say that wouldn't betray my confusion.

"If you love him that much, you'll find a way of letting him know; he'll forgive you for whatever it was you did to him."

I didn't want to find out any more about the man who had conquered Keira's heart, still less be responsible for bringing them back together, but she looked so downcast.

"Maybe you should write to him?"

"It took me three years to teach him to speak good French, as well as some basic English, but he doesn't know how to read yet. And I wouldn't know where to look for him," Keira shrugged.

"He can't read?"

"Did you really come here just to give me back my necklace?"

"And did you really just forget it at my place?"

"What does it matter, Adrian?"

"This isn't just any old pendant, Keira. You do realise that? It has a highly unusual property, which I need to share with you, something far more significant than you could ever imagine."

"Really?"

"Where did your friend buy it? Who sold it to him?"

"Adrian, what planet are you on? He didn't buy it; he found it in the crater of an extinct volcano a hundred kilometres from here. Why are you so worked up about this anyway, what's the big deal?"

"Are you aware of what happens when your pendant is placed close to a strong light source?"

"Yes, I think so. Look, Adrian, when I went back to Paris, I wanted to find out a bit more about this stone, out of sheer curiosity. I tried to date it, with the help of a friend, but we didn't have any success. And then one evening, in the middle of a terrifying thunderstorm, lightning passed through it and I saw a pattern of tiny dots projected onto the living room wall. A bit later on, as I looked out of the window, I thought I might have seen some kind of resemblance between what had appeared on the wall and what I could see in the sky. By chance, you and I crossed paths a while later. That morning in London, when I left your place, I wanted to write you a letter, but I couldn't find the words. So I left you this instead, thinking that if there was something that needed looking into, then it would be more your field than mine. If what you've seen has intrigued or fascinated you in some way, I'm delighted. You can have this necklace: do what you like with it. I've got plenty of work to be getting on with here. Winning this prize, heading up this team and justifying the trust that has been placed in me is a huge responsibility. It's very sweet of you to have come all this way to share your story with me, but if you want to embark on some kind of investigation, that's your call. I dig the ground; I can't afford to have my head in the stars."

There was a tall carob tree in front of us, I went over to sit at its base and invited Keira to join me.

"Why are you here?" I asked her.

"Are you kidding?"

She looked amused when I didn't answer.

"I love wallowing in the mud," she said, "and seeing as there's so much of it around here, I'm like a pig in muck, er make that a big fat hippo."

"Don't be flippant, I'm not asking what you're doing, I want you to explain to me why Ethiopia, rather than anywhere else."

"That's a long story too."

"I've got all night."

Keira took a while. She stood up to find a stick and then came to sit back down next to me.

"A very long time ago," she said, drawing a big circle in the sand for me, "the continents were all joined up."

She drew another circle inside the first one.

"Together they formed a kind of vast and unique continent, surrounded by oceans: the supercontinent of Pangaea. The planet was shaken by dreadful earthquakes, and the tectonic plates began to move. The supercontinent divided in two: Laurasia to the north and Gondwana to the south. Then Africa became detached, almost an entire island in its own right. Not far from where we are now, as a result of extreme high pressure, a natural barrier of mountains rose up. These new summits had a major impact on the climate. Their peaks acted as a barrier to the clouds; without rain, the desertification of the lands to the east began.

The monkeys that lived in the trees, sheltered from

predators, saw their habitat shrinking away. Fewer trees meant less fruit, and so food started to become scarce and the species was threatened with extinction. Now listen carefully, because this is where the story starts to take shape.

Further to the west, opposite a valley where only tall grass now grew, the forest had survived. From the tops of the few remaining trees, the monkeys could catch a glimpse of these lands where food was still abundant. You see, the law of evolution is all about adapting to your environment in order to survive; and the survival instinct is strongest of all. So, overcoming their fear, the monkeys left the foliage behind. On the other side of the plain was an Eden where they'd lack for nothing.

Picture the monkeys, on their way. But moving through the tall grass on four legs, they can't see much; neither the direction they're going in, nor the lurking dangers. What would you have done in their place?"

"I don't know," I murmured, entranced by her voice.

"Like them, you'd probably have stood up on your hind legs to try and see into the distance, and then you'd have fallen back on all fours to carry on with your journey; you'd have stood up once again to check your route before picking up the path, and so on, until you got bored of that particular exercise, until you'd had enough of stretching up and bending down. By feeling your way on all fours, you were constantly veering off your path. You needed to follow a straight line and escape from this hostile plain, where, night after night, predators were attacking animals who looked just like you; your aim was to reach the forest with its appetising fruit as quickly as possible. So, one fine day, to go a bit faster, once you were on your hind legs, you tried to stay upright.

Of course, you walked clumsily, and it was painful because neither your skeleton nor your muscles were adapted to this body position, but you held out, realising that your survival depended on your ability to reach your destination. The number of monkeys who died of exhaustion along the way or who were devoured by the big cats would have convinced you to keep forging ahead, always going faster. If just one couple could reach their goal, the species would be saved. Without noticing it, in the middle of this plain you were no longer the same monkey who, just yesterday, leapt from branch to branch, running on all fours during your brief sorties at ground level; without realising it you were already becoming a man, Adrian, because you were walking. You had forgone the attributes of your own species to invent another, the human being. These monkeys, who succeeded in the risky venture of reaching the fertile lands on the other side of the plain, were our ancestors. And I don't care if what I'm about to tell you still makes the blood of certain scientists boil, because the truth is seldom universally agreed upon in this field.

Twenty years ago, some eminent colleagues discovered the remains of Lucy. Her skeleton became a celebrity. Lucy was three million years old, and everybody was prepared to view her as the grandmother of humanity, but they were all mistaken. A little over a decade later, other researchers brought to light the remains of *Ardipithecus Kadabba*. He was five million years old and the arrangement of his ligaments, as well as the structure of his pelvis and of his vertebral column, proved to us that he was also a biped. Lucy was no longer our earliest ancestor.

More recently, a team found the fossilised bones of a third family of bipeds, which was even older. The Orrorins lived six million years ago. This discovery turned everything we knew up until then on its head. Because not only could the Orrorins walk, but they were even closer to us. Genetic evolution knows no going back. So they relegated everyone who'd been thought of as the grandparents of humanity to the rank of distant cousins, and pushed the assumed moment of separation between the line of monkeys and that of hominids even further back. But who could now claim with any confidence that others hadn't preceded the Orrorins? My colleagues looked to the west for an answer while I set off for the east, to this valley, at the foot of these mountains, because I believe with all my heart that our human forebears are much more than seven or eight million years old; I also believe that their remains are to be found somewhere beneath our feet. Now you know why I'm in Ethiopia."

"At your wildest guess, Keira, how old would you say our ancestors are?"

"I don't have a crystal ball – it's only by making a discovery that I'll be able to answer your question. But what I do know is that all humans carry an identical gene. Whatever the colour of our skin, we are all descended from the same being."

Eventually, the evening chill drove us back down to the camp. Keira set up a folding-bed for me in her tent; she gave me a blanket and blew out the candle. No matter how much I'd tried to suppress my feelings, just being close to her made me feel ridiculously happy – even if we weren't sharing a bed. I heard her turning over.

"Are there really trap-door spiders around?"

"None that I've seen. Good night, Adrian, I'm glad you're here."

*

Rome

Ivory was perched at a café counter in the middle of Fiumicino Airport. He checked the clock just above his head and buried his face again in his newspaper, *Corriere della Sera*. A man sat down on the neighbouring barstool.

"Sorry Ivory, the traffic was even worse than usual. What can I do for you?"

"Nothing much Lorenzo, apart from sharing your information."

"What makes you think I've got something of interest to you?"

"All right old friend, if that's the game you want to play then let's at least keep this fair. I'll go first, why don't I start by telling you everything I know? That the cell has been re-activated, for example, that the target is currently in Ethiopia, that he's joining his archaeologist friend out there; I also know that China has numerous economic interests in the area, and I've still got enough of my wits about me to re-alise that the others must be wondering whether or not to invite the Chinese to the table. Now, let's see, what else can I tell you? That Italy has also kept up some of its contacts in Ethiopia. And that, if you're still the man I once knew, you'll have activated one or two of your agents. Anything else...? I'm racking my grey cells here... Hold on, there must be a few more snippets to report back on. Oh yes, you haven't told anyone what you're up to: it's all about maintaining your interests, perhaps with a view to seizing control at an opportune moment."

"You haven't come all this way to level such grotesque accusations, when a telephone conversation would have sufficed?"

"Lorenzo, do you know where the real power lies nowadays, in your line of work?"

"I'm sure you're about to tell me."

"In not having to rely on any form of technology. Not on your telephone, not on your computer and not on your bank card. Remember how subtle and complex espionage used to be before anyone invented these wretched devices? Today, there's no art or pleasure left in our profession. The first idiot to switch on his mobile phone gets geo-localised in a matter of minutes by a raft of satellites. But nothing will ever replace drinking a good espresso with an old friend in the anonymity of an airport café."

"You still haven't told me what you want."

"You're right, I nearly forgot. I once did you a few favours, if I remember correctly. I won't ask you to repay them now – though I may well need to at some point – no, what I'm after today isn't worth wasting a trump card on, I'd be paying too high a price. All I'm asking is that you give me a slight head start over the others. Of course, I won't tell them anything about your scheming and, in return, you'll keep me apprised of developments in the Omo Valley. I'll be terribly generous: when our lovebirds fly off to other countries, it'll be my turn to keep you informed. I'm sure you'll appreciate that an invisible bishop on the chessboard is a major advantage for the player who's got him on his side."

"I'm strictly a poker-player, Ivory, chess isn't my game. What makes you think they'll leave Ethiopia?"

"Oh please, Lorenzo, give me some credit. If you really believed our astrophysicist had set out just to whisper sweet nothings into his girlfriend's ear, you wouldn't have dispatched your men on the ground."

"I don't know what you're talking about!"

Ivory paid for his drink and stood up. He patted his neighbour on the shoulder.

"It was nice to see you again, Lorenzo. Do pass on my best wishes to your beautiful wife."

The elderly professor bent down to pick up his bag and walked off. But Lorenzo caught him up immediately.

"All right, my men tailed him from Addis Ababa Airport; he chartered a tiny plane to get to Jinka. The link-up took place there."

"Your men came into contact with him?"

"Completely anonymously. They gave him a lift and took the opportunity to plant a small bugging device in his luggage: a medium-range transmitter. His conversation with the young archaeologist you mentioned indicates he hasn't twigged what this is all about yet, but he's not far from the truth, it's just a matter of time; he *has*, on the other hand, found out about some of the object's properties."

"Such as?" asked Ivory.

"Properties we're not familiar with. We didn't hear everything; as I told you, the bugging device is in his luggage. It has something to do with projecting dots when the object is brought close to a powerful light source," Lorenzo answered, without showing much interest.

"What kind of dots?"

"He was talking about a nebula and something to do with a Pelican: I suppose it must be some kind of English expression."

"I'm afraid your ignorance betrays you; the Pelican Nebula is to be found in the Constellation of Cygnus the Swan, not far from that constellation's brightest star, Deneb. Why didn't I think of that earlier?"

Ivory's excitement was so palpable, Lorenzo felt disconcerted.

"Aren't you getting a bit carried away by all this?"

"And with good reason, this piece of information confirms all my suppositions."

"Ivory, you were sidelined by the community because of your 'suppositions'; I'd like to help you out, for old time's sake, but I have no intention of discrediting myself with your asinine blunders."

Ivory grabbed Lorenzo by the tie. He tightened the knot so fast, the latter had no time to react; he was already gasping for air and his face was turning an alarming shade of purple.

"Never, ever talk to me like that again! Asinine, did you say? You're the asses here, frightened of coming close to the truth, just like the most obscure religious fanatics six centuries ago. You're as unworthy of the responsibilities on your shoulders as they were. What a bunch of incompetents!"

People were stopping to stare at them.

Ivory relaxed his grip and smiled at them. The onlookers carried on their way and the barman returned to his duties. Lorenzo had loosened his shirt collar and was taking some deep breaths.

"Next time you do something like that, I'll kill you!" said Lorenzo, trying to suppress a choking fit.

"Just try, you jumped-up nobody! Right, we've argued enough; all I ask is that you show more respect."

Lorenzo sat down on his stool again and ordered a large glass of water.

"So what are our lovebirds up to at the moment?" Ivory inquired breezily, picking up where he'd left off.

"I've already told you, they're a million miles from suspecting anything."

"A million miles, or within an inch?"

"Listen, Ivory, if I were in charge of operations,

I'd have taken possession of that object some time ago, either with their consent or by force, and the problem would have been dealt with. Not only that, but I imagine that sooner or later my approach, as advocated by a certain number of our friends, will be agreed on by everyone."

"I would urge you never adopt such an approach, and to use your influence to ensure that the others follow suit."

"So you want to dictate how I behave now?"

"You say you're worried my asinine behaviour will discredit you; well, how would it be if the community found out we'd met? Of course, you could always deny it, but how many surveillance cameras have filmed us, do you think? I'd even wager that our little skirmish hasn't gone unnoticed. As I pointed out, this ubiquitous technology is rather a nuisance."

"Why are you doing this, Ivory?"

"Precisely because your friends are capable of voting for a proposal as rash as the one you've just outlined. There is no question, I repeat *no question* of anyone raising so much as a little finger against our two lovebirds, given that they might finally embark on the kind of investigation you've all been too frightened of for so long."

"That's precisely what we've been trying to avoid, ever since the first object was discovered."

"But now there's a second object and it won't be the last either. So let's do everything in our power, you and I, to make sure our protégés succeed. After all, isn't it the imperative of knowledge that motivates you?"

"No, it's what motivates you, Ivory."

"Come on, Lorenzo, no one's taken in, not even your highly respectable colleagues."

"If your two lovebirds, as you call them, were to grasp the implications of their discovery and go public, do you realize what a Pandora's Box they'd be opening? What potential dangers they'd be letting loose on the world?"

"Which world are you talking about? The one where the leaders of the most powerful nations can no longer meet without provoking mass riots? Where forests are disappearing while arctic glaciers melt like snow in the sunshine? Where the majority of the population is starving or dying of thirst while a minority dances to Wall Street's tune? The one terrorised by small fanatical groups who murder in the name of imaginary gods? Which one of these worlds frightens you the most?"

"You're insane, Ivory!"

"No, answer my question! Is that why you all forced me to retire? So as not to have to face the consequences of your decisions?"

"And I suppose you think you're a saint?"

"There are no saints, my friend. We're all human beings with our failings and foibles; it's just that some of us are more hypocritical than others. "

Lorenzo stared at Ivory, put his glass down on the counter and got up from his stool.

"You'll be the first to learn what I've found out. I'll give you one day's head start, that's all. Take it or leave it. Think of it as clearing my debts to you. It's not such a high price to pay, is it – given there are no trump cards in poker?"

Lorenzo walked away, Ivory glanced again at the clock above the bar; his flight for Amsterdam was due to take off in forty-five minutes, there was no time to lose.

*

The Omo Valley

Keira was still asleep when I got up and left the tent, making as little noise as possible. The camp was silent. I climbed to the top of the hill: down below, the Omo River was shrouded in a light mist. A few fishermen were already busy by their dugouts. I sat down and took in the scene.

"It's beautiful, isn't it?" breathed Keira, who had come up behind me.

"Those must have been some nightmares you had last night," I told her, turning round. "You were tossing and turning and making all sorts of whimpering noises."

"I don't remember a thing. Maybe I was dreaming about our conversation last night?"

"Keira, could you take me to the place where your pendant was found?"

"Why, what good would that do?"

"I need to find the exact position, I've got a hunch I want to follow up."

"I haven't drunk my tea yet. Follow me, I'm hungry, we can talk about it over breakfast."

Back in the tent, I put on a clean shirt and checked my bag to see if I'd brought everything I'd need.

Keira's pendant had revealed a section of sky to us that was out of kilter with our era. I needed to familiarize myself with the exact place where this object had been left by the last person to use it. The stars we see on a clear night change from day to day. The March sky isn't the same as the October sky. A series of calculations might enable me to find out in which season that four-hundred-million-year-old sky had been viewed.

"From what Hari told me, he found it on an island in the middle of Lake Turkana. It's an extinct volcano. The silt there is fertile and farmers make a point of collecting it to enrich their own soil. He found the pendant during one such trip with his father."

"Well then, since your friend is nowhere to be found, is his father about?"

"Hari is a child, Adrian, who lost both his parents."

I must have betrayed my astonishment, because Keira looked at me and shook her head in disbelief.

"You didn't think, he and I...?"

"I just thought your Hari was a bit older, that's all."

"I can't tell you any more about the exact location where it was found."

"I'm sure a metre more or less won't make much difference. Will you come with me?"

"I can't. Getting there and back will take at least two days and I can't just drop my team like that, I have duties here."

"If you sprained your ankle, you'd have to stop, wouldn't you?"

"I'd wear a splint and carry on with my work."

"No one's indispensable."

"No, but my work is indispensible to me if you want to look at it like that. We've got a 4x4. I can lend it to you, and I should be able to find someone in the village who could act as your guide. If you go now, you'll reach the lake by late afternoon. It's not that far, but the track is virtually impassable; you'll have to drive very slowly. Then you'll need to find a boat to take you to the central island. I don't know how long you're thinking of spending there, but if you're lucky you should make it back by tomorrow evening. That'll leave you just enough time to get back to Addis Ababa for your plane."

"We won't have seen much of each other."

"And whose fault is that? You're the one who's dead set on going to the lake."

I did what I could to hide my glum mood and thanked Keira for the car. She came with me as far as the village, where she discussed matters with the chief. Twenty minutes later, we set off with him in tow. It had been a long time since the chief's previous chance to visit Lake Turkana; at his age, he could no longer make the trip by river, so he was delighted to take up the offer of a lift. He promised to show me

the way to the riverbank opposite the volcano. Once
we were there, he could easily find us a dugout. As
soon as he'd gathered together a few belongings and
we had driven Keira back to her camp, we'd be off.

Keira got out of the jeep and walked round to lean on
my window.

"Don't take too long, we won't have much time together before you fly back. I hope you find what
you're looking for."

What I'd really come looking for was standing in
front of me, but I wasn't ready to admit it yet.

It was time for us to go, and I prepared to drive
back up the little path from the camp towards the
main track. The gearbox crunched, and Keira suggested I push the clutch right in; then, as we were reversing, she started running and caught up with me.

"Could you delay your departure by a few minutes?"

"Yes, of course – but why?"

"So I can pack a bag and tell Eric he's in charge
of the excavations until tomorrow. I don't know what
you're getting me into here."

The village chief had dozed off on the back seat,
and didn't notice that Keira had joined us.

"Are we still taking him with us?" I asked her.

"It wouldn't be very tactful to leave him on the
roadside."

"He can act as your chaperone," I pointed out.

Keira gave me a thump on the shoulder and indicated it was time to drive on.

She hadn't been exaggerating about the track: it was a series of potholes. I gripped the steering wheel, trying to control the direction we were going in and avoid us sinking into a rut. After an hour, we'd barely covered ten kilometres; at this speed, we wouldn't reach our destination that day.

A particularly violent jolt woke our passenger. The village chief had a stretch and then pointed out a path that was barely visible, round the next bend; I understood from his gesturing that he wanted us to take a shortcut. Keira urged me to do as he asked. The path petered out: we were climbing the flank of a hill. Suddenly, a vast plain appeared before us, covered in golden reflections from the sun. The ground had softened up a bit under our wheels, and I was able to accelerate slightly. Four hours later, the chief requested that I stop. He got out of the car and started walking. Keira and I followed him. We trod in our guide's footsteps all the way to the edge of a small cliff. The old man showed us the delta of the river down below, where the majestic Lake Turkana was spread across more than two hundred kilometres. Of its three volcanic islands, the one to the north was visible: we still had a long drive ahead.

On the Kenyan shore, colonies of pink flamingos flew off to form long, graceful curves in the sky. The gypsum laguna gave the waters of the lake an amber tint which, in the distance, turned green. Now I understood why it was nicknamed the Jade Sea.

After getting back into our vehicle, we took a

scree path heading towards the northern part of the lake.

Apart from a herd of antelope, the place was deserted; we travelled for kilometres without coming across a living soul. The light reflected off the salt marshes was a dazzling white. Elsewhere, a semblance of vegetation was encroaching on the desert; from a landscape of tall grass emerged the head of a stray young buffalo.

A sign erected in the middle of nowhere indicated that we had entered Kenya. We travelled through a nomad village: a few mud huts testified to those who had decided to settle there. The path, which seemed to go on forever, deviated from the shore around a rocky plateau, and for a while we lost sight of the lake.

"We'll be at Koobi Fora soon," Keira announced.

Koobi Fora was an archaeological site discovered by Richard Leakey, a pioneering anthropologist whose work Keira admired. He had unearthed hundreds of fossils, including Australopithecus skeletons, as well as a quantity of stone tools. But his most important discovery had been that of the remains of *Homo habilis*, our most direct ancestor, who lived approximately two million years ago. As we were passing an excavation site, Keira turned to look behind and I wondered if she was dreaming of the day when travellers might pass a site made famous by one of her discoveries.

An hour later, we were nearly at the end of our journey.

There were a few fishermen down by the shore. The chief had a word with them and, just as he'd promised us, he managed to get us aboard a canoe with an engine. He said he would prefer to wait on dry land. He had made this long journey to contemplate the magical landscape for one last time.

As we pulled away from the coast, I noticed a cloud of dust in the distance, presumably a car; but my gaze turned back to the central island, also known as Funny Face Island, because three of its craters were formed like a pair of eyes and a mouth.

The small island had twelve craters altogether, with each of the three main craters enclosing a little lake at its centre. We'd hardly stepped out of the boat onto the black sand when Keira made me climb a steep rock face. The basalt ground crumbled under our feet, and it took nearly an hour to reach the top of the volcano. At an altitude of three hundred metres, the sweeping view was impressive. I couldn't help imagining the devastating powers of the monster that slumbered beneath those calm waters.

Keira tried to allay my fears by telling me that the last volcanic activity had been in the dim and distant past, but then she taunted me by letting it drop that in 1974 the crater had started giving off a foul stench; this wasn't, strictly speaking, an eruption, but the rumblings had produced clouds of sulphur vapour that were visible from the banks of the great lake. Was it these convulsions from the bowels of the Earth that had thrown up the pendant she wore around her neck? And if so, how long had it been lying there?

"This is where Hari found it," Keira told me. "Does that help you?"

I got the GPS I'd brought with me out of my backpack and pinpointed our position. We were at 3° 29' to the north of the equatorial point and at 36° 04' to its east.

"Have you found what you were looking for?"

"Not yet, once I'm back in London I'll have to carry out a whole series of calculations."

"To achieve what?"

"To verify that the view of the stars from here fits with the one revealed to us by your pendant. I may hit on some very valuable information."

"Couldn't you have found those coordinates on a map?"

"Yes, but it's not the same as actually being here."

"What's so different?"

"It's just not the same, okay?"

As I spoke, I turned bright red, like a prize idiot. *Subtle as a flying brick*, Walter would have remarked, if he'd been there.

The sun was sinking, and we needed to head down to the black sand beach and rejoin our boat. That evening, we would sleep in the nomad village we'd passed on our way.

As we were approaching the shore, Keira and I noticed something was up. The doors of our jeep had been flung wide open and the village chief was nowhere to be seen.

"I'm sure he's just inside, having a rest," said Keira, offering a rational view of things, but both of us felt alarmed.

The fishermen put us ashore and immediately set off again in order to make it back home before nightfall. Keira rushed over to the car and I followed her, only for our worst suspicions to be confirmed.

The village chief was lying on the ground, face down. A rivulet of blood, already dried, had trickled from his head and vanished between the stones. Keira bent down and turned him over, taking all the necessary precautions, but his glassy eyes left no doubt as to his state. Keira dropped to her knees and, for the first time, I saw her crying.

"He must have been taken ill and then fallen; we should never have left him alone," she sobbed.

I took her in my arms and we stayed there, watching over the body of this old man whose death I found inexplicably poignant.

The deep blue night shone above us and over the final sleep of an old tribal chief. I prayed, on that particular night, for an extra star to glow for him in the sky.

"We'll have to inform the authorities tomorrow."

"Absolutely not," Keira objected, "we're on Kenyan territory here, and if the police get involved they'll keep the body for as long as the investigation takes. If they did an autopsy, it would be a terrible affront for the tribe. No, we need to get him back to his own people, he has to be buried within twenty-four hours. His village will want to honour him in the customary manner, he's an important person for them: their guide, their knowledge and their wisdom. We mustn't infringe their rights. Just the fact of him having died on foreign soil will already be traumatic enough. Many of them will view this as some kind of curse."

We wrapped him in a blanket and, as we were lifting him into the back of the jeep, I noticed tire marks by our vehicle. I remembered the trail of dust I'd glimpsed earlier on, when we were setting out towards the central island. Could it be that this old chief's death wasn't simply the result of a heart attack or a bad fall? What had really happened while we were away? I left Keira to collect herself for a moment, and examined the ground using a flashlight I'd found in the glove compartment. Footprints surrounded our car, too many for all of them to be ours. They could belong to the fishermen who had ferried us, except that I had no recollection of them leaving their boat – I could have sworn we'd gone to meet them. I decided against discussing this with Keira, she was upset enough as it was; and I didn't want to worry her with suspicions that were unfounded, apart from a few tire marks and footprints on the dusty soil of the lake's shore.

We slept for a few hours on the ground.

At dawn, Keira took the steering wheel. As we were heading back to the Omo Valley, she whispered:

"My father went the same way. I'd gone out to do some food shopping, and when I came back I found him lying on the steps to his house."

"I'm sorry," I stammered, clumsily.

"The worst thing about it wasn't seeing him sprawled like that, head first, feet in front of the door; no, the worst was still to come. After they'd taken his body away, I went back into his bedroom and I saw the crumpled sheets. I pictured his routine that morning, his final steps on getting out of bed. I imagined him walking over to the curtain and opening it a little to see what the weather was doing. That ritual mattered more to him than anything he read about it in his paper. I found his coffee cup in the kitchen sink; the butter was still on the table next to a piece of half-eaten toast.

It's when we see everyday objects, like a butter-knife, that we realise someone has gone away and won't ever be coming back; a stupid butter-knife forever carving out chunks of loneliness in our life."

Listening to Keira, I realised why I'd taken her necklace to Greece, why it had come with me everywhere since the day she'd left it on my bedside table before walking out of my house.

We reached the village at dusk. When Keira got out of the car, the Mursis understood that something serious had happened. Those in the main square came over straightaway. Keira wept as she looked at them, but none of them went to console her. I opened the rear passenger door and gently lifted out the old chief, laying him on the ground and lowering my head as a sign of reverence. A sustained lament rose up from those gathered: the women raised their arms to the sky and started wailing. The men came up close to the corpse of their chief. His son lifted the blanket and slowly stroked his father's forehead. Stony-faced, he stood up and gave us a hard stare. I realised we were no longer welcome. They weren't interested in what had happened; as far as they were concerned, their old chief had set out with us alive and we had brought him back dead, end of story. I felt their hostility growing by the second. I grabbed hold of Keira's arm and steered her slowly over to the car.

"Don't look back," I instructed her.

As we were getting into the jeep, the villagers massed around us, circling the vehicle. A spear ricocheted off the hood, a second caught the wing mirror, and Keira just had time to shout at me to duck when a third glanced off the windshield. I'd put us into reverse and the car lurched backwards; I straightened up, did a half-turn and sped off out of the village.

The angry horde didn't follow us, and ten minutes later we reached the camp. Eric was shocked by the state of the 4x4 and by how pale Keira was; I filled him in on what had happened. The entire team of archaeologists gathered around a fire to decide on how they were going to handle things from now on.

Everyone agreed that the future of the group had been compromised. I offered to go back to the village the next day: I'd meet with the chief's son, man to man, and explain to him that we had nothing to do with his father's tragic demise.

My suggestions angered Eric, who thought that I hadn't grasped the seriousness of the situation. We weren't in London now, he argued, and the villagers wouldn't be appeased over a cup of tea. The chief's son would be looking for someone to blame and, according to Eric, it wouldn't be long before the villagers attacked the camp in order to avenge their chief.

"We need to get you both to somewhere safe," Eric declared. "You'll have to go away."

Keira stood up and made her excuses to her colleagues, saying she didn't feel well. As she walked past me, she asked that I find somewhere else to sleep, she needed to be alone. I left the gathering to go after her.

"I hope you're proud of yourself. You've just ruined everything," she snapped, without slowing down.

"For heaven's sake, Keira, it's not as if I killed the old man!"

"We can't even explain to his people how he died, and I'm going to have to abandon my dig to avoid the general carnage. You've destroyed my work and my hopes; I've just lost all standing among my colleagues, and Eric must be rubbing his hands at the prospect of taking over from me. If I hadn't gone with you to your blasted island, none of this would've happened. You're right: it's not your fault, it's mine!"

"Good grief, what's the matter with all of you?! Why behave as if you're guilty? The man died of old age, he wanted to see his lake one last time and we offered him the chance to fulfil his dying wish. I'm going back to the village tonight and I'll talk to them."

"Oh yes – in what language? Do you speak Mursi now?"

Confronted with my own helplessness, I fell quiet.

"Tomorrow morning, I'll drive you to the airport. I plan to spend a week in Addis Ababa, in the hope that things calm down here in the meantime. We'll set out at daybreak."

Keira went inside her tent without even saying goodnight.

I had no desire to rejoin the rest of the group. The archaeologists were still debating their future, around the campfire. The snatches of conversation that wafted my way confirmed that Keira's hunch wasn't so far-fetched: Eric was already asserting his authority over the group. What place would there be for her when she returned from Addis? I walked over to the hill and sat down, taking in the view of the river. Everything looked so calm.

An hour went by and then I heard footsteps. Keira came to sit down next to me.

"This evening I lost everything: my job, my credibility, my future – it's all vanished. The first time it was the Shamal that drove me out of here and now, Adrian, it's you who caused a storm."

"Do you believe in destiny, Keira?"

"Oh please, not now, you're not going to get a tarot pack out and start reading my cards?"

"I've never believed in it, you see. I even hated the idea that destiny might exist; because that would mean denying the existence of free will and the possibility of making our own choices."

"I'm not in the mood to listen to your handbook philosophy."

"I don't believe in destiny, but I've always wondered about chance. If you only knew the number of discoveries that would never have been made, without a little helping hand from chance. You're here because you dream of finding the traces of the first human beings, aren't you? Now, I put this question to you yesterday and you avoided answering it: in your wildest dreams, how old would this 'zero' human be?"

I think Keira replied more in a fit of pique than out of any real conviction.

"I wouldn't be unduly surprised if the first human being was fifteen or sixteen million years old," she told me.

"And if I said you could bump that up by three hundred and eighty-five million years in one fell swoop, what would you say?"

"That you've had too much sun today."

"Well, let me put this another way. Do you still believe that your pendant, which is impossible to date and made of a substance as yet unknown, is just a freak of nature?"

Bull's-eye! Keira was staring at me, with an expression I'd never seen before.

"That night of the storm – when those millions of luminous dots appeared as a result of the lightning – what you saw on the wall was the Pelican Nebula, a cradle of stars in our galaxy."

"I beg your pardon?"

"And that's not all. The section of sky projected by your pendant is not identical to what you can see above us now. It goes back four hundred million years. What does that correspond to, on your geological ladder?"

"To the beginning of life on earth," Keira breathed.

"I have good reason to believe that there are more objects out there, identical to the one you're wearing around your neck. If they're all more or less the same size, and if I've done my sums right, then we would need four more to project the entire sky. Some jigsaw, hey?"

"It's completely impossible that a map of the sky was drawn up four hundred million years ago, Adrian!"

"Weren't you telling me that just twenty years ago, everyone thought our oldest ancestors were only three million years old? Picture, for a moment, the two of us bringing together all the missing pieces, and then somehow – I've no idea how yet – being able to prove that four hundred million years ago, a map of the sky was fashioned with a degree of accuracy requiring methods of observation we can't even guess at... Then what conclusions would you draw?"

The prospect of such an incredible discovery left Keira lost for words.

I could never have predicted that the death of an old man would force her to leave her excavations; but if I were honest, ever since I'd set out from London I'd been hoping to find a way of convincing her to follow me.

We stayed there in silence, staring up at the sky, until late into the night.

After grabbing a few hours' sleep, we said our farewells to the camp at dawn. The whole team gathered around the jeep to see us off. Keira would drop me off at Addis Ababa Airport, as planned; she would then stay in the city as long as it took for things to settle down again. Eric would head up the research during her absence. She would call him regularly, waiting until it was safe for her to return.

In the course of the journey, which lasted two days, we asked ourselves a raft of questions about the mysterious pendant. How had it come to be in that former volcano in the middle of Lake Turkana? Had someone left it there on purpose, and if so why and, above all, *when*?

We both knew, separately, that at least one other such object with similar properties also existed, even if – at Ivory's request – we hadn't talked about it. Five pieces needed bringing together to form a complete sky. But what would haunt us from now on was finding out where they were, and how we could lay our hands on them.

A few months ago, back in the Atacama, I'd never have entertained the idea of combining my expertise as an astrophysicist with that of a paleoanthropologist, in the quest for some unlikely discovery.

We were starting out on our second day of driving when Keira suddenly remembered an article she'd read in a journal a few years earlier. She asked me if I'd ever heard of a bronze-age object resembling an astrolabe that had been found in Germany.

"Of course! Every astrophysicist worth his salt knows about the existence of the Nebra sky disc. Illegal treasure hunters looted it from a site in Upper Saxony in 1999. It weighs about two kilos, and is shaped like a round shield, thirty centimetres across, on which a crescent moon stands out in gold overlay, together with dots believed to represent celestial bodies. Its composition is apparently so remarkable that archaeologists at first took it to be the work of a forger. But a rigorous dating process has confirmed that it is indeed 3,600 years old. Swords and ornaments found in the same spot attested to its authenticity. Aside from its age, the Nebra sky disc has two very noteworthy features. The dots on the shield resemble the Pleiades, a star cluster that appeared in the European sky at around that time. The second noteworthy feature is the presence on the right hand side of an arc of eighty-two degrees. Eighty-two degrees corresponds exactly to the interval between the point where the sun rose at Nebra, at the time of the summer solstice, and the point where it rose at the time of the winter solstice. Several theories have been put forward as to the purpose of the disc: it might have been intended for agrarian purposes, since it depicts both the summer solstice and the appearance of the Pleiades in the sky, announcing the harvest season. Alternatively, the Nebra sky disc might have been a teaching aid to communicate astronomical information. In both cases, human knowledge at the time was infinitely more advanced than had previously been thought.

"So, you see, the Nebra sky disc is the most ancient representation of the sky known to us today. At least until your pendant appeared on the central island of Lake Turkana..."

"Are you saying there's a connection between the Nebra sky disc and my pendant?"

"I have no idea, but I reckon it could be worth our while to make a little trip to Germany," I replied cheerfully.

The closer we got to the capital, the more I could feel Keira clamming up. Was it the prospect of a major discovery that gave me an energy boost, or the idea that I might succeed in convincing Keira to undertake this research with me? Not that my excitement was contagious; each time a road sign announced the number of kilometres to Addis Ababa, Keira became distracted and lost in her thoughts.

A hundred times, I held back from questioning her, and a hundred times, I returned to the lonely business of concentrating on the road ahead.

We parked the jeep in the airport car park, and Keira followed me into the terminal. There was a flight for Frankfurt leaving the next day. I bought two tickets at the airline carrier's desk, but Keira drew me aside.

"I'm not going away with you, Adrian."

She explained that her life was here, and she wasn't ready to give it up. In a few weeks' time, a month at the most, things in the valley would be calm again, and she'd be able to get back to work.

No matter what extravagant claims I made for the discovery we might make together one day, she simply repeated that it was my quest, not hers. Her tone of voice was adamant; there was no point in me going on about it.

We had one evening left in Addis Ababa before my flight, and I asked a last favour of her: to find us a decent restaurant, one that wouldn't leave me with my stomach in knots.

It was a tough call pretending to ignore our imminent

separation, but why spoil the short amount of time we had left together?

I kept up a respectable front throughout dinner, and not once during our walk back to the hotel did I cave in and try persuading her to change her mind.

As I was seeing her back to her room, Keira flung her arms around me and put her head on my shoulder. She whispered in my ear that she would keep the promise I'd asked her to make in London. She didn't kiss me.

I hated the idea of saying our farewells at the airport. The previous evening had been upsetting enough and there was no point in prolonging the agony. At first light, I left the hotel after sliding a note under Keira's door. I can still remember what I wrote: about how sorry I was to have caused her so many problems, and that I hoped with all my heart she'd very quickly get back to the life she had so bravely built for herself. I also owned up to how selfish my attitude had been, and having made a full enough confession of my guilt I told her that, although I had no idea what was in store for me, I had already made one discovery of the utmost importance – just being with Keira made me happy. I knew I'd expressed myself clumsily, and my pen hovered umpteen times over the piece of paper before writing those few words, but at least they were heartfelt.

The airport terminal was heaving with people: it was as if all of Africa had decided to travel that morning.

The queue to board my flight was never-ending. After a long wait, I found myself sitting in the back row of the plane. As the cabin doors were closing, I wondered if I wouldn't have been better off returning to London, putting an end to what might, after all, just be one great illusory dream. The stewardess announced that there would be a short delay, with no further explanation.

And then, suddenly, further down the gangway, in the thick of all the passengers stowing their belongings into the overhead lockers, I saw Keira dragging a bag that must have matched her own body weight. She negotiated with my neighbour to swap seats, which he willingly agreed to, and she sat down next to me with a sigh.

"Two weeks, do you hear?" she said, fastening her seat belt. "In two weeks' time, wherever we are, you'll put me back on a plane to Addis Ababa. Do you promise?"

I promised.

A fortnight to find out the truth about her pendant: two weeks to piece together a puzzle that was four hundred million years old. It seemed an impossible gamble, but who cared? The plane was gathering speed and Keira was sitting next to me, her face pressed against the window, her eyes closed. The fortnight ahead was already far more than I'd dared hope for. During our eight-hour flight, Keira never once referred to the note I'd slipped under her hotel room door. She never mentioned it later on, either.

*

Frankfurt

We were still three hundred and twenty kilometres from Nebra. Despite feeling worn out by the journey, I hired a car in a bid to reach our destination by the end of the afternoon.

Neither Keira nor I had ever imagined this small country town would prove so popular. The spot where the famous sky disc had been unearthed appeared to have been turned into a tourist attraction complete with Visitor Centre. An imposing concrete turret rose up in the middle of a field. From the base of the structure, which sloped like the leaning tower of Pisa, two lines stretched across the ground, each supposedly representing the solar axes of the solstices. The complex also included an eyesore of a museum, in the form of a gigantic timber and glass building on top of the hill.

We didn't learn anything earth-shattering from the Nebra sky disc site. Located a few kilometres away, the heart of the village with its cobbled streets, and the remains of a castle with attractive façades, had

the advantage of being a bit more authentic –
provided we ignored the shop windows displaying an
array of T-shirts, crockery and replicas of the disc.

"Maybe I should make a plan to excavate around
the Asterix theme park," suggested Keira.

Once our hotelier had handed us the keys to his
last available room, I introduced myself properly, informing him of our respective professions; I then
asked if he could arrange a private appointment for
us the next day with the curator of the archaeological
site at Nebra, which he agreed to do.

*

Moscow

Lubyanka Square, where two diametrically opposed worlds face each other: on one side, the huge orange-fronted former KGB headquarters; on the other, the 'Children's World' toy store.

That morning, Vassily Yurenko was in a bad mood because he'd had to pass up breakfast at Café Pushkin. After parking his old Lada alongside the curb, he waited for the toy store to open its doors. On the ground floor, the lit-up roundabout was taking its first few spins of the day, but no child had yet mounted the wooden horses. Vassily refrained from holding onto the escalator handrail: it was filthy. On the first floor, he stopped in front of a display stand containing the most beautiful nesting Russian dolls. He was always tickled by this collection of figurines encased inside each other. When he was a young boy, his sister had owned a collection that would have been priceless today; but his sister had been laid to rest in the Novodevichy cemetery thirty years ago and her collection was just a distant memory.

The elderly sales assistant gave him a big smile and a rather unappetising view of her toothless gums. Yurenko looked away. The babushka picked up a brightly coloured doll, with a red head and yellow body, stuffed it into a paper bag and asked her customer for a thousand roubles. Yurenko paid and moved off. Shortly afterwards, he sat down at a café table, scratched off the paint on the third doll and copied down the numbers that appeared. He caught the Metro, got off at Ploshchad Vosstaniya Station and walked down the long corridor leading to Moscow Railway Station.

At the left luggage, he went to the locker indicated by the third doll, composed the numbers on the combination lock revealed by the fifth doll and picked up the envelope he found inside. It contained a plane ticket, a passport and a telephone number in Germany, as well as three photographs; one was a mug shot of a man, another of a woman, and in the third they were both getting off a plane. Their names had been scribbled on the back of the photo. Yurenko slid the envelope into his pocket and checked the timetable on his plane ticket. He had two hours to get to Sheremetyevo Airport.

*

Rome

Lorenzo was leaning over his office balcony. His cigarette butt dropped into the street below. He watched it roll into a gutter, then shut the windows and picked up the telephone.

"We've got a little problem in Ethiopia. They've left the country," Lorenzo informed the person on the other end.

"Where are they?"

"The trail went cold in Frankfurt."

"What happened?"

"The agents shadowing them ran out of luck. Your two protégés made a trip to Lake Turkana, together with a village chief who was acting as their guide. My men wanted to question him about what the pair were intending to do on a small island in the middle of the lake, but there was an accident."

"What sort of an accident?"

"The old man laid into them – he had a bad fall."

"Who knows about this?"

"I promised you'd be the first to hear any news but, given how events have panned out, I can't leave it any more than a day before I contact the others. And I'm going to have to explain why my men were tailing your two lovebirds."

Lorenzo didn't get the chance to say goodbye to Ivory, who had already hung up.

"What do you reckon?" asked Vackeers, who was sitting in a swivel chair opposite him.

"Ivory won't be fooled for long; in fact, I suspect he's guessed you're already in the know. He's a crafty old fox; you won't trap him like that."

"Ivory's an old friend, and I'm not out to trap him, I just don't want him manipulating us. We have different objectives, and we can't let him call the tune."

"Well, if you want my opinion, I think he's conducting the orchestra even as we speak."

"What makes you think that?"

"I'd be willing to bet that the man waiting down below in the street followed you all the way from your office."

"What, all the way from Amsterdam?"

"For him to be so blatantly visible means either that he's incompetent, or your old friend is sending you a message, along the lines of: '*don't take me for an old fool, Vackeers, I know where you are.*' And seeing as the guy's managed to tail you this far without your noticing, I'd say the second scenario is more likely."

Vackeers leapt to his feet and went over to the window. But the man Lorenzo had just been talking about was already moving off.

*

Upper-Saxony, Germany

"You should put your seat belt on, the roads are narrow round here."

Keira opened her window wide and pretended she hadn't heard. There were times on that trip when I wanted to fling open the passenger door and push her out.

The curator of Nebra Museum welcomed us with open arms. He was so proud of his collection that he explained every item in detail. Swords, shields, spearheads, all sorts of paraphernalia; we had to listen to the history of each individual treasure before he finally showed us the disc.

It was a remarkable object. Visually, it bore no resemblance to Keira's pendant, but we were both fascinated by its beauty and by the ingenuity of its craftsmanship. How had someone been able to pull off such a technical feat in the Bronze Age? The curator invited us to join him in the cafeteria, where he asked how he could be of help. Keira showed him her necklace while I explained its unusual properties.

Fascinated by what I'd just told him, the curator inquired as to its age, and I told him that we had absolutely no idea. The curator, who had spent ten years of his life studying the Nebra sky disc, was thoroughly intrigued by our object. He had a dim recollection of having read something that might interest us, but he would have to put both his thoughts and his archives in order. He suggested meeting up again that evening for dinner. In the meantime, he would do his best to help us. So we had a free afternoon ahead of us. Back in our hotel, we found that two computers were available for guest use; I sent a news update to Walter and I wrote a few e-mails to colleagues – weighing up what I was prepared to reveal and what I preferred to hold back on, so as not to sound like a complete raving lunatic.

*

Frankfurt

The minute he was off the plane, Vassily visited each of the international terminal's four car-hire counters in turn. He showed the same photo to each employee, asking if they recognised the couple featured. Three of them said no, the fourth told him that this kind of information was confidential. Vassily now knew that the people he was looking for hadn't taken a taxi into town; and, more importantly, he knew exactly where they'd rented their car from. Having gotten what he needed, he found a telephone booth and called the car-hire employee he'd just spoken with; when the latter picked up, Vassily explained in near-perfect German that an accident had occurred out in the parking area and his presence was required immediately. Vassily watched the man hang up furiously, abandon his post and rush over to the lifts for the basement. As soon as he was gone, Vassily headed back to the counter, leaned over the keyboard and in no time the printer was humming and whirring. Vassily walked off with a copy of Adrian's car-hire contract in his pocket.

After dialling the telephone number he'd found in the envelope at left luggage in Moscow Station, Vassily learned that the grey Mercedes, licence plate KAPA 521, had been filmed by the CCTV cameras on motorway B43, followed by those on motorway A5 direction Hanover; twenty-five kilometres further on, the vehicle had been seen again on the A7 where it had taken Exit 86. A hundred and ten kilometres from there, the Mercedes had sped along at a hundred and thirty kilometres per hour on the A71; shortly after that, it had turned up on the trunk road towards Weimar. Faulty surveillance devices on the minor roads meant that the car seemed to have vanished off the radar, but thanks to the camera at a set of traffic lights it had reappeared at a crossroads in Rothenberga.

Vassily hired a large saloon car and drove out of Frankfurt, sticking to the itinerary he'd copied down.

Luck was on his side that day: there was only one road continuing on from the point where the Mercedes had been seen for the last time. It wasn't until fifteen kilometres later, when he was driving through Saulach, that he was faced with a choice. Avenue Karl Marx pointed in the direction of Nebra, while a road on Vassily's left was for Bucha. Following Karl Marx didn't appeal, so he took the Bucha road; this passed through a wooded area, before re-emerging between vast yellow fields of oil-seed rape.

At Memleben, as he was approaching a river, Vassily changed his mind; he pulled down hard on the steering wheel and swung into Thomas Müntzer Strasse. The route he'd taken was clearly triangular, because once again there was a road sign to the town of Nebra. When he noticed the car park for an archaeological museum on his right, Vassily opened his window and allowed himself the first cigarette of the day. The hunter could sniff his prey in the vicinity, it wouldn't take him much longer now to track them down.

*

The museum curator had joined us at our hotel, having changed into a corduroy suit, a checked shirt and a knitted tie. Even dressed in the clothes we'd salvaged from our tour of Africa, we still looked more presentable than he did. He took us to an inn and waited for Keira and myself to be seated before cheerily asking how we'd met.

"We've been friends since college days!" I answered. Keira gave me a sharp kick under the table.

"Adrian is more than just a friend, he's my very own personal tour guide; in fact, he often invites me on trips to help me take my mind off things," she declared, kneading my toes with her heel.

The curator changed the subject by calling the waitress over and ordering our meal.

"I have something that might interest you," he told us. "When I was carrying out my research on the Nebra sky disc, and God knows I did enough of it, I came across a document in the National Library. For a while, I thought it would help me in my work, but it proved to be a red herring; though perhaps not as far as you're concerned. Now, despite having spent the afternoon rummaging through my files, I haven't been able to lay my hands on it, but I've got a fairly good recollection of its content. It was written in Ge'ez, a very ancient African language whose characters are relatively close to the Greek alphabet."

Keira suddenly perked up.

"Ge'ez," she explained, "is a Semitic language that contributed to the development of Amharic in Ethiopia and of Tigrinya in Eritrea. The writings that gave birth to Ge'ez go back about three thousand years. But what's most astonishing are the similarities between Ge'ez and Ancient Greek, not only in the alphabet but also in the litany. According to the beliefs of the Ethiopian Orthodox Church, Ge'ez was a divine revelation made to Enos. In the book of Genesis, Enos is the son of Seth, the father of Kenan and the grandson of Adam; in Hebrew, '*enosh*' implies the notion of humanity. In the Ethiopian Orthodox bible, Enos was born in the three hundred and twenty-fifth year after the creation of the world; in other words, we're going back to the thirty-eighth century BCE, before the Flood in Hebrew mythology. What's the matter?"

I must have given Keira a funny look because she broke off, adding that she was relieved I'd finally noticed her real job didn't involve helping me re-write the *Rough Guide*.

"Do you remember what that Ge'ez text was about?" Keira pressed the museum curator.

"Just to be clear, although the original was written in Ge'ez, what I had in my hands was rather more recent: it was a retranscription that only dates back to the fifth or sixth century BC. If my memory serves me correctly, it talks about a sky disc, a sort of map where each piece would serve as a guide to the world's population. The translation was muddled and open to all sorts of interpretations, but what I do remember was that at the heart of the text was the concept of *'reunification'*. It was impossible to tell whether it predicted the accession of the world or its destruction. I would imagine that it's a fairly religious text, another prophecy if you like. In any case, it was much too old to refer to the Nebra sky disc. You'll have to go to the National Library, where you can take a look at the text and make up your own minds. I don't want to raise your hopes, there's little likelihood of that text having anything to do with the object you're wearing around your neck, but if I were you I'd pay a visit all the same. You never know."

"And how do we find the document? The National Library is vast."

"I'm pretty sure I consulted it in Frankfurt; I went to the library in Munich several times, as well as the one in Leipzig, but I think this particular manuscript was in Frankfurt. Yes, it's coming back to me now: it was in a manuscript, but which one? This was all ten years ago. I really must sort out my papers. I'll make a start tonight, and if I find anything I'll let you know straightaway."

After the curator had left us, Keira and I decided to walk back. The old town of Nebra was attractive enough and a walk would help us digest the copious meal.

"I'm sorry – it looks like this is turning out to be a wild goose chase."

"You are joking, I hope?" said Keira. "You're not getting cold feet just as things start to get interesting? I don't know what your plans are for tomorrow morning, but I'm going to Frankfurt."

We were crossing a little square with a picturesque fountain when a car suddenly appeared in front of us, headlights blazing.

"Shit, that idiot's headed straight for us!" I shouted to Keira.

I pushed her into a doorway just in time; the car brushed against me and skidded in the middle of the square before disappearing off down the main street. If the crazy driver's intention was to give us the scare of our lives, he'd succeeded. I didn't even get a chance to catch his plate number. As I reached for Keira's arm, she looked at me in a dazed state: had that guy deliberately just tried to mow us down? I was at as much of a loss as she was.

I suggested finding somewhere we could drink a pick-me-up. But Keira felt too shaken and said she'd rather go back to the hotel. When we got to our floor, I was surprised to find the landing in darkness. I could have understood it if just one bulb had gone, but the whole corridor...? This time, it was Keira who had the presence of mind to hold me back.

"Don't go down there."

"I'm not sure we've got any choice, what with our room being at the end of the corridor."

"Come back down to reception with me. Don't play the hero – something's up, I can tell."

"The fuses have blown, that's what's up!"

But I could sense that Keira was worried and we went back downstairs.

The receptionist kept apologising profusely, insisting that nothing like this had ever happened before. It was all very odd since the first and ground floors also relied on the same fuse and, clearly, all the lights were working there. He grabbed a flashlight, asked us to wait in the lobby and promised he'd be back as soon as he'd got the electrics up and running again.

Keira led me over to the bar: perhaps a glass of schnapps would help her get to sleep, after all.

The receptionist had been gone for twenty minutes.

"Stay here. I'm going to find out what's going on, and if I'm not back in five minutes, call the police."

"I'm coming with you."

"No, stay here, Keira, listen to me for once – or,

one of these days, I really will end up opening the passenger door. And don't look at me like that, *I* know what I mean!"

I was feeling guilty about letting the receptionist go up on his own, given that Keira had already sensed danger in the air. I climbed the stairs, listening for any suspicious noise; I tried calling out all the German first names I could think of, tiptoed down the dark corridor and came across the flashlight (by accidentally treading on it) before finding our receptionist sprawled on the floor. His head lay in a pool of blood that was seeping from a nasty wound to his skull. The door to our room was open, and so was the window. Our suitcases had been emptied, and all our belongings scattered. But it didn't look like anything had been taken.

The police officer read my statement back to me; I had nothing else to add. I signed at the bottom of the document; Keira did likewise and we left the police station.

The hotel manager had helped us to find somewhere else to stay in town. But neither Keira nor I managed to get any sleep. The violence of the episode had brought us closer together. That night, in the bed where we sought refuge in each other's arms, Keira broke her promise: we kissed.

Strictly speaking, this wasn't the romantic set-up I'd been dreaming of, but I wasn't complaining; as she fell asleep, Keira took my hand in hers and that gesture of tenderness was even more irresistible than a kiss.

The next morning, we ate breakfast on a café terrace.

"I've got a confession to make: this isn't the first time events have taken a dramatic turn for me, of late. Which makes me wonder whether our hotel room door really was forced by an ordinary burglar? And I've also got a question or two about that reckless driver who nearly killed us."

Keira put down her croissant and stared at me: I could detect something in her expression, and it wasn't astonishment.

"Are you trying to say someone's after us?"

"Or after your pendant, at any rate. Before I became interested in it, my life was one hell of a lot less eventful... apart from an attack of altitude sickness, that is."

I told Keira all about what had happened to Walter and me in Heraklion; the way the professor had tried to seize the necklace, how Walter had set about dissuading him, and the chase that had ensued.

Keira started to giggle: I failed to see what was so funny.

"You smashed some guy in the face because he wanted to borrow my necklace for a few hours to study it, you knocked out and handcuffed a security guard, you fled the place like thieves and now you think you're bang in the middle of some kind of conspiracy?"

Keira clearly found Walter's behaviour equally ridiculous, not that this made me feel much better about things – although it did help a bit.

"And while you're at it, I suppose you think the old Mursi chief's death wasn't an accident either?"

I didn't answer.

"You're mad! How could anyone have known where we were?" she demanded.

"I don't know, but there were footprints and tire marks around our car. I don't want to blow things out of proportion, but I do think we should be a bit more careful."

The museum curator spotted us from a distance and hurried over. We invited him to sit down with us.

"I heard about last night's dreadful events. It really is appalling how drugs are destroying our country. For the price of a heroin fix, young people will commit all sorts of crimes. We've had several bag-snatchings in tourist-spots, and a few hotel rooms broken into, but never any violence before."

"Maybe it was an old-timer who wanted a fix – the old guys can be the worst," Keira remarked drily.

I gave her a discreet nudge on the knee under the table.

"No, I'm serious, why does everything always get blamed on the young?" she carried on.

"Perhaps because older people are less comfortable shinning down a drainpipe to make their get-away – after they've broken into a hotel room," replied the curator.

"Now, despite all this upset, I do have two bits of good news for you. The first is that the receptionist is no longer in critical condition. And the second is that I've found the shelf number of the manuscript in the National Library. It was really niggling me; I spent half the night opening up boxes and files and in the end I found a small notebook in which I had indexed all the documentary material I'd consulted at the time. When you go to the Library, you should request this reference number," he said, holding out a small slip of paper. "A manuscript like that is much too old and far too fragile to be accessed by the general public, but your professional accreditation means you'll be allowed to see it. I took the liberty of sending a fax to a colleague of mine – she's the conservationist at the Frankfurt Library, and she's bound to give you a warm welcome."

We thanked our host for all the trouble he'd gone to and set out from Nebra, with mixed memories of our visit.

Keira wasn't very talkative during the journey and I was thinking about Walter, hoping he'd respond to my e-mail. We reached the National Library by lunchtime.

The two-storey building was relatively new. The glazed rear façade overlooked a large garden. We presented ourselves at the desk and, a few moments later, a woman in a sharply tailored suit came to meet us.

She introduced herself as Helena Weisbeck and invited us to follow her to her office. There she offered us coffee and biscuits which Keira, not having eaten any lunch, wolfed down.

"This manuscript is certainly starting to pique my curiosity; nobody's bothered with it for years and now you're the second people today who want to consult it."

"Someone else came to see you about it?" asked Keira.

"No, but I received a request by e-mail this morning. The book in question isn't actually here, it's archived in Berlin – we house more recent documents – but this kind of text, along with plenty of other works, has also been digitised for posterity. If you'd put in an e-mail request, and I would have sent you a copy of the relevant pages too."

"Could I ask who made a similar request to ours?"

"It came from a foreign university, I'm afraid I don't remember any more than that, I just signed off the request. It was my secretary who handled it and she's on her lunch break now."

"You don't remember which country this university was in?"

"Holland, I seem to remember, yes, I think it was the University of Amsterdam. In any event, it came from a professor, but I don't recall the name, I sign so many pieces of paper every day, we really are mired in red tape."

Helena Weisbeck held out a brown paper envelope –

inside was a colour facsimile of the document we wanted to examine. The manuscript was indeed written in Ge'ez, and Keira studied it closely. The conservationist coughed, indicating that the copy she'd just given us was now ours to do with as we wished. We thanked her and left the building.

There was a sprawling cemetery on the other side of the street, which reminded me of London's Brompton Cemetery, where I often used to go for a walk, enjoying the unexpectedly pretty wooded park in the middle of a great metropolis.

We went to sit on a bench below an alabaster angel perched on its pedestal, which seemed to be spying on us. Keira gave it a wave and then pored over the copy of the manuscript. She compared the characters with the rudimentary English translation that accompanied it. The text had also been translated into Greek, Arabic, Portuguese and Spanish, but what we were reading in English made little sense:

Beneath the trigonal of stars, I have entrusted to the magi the disc of powers, separated from the parts which link the colonies.

May they remain concealed under the pillars of abundance. Let no one know where the zenith is, the night of one is guardian of the prelude.

Mankind must not disturb it, the end of the region is drawn at the junction of imaginary times.

"Well, this isn't much use!" said Keira, putting the document back in its envelope. "I've got no idea what it means, and I can't translate it for myself either. Where did the curator at the Nebra Museum tell us this manuscript was found?"

"He didn't. He just mentioned that it went back to the fifth or sixth century BC. And pointed out that the manuscript in question was itself a retranscription of a much older text."

"So this looks like a dead-end."

"Don't you know anyone who might be able to cast an eye over this?"

"Yes, but he lives in Paris."

Keira sounded unenthusiastic, as if the prospect somehow pained her.

"Adrian, I can't go on with this trip; I haven't got a cent left and we haven't got a clue where we're going, let alone why."

"I've got some savings and I reckon I'm still young enough not to have to worry about my pension just yet. Paris isn't far, we could even travel by train if you prefer. Come on, let's share this adventure."

"You've just put your finger on it, Adrian – you talk about sharing but I've got nothing left to share."

"We can strike a deal, if you like. Just suppose for a minute that I lay my hands on some kind of treasure: I promise I'll deduct half our expenses from your share of the spoils."

"And what if I'm the one who finds the treasure?

After all, I'm the archaeologist here!"
"In that case, I will have made a good deal!"
Keira finally agreed to us going to Paris.

*

Amsterdam

The office door was flung open, catching Vackeers off-guard. He reached for his desk drawer in a flash.

"Shoot me, why don't you? You've already stuck the knife in my back."

"You could have knocked, Ivory! I'm too old for scares like that," Vackeers berated his surprise visitor, pushing his gun to the back of the drawer.

"You're not wrong about getting old, my friend – your reflexes definitely aren't what they used to be."

"Look, I don't know what you're so worked up about, but sit down and let's see if we can't have a civilised conversation."

"Forget the niceties, Vackeers. I *had* thought I could trust you."

"Oh yes? So why did you have me followed to Rome?"

"I never had you tailed; I didn't even know you'd been to Rome."

"Really?"

"Really."

"Well, if it wasn't you, I find that even more alarming."

"An attempt was made on our protégés' lives, Vackeers. This is wholly unacceptable!"

"Get off your high horse, Ivory! Look, if one of us had wanted to kill them, they'd already be dead. We just meant to intimidate them; there was never any question of endangering them."

"Liar!"

"The decision was a stupid one, I'll grant you that – and, for the record, I was against it. Lorenzo has been a bit of a loose cannon recently. This may be small consolation for you, but I made it clear how much we disagreed with his method of operating. That's why I went to Rome. All the same, the cell *is* very preoccupied by the turn events are taking. Your protégés, as you call them, have got to stop stirring things up the world over. So far there's been no major mishap, but I fear our friends might resort to more radical methods if things carry on like this."

"So you don't consider the death of an elderly tribal chief to be a 'major mishap'? What world are you living in?"

"In a world they're putting at risk."

"I didn't think anybody took my theories seriously. But it seems even fools change their minds in the end."

"If our organisation fully subscribed to your theories, then Lorenzo's envoys wouldn't have been the only ones trying to thwart your two scientists. The cell doesn't want to take any risks; if you really do care about your two researchers, I would strongly recommend you dissuade them from pursuing their line of inquiry."

"Vackeers, you and I have spent many an evening playing chess together, and if there's one thing I do know, it's that I *will* win this game – alone against everybody else, if needs be. Warn the cell that it's already in checkmate. If your members dare to make another attempt on these scientists' lives, they will lose an important player."

"Which one?"

"You, Vackeers."

"You flatter me, Ivory."

"I never underestimate my friends, Vackeers, which is why I'm still alive. I'm going back to Paris now; please don't go to the trouble of having me followed."

Ivory stood up and walked briskly out of Vackeers' office.

*

Paris

The city had changed a great deal since my last visit. There were bicycles everywhere: if it weren't for them all being identical, I could have been in Amsterdam. The place itself was more beautiful than ever. The traffic might have been worse than I remembered, but the pavements had got wider and the façades whiter. Only the Parisians were the same as twenty years ago: crossing the road when the lights were against them, barging into people without apologising. And queuing, of course, was completely alien to them; in the taxi queue at Gare de l'Est, people pushed in front of us twice.

"Paris is the most stunning city in the world," insisted Keira, "and that's a fact."

The first thing she wanted to do on arrival was visit her sister. She begged me not to let on about what had happened in Ethiopia. Jeanne was a worrier by nature, especially when it came to Keira, so there was no question of mentioning the tensions that had forced her little sister to leave the Omo Valley; chances were, she'd chain herself to the runway rather than let Keira catch a plane back there, if she found out. So we'd just have to make up a reason for being in Paris. But when I suggested Keira say she was here to visit me, she scoffed that her sister would never fall for a bullshit story like that. I pretended I didn't mind, though of course I did.

Keira rang Jeanne, without saying that we were already on our way to see her. Once the taxi had dropped us off at the museum she called her big sister from her mobile, suggesting she look out of her office window to see if she recognised the person waving in the garden. Jeanne was down in a flash and joined us at our table. She hugged her sister so tightly that Keira looked like she was about to suffocate. And in that moment, I wished I had a brother I could spring such a surprise on; I thought about Walter and our burgeoning friendship. Jeanne looked me up and down, then said hello – and I said hello back. She was clearly curious to find out more about me, and inquired whether I was English. I'd have thought my thickly accented French was a dead giveaway, but out of politeness I felt obliged to confirm this fact.

"So you're an Englishman from England?"

"You've got it!"

"I mean an Englishman from London, England?" asked Jeanne, blushing.

"Absolutely."

"I see."

I didn't fancy interrogating Jeanne about what exactly it was that she saw, or why my answer made her smile.

"I was wondering what on earth could have torn Keira away from her wretched valley," she said, "now I've got a bit more of an idea..."

Keira looked daggers at me. I tried to make myself scarce, pointing out that they had plenty to catch up on, but Jeanne insisted I stay. We had a convivial enough time together, with Jeanne constantly asking me about my work, as well as my life in general; I felt almost embarrassed that she seemed more interested in me than in her sister, who ended up getting annoyed.

"Look, why don't I just leave you both to it? I'm obviously in the way here, so I'll pop back at Christmas," she announced, in the middle of Jeanne asking (I've no idea why) whether I'd gone with Keira to visit their father's grave.

"No, we don't know each other well enough for that yet," I said, teasing Keira a bit.

Already starting to make evening and weekend plans, Jeanne hoped we'd stay the whole week. But Keira said we were only there for a day or two, at most. When Jeanne asked us, disappointedly, where we were staying – pointing out that she'd successfully rented out Keira's studio to a friend, as instructed – Keira and I exchanged embarrassed glances: we didn't have a clue. Jeanne invited us over to her place.

During supper, Keira managed to get hold of the man who might be able to shed some light on the manuscript we'd found in Frankfurt. We were to meet him the following morning.

"I think it'd be better if I went alone," Keira suggested, taking her place again at the table.

"Went where?" asked Jeanne.

"To see one of her friends," I explained, "a fellow archaeologist, if I've got it right. We need him to help us translate a text written in an ancient African language."

"Which friend?" niggled Jeanne, who was being far more prying than I'd been on the subject.

Keira abruptly volunteered to go and fetch the cheese plate.

"I hope you're not going to see Max?" Jeanne called out to Keira in the kitchen.

No answer.

"If you want a text translated, I've got all the specialists you could ever need at the museum."

"Mind your own business, big sister," snapped Keira as she came back into the living room, brandishing the cheese.

"Who's Max?"

"A friend of mine Jeanne likes A LOT!"

"If Max is a friend, then I'm a nun," muttered Jeanne, before declaring out loud: "Well then, since Max is a *friend*, Keira, he'll be delighted to meet Adrian. Friends of friends generally hit it off, isn't that right?"

"Which bit of 'mind your own business' don't you get, Jeanne?"

I told Keira I'd be only too happy to join her for the meeting the next day.

The following morning we took the metro to Max's print works, on a street off Boulevard de Sébastopol. He welcomed us in friendly fashion and invited us up to his office, on the mezzanine floor. I've always admired the architecture of these old industrial buildings constructed at the time of the Eiffel Tower, with their girders from the steelworks of Lorraine.

Max hunched over our document, grabbed a notepad and pencil and set to work with an ease that fascinated me. It was like watching a musician deciphering a score and playing it at the same time.

"This translation is riddled with mistakes; I'm not saying mine will be perfect, I'll need time to do the job properly, but I've already spotted some howlers in this. Move in closer so I can show you."

With the pencil resting on the sheet of paper, he ran through the text, indicating the Greek equivalents he deemed erroneous.

"These aren't 'magi' being referred to here but magisteries. The word 'abundance' is a silly mistake: we should read the word 'infinity' in its place. Abundance and infinity can sometimes be close in meaning, but 'infinity' is the correct word here. A bit lower down, it's not the word 'mankind' either but 'nobody'."

He pushed his glasses down to the tip of his nose. When I have to wear glasses, I'll remember never to do that; it's ludicrous how such a gesture ages you, all of a sudden. Although I was in awe of Max's erudition, I was less keen on the way he was ogling Keira; but what really bugged me was that I appeared to be the only person who noticed – she just carried on blithely.

"I think there are a few grammatical mistakes too and I'm not sure the sentence order is quite right, which could change the whole meaning of the text. Of course, I'm just doing a bit of preliminary groundwork for now, but the segment '*under the trigonal of stars*', for example, isn't in the right place. We'll have to reverse the words and put them at the end of the sentence – it's nearly as persnickety as English, wouldn't you say?"

Max clearly wanted to spice up his lecture with a bit of humour, but I didn't rise to the bait. He tore the sheet of paper off the notepad and held it out to us. Now it was Keira's and my turn to lean over his translation, and read it (without glasses):

I have split up the table of memoranda, and entrusted the parts it combines to the magisteries of colonies.

May the shadows of infinity remain concealed beneath the trigonal of stars. Let no one know where the zenith is, the night of one is guardian of the prelude. Let nobody disturb it, the end of the region is drawn at the junction of imaginary times.

"That makes it a whole heap clearer!"

My jibe didn't amuse Max, but Keira was tickled.

"In writings as ancient as these, the interpretation of each word counts as much as the overall translation."

Max got up to photocopy the document; he promised to spend his weekend working on it and asked Keira where he could get hold of her; she gave him Jeanne's telephone number. Max wanted to know how long she'd be staying in Paris, to which Keira replied she had no idea. I felt invisible. Luckily, a foreman called Max over because there was a problem with one of the machines. I pounced on the opportunity to declare that we'd already overstayed our welcome and we should let him get back to work. Max showed us out.

"By the way," he pondered on the threshold, "why are you interested in this text? Is it to do with your research in Ethiopia?"

Keira shot me a look and promptly lied to Max, saying that a tribal chief had given it to her. When he asked me if I was as fond of the Omo Valley as she was, Keira put on a convincing show of declaring me to be one of her most valued colleagues.

We went to have a coffee in a *brasserie* in the Marais. Keira hadn't said a word since we'd left Max.

"He's awfully bright for a printer."

"Max was my archaeology professor; he had a career change."

"Why?"

"His safe, middle-class upbringing left him with no taste for adventure or fieldwork and then, after his father's death, he took over the family business."

"Were you together for a long time?"

"Who said we were together?"

I raised an eyebrow over my coffee cup.

"Oh come on, don't tell me you're jealous of Max? That would be pathetic!"

"Why would I be jealous of anyone, given I'm a friend one moment and a valued colleague the next?"

I quizzed Keira on why she'd lied to Max.

"It just came out like that."

I wanted to change the subject. I also wanted us to get away from Max's print works and Paris in general as quickly as possible. I suggested to Keira that we pay a visit to someone I knew in London, who might be able to help us decipher the document; someone a lot more learned than her printer.

"Why didn't you mention them before?" she wanted to know.

"Because it didn't occur to me."

Keira didn't have a monopoly on lying, did she?

While Keira was saying her goodbyes to Jeanne and getting her belongings together, I called Walter. I caught up on his news, before asking him a favour which he construed as decidedly odd.

"You want me to find someone at the university who's an expert on ancient African dialects? Have you been smoking the wacky baccy again, Adrian old chap?"

"It's a delicate matter, Walter, and I made a rather hasty promise; we're catching the Eurostar in two hours' time and are due into London this evening."

"That's great news about the travel plans at least;

but as for this witch-doctor I'm supposed to unearth, that's more complicated. Did I hear you mention '*we*'?"

"You did."

"Aha! Didn't I say you were better off going to Ethiopia on your own? Now there's the mark of a true friend! All right, I'll try to track down your wizard."

"What I need, Walter, is a translator of ancient Ge'ez."

"That's right, and I need a magician to make him appear out of thin air. Let's have dinner together tonight – call me when you get to London, I'll see what I can do between now and then."

And Walter hung up.

*

On the Other Side of the Channel

We'd emerged from the tunnel a while ago and the Eurostar was cutting through the English countryside. Keira had dozed off on my shoulder, sleeping for a good chunk of the journey. I had pins and needles in my arm, but I wouldn't have changed position for anything in the world. As the train slowed down for its approach into Ashford Station, Keira's elegant stretching was cut short by a sneezing fit; she sneezed violently three times, loud enough to startle the whole carriage.

"It's something I inherited from my father," she apologised. "Is it far now?"

"Another half hour."

"We can't be dead certain this document is linked in any way to my pendant, can we?"

"That's true, but then again I've always felt wary of being dead certain about anything."

"But you'd like to think there's some kind of connection between the two?" she went on.

"Keira, when we're searching in the infinitely big for a dot that is infinitely small, such as a light source from unimaginably far away, or when we're listening out for a noise from the depths of the universe, there's only one thing we can be dead certain of: our desire to find it. I know it's the same for you when you're excavating the ground. So yes, you're right, we haven't found anything yet that confirms we're onto something, aside from this instinctive belief we both have – which is already a start, wouldn't you say?"

It wasn't as if I'd said anything earth-shattering, and Ashford Station is hardly the most romantic of places, so I still catch myself wondering *why then*? Keira turned to face me, put her hands on my cheeks and kissed me as if for the first time.

For months, I've thought back to that moment, not only because it will always be one of my most treas-ured memories, but also because I've sought in vain to understand what I could have done to prompt that sudden outburst of affection. Later on, I even plucked up the courage to ask her, but I only got a smile for an answer. In the end, I decided that not knowing is a good thing. It means I can keep asking myself the same question, re-living that kiss in Ashford Station at the end of a glorious afternoon.

*

Paris

Ivory moved the knight on the marble chessboard that occupied pride of place in his sitting room. He owned some very old chess sets indeed, the finest example being located in his bedroom: a Persian set that was entirely ivory-coloured, dating back to the sixth century. Chaturanga is an ancient Indian game with four kings which preceded chess. A board of eight squares by eight, whose tally of sixty-four explained the passage of time and the passing of the centuries. The business of black and white came later; prior to which the Indians, Persians and Arabs played on a monochrome board, and sometimes on a grid marked out on the ground. Before becoming a secular game, the chessboard layout served as a sort of astrological map of Vedic India at the time when the temples and cites were created. It symbolised the cosmic order, and the four central squares related to God the Creator.

The hum of the fax machine stirred Ivory from his reverie. He went into the library where he kept his fax and removed the page that had just been spewed out.

It was written in a very ancient African language, followed by a translation. The sender asked Ivory to call as soon as he'd received it, which he did.

"She came to see me today," said the voice on the other end of the line.

"Was she alone?"

"No, she had some kind of English boyfriend in tow. Have you had a chance to cast your eye over the document?"

"I've done just that – is this your translation?"

"I did my best, given the time constraints."

"It's a nice job: consider your financial worries a thing of the past."

"Can I ask why you're so interested in Keira? And what the importance of this text is?"

"Not if you want the money to bail out your print works by tomorrow, as promised."

"I tried to get hold of her just now. Her sister told me Keira had gone to London, before promptly hanging up on me. Is there anything else you need to know?"

"As agreed, let me know if she gets back in touch."

Once the call was over, Ivory went back to his sitting room. With the text in one hand, he put on his glasses and started honing the translation in his turn. From the very first line, he introduced some small changes.

*

London

The prospect of spending a few days in my own home was rather appealing. Keira made the most of a warm end to the day by going for a stroll through the streets of Primrose Hill; as soon as I was alone, I called Walter.

"I'm warning you, Adrian, before you say anything, I did my best. It may be news to you, but one doesn't just pick up a translator from ancient Ge'ez on the Tottenham Court Road, or at Camden Lock for that matter, and they're not listed in the Yellow Pages either, I checked."

I held my breath. My heart sank at the prospect of having to admit to Keira I'd been bluffing all along, with the sole aim of getting her out of Max's clutches.

"Didn't you say that you were lucky to have me as a friend, Adrian? Well, I've managed to get hold of somebody top-notch who will definitely be able to help you. I have to say, old chap, I'm astonished at my own resourcefulness. So, I was talking about your problem with a friend of mine, who happens to have a close relative who's a regular member of the congregation at the Ethiopian Orthodox Church of St Mary of Zion in Leyton, East London. This person has had a word with a priest, a holy man whose erudition is apparently unparalleled. He is not just a man of the Church, but also an historian and a very great philosopher. He's been a political refugee in England for the past twenty years, and is acclaimed as one of the great specialists in the subject that interests you. We're meeting him tomorrow morning. And now you're allowed to say: 'Walter, you're a super-hero!'"

"And who is the friend to whom we owe this amazing favour?"

"Miss Jenkins," said Walter, sounding a little embarrassed.

"Now that makes this piece of news twice as heart-warming. You're a genius, Walter."

Thrilled at the prospect of a catch-up, I invited Walter to spend the evening round at my place. Over dinner, Keira and Walter got to know each other a little better. We took it in turns to tell him about our adventures and mishaps in the Omo Valley, as well as the Nebra escapade and the episodes in Frankfurt and Paris. We showed him the text we'd found in the German National Library, along with Max's translation. He couldn't make head nor tail of it, but paid it close attention all the same. Whenever Walter joined me in the kitchen or we found ourselves alone at the table, he insisted on telling me how fantastic he thought

Keira was – that she was a real beauty and quite charming. He'd clearly fallen under her spell too, and it's true that Keira was particularly bewitching that evening.

What Walter had neglected to tell us was that we would have to attend the service before being able to speak with the priest. I'll admit to dragging my feet that Sunday morning, my links with God having grown distant since childhood, but the service turned out to be deeply moving. I was struck by the beautiful singing and the sincere contemplation. Once the service was over, as people were filing out, the priest came to find us and invited us to follow him to the altar.

He was a small man, very hunched, perhaps from the weight of his congregation's confessions, or from a past that had seen wars and genocide. It was as if nothing evil could ever exist in him. His voice was deep and captivating and made you want to follow him anywhere.

"It's a surprising document, to say the least," he announced, having re-read it twice.

To my amazement, he paid no attention to the accompanying translations.

"Are you sure that it's authentic?" he asked.

"Yes."

"The problem here isn't one of translation but rather of interpretation. We can't translate poetry word for word, can we? And the same goes for ancient writings. It's easy to make a holy text say roughly what you want it to say; and there are people who'll gladly deform the well-intentioned word, twisting it in order to grant themselves unwarranted powers and to obtain what they want from their followers. Holy writings neither threaten nor command; they indicate a path and leave humans to choose the one that will guide them, not in their life, but towards life. Those who claim to understand and to perpetuate the word of God don't always interpret it in this way, and abuse the naïveté of those they rule over."

"Why are you telling us this, father?" I asked.

"Because I'd like to know what your intentions are, before I tell you anything further about this text."

I explained that I was an astrophysicist and Keira an archaeologist; the priest surprised me by saying that it was no coincidence we were together.

"You're both looking for something that is terrifying to understand – are you sure you're ready to deal with the answers you might find along the way?"

"What's so terrifying about it?" asked Keira.

"Fire is a precious ally for humans, but it is also dangerous for the child who doesn't know how to use it. The same goes for certain knowledge. On the scale of humanity, adults are but children; look at the world and see how uneducated we still are."

Walter assured him that Keira and I were highly respectable, and worthy of his trust in every way. This made the priest smile.

"What do you really know about the Universe, my astrophysicist friend?" he asked me.

There was nothing arrogant about his question, and no smugness in his tone of voice, but before I could answer he gave Keira a kindly look and inquired of her:

"So you think my country is the cradle of humanity – but have you asked yourself why?"

We were both psyching ourselves up to give him some pithy scientific answers, but he immediately asked us a third question.

"Do you believe your encounter to be an accident of fate? Do you really imagine that such a document landed in your hands purely by chance?"

"I don't know, Father," stammered Keira.

"You're an archaeologist, young lady; in your opinion did humans discover fire or did fire appear to us, when the time was right?"

"I think that the nascent intelligence of humans enabled us to tame fire."

"So you'd call that providence?"

"If I believed in God then yes, I probably would."

"You don't believe in God and yet it is to a man of the Church that you turn to try to solve a mystery that eludes you. I would ask you not to forget this paradox; the time will come when you'll need to remember it."

"What time is that?"

"When you have understood where this road is taking you, because neither of you has even begun to grasp that for now. If you had, would you pursue this path? I doubt it."

"Father, I'm not sure I fully understand what you're saying here; can you shed any light on the meaning of this text for us?" I ventured.

"You haven't answered my question, my astrophysicist friend, what do you know about the Universe?"

"Rather a lot, as a matter of fact, and I can happily vouch for that," Walter chipped in on my behalf. "I was his student for a few weeks and you've no idea how much knowledge I had to assimilate; it was impossible to hold it all in my head."

"Numbers, the names of stars, positions, distances, movements – all these are just observations; you and your colleagues are beginning to catch a glimpse, but what have you really understood? Would you be able to tell me what the infinitely big or the infinitely small is? What do you know about the beginning of all this, and can you guess at how it will end? Do you know who we are, what it means to be human? Would you be able to explain to a child of six about the intelligence your friend just mentioned: that which allowed humans to tame fire?"

"Why a six-year-old child?"

"Because if you can't explain an idea to a six-year-old child, then you don't understand it yourself!"

The priest had raised his voice for the first time and its echo voice rang out between the walls of St Mary's.

"We are all six-year-old children on this tiny planet," he declared, sounding calmer now.

"No, I can't answer any of those questions, Father, nobody can."

"Not yet, but if those answers were offered to you, would you both feel ready to hear them?"

The man of the Church sighed as he spoke, as if something pained him.

"You want me to light your way? There are only two ways of understanding light, two ways of advancing towards it. And humans know just one of them. That's why God is so important to us. To the six-year-old child who asked you what intelligence is, you could have answered in a word: love. There's a thought that will exceed our understanding for a long time to come. There'll be no going back when you decide to cross that frontier. Once you know, it will be too late to change your minds. That's why I'm putting this question to you once again. Are you ready to go beyond what you know, to risk abandoning the life you've known up until now? Do you understand that studying the universe has nothing to do with understanding it?"

Neither Keira nor I gave an answer. I wish I'd understood then what his wisdom was trying to reveal to us; that I'd been able to guess at what he was so keen to protect us from.

He leaned over the piece of paper, sighed again and stared hard at Keira and myself.

"This is the way to read this scripture," he told us.

A tiny hole, barely nine millimetres in diameter, erupted in the stained-glass window. The projectile crossed the church at a thousand metres per second. The bullet pierced the priest's neck, severing the jugular before burying itself in his second cervical vertebra. The man opened his mouth, gasping for air, but instantly collapsed.

We didn't hear the gunshot, or the shattering of the stained-glass window above the nave. If blood hadn't oozed from his mouth, and if that same blood hadn't started trickling down his neck, we'd have thought the priest had merely fainted. Keira screamed, Walter pushed her down and dragged her towards the church doors.

The priest was writhing, face-down, hands trembling; I stood rooted to the spot, as death overtook him. I knelt down and turned him over. His eyes were staring at the cross now, and it seemed to me that he was smiling. He turned his head and saw the pool of blood forming around him. I understood from his eyes that he wanted me to come closer.

"The hidden pyramids," he whispered with his last living breath, "the knowledge, the other text. If you find it one day, I beg you to let it sleep, it is too soon to rouse it, don't do something that can never be undone."

Those were his last words.

As I knelt there in the deserted nave, I heard Walter's voice in the distance ordering me to join him. I passed my hands over the priest's eyes to close them and picked up the text that was now stained with his blood. I left the church in a daze.

Keira was sitting on the steps in front of the church; she looked at me, trembling and unable to believe what had happened. Perhaps she was hoping I'd tell her it was all just a nightmare, that with a snap of my fingers I could bring her back to reality, but it was Walter who took charge.

"Let's get out of here, Adrian. Keira, let's go! If the killer is still in the vicinity, he won't want to leave three witnesses behind, and we're fully exposed right now!"

"If they'd wanted to kill us, we'd be dead already."

I should have kept my mouth shut – a piece of stone shattered at my feet. I grabbed Keira's arm and dragged her towards the street, with Walter following on our heels. All three of us ran until we were out of breath. A taxi sailed past the end of Coopers Lane; Walter hailed it, and the car's reversing lights came on. The driver asked us where we wanted to go and we piled in gratefully, silently thinking: *as far away from here as possible.*

Back at my place, Walter insisted I change my shirt: the one I was wearing was stained with the priest's blood, and Keira's clothes were splattered too. I steered her into the bathroom. She took off her sweater and let her trousers slide down her legs, before stepping into the shower with me. I remember washing her hair, as if trying to rinse away that feeling of being sullied that clung to our skin. She put her head against my chest, the hot water reviving our frozen bodies. Keira looked up and stared at me. Words failed me, only my hands could provide any reassurance.

Back in the living room, I offered Walter some clean clothes to change into and he disappeared upstairs.

Keira and I stared at each other, not knowing what to say.

"We've got to stop everything," whispered Keira, "the village chief, now this priest. What have we done, Adrian?"

"The priest's murder has nothing to do with you or your journey," insisted Walter, re-joining us. "He was a political refugee, and that wasn't the first time he'd been targeted. Miss Jenkins told me all about him; he spoke at conferences, fought for peace, worked for the reconciliation of ethnic communities in East Africa. Men of peace have many enemies. We just happened to be in the wrong place at the wrong time."

I suggested going to the police, our witness statements might help them in their investigation, and the perpetrators had to be caught.

"Give a witness statement about what?" asked Walter. "Did you see anything? We're not going anywhere! Your fingerprints are everywhere, Adrian, at least a hundred of the congregation would have seen us at mass, and we were the last people in the priest's company before he was killed."

"Walter's got a point," Keira continued. "We fled the scene; they'd want to know why."

"Isn't having someone firing at you reason enough?" I exploded. "If that man was under threat, why didn't the government provide some kind of protection?"

"Perhaps he didn't want it?" suggested Walter.

"And what are the police going to suspect us of? I don't see there's anything that could link us to this murder."

"I do!" whispered Keira. "I've spent a fair number of years in the priest's native Ethiopia. I've worked in border regions where his enemies live: that might be enough for the investigators to suspect me of being in contact with the people behind this crime. Plus there's the small matter of what I'm going to say, if they ask me why I left the Omo Valley so suddenly? How's it going to look when I have to explain it was the death of a village chief – who was accompanying me at the time – that forced me to flee the country? And that after returning his corpse to his tribe, I ran away like a criminal, without reporting his death to the Kenyan police? That you and I were together when that old man died, as we were when this priest was murdered? You're right, the police will lap it up! Put it this way – if we went over to the station now, I'm not sure we'd be back in time for dinner."

Everything in me wanted to deny the disastrous picture Keira and Walter were painting.

"The forensic examination will quickly establish

that the shot was fired from outside, so we've got no reason to be worried," I argued, but even I was starting to sound unconvinced.

Walter was pacing up and down, scowling. He made for my alcohol stash and poured himself a double scotch.

"Keira has listed all the reasons why you might be seen as the ideal culprits. The kind that would satisfy the authorities, so they could wrap up the investigation quickly with an outcome that would appease everybody. You'd be playing into the police's hands if they could make a quick-fire announcement about already having taken the priest's killers in for questioning; and, furthermore, about them being Europeans."

"But why, for heaven's sake? This is insane."

"To avoid unrest in the area where he lived and to prevent some kind of community uprising," Keira answered, with rather more political acumen than I had.

"Look, it's not all doom and gloom," Walter went on. "The possibility remains that we might be cleared of everything. That said, those who will go as far as killing a man of the Church are unlikely to have any scruples when it comes to witnesses; I wouldn't value our lives very highly if our faces were splashed all over the tabloids."

"And that's not viewing everything as 'doom and gloom'?"

"Not at all; if you really want a grim picture, I can talk to you about our respective careers. Take Keira —

402

add the priest's death to that of the village chief, and I don't see her going back to work in Ethiopia any time soon. As for us, Adrian, I'll leave you to imagine the reactions of the powers-that-be at the university if we were implicated in such a gruesome case. Believe me, the only thing for it is to try and forget all this and wait for a modicum of order to be re-established."

Once Walter had finished speaking, all three of us stood there, staring at each other in complete silence. Things might calm down in the end, but we knew that none of us would ever forget this dreadful morning. I only had to close my eyes to see the way the priest had looked at me as he lay dying in my arms: his expression was so peaceful as life left him. I recalled his final words: '*The hidden pyramids, the knowledge, the other text. If you find it one day, I beg you to let it sleep.*'

*

"Adrian, you're talking in your sleep."

I woke with a jolt and sat up in bed.

"I'm sorry," whispered Keira, "I didn't mean to frighten you."

"No, *I'm* sorry, I must have been having a nightmare."

"You're lucky, at least you were sleeping – I've been awake all night."

"You should've woken me earlier."

"It was nice watching you."

The bedroom was shrouded in half-shadow and felt hot and stuffy; Keira gazed on sleepily as I got up to open the window. The moonlight revealed the curves of her body; she kicked back the sheet and smiled at me.

"Come back to bed," she whispered.

Her skin tasted of salt, the smell of amber and caramel rose up from between her breasts; her belly button was so intricately formed that I loved letting my lips wander over it; my fingers stroked her stomach, and kissed it where beads of sweat had made it moist. Keira wrapped her legs around my shoulders, her feet caressing my back. She took my chin in her hand, to guide me to her mouth. We heard a starling through the window and it was as if its song was echoing our rhythm: when it fell quiet, Keira held her breath. Her arms tore themselves from mine and she pushed my body away one moment, only to cling to it even more tightly the next.

The memory of that night still haunts me as a moment of intimacy in which we were fending off death; even then, I knew that no other woman would ever embrace me like that, and it frightened me.

Day was breaking over the silent street below; Keira walked, naked, over to the window.

"We've got to leave London," she told me.

"To go where?"

"To a place where the land crumbles into the sea, to the south coast of Cornwall. Have you ever been to St Mawes?"

I confessed I hadn't.

"You said some weird things while you were asleep last night," she went on.

"I was dreaming about the priest's final words before he left us."

"He didn't leave us, he's dead! Anymore than my father '*set out on a long journey*', as the pastor said at his funeral service. Dying is the right word; the only place you'll find him is in his grave."

"When I was a kid, I used to believe that every star was a soul that shone in the sky."

"That would make for a lot of stars in your sky, if you were to count every soul since the beginning of time."

"There are hundreds of billions of stars, far more than the number of people who've ever walked the planet."

"Well, who knows, but twinkling in chilly outer space would bore me to tears."

"That's one way of looking at it. I've got no idea what's in store for us afterwards; I don't think about it very often."

"I do, all the time. It must be part of my job description. Each time I unearth some remains, I start asking myself questions. I find it hard to accept the only thing that's left after an entire lifetime is a fragment of femur or a molar."

"Bones aren't the only things we leave behind, Keira, there's also the memory of what we've been. Every time I think of my father, every time I dream of him, I tear him away from his death, like jolting someone out of sleep."

"Well, mine must have had enough of that by now," said Keira, "I don't let him sleep very often."

Keira was keen to go to Cornwall, so after lunch we slipped quietly out of the house leaving a note for Walter promising to be back soon. My old car was waiting for us in its garage, and it even started up first time; by midday, we were driving through the countryside, with the roof rolled down. Keira was singing at the top of her voice, miraculously drowning out the sound of the wind in the car.

Approaching Salisbury, we caught sight of Stonehenge's monoliths, whose massive forms stood out against the horizon.

"Have you already been there?" I asked Keira.

"What about you?"

I've got Parisian friends who've never climbed the Eiffel Tower, friends from Manhattan who've never been up the Empire State Building and, as an Englishman, I was forced to admit I'd never set foot on the ancient site which tourists the world over come to visit.

"If it's any consolation, I've never been there either," Keira confessed. "Why don't we stop and take a look?"

I knew that access to the four-thousand-year-old site was tightly controlled. During opening hours, visitors are channelled along a cordoned path, hurried by the guide's whistle; no one is allowed to stray from the official path. I strongly doubted we'd be allowed to stroll freely.

"It'll be dark soon – the sun will be setting in an hour and there isn't a soul in sight," Keira went on, clearly tickled by the thought of breaking the rules.

After our horrendous experience the day before, we were entitled to some fun – it's not every day you get shot at. I yanked the steering wheel and turned the car into the narrow track leading to the headland where the monoliths stood. A mass of barbed wire barred our way. I switched off the engine; Keira got out of the car and walked across the deserted car park.

"Come on, it's easy to get in," she called out.

To slip under the barbed-wire barrier, all we had to do was flatten ourselves against the ground. I wondered if our intrusion would set off an alarm, but I couldn't see a device installed anywhere, and there were no CCTV cameras either. In any case it was too late: Keira was waiting for me on the other side.

The site was far more impressive than I'd expected. The first enclosure of dolmens formed a circle with a diameter of one hundred and ten metres. By what miracle had men been able to build such an edifice? The plain stretched out all around us, uninterrupted by a single rock. Each dolmen in this first ring must have weighed tens of tonnes. How had they been transported here?

"The second circle measures ninety-eight metres in diameter," Keira told me. "It was plotted using string, which was extraordinary for the time. The third ring is made up of fifty-six pits, known as the Aubrey holes, all equally spaced. Charcoal and charred bones have been found there; these were probably the incineration chambers. A sort of funeral enclosure."

I stared at Keira, flabbergasted.

"How do you know all that?"

"I'm an archaeologist, remember?"

"So that means you know about every archaeological site in the world?"

"Come off it, Adrian! Everyone learns about Stonehenge at school."

"Maybe, but I don't remember half of what I was taught at school!"

"Me neither. But I can remember what I've just read on the little sign behind me. Right, let's get walking."

We headed towards the middle of the monumental structure, crossing the outer circle of blue stones. Later, I found out that it was originally made up of seventy-five monoliths of blue sandstone, with the heaviest of these monsters weighing in at fifty tonnes. The stones had been assembled as a framework, but how had the orthostates been raised upright and the lintels hoisted? We admired this prodigious feat in stunned silence. The sun was sinking, its rays sliding under the porticos. And suddenly, for a brief moment, the single dolmen lying in the middle began to glow; the light coming off it was like nothing I'd ever seen.

"Some people believe that Stonehenge was erected by Druids," said Keira.

I remembered reading articles about it in popular science magazines. Stonehenge has whetted the curiosity of all sorts of minds, and multiple theories abound, from the crackpot to the highly rational. But where did the truth lie? Here we were in the early twenty-first century, nearly four thousand eight hundred years after work on it had commenced, forty-eight centuries after the first embankments were dug, and still nobody could explain the meaning of this site; why did the men who lived here all those years ago put themselves through so much physical pain and labour to build this? How many of them had sacrificed their lives?

"Some believe there's an astrological reason behind the alignment of the stones. The positioning of the block enables the winter and summer solstices to be determined."

"Like the Nebra sky disc?" Keira asked me.

"Yes, like the Nebra sky disc," I answered dreamily, "but on a much bigger scale."

She stared up at the sky, but there were no stars to be seen that night; a thick front of cloud was rolling in from the sea. She swivelled round to face me.

"Could you repeat the priest's last words?"

"He was talking about the hidden pyramids, about another text, about someone who should be allowed to sleep... If only we could understand. But understand what? I'm buggered if I know!"

"Triangles and pyramids are similar, aren't they?" asked Keira.

"From a geometric point of view, yes."

"Don't people say that the pyramids were linked to the stars?"

"Yes, as far as the Mayan pyramids go, people talk about the Temple of the Moon and the Temple of the Sun; you're the archaeologist, you'll know better than me."

"Hmm... but the Mayan pyramids aren't hidden," she reflected.

"There are lots of archaeological sites to which astrological functions have been attributed, rightly or wrongly. Stonehenge might have been a gigantic Nebra sky disc, but it's certainly not pyramid-shaped. What we need to find out is the location of those that are still undiscovered."

"When every desert in the world's dug up," said Keira, "when every possible jungle has been searched and the depths of the oceans explored, I might be able to give you an answer."

A streak of lightning flashed through the sky and the thunder started rumbling a few seconds later.

*

Madrid

The private jet landed at Barajas Airport in the late afternoon, lining up alongside similar small aircraft on the apron. Tight-faced Vackeers was the first to alight. Lorenzo (who had come aboard during a stop-off at Rome) followed closely behind, with Sir Ashley bringing up the rear. A limousine was waiting for them in front of the terminal reserved for business jets. The car dropped them off at the town centre, and they walked into one of the twin towers of Plaza de Europa.

Isabel Marquez, codename Madrid, greeted them in a conference room with the blinds drawn down.

"Berlin and Boston will be joining us later on," she said, "and we're expecting Moscow and Rio at any moment: they ran into adverse weather conditions."

"We experienced a fair amount of turbulence ourselves," replied Sir Ashley.

He wandered over to a table laid out with refreshments, and poured himself a large glass of water.

"How many are we going to be this evening?"

"If the storm that's heading our way doesn't force the authorities to close the airport, thirteen of our friends will be gathered around this table."

"So, the operation two days ago ended in failure," sighed Lorenzo, flopping into a chair.

"Not exactly," retorted Sir Ashley, "that priest may have known more than we'd suspected."

"How did your man manage to miss his target?"

"He was two hundred metres away and aiming with infrared sights, so what can I say: *Errare humanum est.*"

"His clumsiness led to the death of a man of the Church, I find your Latin humour in bad taste. I imagine the pair you were aiming for are now fully on their guard?"

"We can't be sure about that, but for the time being we've relaxed the reins and we'll watch them from a distance."

"Why don't you just admit you've lost their trail?" Isabel Marquez interrupted Sir Ashley and Lorenzo.

"We haven't gathered here to argue but to reach a consensus on what to do next. Let's wait until everyone is present and try to work out a plan together. We have some serious decisions to reach."

"It was pointless calling this meeting, we all know what decisions need taking," grumbled Sir Ashley.

"Not everybody shares your point of view, Sir Ashley," declared the woman who'd just walked into the conference room.

"Welcome, Rio!"

Isabel stood up to greet her guest.

"Isn't Moscow with you?"

"Here I am," said Vassily, just behind Rio.

"We're not going to wait indefinitely for no-shows, are we?" griped Sir Ashley. "Let's make a start!"

"Fine, if that's the way you want it, but we won't vote on any decision without the full cell," replied Madrid.

Sir Ashley sat down at the end of the table, to the right of Lorenzo; Vassily took the place to his left and Paris occupied the next chair, with Vackeers opposite. In the half hour that followed, Berlin, Boston, Beijing, Cairo, Tel-Aviv, Athens and Istanbul joined them; the cell was complete.

Isabel began by thanking everybody for being there. The situation was sufficiently serious to justify summoning them all. Some had already met in the past to discuss this very same case; others like Rio, Tel-Aviv and Athens, were replacing their predecessors.

"Individual initiatives have backfired. We can only control our two researchers through cooperation and faultless communication."

Athens complained about this, the Heraklion incident couldn't have been foreseen. Lorenzo and Sir Ashley exchanged glances.

"I don't see that this assignment has ended in failure," stated Moscow. It wasn't a question of eliminating them at Nebra, for example, we just wanted to give them a scare."

"Could we please get back to the problem in hand," requested Isabel. "We now know that the theories of one of our colleagues – whose stubbornness in former times resulted in his being sidelined – are probably not as absurd as we first thought."

"We all wanted to believe he was wrong, because it suited us!" Berlin retorted. "If we hadn't refused him the funding he requested at the time, we wouldn't be where we are today. It would all be under control."

"Just because another fragment has popped up from goodness knows where, it doesn't mean that old nutter Ivory is right about everything," exclaimed Sir Ashley.

"Whatever the case may be, Sir Ashley," Rio fiercely objected, "nobody authorised you to make an attempt on the life of the young scientist."

"Since when does one have to ask permission to act on one's own territory and, moreover, against one of one's own nationals? Is there some new rule I've missed? If our German friends want to appeal to Moscow to intervene on their behalf, that's their business, but don't lecture me on my home soil."

"Will you please *stop*!" shouted Isabel.

"Let's stop pretending and save ourselves some time," urged Athens, standing up and eyeing the room scornfully. "We now know that there are at least two identical fragments that probably fit together. From all the evidence, and whatever Sir Ashley's views, Ivory was right. We can no longer ignore the fact that there might also be other fragments out there, but we don't know where. The situation is as follows: we can easily envisage the potential danger if these objects were to be reunited and if the world were to get an inkling of what they might reveal. On the other hand, we could learn a lot from them. Today we have within our grasp a couple of scientists who appear, and I stress *appear*, to be on the trail of the other fragments. Let's hope that despite certain regrettable incidents, they don't suspect us of spying on them. We can let them get on with their research, and it won't cost us anything. If they succeed, all we have to do is intercept them at the right moment and seize possession of their work. Are we prepared to take the risk that they might elude us, which is unlikely if we coordinate our efforts as Madrid suggests? Or would we prefer, as Sir Ashley wishes, to nip their curiosity in the bud before they go any further? And we're not just talking about the killing of two eminent scientists here. Would we rather remain in ignorance, for fear that what they might find risks jeopardising a certain world order? Will we choose the camp of those who wanted to burn Galileo?"

"The works of Galileo and Copernicus didn't have consequences on the scale of those that could be triggered by your astrophysicist and his archaeologist friend," Beijing retorted.

"None of you is in a position to deal with this, or

to prepare your country for it. We need to dissuade this pair as quickly as possible, and by whatever means," stipulated Sir Ashley.

"Athens' point is sensible and worth consideration," advocated Rio. "In the thirty years since the first fragment appeared, we've relied on guesswork. Do I have to remind you that, for a long time, we believed the fragment to be unique? Together, this astrophysicist and this archaeologist have every chance of finding some convincing evidence. We would never have had the idea of bringing together two individuals whose respective areas of expertise, though worlds apart, have proved so complementary. The idea of allowing them to carry on with their research, while keeping a close eye on their movements, seems eminently sensible to me. We're not going to be here forever. If we eliminate them, since that's what this evening's discussion is about, what do we do next? Wait for the other fragments to surface? And even if that does happen in a century or two, what difference will it really make? Wouldn't you like to belong to the generation that discovers the truth at last? Let them get on with it, we can step in when the time is right."

"I think everything has been said, let's vote now on these two motions," concluded Isabel.

"I'm sorry," Beijing interjected, "but what guarantees are we giving each other?"

"How do you mean?"

"Which of us will decide when the moment has

come to intercept our two scientists? Let's say that Ivory has foreseen everything correctly, and that there are indeed five or six fragments – who will be their keeper once they've been brought together?"

"That's a good question and one that deserves further discussion," said Cairo.

"As you're all well aware, we'll never come to an agreement on that," complained Sir Ashley, "which is yet another reason not to get involved any further in this reckless venture."

"On the contrary: for once we'll all be joined at the hip," pointed out Tel-Aviv, "with the result that if one party betrays us we'll all face the same catastrophe. If the mystery that is solved by the uniting of the fragments were to come out into the open one day, the problem would be the same in each of our countries: our stability and interests would be equally compromised, including for the person who had broken the agreement."

"I know a way of protecting us from that."

All faces at the meeting turned to Vackeers.

"Once we can actually hold the proof in our hands, I would suggest that each of the fragments be re-dispersed: one per continent. That way we know they'll never be reunited again."

It was Isabel's turn to speak.

"We need to vote, what is the motion being proposed?"

Nobody moved.

"Let me put it another way: who wants to put a

stop to the journey of our two young scientists?"

Sir Ashley raised his hand, Boston followed suit, Berlin hesitated but ended up raising his arm too; Paris also joined the yes-vote, as did Lorenzo. Vackeers sighed but didn't move.

Five votes to eight, the motion was rejected.

Sir Ashley stood up furiously and left the table.

"You think you can play at sorcerers' apprentices, but you grossly underestimate the risks you're making us take."

"Sir Ashley, are we to understand by this that you intend to go it alone?" pressed Isabel.

"I shall respect the committee's decision; my surveillance services will be at your disposal to monitor your two free radicals and, believe me, you'll need our help."

Sir Ashley stormed out of the room. Shortly after his departure, Isabel Marquez declared the meeting closed.

*

London

Keira had abandoned the idea of St Mawes. Another time, she said. We headed back to London in the middle of the night and in a sorry state. The storm had done its worst, we were soaked through, but Keira had been right about one thing: we'd had an unforgettable time at Stonehenge.

Days like that form the fabric of a relationship: a love affair is woven out of a series of moments, until one day you can begin to imagine a future together.

My house was empty, and this time it was Walter who had left us a note. He asked us to contact him as soon as we were back.

We met up with him the following day at the university. I showed Keira around and she was blown away when we visited the great library. Walter found us in there, and disclosed a troubling fact: no newspaper had reported the murder of the priest – the press appeared to be involved in some kind of a cover-up.

"I don't know what to think," said Walter, sounding serious.

"Perhaps they don't want to stir things up?"

"Have you ever known the tabloids hold back on printing anything that might sell papers?" said Walter.

"Or else the police have hushed up the affair to give their investigation a better chance."

"What I do know is that I'd pin more hope on us emerging from this unscathed if it's kept under wraps."

Keira looked at each of us in turn, and raised her hand as if asking permission to speak.

"Hasn't it occurred to you that the priest might not have been the target in the church?"

"Of course it has," Walter confirmed, "and that's the question I keep asking myself. But why would someone have such a serious grudge against you?"

"Because of my pendant!"

"That might perhaps answer why, but I still don't understand who would benefit from the crime?"

"The person who wants to get their hands on the pendant," Keira went on. "It was never the right moment to tell you about this before, but my sister's apartment was burgled. At the time, I didn't think it had anything to do with me, but now..."

"Now you're wondering if that driver in Nebra wasn't deliberately trying to run us over?"

"Let's stay calm, here," Walter intervened. "I appreciate all this is pretty unsettling, but from that to believing yourself to be the target of a burglary or concluding that someone tried to kill you... I mean, let's be reasonable!"

420

But Walter was just as rattled as we were, and only saying this to reassure us. The proof being that, not long after, he insisted we leave London, until things had "quietened down".

Keira was mesmerised by the sheer number of tomes in the college library; she walked down aisle after aisle lined with impressive titles and asked Walter for permission to take a book off the shelf.

"Why are you asking him?"

"I don't know," she teased me, "Walter seems to have more authority here than you do."

My colleague did little to hide his smugness.

I promptly sat down at a table opposite Keira, and it stirred up old memories. I grabbed a sheet from a notepad that someone had left on the table, rolled it into a ball and started chewing as loudly as I could. Then I ripped off another page. Without looking up, Keira smirked and said:

"Swallow that, I forbid you to spit it out!"

I asked her what she was reading.

"Something on the pyramids. It's a book I've never seen before."

Playing the part of the invigilator, she now looked disdainfully at both Walter and me, as if we were two impatient kids.

"Why don't you both do me a big favour, and go for a walk? You could even indulge in a bit of work if that's something you ever do, but kindly leave me in peace to read this book. Go on – I don't want to see either of you before closing time! Have I made myself clear?"

So we made ourselves scarce, as instructed.

*

Paris

A Bach partita softly filled the apartment. With a cup of tea in one hand, Ivory was playing a game of chess against himself in the sitting room. There was a ring at the door. Ivory glanced at his watch; he wasn't expecting anybody. He padded over to the door, lifted the lid off the mahogany box on the table, took out the pistol and slipped it into his dressing gown pocket.

"Who's there?" he called, standing to the side of the door.

"An old enemy."

Ivory put the pistol back in its hiding place and opened the door.

"What a surprise!"

"I was missing our games of chess, my dear friend, can I come in?"

Ivory ushered Vackeers through.

"Were you playing all by yourself?" Vackeers inquired, settling into an arm-chair opposite the chessboard.

"Yes, and so far I'm unbeatable; it's most tedious."

Vackeers moved the white bishop from c1 to g5, threatening the black knight.

Ivory promptly shifted a pawn from h7 to h6.

"What brings you here Vackeers; you didn't travel from Amsterdam just to try and take a knight off me?"

"Actually I've come from Madrid. The cell members met yesterday," replied Vackeers, taking the black knight.

"And what did they decide?" Ivory quizzed him.

The queen on d8 knocks the white bishop off f6.

"To let your two protégés continue their search, but to seize their findings when they reach their goal, if they reach it."

The white knight moves out from base to c3.

"They'll get there," Ivory commented tersely, as he nudged the pawn from b7 onto b5.

"Are you quite certain about that?"

The second white knight slides from c4 to b3.

"As certain as I am that you'll lose this game. You can't have been very pleased with the cell's decision."

The black pawn protecting the rook on a7 advances two squares.

"Don't you believe it, I was the person who convinced them. I should add that there were some around the table who'd have preferred to put a stop to these globetrotting adventures, and in a rather brutal way."

The white pawn guarding the rook moves from a2 to a3.

"Only fools never change their minds," Ivory pointed out, sliding his bishop from f8 to c5.

"Sir Ashley got a priest shot in London. It was an accident."

The white knight jumps from g1 to f3.

"An accident? They killed a priest by accident?"

A black pawn shifts from d7 to d6.

"Your astrophysicist was the real target."

White queen from d1 to d2.

"I'm appalled – and I'm referring to Sir Ashley, not your last move, though that said...!"

The black bishop glides from c8 to e6.

"I'm concerned our English friend won't abide by the Madrid resolution. I suspect he wants to act alone."

The white bishop takes his black cousin.

"You're saying that he'd go against the will of the group? That's a serious matter. I was forced into retirement for considerably less. But why have you come to tell *me* this? You should have voiced your concerns to the others!"

The black knight gobbles up the white bishop, which has unwisely ventured onto e6.

"It's just a hunch I've got; I can't openly accuse Sir Ashley without any proof. But if we have to wait around for concrete evidence, I'm afraid it'll be too late for your young archaeologist friend. Did I mention that Sir Ashley wanted to eliminate her as well?"

The white king castles.

"I've always found him offensively arrogant. So what do you want from me, Vackeers?"

Black pawn from g7 to g5.

"I don't like this tension between us. I've told you, I miss our games of chess."

Vackeers nudged a white pawn from h2 to h3.

"The game we're playing isn't of our own making, you know that and you also know how it ends. It's not so much the way you sidelined me in Amsterdam that hurt me, it's that you didn't think I'd see through your double game."

The black knight jumps from b8 to d7.

"You're leaping to hasty conclusions, my friend; if it weren't for me, we'd be rather less well-informed than we are at present."

The white knight retreats from f3 to h2.

"If our two scientists are in Sir Ashley's sights, they'll need protection; and that won't be easy, especially in England. They should be urged to leave as quickly as possible," Ivory continued, moving the black pawn guarding the second rook from h6 to h5.

"After what they've just experienced, it's going to be difficult to lure them out of their hiding place."

Vackeers advanced his white pawn from g2 to g3.

"I know a way of making them leave London," said Ivory, moving his king.

"And how do you plan to proceed?"

Now it's the white king's turn to move. The black pawn on d6 advances to d5 in preparation for an attack.

"You still haven't told me what made you change your mind," said Ivory, staring at Vackeers. "Up until very recently, you'd have pulled out all the stops to ensure they never got any further."

"Not to the point of killing two innocents, Ivory – that's not my style."

White pawn from f2 to f3.

"You're not motivated by saving a couple of lives, Vackeers; I want to hear what's really on your mind."

Black knight retreats from d7 to f8.

"Like you, Ivory, I'm getting old and I'm ready to find out now. The desire to understand has finally got the better of my fears. Yesterday, in the course of our meeting, Rio asked whether we wanted to be counted among those who will get to know the truth, or whether we'll choose to leave that discovery to future generations. Rio's got a point, the truth will come out in the end – whether tomorrow or in a hundred years' time, what difference does it make? I don't want to be part of the old guard, standing in the way of progress," Vackeers admitted.

The white knight retreats from c3 to e2. The black knight launches into a new offensive and ends up next to its queen.

"If you really do know how to protect this astro-physicist and his archaeologist friend, then go ahead, Ivory, but act now," urged Vackeers, sliding a white pawn forward from c2 to c3.

The black rook shoots from a8 to g8.

"Her name is Keira."

Vackeers moved a pawn from d3 to d4.

The black bishop withdraws from c5 to b6. A white

pawn devours a black pawn on e5. The black queen immediately exacts her revenge, destroying the piece that has dared venture too close to her.

For the next twenty-three moves neither Ivory nor Vackeers uttered a word.

"If you're prepared to concede there might actually be something to my theories, and if you'll agree to do what I tell you, then together we might stand a chance against Sir Ashley and his lunatic plans."

Ivory picked up his rook and triumphantly positioned it on h4.

"Checkmate, Vackeers! But you knew that from the fifth move."

Ivory stood up and went to fetch the Ge'ez text from one of his desk drawers; he'd finished translating it in the small hours.

*

London

Keira hadn't budged from the college library. We went to find her so we could all go out to dinner, but she wanted us to leave her in peace to finish her reading. She barely bothered to look up as she waved us away.

"Why don't you two enjoy a boys' dinner? I've got work to do, go on, clear off!"

Walter tried to explain that it was closing time, but she didn't care; so my colleague had to appeal to the security guard on night-duty to let Keira stay and read for as long as she wanted. She promised to join me at home later on.

By five o'clock in the morning, she still wasn't back. Alarm bells were starting to ring for me, so I went to get my car. The college entrance hall was empty and the security guard was snoozing in his booth, but came to with a jolt when I appeared. Keira wouldn't have been able to leave the premises because the entrance gates were locked and, without a pass, she couldn't open them. I almost ran down the corridor to the great library, with the security guard on my heels.

Keira didn't even notice I was there; I watched her through the glass doors, totally absorbed in what she was reading. From time to time, she scribbled something in a notebook. I coughed to let her know I was there: she looked up at me and smiled.

"Is it late?" she wondered, stretching.

"Or early, depending which way you look at it. The sun's just up."

"I'm starving," she declared, closing her book.

Keira tidied up her notes, put the book back in its place on the shelf and, linking arms with me, asked me to take her out for breakfast.

There's a fairy-tale quality to crossing a city in the silence of early morning. We passed a milk float just setting off on its rounds. Not everything had changed in London, after all.

I parked in Primrose Hill. The metal shutters of a tea-room had just gone up and the proprietor was putting the tables out on the terrace. She took our order.

"So... what was so fascinating about that book, for you to be absorbed in it all night?"

"I remembered that the priest hadn't talked to you about pyramids to be unearthed but *hidden pyramids*, which isn't the same thing. I was curious and consulted several works on the subject."

"Sorry, but I'm not sure I get the difference."

"There are three places in the world where pyramids might be hidden: some temples were discovered and instantly forgotten about in Central America (they're overgrown again now); in Bosnia, satellite pictures have revealed the presence of pyramids – we still don't know who built them or why; and in China, well, that's a whole other story."

"There are pyramids in China?"

"Hundreds of them. They were completely unknown to the western world until around 1910. Most of them are to be found in Shaanxi Province, within a radius of a hundred kilometres around the ancient city of Xi'an. The first were discovered in 1912 by Fred Meyer Schroder and Oscar Maman; others were found in 1913 by the members of the Segalen Mission. In 1945, a United States Air Force pilot who was flying from India to China took an aerial photo, as he crossed over the Qinling mountains, of what he called the white pyramid. No one's ever been able to locate it with any degree of accuracy, but it would be much bigger than the Great Pyramid of Giza. An article about it was published in the *New York Sunday News* in spring 1947.

Unlike their Mayan and Egyptian cousins, the Chinese pyramids aren't built out of stone, for the most part, but from earth and clay. We do know that they were used as burial places for emperors and the families of great dynasties, like in Egypt. The pyramids have always fascinated people; they've given rise to any number of far-fetched theories. For thousands of years, they were the greatest edifices built on earth –

whether we're talking about the Red Pyramid at the Necropolis of Dahshur on the west bank of the Nile, or the Giza Pyramid, the only one of the seven wonders of the Ancient World that still exists. But there is one problem: the most important pyramids were all built at around the same time, without anybody understanding how civilisations that were so far apart from each other managed to replicate such a similar architectural model."

"Maybe people travelled more at that time than we imagine," I suggested.

"Well, what you're saying might not be so far-fetched. While I was in the library, I consulted an article in the *Encyclopaedia Britannica* of 1911. The links between Egypt and Ethiopia go back to the twenty-second dynasty of the Pharaohs; from the twenty-fifth dynasty, the two countries were even placed under the same authority; the capital of the two empires was situated in Napata, in the north of what is now Sudan. The first accounts of relations between Ethiopia and Egypt are even older. Three thousand years ago, merchants wrote about the Land of Punt, which occupied an area south of Nubia. The first known journey to Punt took place during the reign of the Pharaoh Sahure. But, get this, frescos from the fifteenth century BC found in the sanctuary of Deir el-Bahari, depict a group of nomads bringing back incense, gold, ivory, ebony and, above all, myrrh; which leads us to suppose that trade with Ethiopia goes back to the earliest Egyptian times."

"What's all this got to do with your Chinese pyramid?"

"I'm coming to that. What we're trying to establish here is whether there's a relationship between this manuscript and my pendant. Our ancient Ge'ez text refers to the pyramids. Remember the third sentence: *Let no one know where the zenith is, the night of one is guardian of the prelude.* As Max told us, it's not about translating this literally but rather interpreting the text. The word 'prelude' might mean the 'origin'; which gives us this instead: *Let no one know where the zenith is, the night of one is guardian of the origin.*"

"It sounds nicer, but I'm afraid I still can't see what you're driving at."

"We found my pendant in the middle of a lake a few kilometres from the disputed Ilemi Triangle, in the Land of Punt, which, as I just mentioned, bordered what is now Ethiopia, Kenya, and the Sudan. Do you know what the Egyptians called Punt?"

I didn't have a clue. Keira looked at me triumphantly and moved in closer.

"They called it '*Ta Neteru*' which means 'Land of the Gods', or 'country of origin'. It is also in the region of the Blue Nile, where the source of the Nile is; all you have to do is travel downriver to arrive at the first and oldest of the Egyptian pyramids – the Pyramid of Djoser – at Saqqara. My pendant may have reached the middle of Lake Turkana via that navigable route. Right, now back to China, which I spent the second half of the night reading up on. If that American pilot's report is genuine (and the white pyramid's existence is still disputed), then the pyramid he photographed would have risen to more than three hundred metres, making it the tallest in the world."

"Are you saying you want us to make a trip to the Qinling Mountains in China?"

"That may be what the Ge'ez text is suggesting. The hidden pyramids... Central America, Bosnia or China? It's a gamble, a one in three chance, and I'd go for the highest of the lot! But what you have to remember is that thirty-three percent is already enormous for a researcher – plus, I trust my intuition."

I was struggling to get to grips with Keira's sudden change of tack. Not long ago, she was constantly reminding me of how much she missed Ethiopia. I knew how much willpower it had taken for her not to call Eric. As the days went by, I grew to dread the moment when she'd inform me that everything had returned to normal in the Omo Valley, and that she'd be setting off again. And yet here she was suggesting that we travel even further away from her beloved Africa and her excavations.

I should have been overjoyed at the prospect of a trip to China with her, but in fact it worried me on many fronts.

"You do realise we'll be looking for a needle in a haystack, and a haystack the size of China!"

"What's got into you, Adrian? You don't have to

come, you know; if you'd rather teach your nice students, then by all means stay in London, I'll understand, at least you've got a life here."

"What does that mean, *at least I've got a life here?*"

"It means that I spoke to Eric on the phone yesterday: the Ethiopian police came to the camp and if I set foot there right now, it would be to answer a summons to appear before a judge. So, thanks to my impulsively joining you on that little trip to Lake Turkana, I've been driven away from my own excavations for the second time in less than a year! I don't have a job anymore, I've got nowhere to go, and in a few months I'll have to report back to the Walsh Foundation which has entrusted me with a fortune to find something in Ethiopia. What's the alternative? Stay in London, doing whatever shitty job I can get while I wait for you to come home from work?"

"You were burgled in Paris, our room was raided in Germany, a priest was mown down before our eyes, and don't tell me you haven't done some soul-searching as to the causes of the village chief's death. Don't you think we've both had enough trouble since we became interested in your pendant? What if you'd been the one who got a bullet in the neck, or if the driver in Nebra hadn't messed up?"

"I've chosen a dangerous career Adrian; I'm constantly having to take risks. Do you think the people who discovered Lucy's skeleton had a map of the cemetery, or that the right GPS coordinates just

435

dropped out of the sky? Of course not! Instinct, that's what defines discoverers: they've got a nose for it, like the best detectives."

"But you're not a detective, Keira."

"You do what you like, Adrian, I'll go on my own if you've got cold feet. Do you have any idea how important it would be, if we managed to prove my pendant was really four hundred million years old? Do you understand the implications? It would turn everything on its head! I'd be prepared to search through every haystack on Earth to find out, given half a chance. Remember, you're the one who first suggested factoring in an extra three hundred and eighty-five million years in the quest for our origins. And now you want me to throw in the towel? Would you give up on the chance to witness the moment the Universe was created, just because the telescope through which you could glimpse that magical mo-ment was a bit inaccessible? You nearly died at an al-titude of five thousand metres, trying to get a closer view of your stars! But if you want to stay in your safe, rainy little life, I guess that's your choice. All I ask is that you help me out: I don't have the means to finance this trip, but I promise to pay you back every last penny one day."

I didn't say anything because I was furious; furious with myself at having dragged her into this business in the first place, furious at feeling guilty about her losing her job, and powerless in the face of the dangers I sensed closing in on us. How many times have I gone back over that horrible shouting match? I must have cast my mind back a hundred times to the moment when I was terrified of losing her because I risked disappointing her. And today I feel even more furious with myself at having been so cowardly.

In need of a friend, I went to see Walter. If I couldn't dissuade Keira from undertaking this trip, perhaps he'd find a way to make her listen to reason. But this time he refused to help me out. In fact, he seemed positively happy we were getting out of London. At least, he told me, nobody would think of looking for us in China. He added that he thought Keira's viewpoint was entirely justified, and even asked whether I'd lost all taste for adventure. Hadn't I taken unnecessary risks in the Atacama...? They were ganging up on me, now.

"Yes, but I was the one running those risks, not her!"

"Stop playing at being the knight in shining armour, Adrian. Keira's a big girl: before she knew you she was living on her own in the middle of Africa, surrounded by lions, tigers, leopards and heaven knows what other beasts. So this 'I'm so worried' act is all well and good coming from your mother, but in a man of your age it is – how can I put it – a bit ridiculous, old chap!"

I booked our flights. The agency Walter recommended to me (the one that had done such a great job on his trip to Greece) warned us that it would take at least ten days to get our visas. I was hoping this stay of execution would give Keira time to change her mind, but in fact we received a call two days later; we were in luck, the Chinese embassy had already dealt with our applications, and our passports awaited us. We were on our way.

*

London

The meal was drawing to an end and Vackeers had enjoyed a pleasant lunch in his colleague's company. He did wonder if he hadn't committed a culinary *faux pas* by taking his guest out to a Chinese restaurant, but then again it was supposed to be one of the best in London, and Beijing seemed to have tucked in with gusto.

"We'll carry out close but discreet surveillance," he assured Vackeers. "The others have nothing to worry about, we're highly efficient."

Vackeers had no doubts about that. As a young man, he had spent a few years working on the Burmese border, and knew from first-hand experience that Chinese discretion was far from being a myth. When their commandos made an incursion into foreign territory, nobody heard them arrive or leave – their victims' bodies were the only sign they'd paid their neighbours a visit.

"The funny thing is," said Beijing, "that I'll be on the same plane as our two scientists. When they go through customs, their luggage will be checked (a mere formality, and all perfectly friendly) but it will allow us to plant bugging devices in some of their belongings. We've rigged the satnav in the hire car that they'll be picking up on arrival. Have you done the necessary on your side?"

"Sir Ashley was only too happy to help out," Vackeers explained. "I hadn't realised just how worried he is about this operation – he'd steal the crown jewels if that was the surest way not to lose the trail of our two scientists. Things will proceed as follows: the security gates at Heathrow will be set to the highest sensitivity levels; to get through without setting off all the alarms, the astrophysicist will have to put all his personal belongings on the X-ray conveyorbelt; while he's being frisked by a particularly thorough officer, Sir Ashley's men will tamper with his watch."

"What about the archaeologist? Isn't there a chance that she'll smell a rat?"

"We'll make sure she's distracted. As soon as they've been fitted up, Sir Ashley will provide you with the transmitter frequency, which I have to say worries me somewhat, because it means he'll have access to them as well."

"Rest assured, Amsterdam; those kinds of devices are short-range. Sir Ashley may have the means to bribe all the personnel he wants to on British soil, but as soon as the pair reach my country, I doubt he'll be able to find out anything much. You can count on us:

440

reports on their activities will come through on a daily basis to the cell as a whole, without Sir Ashley getting a first look."

Vackeers' mobile phone emitted two high-pitched beeps. He read the text message and apologised to his guest; he had another meeting to attend.

Vackeers leaped into a taxi and asked for South Kensington. The car dropped him off at Bute Street, in front of the French Bookshop. On the pavement opposite, just as his informant had said, a young woman was drinking a coffee outside a delicatessen and reading *Le Monde*.

Vackeers sat down at the next table, ordered a tea and opened up a copy of *The Economist*. He stayed there for a short while, paid for his drink and then stood up, leaving his magazine on the table.

Keira happened to notice, grabbed the magazine and called out to the man who was heading off, but he had already turned the corner of the street. Vackeers had kept his promise to Ivory and would be flying back to Amsterdam that evening.

As she put the magazine back down on the table, Keira noticed a letter sticking out of it. She gently pulled at it and was shocked to find her name on the envelope.

My dear Keira,
Forgive me for not handing you this note myself, but for reasons too tedious to explain it is best if we are not seen together. I am not writing to alarm you

in any way; quite the opposite, in fact, I wish to congratulate you and to provide you with some news which I think you will be rather pleased about. I am delighted to learn that the fascinating legend of Tikkun Olam, which I discussed with you in my office, has aroused your interest at last. I know that when we talked in Paris, you must have had occasion to think I was too old still to be of sound mind. Deeply as I regret the events that have taken place over the past few weeks, they may at least have the advantage of making you revise your opinion of me.

I promised you some good news, here it is. I believe that you have come across a very ancient text; I was already aware of its existence, as it happens, but it is thanks to you and your pendant that I have finally been able to make some progress in understanding the writing which, for a long time, eluded me. I am still transcribing it even now. On which subject, the document in your possession is incomplete, there is a line missing; it was removed from the manuscript. I found the original traces of it in a very ancient Egyptian library, when I was reading a translation which I shall spare you, since it was not very good. Although I cannot be by your side, much as I would like to be, I shall not be able to resist giving you a helping hand every time it is within my power to do so.

The missing sentence is as follows: 'The lion sleeps on the stone of knowledge.'

All this is a mystery, is it not? It is the same for

me. But my instincts tell me this information might be very valuable to you one day. There are plenty of sleeping lions at the feet of pyramids – don't forget that some of them are wilder than others, more enamoured of their freedom, and that the most solitary live far from the pride... But I realise I am not telling you anything new: with your knowledge of Africa, you are used to lions. Take good care, dear friend, you are not alone in your enthusiasm for the Tikkun Olam legend. And even if it is only a legend... some dreams, often the most far-fetched ones, can lead to the most surprising discoveries. Have a wonderful journey. I am so pleased you are embarking on it.

With my endless devotion,

Ivory

PS: You must not tell anyone about this letter, not even those close to you. Memorize its contents and then destroy it.

Keira did as Ivory had instructed. She re-read the letter twice and didn't tell anybody about it, not even me, or at least, not until long afterwards. But instead of destroying it, she put it in her pocket.

I can remember that Friday as if it were yesterday. We said our farewells to Walter and boarded our long-haul flight for Beijing, setting off at 8.35pm.

Getting through security was a nightmare. I found myself swearing I'd avoid travelling from Heathrow at all costs from now on and Keira was equally furious at the way we were being treated by the overzealous staff. Thankfully, I managed to calm her down just before we were threatened with a strip search.

The flight took off on time and once we'd reached cruising altitude Keira finally began to relax. I decided to use the ten-hour flight to try and learn a few words of vocabulary that would help me with the basics: *hello*, *goodbye*, *please* and *thank you*... Hello to whom, thank you for what, I had no idea. But I gave up on my fast-track Mandarin lessons fairly quickly and reverted to reading matter more in keeping with my usual tastes.

"What's the book?" Keira asked me, mid-flight.

I showed her the cover and recited the title: *A Treatise on Particle Emissions at the Periphery of Galaxies*.

I wasn't quite sure what to make of her "mmm".

"What?"

"Looks like a real page-turner," she remarked, "I bet the film'll be even better. Do you reckon they'll make the sequel...?"

She turned her back and switched off her overhead reading light.

*

Beijing

We landed in the early afternoon, feeling pretty jet-lagged. The formalities at customs were relatively smooth: just a routine check carried out by officials who were a lot more pleasant to deal with than their counterparts back at Heathrow. With the help of the travel agency in London, I'd managed to book the Chinese equivalent of a 4x4. The contract had already been made out in our names at the airport car-hire counter, and a brand new vehicle was waiting for us in the car park.

Given that all the street names were written in Chinese (making them illegible for most westerners) it was lucky our car was fitted with satnav. I punched in the address of the hotel where I'd reserved a room; all I had to do was follow the little arrow that would guide me to the town centre.

The traffic was heavy. Suddenly, the walls of the Forbidden City loomed on our right. A bit further on our left, the Monument to the People's Heroes rose up, and further away still Tiananmen Square evoked sad memories. We had just passed the dome of the National Theatre, whose modern architecture stood out in the urban landscape.

"Are you feeling wiped out?" Keira asked me.

"Not too bad actually," I replied. The thrill of being in this legendary place had given me a second wind.

"Then why don't we carry on towards Xi'an?"

I was impatient as she was, but we had a thousand-kilometre drive ahead of us; a decent night in Beijing would do us no harm. And we couldn't be *this* close to the Forbidden City and not visit it. We had a brief stop-off at our hotel to change clothes. From our bedroom, I could hear the water running in the bathroom where Keira was taking a shower and just the sound of it suddenly made me feel happy, washing away the worries that had nearly prevented me from setting out on this trip together in the first place.

"Are you still there?" she called out.

"Yes, why?"

"No reason..."

I was frightened of us getting lost in the maze of streets that all looked so alike. A taxi dropped us off in Jingshan Park: I'd never seen such a beautiful rose garden; in front of us, a stone bridge arched across a lake. Like a hundred other tourists before us that day, we crossed it, and like a hundred other tourists we walked along the park's paths and alleyways. Keira took my arm.

"I'm so glad to be here," she said.

If I could freeze time, I would stop it at that precise moment. If we could rewind the clock, that's where I'd go back to: a path in Jinghsan Park by a white rose bush.

We entered the Forbidden City by the North Gate. I'd have to fill more than a hundred pages of this notebook to describe all the beautiful things that met our eyes: the ancient pavilions, where so many dynasties had succeeded each other, the imperial garden where the courtesans had strolled in times gone by, the Temple of Heaven, those dementedly curved roofs on which golden dragons appeared to be nosing around, or the bronze herons staring at the sky, frozen there for all eternity, as well as marble staircases carved as intricately as lace. A very elderly Chinese couple, sitting on a bench near a tall tree, were having a fit of giggles about something; we had no idea what, but their mirth was infectious.

I like to think they still go back to that bench in the middle of the Forbidden City and that they're still there laughing conspiratorially together.

By now, exhaustion really had got the better of us. Keira could barely stand up, and I wasn't much better. We headed back to the hotel.

We slept like babies. Then, after a hasty breakfast, we left Beijing. The road ahead was long and I doubted that a day would be enough to complete the journey.

As the city gave way to countryside, the plain

looked as if it stretched on forever; and the mountains, which we could make out on the horizon, didn't seem to be getting any closer. We'd put three hundred kilometres behind us; from time to time we passed through industrial towns that had sprung up in the middle of nowhere, making a change to the monotonous landscape. We stopped at Shijiazhuang to fill up with gas. At the service station, Keira bought a sandwich that bore a passing resemblance to a hotdog, except that the sausage was unidentifiable. I refused to try it, but Keira swallowed each mouthful with what I suspected was exaggerated relish. Fifty kilometres later, by which time my passenger had dramatically changed colour, I pulled up on the hard shoulder as a matter of urgency. Bent double, Keira rushed behind a bush. When she got back into the car ten minutes later, I didn't dare say a word.

Keira drove from there, to take her mind off feeling sick. By the time we reached Yangquan, we'd covered four hundred kilometres. Spotting what looked to be a deserted small stone village on the top of a hill, Keira pleaded to leave the road and follow the dirt track leading up to it. I'd had enough of the asphalt road by then, and it was high time the four-wheel drive was put through its paces.

A battered path got us as far as the entrance to the hamlet. Keira had been right, nobody lived there any more: most of the houses were in ruins, though some had kept their roofs. The lugubrious atmosphere was thoroughly uninviting, but Keira was already exploring the ancient streets; I had no choice but to follow her through that ghost village. In the middle of what must once have been the main square, we came across a water trough and a wooden edifice, which seemed to have weathered the onslaughts of time better. Keira sat down on its steps.

"What is this?" I asked.

"An ancient Confucian temple. Confucius had numerous disciples throughout ancient China; his wisdom guided many generations."

"Shall we go in?" I suggested.

Keira stood up and went over to the door. A gentle push and it opened.

"Yep, we're going in!" she answered.

Inside, it was empty: a few stones lay scattered on the weed-infested ground.

"What do you think happened for the village to be deserted like this?"

"The water source ran dry or an epidemic wiped out the inhabitants, I don't know. This site must be at least a thousand years old. What a shame to have left it in this state."

Keira noticed a small square of earth at the back of the temple. She knelt down and started digging carefully with her bare hands. With her right hand she extracted stones, sweeping them to the side with her left hand. I could have been reciting Confucius's precepts verbatim, and she still wouldn't have paid me the slightest bit of notice.

"What are you doing?"

Marc Levy

"You're about to find out."

And suddenly, the fine curves of a bronze bowl emerged from the earth she'd been raking. Keira changed positions; sitting cross-legged, she spent nearly an hour rescuing the bowl from the dry silt that imprisoned it. And then, as if by magic, she lifted it up and gave it to me.

"There you go," she said, clearly chuffed to pieces.

I was blown away, not only by the object's sheer beauty, caked in earth as it still was, but by the magical way in which it had surfaced from oblivion.

"How did you do that? How did you know it would be there?"

"I've got a knack for finding needles in haystacks," she told me, getting to her feet, "even when those haystacks are in China. Handy, eh?"

I had to badger her for a long time before she agreed to reveal her secret. In the place where Keira had started digging, the grass was shorter, there was less vegetation, and it wasn't as green as elsewhere.

"That's generally what happens when an object is buried in the ground," she confided in me.

Keira dusted off the bowl.

"Well, this certainly wasn't made yesterday," she remarked, putting it down gently on a stone.

"Are you leaving it here?"

"It doesn't belong to us, it's part of the history of the people from this village. Someone'll find it and they'll do as they see fit with it; come on, we've got other haystacks to search!"

At Linfen the landscape changed; the city was one of the ten most polluted in the world, and the air suddenly turned a shade of amber as a foul-smelling toxic cloud darkened the sky. I thought back to those crystal clear nights in the Atacama: could these two places belong to the same planet? It was crazy to see the extent to which humans had destroyed nature and I wondered which environment, the Atacama or Linfen, would win out. We had closed the windows; but Keira still kept coughing and the road ahead went blurry because my eyes were stinging.

"This stuff really stinks!" complained Keira, promptly bursting into another coughing fit.

She'd turned to face the backseat, where she was rummaging in her bag for some cotton clothing to fashion makeshift masks; suddenly, she let out a yelp.

"What's the matter?"

"Oh nothing, I just caught myself on something in the lining of my bag; I guess it must be a needle or a staple or something."

"Are you bleeding?"

"A bit," she admitted, still leaning over her bag.

I was driving and the visibility was so poor I had to keep both hands on the steering wheel.

"Look in the glove compartment, there's a first aid kit in there, you should find some plasters."

Keira opened the compartment, got out the first aid kid and extracted a small pair of scissors.

"Are you really hurt?"

"No, I'm fine, but I want to know what on earth

pricked me like that. I paid a small fortune for this bag!"

She proceeded to contort her body in a crazy gymnastic routine as she searched the lining of her bag.

"Have you found it?" I inquired, when her knees started poking me in the ribs.

"I'm unstitching."

"Unstitching what?"

"This bloody lining! Now shut up and drive."

"What the hell is *that*?" I heard Keira muttering to herself.

She scrambled back into her seat clutching a small metallic brooch, which she waved at me victoriously.

"It's a needle!" she exclaimed.

It looked like a sort of lapel pin, except that it was grey and dull and bore no logo.

Keira inspected it more closely and I saw her turn pale.

"What's the matter?"

"Nothing," she replied, but the look on her face told another story. "It's probably some kind of bag-making tool that accidentally got left behind inside the lining."

Keira signalled that I should keep quiet and park up on the side of the road as soon as possible.

Leaving the outskirts of Linfen behind, the road began to wind as we headed up the mountainside. Once we'd reached an altitude of three hundred metres, the layer of pollution fell away and abruptly, as if we'd pierced a cloud, we saw something resembling blue sky once again.

Pulling out of a bend, we noticed a small parking area where I could stop. Keira left the small badge on the dashboard, got out of the car and signalled for me to follow her.

"You're behaving weirdly," I told her, catching up.

"I'll tell you what's weird, and that's finding a goddam bugging device in my bag."

"A what?"

"That's no needle, it's a microphone; believe me I know what I'm talking about."

I didn't have much experience when it came to spying, but I found what she was telling me hard to believe.

"Right, we're going to go back into the car now: take a closer look and you'll be able to see for yourself."

Keira was right: it was indeed a tiny transmitter. To discuss the situation away from twitching ears, we got out of the car again.

"Why would anyone plant a microphone in my bag?" said Keira.

"How about the Chinese authorities are greedy for information on foreigners travelling through their territory?" I suggested. "For all we know this could be standard tourist procedure."

"There must be millions of visitors who come to China every year. Are you seriously telling me they'd put that many microphones into people's luggage?"

"How should I know? Maybe they bug tourists at random."

"Oh come off it! If that was the case, we wouldn't be the first to find out about it, and the western media would've blown their cover."

"It could be a relatively recent development."

I said that to reassure her, but the fact was I found the situation every bit as strange and disturbing as she did. I tried to remember the conversations we'd had in the car, but couldn't recall anything compromising; apart, perhaps, from Keira's remarks about the filthy, stinking industrial towns we'd passed through, not to mention her comments on the dodgy food she'd eaten at midday.

"Well, now that we've found this wretched thing, we can ditch it and carry peacefully on our way," I suggested.

"No, let's keep it with us. All we've got to do is say the opposite of what we're thinking, lie about the direction we're taking and, that way, we'll fox whoever's spying on us."

"Excuse me, but what about our privacy?"

"Adrian, please don't go all English on me. We'll take a good look at your bag this evening: if they've bugged mine, I bet they've done the same with yours."

I hurried back to the car, tipped out the paltry contents of my luggage directly into the boot, and flung the bag as far away as I could. Then I got back behind the steering wheel and tossed the bugging device out of the window.

"I don't like the idea of some randy Chinese secret

service agent Stasi getting off on listening to me telling you how much I love your breasts!"

I started the engine before Keira had time to say a word.

"You like my breasts?"

"Yup!"

We drove the next fifty kilometres in complete silence.

"But what if I had to have a breast removed one day, or even both of them?"

"In that case, I'd start fantasising about your belly-button; I never said I *only* liked your breasts!"

We drove a further fifty kilometres without speaking.

"You could draw up a list of things you like about me," Keira said coyly.

"I could, but not now."

"When?"

"When the time's right."

"And when might that be?"

"When I feel like drawing up a list of things I like about you!"

Night was beginning to fall, and I could feel tiredness getting the better of me. The satnav indicated that we still had over a hundred kilometres to go before reaching Xi'an. My eyelids were drooping and I was struggling to stay awake. Keira was already out for the count, with her head against the window. The car swerved slightly round a bend. It only takes a moment's inattention to throw your life away, and I valued my passenger's life too much to take any risks. Whatever we'd set out to find, it could wait another night. I parked up on the side of a track that met our road, switched off the engine and instantly fell asleep.

*

London

A dark blue Jaguar crossed Westminster Bridge, skirting Parliament Square, passing HM Treasury and turning off towards St James's Park. The driver parked up alongside a bridle path and the passenger stepped out, continuing on foot into the park.

Sir Ashley sat down on a bench opposite a lake where a pelican was drinking. A young man approached and sat down beside him.

"What's the news?" inquired Sir Ashley.

"They spent the first night in Beijing and are now a hundred and fifty kilometres away from Xi'an, which is where they seem to be headed. They were presumably sleeping when I left the office to come and join you; the car hasn't moved for more than two hours."

"It's five o'clock here which makes it ten at night there, so that's plausible. Have you found out what they're planning to do in Xi'an?"

"We don't know anything for the time being. They've mentioned a white pyramid once or twice."

"That explains why they're in that province, but I doubt they'll find it."

"So what's all that about?"

"Oh, some figment of an American pilot's imagination; our satellites never found the pyramid in question. Do you have anything else for me?"

"The Chinese have lost two transmitters."

"What do you mean *lost*?"

"They've stopped working."

"Do you suppose they found them?"

"It's possible, Sir Ashley, but our contact on the ground believes it's more likely to be a technical fault. I hope to have more information tomorrow."

"Are you going back to the office?"

"Indeed."

"Send a message to Beijing on my behalf. Thank him and tell him that silence is still the order of the day. He'll understand. Kindly activate the protocols for an imminent departure to China; if I deem it necessary to go, I'd prefer us to be prepared."

"Should I cancel your appointments for the week?"

"Certainly not!"

The young man took his leave of Sir Ashley and walked off down the path.

Sir Ashley called his butler and asked him to pack a suitcase. It was to contain the wherewithal for a two- to three-day trip.

*

Province of Shaanxi

Someone was knocking on the car window. I woke with a start to see the face of an old man smiling at me in the dark, a bundle on his shoulder. When I lowered the window, the man put his hands together and laid his cheek on them, by which I understood he wanted me to let him into our car. It was cold, the walker was shivering and I thought back to that Ethiopian who had shown me such hospitality when I'd stepped off the light aircraft at Jinka and found myself all alone. So I opened the passenger door and pushed our belongings onto the car floor. The man thanked me and settled down on the back seat. He opened up his bundle and offered to share his supper of biscuits with me. I took one, more to please him than anything. We couldn't use words to communicate, but looks were enough. He gave me another biscuit for Keira who was fast asleep, so I put it on the dashboard in front of her. The man seemed content. Having shared his meagre meal, he stretched out and closed his eyes; I did likewise.

The pallid light of day woke me first. Keira stretched and I signalled for her not to make any noise: we had a guest sleeping on the back seat.

"Who is he?" she whispered.

"Haven't got a clue. Probably a beggar – he was walking along this track, and it was a freezing night."

"You did the right thing giving him the guest bedroom. Where are we?"

"In the middle of nowhere, and a hundred fifty kilometres from Xi'an."

"I'm hungry," Keira announced.

I pointed to the biscuit. She took it hesitantly and sniffed it, before wolfing it down.

"I'm still ravenous," she declared, "I could do with a shower and some breakfast."

"It's very early, but we'll find somewhere to pick up food along the way."

The man woke up. He unrumpled his clothes and greeted Keira by putting both hands together. She greeted him in the same way.

"You idiot, he's a Buddhist monk," she told me. "He must be making a pilgrimage."

Keira made an effort to communicate with our passenger, and they exchanged a multitude of signs. Keira turned round to face me, pleased with herself – though I wasn't sure what about.

"Get driving, we'll drop him off."

"You mean he's given you the address of where he's going and you've understood straight off?"

"Trust me, drive up this track..."

The 4x4 lurched and jolted towards the crest of
the hill. The countryside was stunning, but Keira
seemed to be on the lookout for something else. The
track forked at the top of the ridge, heading back
down towards pine and larch trees; as we emerged
from the woods, it petered out altogether. Our back
passenger signalled for me to switch off the engine:
we would have to go on foot from here. At the end
of a footpath we came across a stream, which the
man indicated we should follow. A hundred metres
further on we reached some stepping stones. We
crossed the stream and climbed the slopes of another
hill from where the roof of a monastery suddenly appeared before us. Six monks came out to greet us.
They bowed before our guide and invited us to follow them.

We were taken into a huge room with white walls
and no furniture; there were just a few rugs covering
the earth floor. They brought us tea, rice and *mantous* –
little steamed buns.

After laying out these offerings the monks retired,
leaving Keira and myself alone.

"Would you mind telling me what we're doing
here?" I whispered.

"We wanted some breakfast, didn't we?"

"I was thinking more along the lines of a restaurant than a monastery."

Our guide came back into the room. He had shed
his old rags and was now wearing a long toga belted
with a finely embroidered red silk scarf. The six

monks who'd welcomed us were also in tow and sat down, cross-legged, behind him.

"Thank you for giving me a lift," he said, bowing his head.

"You didn't tell us you spoke perfect French!" gasped an astounded Keira.

"I don't recall saying anything at all last night, or this morning for that matter. I have travelled the world and studied your language," he told Keira. "What are you looking for here?"

"We're tourists and we're visiting the region," I replied.

"Is that so? Well, Shaanxi province is teeming with undiscovered treasures. There are over a thousand temples in this region. And this is a good season for tourists. The winters are terribly harsh here: the snow may look pretty, but it does complicate life. You are welcome as our guests. A washroom is at your disposal. My disciples have laid out mats for you in the room next door. Do rest and make the most of this day; a meal will be served at noon. I shall meet up with you again later, but I must leave you now, I need to report on my journey and to meditate."

The man withdrew, and the other monks stood up and left with him.

"Do you think he's their boss?" I asked Keira.

"I don't think that's the right word for it; hierarchy is more spiritual among the Buddhists."

"He just seemed like a simple beggar going along the road."

"Asceticism is one of the characteristics of these monks: their only possession is thought."

After freshening up, we went for a walk in the surrounding countryside. We stood under a willow tree where we were both lulled by the gentleness of a timeless place far from civilisation.

The day took its course. When dusk fell, I pointed out the stars to Keira as they appeared in the sky. Our monk joined us again and came to sit nearby.

"So, you're keen on the stars," he commented.

"How did you know?"

"Simple observation. At dusk, people generally watch the sun setting, but your eyes are already raised to the sky. It is a discipline that also fascinates me. It is hard to take the path towards wisdom without thinking about the greatness of the Universe, without pondering the question of infinity."

"I'm not what you might call a wise man, but I've been asking myself these questions since I was a child."

"As a child, you were nothing but wisdom," said the monk. "As an adult, it's your child's voice that guides you even now; I'm glad you can still hear it."

"Where are we?" asked Keira.

"In a hermitage – you'll be protected in this private place."

"We weren't in any danger," Keira objected.

"That's not what I said," responded the monk, "but if you were, you'd be safe here, provided that you abided by our rules."

"And what are they?"

"Don't worry, we only have a few: one, to rise before daybreak, two, to work the land so as to deserve the food it provides us with, three, not to violate any life form, whether human or animal – although I'm sure you have no such intentions – and four, not to tell lies."

The monk turned to face Keira.

"So your companion is an astronomer. What about you, how do you fill your days?"

"I'm an archaeologist."

"An archaeologist and an astrophysicist, what a perfect match."

I glanced at Keira, who seemed to be completely absorbed by what the monk was saying.

"And has this tourist trip helped you to discover new things?"

"We're not exactly tourists," Keira confessed.

I coughed disapprovingly.

"The deal is no lies here!" she defended herself, before going on. "We're more like..."

"Explorers?" asked the monk.

"Sort of, yes."

"What are you looking for?"

"A white pyramid."

The monk burst out laughing."

"What's so funny?" Keira wanted to know.

"And have you found your white pyramid?" inquired the monk, his eyes still twinkling with humour.

"No, we've got to get to Xi'an. We think it's ahead of us, somewhere along the way."

The monk was laughing even more loudly now.

"What have I said that's so funny?"

"I doubt you'll find this pyramid in Xi'an, but you're not completely mistaken either; it is indeed along your way and in front of you too, for that matter," the monk added, beaming.

"I think he's making fun of us," said Keira, who was starting to get irritated.

"Not in the slightest," the monk assured her.

"Well then, why do you burst out laughing every time I open my mouth?"

"I would ask that you refrain from telling my disciples how much fun I've had in your company; as for the rest, I promise to explain everything tomorrow. It's time for me to meditate again now. I'll see you again at dawn. Don't be late."

The monk stood up and took his leave. We could tell, as we watched him head off up the path that led to the monastery, that he was still laughing.

*

We slept deeply. I was still dreaming when Keira woke me.

"Come on," she said, "it's time! I can hear the monks in the courtyard, it won't be long before sunrise now."

Simple provisions had been laid out at the entrance

to our room. A disciple showed us to the washroom, signalling for us to clean our hands and faces before touching the food. Once we had washed, he invited us to sit down and enjoy our meal.

We left the enclosure of the hermitage and made our way across the field to the willow tree where we were due to meet the monk. He was already waiting for us.

"I trust you had a good night?"

"I slept like a baby," said Keira.

"So, you're looking for a white pyramid? What do you already know about it?"

"According to the information I have," said Keira, "it's over three hundred metres high, making it the world's tallest pyramid."

"It's even taller than that," said the monk.

"So it does exist?" asked Keira.

The monk smiled.

"Yes, in a certain way, it does exist."

"Where is it?"

"As you yourself remarked yesterday, it's right in front of you."

"I'm sorry, but I'm not very good at riddles, so if you could give us a bit more of a clue..."

"What can you see on the horizon?" asked the monk.

"Mountains."

"The Qinling Mountain range. Do you know what the most important mountain is called, the one we can see over there, opposite us?"

"I'm afraid not," Keira admitted.

"Hua Shan – it's beautiful, isn't it? It is one of our five holy mountains, and its history is rich with teachings. A little over two thousand years ago, a Taoist temple was built at the foot of the western slopes. The temple was inhabited by wise men, who believed that the God of the Hidden Worlds lived among its peaks. Kou Qianzhi, a fifth century monk, founded the Celestial Order of the North; he claimed to have made a major discovery there, what he called a revelation. Mount Hua comprises five peaks, east, west, north, south, plus the peak in the middle; but how would you describe its overall shape?"

"Er.... pointed?" suggested Keira.

"I'm inviting you to open your eyes and to look carefully at Hua Shan; think again."

"It's triangular," I told the monk.

"Indeed it is. And at the beginning of December, the highest peak is clad in a magnificent mantle of snow. In the old days, these snows lasted forever, but now they melt at the end of the spring to reappear the following winter. I'm sorry you won't be able to stay long enough to witness Mount Hua in that season; an incomparable beauty transforms the landscape. One last question, what colour is the snow?"

"White...," whispered Keira, who was beginning to catch on.

"So you see, your white pyramid is right there, in front of us; now perhaps you can understand why I laughed so much when I was listening to you yesterday."

"We've absolutely got to go there!" declared Keira.

"That mountain is extremely dangerous," the monk warned. "There is a path hewn out of the rock along each flank, it is a sacred path that leads to the highest peak – not only of Mount Hua but also of China's five holy mountains; we call it the Pillar of the Clouds."

"Did you say pillar?" quizzed Keira.

"Yes, that's what the peak was known as in ancient times. Are you quite sure you want to go there? Climbing that path is a perilous undertaking."

All I had to do was glance at Keira to understand that, whatever the risks, we'd be climbing towards the peaks of Mount Hua. She was more determined than ever. The monk described what was in store for us in minute detail. Fifteen kilometres of steps carved out of the mountainside would lead to the first ridge; from there, a system of plankwalks and footbridges was secured to the sheer rockface, crossing dizzying precipices. The sacred path enabled the most fool-hardy and determined, or those spurred on by un-shakeable faith, to reach the Temple of God, which was built at an altitude of two thousand six hundred metres, at the summit of the northern peak.

"The tiniest slip would be fatal, as would the smallest deviation from the path. Beware of the ice which, even in this season, often covers the highest stone steps. You can't afford to lose your footing, as there's nothing to cling on to. If one of you falls, the other should *under no circumstances* make a rescue attempt – or both of you will plunge to your deaths."

We had been duly warned, but the monk wasn't trying to discourage us. He suggested we change into something more practical and leave our clothes there. The car would be fine where it was, at the edge of the woods. Mid-morning, we set out in a donkey cart. The monk driving the cart dropped us off by the main road, where he stopped a passing pick-up truck, had a word with the driver and got us settled in the back. An hour later, the truck ground to a halt halfway up the mountain. The driver pointed out a path through the pine forest.

As we ventured through the woods, Keira could see the steps the monk had told us about in the distance. The next three hours were far more challenging than I'd anticipated. The further we climbed, the higher the steps ahead seemed to loom; and it was no optical illusion either, the gradient really was getting steeper. From now on, it wasn't so much a flight of stairs we were climbing as an almost vertical stone ladder. Looking down was madness; the only way to make any progress was to keep our eyes firmly fixed on the peaks.

The first part of the ascent led us towards the Steps of Paradise. These levelled off along a ridge, but the deadly accuracy of their name wasn't lost on me: whoever slipped here would go straight to paradise. The climb became steep again a little further along.

"What was I thinking?" moaned Keira, clinging to the sheer rockface.

"What do you mean?"

"Dragging you here like this! I'd have been better off listening to the monk; it's not as if he didn't warn us about the dangers."

"I'm just as much to blame, and now is no time for second thoughts. Remember what he said, the slightest lapse of attention can be fatal, so concentrate!"

We were approaching the plateau of Canglong, from where we spotted a few umbrella pines dotted across the mountainside; they vanished once we'd made it over the Jinsud Pass.

"Have you got any clue what we're looking for?" I asked Keira.

"No, but I'll know when I find it."

I couldn't even feel my legs anymore; the rest of my muscles were killing me. Three times we nearly came unstuck, three times we caught our balance just in time. The sun was reaching its zenith. At the end of the pass we were faced with a choice of two trails, one leading to the west peak, the other to the north peak. We continued along a plankwalk that hugged the rockface; as the monk had said, there was nothing else to hold on to.

"The landscape is truly breathtaking, but don't look down," implored Keira.

"I wasn't planning to."

At this point in the climb, the danger factor felt overwhelming. The wind had whipped up, forcing us to crouch down and huddle together to avoid being blown over into the void. A crevice in the rock offered us meagre shelter. How long would we have to stay like this? I had no idea, but if the weather got any worse we'd have no chance of making a move after dark.

"Do you want to turn back?" asked Keira.

"No, not now, plus I know what you're like – you'll only start all over again tomorrow morning – and I'm not going through this again, not for all the tea in China!"

"Well, let's just wait for this wind to die down then."

Keira and I clung to each other. The wind blew in great gusts; in the distance, we could just make out the tops of the pine trees bending each time a squall hit the mountainside.

"I'm sure this wind'll die down eventually," insisted Keira.

I refused to imagine us meeting our end here, or the twenty-four-hour news services in London and Paris briefly reporting the deaths of two tourists foolhardy enough to attempt Mount Hua.

Keira had developed cramps in her legs and the pain was becoming unbearable.

"I can't take this anymore, I've got to stand up," she winced, and before I had time to realise what was happening, her foot had slipped. She screamed as she lurched over into the void. I leaped up, miraculously managing to keep my balance, grabbed hold of her jacket collar and just managed to catch her arm. She was dangling above the abyss; the wind redoubled its efforts, lashing us mercilessly. I can still hear her screaming:

"Adrian, don't let me goooooo!"

No matter how strenuously I exerted myself to haul her back up again, the wind was tugging her down. She clung to the rockface as I lay gingerly on the edge and tried to winch her up by her clothes.

"You've got to help me," I yelled, "push with your feet, for God's sake!"

It was an extremely dangerous manoeuvre. To stand any chance of making it out alive, she'd have to find the courage to let go with one hand and grab hold of me instead.

If the God of Hidden Worlds does indeed exist, he must have heard Keira's prayers. Unexpectedly, the wind let up. She unclenched the fingers of her right hand, swung sickeningly over the void and gripped me for all she was worth. This time, I managed to get her back up onto the plank walkway.

It took a good hour for our panic to subside. We were still terrified, but turning back was as frightening a prospect as continuing our ascent. Keira stood up slowly and helped me to my feet. When we saw the rockface that awaited us, the fear kicked straight back in, but magnified. How could I have been stupid enough to refuse Keira earlier, when she'd suggested turning round and retracing our steps? Was I out of my mind? Presumably having similar thoughts, Keira looked up and calculated the distance to the summit. The temple perched on top of the high peak was still

a long way off. A metal ladder climbed vertically upwards. If the rungs hadn't been so slippery, and if the
valley weren't spread out two thousand metres below
us, it might just have been a regular ladder – although
one with five hundred rungs. Our salvation lay a hundred and fifty metres above our heads. The important
thing was to keep our wits about us. Keira asked me
if I was ready to recite the list of things I liked about
her.

"It's the perfect time," she told me. "It'd help take
my mind off everything else."

I wished I was up to the task: the list was long
enough to keep her on tenterhooks until we'd reached
that wretched temple. But I was only good for checking where I put my hands. We carried on climbing in
total silence.

And our difficulties weren't over yet. We still had
to pick our way across another long plank walkway,
scarcely more than a foot wide.

When it got to nearly 6pm and dusk was approaching,
I signalled to Keira that if the monastery wasn't in
sight within half an hour we'd have to seriously start
thinking about a shelter for the night. This was, of
course, a preposterous suggestion: we were flanking
a sheer rockface and there was no possibility of shelter, either ahead or behind us.

Keira was beginning to overcome her vertigo. Her
movements became more fluid, her body language increasingly agile. Perhaps she was doing a better job

of conquering her fear than I was. And then at last, behind the slope we were climbing, a long ridge appeared that stretched towards the highest point of the mountain. It was a plateau jutting out over the valley from which, as if in a dream, a red-roofed monastery rose up.

In the shadow of the tall pine trees Keira knelt down on the gentle slope, exhausted. The air was so pure it burned our throats.

The temple was impressive. Its base was hewn out of the rock, while its façade rose up two floors and featured six large window frames. A staircase led all the way to the entrance. In front of a narrow courtyard a pagoda had been erected, and the overhang of its roof cast further shadows. I reflected on the excruciatingly difficult path that had brought us this far and wondered by what miracle men had been able to construct such a building. Had the wooden frames been carved on site before being assembled?

"We've made it," breathed Keira, tears welling up in her eyes.

"Yes, I suppose we have."

"Look behind you," she told me. I turned round and saw a stone sculpture, a strange-looking dragon with a thick mane.

"It's a lion," she whispered, "a lonely lion, and beneath its paw... a globe!"

Keira was crying and I put my arms around her.

"What's all this about?"

She took a letter out of her pocket, unfolded it and

read to me: *The lion sleeps on the stone of knowledge.*

We walked across to the statue. Keira leaned right over it to get a better look, examining the sphere on which the lion rested his paw, like a proud guardian.

"Can you see anything?"

"There are some fine grooves around the globe, but that's all; the stone's been badly eroded and I suspect the crucial part's missing."

I watched the sun sinking on the horizon. It was far too late to contemplate going back down, we'd have to spend the night here. The temple would shelter us from the cold, but it was open to the wind and I was worried about the two of us freezing to death in the middle of the night. I left Keira leaning over the globe that so entranced her, and made for the pine trees that rose up from the ridge. At their feet I gathered all the dead branches I could carry back with me, together with a few cones that gave off a strong scent of resin. Back in the courtyard I started preparing a fire.

"I've never felt this tired before," said Keira, coming to find me, "or this cold," she added, rubbing her hands in front of the first flames. "If you tell me you've got something to eat, I'll marry you!"

I'd carefully stashed away the biscuits which the monk had slipped into my pocket before we set out. I waited a bit before offering her one.

We found shelter in a room that was better protected

from the wind and, in spite of our less than cosy sleeping conditions, it didn't take us long to drop off.

The cry of an eagle woke us in the early hours. We were frozen stiff. My pockets were now as empty as our stomachs, and we were thirsty too. The way back would be just as dangerous, even if gravity was on our side this time. Keira tried desperately to lift the lion's paw and snatch that globe from him, so that she could study it in her own time. But the stone beast guarded it like a treasure.

Not much of the fire remained as Keira stood there staring at the ashes. Suddenly she rushed over and knelt down to push aside the embers that were still glowing.

"Help me gather up the bits of charcoal that aren't alight, I need two or three pieces."

She grabbed one, thick as a piece of child's drawing charcoal, and ran back towards the lion. Then she started blackening the spherical stone. I watched her, doubtfully. Vandalism wasn't one of Keira's usual pastimes, so why was she stamping her messy mark all over this ancient stone?

"Didn't you ever use crib sheets at school?" she asked, glancing up at me.

I had no intention of being the first to own up to breaking the rules; that would be too much, especially given how we'd first met.

"Are you finally admitting to your past crimes?"

I asked, with the air of an exam invigilator all over again.

"I wasn't talking about *me*."

"I've no recollection of cheating, no. And even if I did, do you think I'd tell you?"

"Right, one day I'll swap my confession for that famous list of things you like about me. But for now, grab a piece of charcoal and help me cover this stone."

"What are you playing at?"

As Keira meticulously blackened the stone, a series of marks began to appear. It was like that secret writing game we used to play as kids. You engraved the letters onto a sheet of paper with the point of a compass, and then went over it with a wax crayon to reveal the hidden words.

"Look!" exclaimed Keira, feverishly.

A sequence of figures was emerging amid intersecting lines and dots. This stone, so preciously guarded by the lion, was a sort of astrolabe, demonstrating the incredible astrological knowledge of those who had created it, centuries and centuries before our time.

"What is it?" asked Keira.

"A sort of *mappa mundi*, but instead of representing the Earth it depicts the celestial sphere; in other words, the representation of the two skies above and below our heads, one visible from the Northern hemisphere and the other from the Southern hemisphere."

The discovery Keira had just made was stupendous; she demanded I explain every detail to her.

"Around the median line which you can see here, this big circle marks the intersection of the equatorial plane with the sphere – we call it the celestial equator, and it divides the sphere in two halves: north and south. Any point can be projected from the Earth onto the celestial sphere; all the stars can be represented there, including the Sun."

I showed her the two polar circles, the tropics, and the ecliptic, the path traced by the Sun as marked out by the zodiacal constellations, and there was the colure of the solstices and equinoxes too.

"When the Sun crosses the equatorial plane, which is to say at the time of the equinoxes, the length of the day is equal to that of the night. The other circle you see is the projection of the Sun's trajectory onto the sphere. Here's what the Greeks called *Alpha Ursae Minoris*, and what we know as the Pole Star; it's so close to the North Pole that it seems to stay in the same place in the sky. This other big circle is a celestial meridian."

The representation was so complete that I swore to Keira I'd never seen anything like it in my life. The first astrolabes had been perfected by the Greeks in the third century BC, but the inlay carved into this stone was a lot older than that. It appeared the Chinese had knowledge of the solar system that predated even the Greeks.

Keira turned over the letter she'd kept in her pocket and on the back of it she copied the inscriptions

478

that appeared on the sphere. She had a real flair for sketching.

"What are you doing?" she asked, looking up from her drawing.

I showed her a small camera I'd kept hidden in my pocket since we'd got to China; I don't know why I hadn't dared own up earlier to the fact that I hoped to capture some moments of our trip.

"What's that?" she asked, knowing full well what it was.

"It was my mother's idea... a disposable camera."

"What's your mother got to do with this? And, more to the point, how long have you had it?"

"I bought it in London before we left. Consider it a camouflage kit – have you ever seen tourists without a camera?"

"Have you already used this?"

Being a dreadful liar, I decided to come clean straightaway.

"I might have photographed you once or twice when you weren't noticing: while you were asleep, or when you were puking behind that roadside bush, for example. Don't pull that face, I just wanted a few holiday souvenirs."

"How many shots are there left in this camera?"

"Actually this is the second camera and it hasn't been used yet, but I've finished the first one."

"How many of these disposable thingies did you buy?"

"Four... maybe five."

I felt rather embarrassed and didn't want to pursue this conversation, so I went up to the lion and started photographing the spherical stone, recording each detail.

Between us, we'd gathered enough material to be able to reconstruct all the information carved on the stone. I'd measured its dimensions with the aid of my trouser belt, so that we'd have a sense of scale when we got back. By assembling the shots I'd just taken, together with Keira's drawing, we'd have a faithful copy in the absence of the original.

The time had come to leave the holy mountain. Judging from the sun's position, I reckoned it was about 10am; if there were no obstacles on our way down, we would make it back to the monastery before nightfall.

*

We collapsed on arrival. The monks had prepared everything for us: hot water to wash with, a meal with plenty of soup to rehydrate us and generous helpings of rice to restore our energy. The head monk didn't show up that evening. The others explained that he was meditating and wasn't to be disturbed.

But we did meet up with him again the following morning. Apart from a few grazes, plus a crop of blisters on our hands and feet, we were in surprisingly good shape.

"Were you happy with your journey to the white pyramid?" asked the monk, coming over to us. "Did you find what you were looking for?"

Keira shot me a quizzical look: should we let him in on our secret? Given that the monk had demonstrated his interest in astronomy on the evening before our departure, how could we keep this fascinating discovery from him? He might be able to shed some light on it for us. I told him that we'd found something even more incredible than what we'd been expecting. He was curious now, but in order for me to explain properly I needed to get my photos developed: this was a case of pictures speaking louder than words.

"You've got me intrigued," he told us. "But I'll be patient and wait for the photographs. My fellow monks will take you to your car. Drive eastwards and after seventy kilometres you'll get to Lingbao, one of the modern cities that mushroomed over the last few years; you'll find everything you need there."

The cart took us to our 4x4. Two hours after leaving the monastery, we arrived in the centre of Lingbao. Along the sprawling main commercial drag were countless electronics goods shops, intended as much for the home market as for tourists. We chose one at random. I handed my disposable camera to the shop assistant and, fifteen minutes later, at a cost of a hundred yuan, he presented us with a set of twenty-four photos taken on Mount Hua, as well as a memory card onto which they'd been digitised.

A funny-looking machine caught my attention. It consisted of a screen and a keyboard, and was fitted with different-sized slots into which you could insert the sort of memory card the shop assistant had just sold me. By inserting a few coins, you could send your photos via the Internet to anywhere in the world.

I invited Keira to join me and, in a matter of minutes, I'd managed to e-mail two friends, Erwin in the Atacama and Martin at Jodrell Bank. I asked each of them to study the pictures very carefully and to tell me what they reminded them of, as well as apprising me of whatever conclusions they might draw. Keira didn't have any photos to send to Jeanne, so she just wrote her a few lines pretending to be in the Omo Valley, letting her know that everything was fine and that she missed her.

We made the most of our city visit by stocking up on a few necessaries. Keira was desperate for shampoo; we spent nearly an hour looking for the brand she insisted on. When I remarked that scouring the shops for a particular brand might be a bit obsessive, she pointed out that if she hadn't steered me out of there, we'd still be in the electronics goods shop.

We'd had our fill of rice, soup and crackers, and neither of us could resist the mouth-watering sights through the window of a fast-food joint where they served real hamburgers, with chips and melted cheese. Five hundred calories a pop, Keira informed me, adding that they would be five hundred calories of pure pleasure.

After lunch, we headed straight back to the monastery. This time, our monk wasn't meditating; he even seemed impatient for our return.

"So what about these photos, then?" he inquired.

I showed him the prints and explained how we'd made the celestial sphere, which was carved into the stone, appear before our eyes.

"You've certainly made a very impressive discovery. I hope you returned the stone to its original state?"

"Yes," Keira reassured him, "we washed it with leaves that were still damp with snow."

"A sensible precaution. How did you know it was the lion you were looking for?" the monk wanted to know.

"It's a long story, a story as long as this entire trip."

"What are your plans now?"

"To go wherever the twin to this is to be found," said Keira, showing her pendant to the monk. "And we believe the celestial sphere we discovered on Mount Hua should help us locate it. We don't know how yet, but with a bit of time perhaps we'll see things more clearly."

"And what is the proper purpose of this rather beautiful object?" asked the monk, studying Keira's pendant more closely.

"It's a fragment from a map of the sky that was

drawn up a very long time ago, even before the celestial sphere we found under the lion's paw."

The monk looked us both directly in the eye.

"Follow me," he said, leading us away from the
monastery.

He took us to the foot of the willow tree, where
our last conversation had taken place, and asked us
to sit down. In return for his hospitality, would we
agree to tell him our long story, because he was fascinated by it? We felt indebted to him and willingly
agreed to his request.

"If I've understood this correctly," he summarised,
"the object that you're wearing around your neck is
a map of the sky as it appeared four hundred million
years ago; which, as I'm sure you'll agree, would
seem impossible. You tell me there are other fragments of this map which remains incomplete, to this
day, and that by bringing them together you would be
able to prove its authenticity?"

"Exactly."

"Are you quite sure that's the only thing it would
prove? Have you thought about the implications of
your discovery, about all the accepted truths in this
world that might also be overturned?"

I confessed that we hadn't had much time to draw
up a list. But if reuniting the fragments enabled us to
find out more about the origins of humanity and, who
knows, even about the birth of the Universe, then the
discovery would be invaluable.

"Are you certain about that?" the monk repeated.

"Have you asked yourselves why nature chooses to wipe clean all our earliest childhood memories? And why none of us have any knowledge of our first moments on Earth?"

Neither Keira nor I had an answer for this.

"Do you have any idea of the difficulties a soul must brave in order to unite with a body, giving birth to life in the form that we know? As an astronomer, I can appreciate how fascinated you must be by the creation of the Universe, by those first moments, the famous Big Bang, that phenomenal explosion of energy giving birth to so much matter. Do you really think the first moments of a life are any different? Isn't it just a question of scale? The Universe being infinitely big, when we are infinitely small. What if these two births were in some way similar? Why do people always have to go so far to search for something so close?

"Perhaps nature chose to erase the memory of our first moments and to protect us so we don't remember the suffering we endured in order to enter life. And, possibly, so that we would never betray the secret of those first moments? I often wonder what would become of humanity if we genuinely understood that process. Man might mistake himself for a god – if we knew how to create life at random, what is there to stop us from destroying everything? Would life still be as valuable if we could uncover the mystery of its creation?

"It's not my place to tell you to abandon this jour-

ney, any more than it is to judge your approach. Perhaps ours is not a chance meeting. This Universe,
which inspires you so much, has unimaginable qual-
ities, and we are far from having even the faintest
notion of what is chance and what is not. I am merely
asking you to think long and hard about what you
are really undertaking. If this journey has already
enabled you to meet each other, then perhaps that was
its primary purpose, and perhaps it would be wise to
stop there."

The monk handed us back the photographs. He
stood up, took his leave and walked back towards the
monastery.

The next day, we returned to Lingbao. We'd spotted
an Internet cafe, where we managed to go online and
check our e-mails. Keira had some news from her sister, and I had heard from my astrophysicist friends –
both of them asking me to ring them immediately.

I got hold of Erwin first.

"I don't know what you're up to this time, but
you've got me hooked. I must be a fool to spend so
many hours slaving away at this when you don't tell
me anything, but I guess it's because I'm your friend.
That said, you've got some explaining to do. Oh, and
you owe me a slap-up meal – for the second sleepless
night you've just inflicted on me."

"What have you found out, Erwin?"

"Your celestial sphere is set on a precise axis. I made
a triangulation, crossing the equatorial coordinates

(these being the equator and the meridian of your astrolabe) to determine the straight ascension and the declination. I spent several hours looking for which star this pointed to, but I'm afraid I couldn't find anything. I saw you'd also asked your friend Martin to apply himself to the same question, so see what he's found out – I'm stumped."

After finishing my conversation with Erwin, I called Martin. He'd only just woken up and I apologised for getting him out of bed.

"That's some riddle you sent over, Adrian! But don't think you can get me that easily, I've seen through your trap."

I let him speak, feeling my heart beat faster every second.

"Of course," Martin went on, "not having the horary coordinates to measure the angles, I wondered what you were playing at. It's a sublime astrolabe, more complete than anything I've ever seen and, most importantly of all, it's accurate – unbelievably so! I was puzzled about which star it referred to, until I realised the sphere wasn't indicating a point in the sky, but rather *from* the sky it was designating a point on Earth. The only snag being that I entered the current horary coordinates and, by my calculations, this point is in the middle of nowhere, right out in the Andaman Sea, to the south of Burma."

"Would you be able to modify those calculations by making the horary coordinates three thousand five hundred years old?"

"Why that date especially? "Martin queried.

"Because that's the age of the stone I found at those coordinates."

"I'd have to recalculate a lot of parameters. I'll try to free up a computer, but I'm not promising anything – give me twenty-four hours."

I thanked my friend for all the trouble he'd gone to. Then I called Erwin back straightaway, to keep him up to speed and to set him the same challenge. Erwin huffed and puffed, but then he always did; and, in the end, he also promised to update me the next day.

I told Keira about all the progress we'd made in a relatively short space of time. I remember how happy we were, how enthusiastic, buoyed up by the promise of what lay in store. We didn't pay any heed to the monk's warnings. All that counted now was the science, and feeding our appetite for discovery.

"I don't fancy going back to our monastic bed-and-breakfast," Keira said. "Not that I've got anything against our host, but his moral lectures are wearing a bit thin. We've got to wait until tomorrow anyway, so why don't you and I do the tourism thing for once? Let's pay a little visit to the Yellow River, seeing as it's nearby. I'll even let you take some photos of me when I *am* looking, if you like; and if we find a nice quiet spot to swim, I can guarantee you a real eyeful!"

That afternoon, we went skinny dipping in the river. It was blissful for both of us. I forgot all about the Atacama, London and the rain sluicing down the rooftops of Primrose Hill; I forgot all about Hydra, my mother, Aunt Elena, Kalibanos and his two-speed donkeys; I forgot about the fact that I'd probably missed out on the chance of teaching next year at the university. But I didn't mind about any of that. Keira was in my arms, and we were making love in the clear waters of the Yellow River. What else mattered?

*

We didn't go back to the monastery, opting instead for a hotel room. Keira was desperate for a decent bath and a good dinner.

Our night of romance in Lingbao: writing about it still brings a smile to my face. We strolled through the streets of that unlikely city. By now, Keira had caught the photography bug. We'd nearly finished the film down by the riverbank, and Keira had bought another disposable camera to snap us in the city streets. She didn't want to get them developed then and there, reasoning it would spoil all the fun of revisiting those moments when we were back in London.

Out on the restaurant terrace, Keira asked me if I was finally ready to recite the list of things I liked about her. I replied that I still wanted to know whether or not she'd cheated in that exam room where we'd first met. She refused to answer and the famous list remained a secret.

The bed in our hotel room was so comfortable that

it made us forget the coarseness of the mats in the monastery. Not that we did much sleeping that night.

Given the twelve-hour time difference with Chile, it was 10am in Lingbao and 10pm in the Atacama when I rang Erwin.

Something was up with one of the telescopes, and I realised I was disturbing him in the middle of a maintenance operation. But he took my call and went to great pains to point out that while I was drifting around China, he was on a metal walkway, doing battle with a nut that wouldn't unscrew. I heard him let out a roar followed by a torrent of expletives. He'd just nicked his finger and was furious.

"I did the sums you asked me to," he said, sounding as if he was wincing. "I don't know why I'm putting myself out like this, Adrian, but I'm warning you, it's the last time! Your coordinates are still in the Andaman Sea, but with the adjustments I made you'd be on dry land this time. Have you got pen and paper there?"

I grabbed a pen and a sheet of paper and checked, feverishly, to make sure the pen had ink.

"13° 26' 50" latitude North; 94° 15' 52" longitude East. I checked for you and it's the island of Narcondam, four kilometres by three and not a living soul. As for the exact position of the coordinates, they'll lead you to the arsehole of a volcano; but I've saved the good news until last – it's extinct! Now, some of us have got work to do, so if you don't mind I'll leave you to your rice and chopsticks." Erwin hung up before I could even thank him.

I checked the time by my watch: Martin was still working night-shifts, but I was too impatient to worry about whether I might be waking him up.

He communicated the exact same coordinates.

Keira was waiting for me in the car. I told her all about the phone conversations. When she asked where we were headed, I amused myself by entering into the satnav the figures that Erwin and Martin had given me: 13° 26' 50" N, 94° 15' 52" E, before revealing to her that our next stop was south of Burma, on an island whose name meant Hell's Well.

The island of Narcondam was two hundred and fifty-six kilometres from the southernmost tip of Burma. We studied a map to figure out the different routes from our current location, aware that it would be very difficult to obtain visas for Burma. We went into a travel agent's to ask for advice, and found that the man in there spoke reasonable-ish English.

A two-hour drive would get us to Xi'an, from where we could catch an evening plane to Hanoi and wait two days for the charter flight to Rangoon that ran twice a week. Once we'd got to the south of Burma, we'd need to find a boat. Best case scenario: it would take us three to four days to get to the island, not to mention obtaining visas, and goodness knows how long that might drag on.

"There must be a simpler and faster way. How

about if we were to go back to Beijing?" The travel agent picked up on everything we said. He leant over his counter and inquired if we had foreign currency. I always travel with dollars in my pocket – there are plenty of countries in the world where a few greenbacks displaying Benjamin Franklin's face will sort out all sorts of problems.

The agent told us about one of his friends, a former fighter pilot in the Chinese air force who'd bought up an old Lisunov from his former employer. He offered his services to thrill-seeking tourists, these air baptism flights aboard his Russian version of a DC3 actually serving as a cover for trafficking goods of all kinds.

In South Asia, there were countless clandestine companies that hired former pilots, retired from the air force and feeling cash-strapped on their stingy pensions. Drugs, alcohol, weapons and currencies transited right under the noses of the customs authorities, between Thailand, China, Malaysia and Burma. The planes making these trips didn't conform to any effective standards, but who was worried about that? The travel agent assured us he could fix it all up on our behalf. This was much better than landing in Rangoon, where we'd have to travel by boat for another ten hours, ditto for the return journey; his pilot friend would drop us off at Port Blair, the capital of the Andaman and Nicobar Islands. From Port Blair, the island we wanted to reach would be no more than seventy nautical miles away.

The door swung open and a customer walked into the agency, giving us a few minutes to think the offer over.

"We nearly lost our lives on that mountain; do you really want us to push our luck in a ropey old plane?" I asked Keira.

"How about the glass half-full approach? Given we didn't break our necks, despite dangling two and a half thousand metres above the void like a couple of dummies, what are we risking in a bashed-up plane?"

Keira's point of view was optimistic but not un-reasonable. Flying by the seats of our pants had its dangers – we had no idea what kind of cargo would be travelling with us, or what risks we'd be running if our plane was intercepted by the Indian coast-guards – but, in the best-case scenario, we would reach Narcondam Island by boat the next evening.

The customer stepped outside and we were alone again with our man. I put down a deposit of two hun-dred dollars, which he gleefully pocketed; but he kept staring at my watch, having clearly earmarked it for his commission. I took it off and he wasted no time in transferring it to his wrist. I promised to give his pilot friend all the cash I had, provided he landed us safely and in the right place. Half would be payable on the way out, and the other half on the way back.

The deal was done. Our fixer closed the door of his agency and the three of us left via the back way.

A scooter was parked in the small courtyard; the agent climbed on and got Keira settled in the middle, leaving me a tiny patch of saddle and the luggage-rack to cling onto. The scooter spluttered to life and we left the city only to find ourselves, fifteen minutes later, racing hell for leather along a country road. The airfield was just a strip of earth marked out in the middle of a field that also housed a rusty old hangar with two crates snoozing inside. Ours was the bigger one.

The pilot could have been a buccaneer straight out of *The Pirates of the Caribbean.* Craggy-faced, with a great big scar on his cheek, he really did look like a South Seas pilot. Acting rather oddly, our travel agent had a chat with him. The pilot, who didn't bat an eyelid, came over and held out his hand for me to settle up. Satisfied, he showed me the ten or so boxes at the back of the hangar and made it clear that if I wanted us to take off, it was in my interest to give him a helping hand. Each time I passed him a package and saw the cargo disappearing into the back of the cabin, I tried not to think about the type of goods that would be travelling with us.

Keira was sitting in the co-pilot's seat and I had the navigator's chair. Our buccaneer pilot leant towards Keira and informed her, affably enough, that the machine we were flying in was postwar. Neither Keira nor I had the nerve to ask him which war.

He asked us to fasten our safety belts; I apologised

for not complying with the safety procedures, but the belt that went with my chair had disappeared. The instrument panel lit up or rather a few screens did; on others the needles remained inert. The pilot looked like he knew what he was doing, as he pulled down on two levers and pressed a series of buttons; the two Pratt & Whitney engines (I'd spotted the make emblazoned on the hood) belched out thick smoke. There was a spray of flames and the propellers started turning. The tail swivelled round and, sliding as if on ice, the plane lined up on the runway. The noise in the cockpit became deafening and everything shuddered. Through one of the portholes I saw our travel agent waving manically at us as, shaken like plum trees, we picked up speed. The end of the runway was zooming towards us in alarming fashion. I suddenly felt the tail lift up and at last we rose into the air. I'm sure we sliced a few centimetres off the treetops but we were gaining height by the second.

The pilot explained that we wouldn't be flying very high, so as to keep below the radar. He said this with a broad grin and I reached the conclusion that there was no point worrying.

For the first hour we flew over a plain, then the pilot climbed a bit as the landscape rose ahead of us; two hours later, we were north-east of Yunnan. The pilot changed course, heading southwards. It was a longer route, but the best way of leaving China was to follow the border with Laos, where aerial surveillance was almost non-existent. I wouldn't say the flight was particularly comfortable up until that point, but it was nothing compared to the turbulence we encountered while flying over the Mekong. As we approached the river, the pilot made the plane nose-dive in order to fly just above water level. Keira thought this was terrific, and the view may well have been – I couldn't say, my eyes were glued to the al-timeter. Each time our pilot tapped it, the needle jig-gled about then plummeted straight back down again. We flew over Laos for fifteen minutes prior to enter-ing Burmese air space. Two other dials held my at-tention: the fuel gauges. From what I could see, the tanks were only a quarter full. I asked our pilot how much longer he thought it would be before we ar-rived. He proudly held up two fingers and bent the third. Given how much fuel we'd consumed since setting out, if we really did have two and a half hours still to fly, by my reckoning we'd run out of fuel be-fore reaching our destination. I shared these deduc-tions with Keira, who just shrugged. All I could see were mountains: there was no potential stop-off for refuelling. I'd forgotten the travel agent had told us his friend was a former fighter pilot. While we were flying between two passes, the plane swooped down before performing a stomach-lurching stall on a wing. The engines screeched, the cabin shook, the plane righted itself into a quasi-normal position and we saw a road of sorts appear, flanking a paddy field. Keira closed her eyes; the plane effortlessly touched down and came to a halt. The pilot switched off the ignition, undid his seat belt and asked me to follow him; he led me behind the cabin, undid the straps holding in two big casks and made it clear that I now had to help him roll them under the wings. What could I say? The in-flight entertainment was certainly original. As I was pushing my cask towards the right wing, I noticed a cloud of dust rising up at the end of the road. Two jeeps were driving towards us: once they were level, four men got out. They exchanged a few words with our pilot, along with a wad of notes – I couldn't see what currency they were, and, in a few minutes, unloaded the boxes it had taken us considerably longer to load up. They set off again in much the same style – without waving goodbye or helping us fill the tank.

The refuelling operation was carried out with the help of a small electric pump and took a good half hour, during which time Keira stretched her legs. We loaded the empty casks into the back of the plane (we'd need them on our return trip) and then each of us took our place back on board. The same cloud of blackish smoke, the same spitting of flames, the propellers spun again and the plane rose up into the sky, narrowly squeezing between the two passes where we'd nose-dived earlier.

Our flight over Burma, at an even lower altitude to avoid detection, was uneventful. The pilot indicated that we'd soon reach the coast, and sure enough we saw the wide blue of the Andaman Sea. The plane took a southwards course, flying almost at wave-level now, because the Indian coast-guards were rather more vigilant than their Burmese neighbours. The pilot checked the portable GPS strapped to the instrument panel: it was at least a more robust and accurate model than those sold to motorists.

"Land!" the pilot's announcement rang out in the cockpit.

We changed direction again to fly round the island's east coast, and after an initial hedge-hopping manoeuvre the plane touched down gently in the middle of a field.

Port Blair was a ten-minute walk away, through the countryside. The pilot gathered his belongings and trotted along beside us; he knew a small family-run place that rented out rooms. We had the rest of the day to make our sea voyage; the flight back was set for the next morning. The pilot was adamant about flying back over the Chinese border at midday, on the basis that, when the radar operators were on their lunch breaks, they didn't keep an eye on their control screens.

*

Port Blair

Sitting outside an ice-cream parlour, where we'd invited our pilot to join us, we began to recover from our trip.

During the first Anglo-Burmese War in the 1820s, Port Blair became the naval base for British war ships transporting soldiers to the front. The ships' crews were regularly attacked by natives from the island rebelling against the invader. When the British Empire started to crumble, the Indian uprisings provided His Majesty's government with more prisoners than its jails could accommodate; so a prison was built above the port where we now sat. How much brutality did my fellow citizens mete out to the islanders here? I knew that torture, maltreatment and hanging were the daily lot of the prisoners, most of them political detainees, until India's independence brought an end to such abominations. Port Blair, in the middle of the Andaman Sea, is now a holiday resort for Indian tourists. In front us two children were gorging themselves on ice-cream, while their mums combed the shops. Glancing up at the prison, whose walls still rise above the port, I wondered if anyone remembered those who had died here in the name of freedom.

After eating, our pilot helped us find a small boat that would take us to Narcondam. A captain agreed to let us have one of his fast launches. By a stroke of luck, he also accepted credit cards. Keira rightly pointed out that at this rate, the trip was going to bankrupt me.

Before setting off, I asked our pilot whether he'd mind lending us his navigation device; my excuse being that I wasn't familiar with the region, and feared the on-board compass might not be enough. Less than thrilled at the prospect of lending me his GPS, he explained that if I lost it we wouldn't be able to get back to China. I promised to be extra-careful.

The weather was perfect, the sea like a mill-pond, and with the two 300-hp outboard motors we'd reach Hell's Well Island in two hours, tops.

Keira was sitting up at the prow. Perched astride the rail, she was basking in the sun and the gentle breeze. A few miles from the coast there was more of a swell, forcing her to join me in the cabin. The boat sped along, hopping over the crests of the waves. It was 6pm by the sun when the coast of Narcondam loomed up ahead. I steered round the tiny island and spotted a beach at the end of an inlet where I'd be able to run the speedboat aground.

Keira started walking up from the foot of the volcano: we had seven hundred metres to climb through shrubs and undergrowth before reaching the top. I switched on the GPS and punched in the coordinates Erwin and Martin had given me.

*

London

13° 26' 50" N, 94° 15' 52" E.

Sir Ashley folded the piece of paper his assistant had given him.

"What does that mean?"

"I don't know, sir, I have to confess it's rather baffling. Their car is parked in a street in Lingbao, a city in the north of China, and it hasn't moved since yesterday morning. They've simply entered these coordinates into the car's satnav, but I strongly doubt they're planning on reaching this destination by road."

"Why not?"

"Because these coordinates lead to a tiny island in the middle of the Andaman Sea; even with a jeep, it's not the kind of place that's easily accessible by car."

"And what's so special about this island?"

"Well that's just it, sir, nothing – it's a miniscule volcanic island. Apart from a few birds, it's entirely uninhabited."

"And is the volcano active?"

"No, it hasn't erupted for over four thousand years."

"And they've left China to go to this miserable island?"

"No, not yet; we've checked with all the airlines, and they weren't on any of the passenger records; according to the bugging device we inserted into the astrophysicist's watch, they're still in the centre of Lingbao."

Sir Ashley pushed back his chair and stood up.

"This pantomime has gone on long enough! Reserve me a seat on the first flight to Beijing. I want a car and two men waiting for me when I get there. It's high time we put an end to all this before it's too late."

Sir Ashley took his chequebook out of the desk drawer and a fountain pen from his jacket pocket.

"Pay for my ticket with your own credit card; I'll leave you this cheque to fill out the sum necessary to reimburse you. I'd prefer nobody to know where I'm going. If anyone tries to get hold of me, take a message; say that I'm unwell and resting in the country."

*

Hell's Well

By my calculations, the sun would set four hours from now. I didn't want to be sailing back in the dark, so we didn't have much time to play with. Keira was the first to reach the top.

"Hurry up, it's quite a sight!" she called out.

I put on a spurt to join her and realised she hadn't been exaggerating, when I saw all that thick vegetation covering the crater. A toucan we'd disturbed flew up into the sky. Then I checked my navigational device, which was accurate up to five metres: the flashing dot was approaching the centre of the screen, so we weren't far from our goal.

Looking at the landscape stretched out below us, I realised I could do without the GPS our pilot had lent us. Right in the middle of the volcano, we could see a small patch of land where the grass hadn't grown. Keira rushed over to it. I wasn't allowed anywhere near. Kneeling down, she scraped at the earth. Then, taking a big stone, she marked out a square and started digging, as her fingers hollowed out the dirt.

An hour went by and still Keira kept on digging. A small pile had formed next to her. She was exhausted, her forehead dripping with sweat; I wanted to give her a break, but she ordered me to keep my distance; and then, all of a sudden, she roared my name at the top of her voice.

In her feverish hands shone a fragment made of a substance as smooth and hard as ebony; its near triangular form was the colour of ebony too. Keira took off the necklace she was wearing and brought her pendant close to the new find. The two pieces were clearly attracted to each other, uniting to form one.

As soon as they were joined, they changed colour from ebony black to midnight blue. Suddenly, millions of dots started glowing on the surface of these united fragments: millions of stars, just as they had appeared in the sky four hundred million years ago.

I could feel the heat of the object beneath my fingers. The dots shone even more strongly, one brighter than all the rest. Was this the star of the First Day, which I'd set out to find by exiling myself to the highest Chilean plateaux?

Keira put the object carefully down on the ground. She hugged me tightly and kissed me. Despite the bright sunlight, there gleaming at our feet was the most beautiful night sky I'd ever seen.

It wasn't easy to separate the two fragments again. No matter how hard we tugged, nothing happened.

And then the glowing dimmed and faded away, at which point a gentle tweak was enough to pull them apart. Keira put her necklace back on and I stowed the other fragment deep in my pocket.

Neither of us looked at each other; we were both wondering what on earth would happen if, one day, we were able to bring together the five fragments.

*

Lingbao, China

The Lisunov touched down on the airstrip and taxied to its hangar. After the pilot had helped Keira out of the plane, I handed him my last remaining dollars and thanked him for bringing us back safe and sound. Our travel agent was waiting for us on his scooter and in no time dropped us off at our car. I promised to recommend his agency to all our friends and he grinned from ear to ear, bobbing up and down in a goodbye bow.

"Have you still got the energy to drive?" asked Keira, yawning.

I didn't like to admit I'd dozed off while we were flying over Laos.

I turned the ignition key and the engine of the 4x4 revved up. We needed to retrieve our belongings from the monastery and would take the opportunity to thank the monk for his hospitality; the plan was to spend one last night there before heading back to Beijing the next day. Impatient to see the image that the new fragment would project once exposed to a laser, we wanted to get back to London as quickly as possible. What constellations would we discover this time?

As we were driving along by the Yellow River, I reflected on all the truths this strange object might reveal to us. I had a few ideas flying around my head, but before sharing them with Keira I wanted to be in front of the proper equipment so that I could see the phenomenon with my own eyes.

"I'll call Walter tomorrow," I told Keira. "He'll be as excited as we are about this."

"I must remember to call Jeanne," she added.

"What's the longest you've ever gone without being in touch?"

"Three months!" Keira admitted, sheepishly.

A large saloon car was right on our tail. Its driver could flash his headlights at me all he liked, but the winding road was too narrow for overtaking. On one side was sheer mountain face, on the other the bed of the Yellow River. I waved to indicate that I'd move over and let him pass just as soon as I could.

"Just because you don't call someone, it doesn't mean you're not thinking about them," Keira defended herself.

"So why not call them anyway?" I goaded her.

"Sometimes, distance makes it hard to find the right words."

*

Paris

Ivory enjoyed the weekly ritual of going to the market in Place d'Aligre. He knew each of the stallholders by name: Annie the baker, Marcel the cheese-maker, Étienne the butcher, Monsieur Gérard the ironmonger who had been sourcing items for his stall, guaranteed to turn the heads of passers-by, for the past twenty years. Ivory loved Paris, the island where he lived in the middle of the Seine, and the covered market of Place d'Aligre, with its distinctive roof shaped like an overturned ship's hull.

On returning home, he put his shopping bag down on the kitchen table, methodically tidied away his modest purchases and walked into the sitting room munching on a carrot.

The telephone rang.

"There's some news I'd like to share with you – it's got me worried," said Vackeers.

Ivory put the carrot back down on the coffee table and listened to what his chess partner had to say.

"We had a meeting this morning: our two scientists are causing quite a stir. They're in Lingbao, a small city in China, but they haven't moved for several days. Nobody can work out what they're doing there. All we know is that they've punched coordinates into their GPS which are eyebrow-raising, to say the least."

"And where are the coordinates for?" asked Ivory.

"A small island in the middle of the Andaman Sea and of no real interest."

"Is there a volcano on this island?" asked Ivory.

"Yes, I believe there is, how did you know?"

Ivory didn't reply.

"So what's bothering you, Vackeers?"

"Sir Ashley reported in sick and didn't attend the meeting. I'm not the only person alarmed by this: everybody's aware of his hostility to the motion passed at our last meeting."

"Do you have reason to believe he may be better informed than us?"

"Sir Ashley has a lot of friends in China," Vackeers confirmed.

"Lingbao, you said?"

Ivory thanked Vackeers for his call. He stepped outside to lean on the balcony and stayed there for a short while, deep in thought. The meal he'd planned to cook would have to wait. He went into his bedroom and sat down at his computer, booking himself onto a flight leaving for Beijing at seven o'clock that evening, with a connection to Xi'an. Then he packed a travel bag and rang for a taxi.

*

The Xi'an Road

"Why don't you just let him overtake us?"

I didn't disagree with Keira's sentiment, but the car behind us was going too fast for me to brake; and the road was still too narrow for it to overtake. I decided to ignore the impatient driver's blasts of the horn – he'd just have to wait a bit longer. Coming out of a bend, with the road climbing upwards, he got dangerously close and I saw the radiator grille of his saloon looming in my rear-view mirror.

"Put your seat belt on," I instructed Keira, "this jerk's going to send us into the ravine at this rate."

"Slow down, Adrian, please."

"I can't slow down, he's right on our tail."

Keira turned around and looked through the rear window.

"They're out of their minds to be driving like that!"

The tires screeched and the 4x4 swerved. I managed to maintain control of the steering wheel and pressed my foot down hard on the accelerator in order to shake off the maniacs behind.

"They really seem to have it in for us," said Keira, "the guy at the wheel has just given me the two-fingered salute!"

"Stop looking and fasten your seat belt. Are you belted in?"

"Yes."

Not that I'd got my seat belt on, but I couldn't let go of the steering wheel.

We felt a violent jolt which sent us lurching forwards. Our pursuers were playing at dodgems, as our back wheels went spinning sideways and the mountain-side scratched Keira's door. She was gripping the wrist strap so hard her knuckles turned white. The 4x4 was holding the road well, but we were thrown around at every bend. They rammed us again, knocking us sideways, and then the saloon finally retreated in the rear-view mirror. But moments after I'd miraculously got us back on track, the saloon bore back down on us once more. The bastard was gaining ground. The needle on my speedometer was approaching seventy, an untenable speed on such a winding mountain round. We'd never get round the next bend.

"Slow down, Adrian, please!"

The third shunt was even more forceful, the right fender struck the rock, and the headlight shattered. Keira pushed herself deep into her seat. The vehicle swung sideways and spun round. I saw the parapet shatter as we hit it. For a moment, it felt as if we were being lifted off the ground, then we remained frozen, suspended in mid-air for a second before the front wheels plunged down into the precipice. The first somersault turned us onto the roof, and then the car slid down the slope towards the river. We hit a rock, and a fresh somersault righted us; the roof had been heavily dented and we continued plummeting towards the river. There was absolutely nothing I could do about it. We were heading straight for a pine tree when the 4x4 skidded sideways, narrowly avoiding it. Nothing could stop us, it seemed. Then a pile of rubble and rocks blocked our path: the radiator grille rose up into the sky, the car glided through the air and I heard a great deafening thud, followed by a sharp jolt: we had just plunged into the waters of the Yellow River. I turned instantly to Keira, who had a nasty gash on her forehead and was bleeding, but was still conscious. The vehicle was floating, though not for long – the hood was already submerged.

"We've got to get out of here," I yelled at Keira.

"Adrian, I'm stuck."

Due to the shock of impact, the passenger seat had come out of its tracks and the release handle for her seat belt was completely inaccessible. I yanked on the strap but nothing happened. I must have broken some ribs – every time I breathed, a searing pain shot through my chest, but the water was flooding in and I had to free Keira. The water level just kept on rising, we could feel it lapping at our feet, and the windshield was almost submerged now.

"Get out, Adrian! Get out while you still can!"

I turned round looking for something with which to cut the seat belt. The pain surged through me and I could hardly breathe, but I refused to give up. I leaned over Keira's knees to try and open the glove box. She put her hand on my neck and stroked my hair.

"I can't feel my legs anymore, you won't be able to get me out of here," she whispered, "you've got to go now."

I took her head in my hands and we kissed. I'll never forget the taste of that kiss.

Keira looked at her pendant and smiled.

"Take it," she said, "we didn't put ourselves through all this for nothing."

I refused to let her take it off: I wouldn't go, I'd stay right here with her.

"I wish I could have seen Hari again one last time," she murmured.

The water kept flooding into the car as the current slowly dragged us down.

"I wasn't cheating in the exam room," she told me. "I just wanted to attract your attention, I liked you even then. In London, I turned back at the end of your road; if a taxi hadn't passed by, I would have come back to bed with you; but I was scared, perhaps of being too much in love."

We embraced. The car was still sinking and the daylight finally disappeared. The water was shoulder-level now. Keira was trembling as fear gave way to sadness.

"You promised me a list, you'll have to hurry up with it now!"

"I love you."

"That's a beautiful list – you couldn't have made a finer one."

I'll always stay with you, my love: I stayed with you right to the end, and beyond. I never left you. I kissed you as the waters of the Yellow River were drowning us, and I gave you my last breath. The air in my lungs was your air. You closed your eyes when the water covered our faces; I kept mine open until the very last moment. I had set out to find answers to my childhood questions in the fathomless Universe, in the furthermost stars, and there you were, right next to me. You smiled, your arms gripped my shoulders but I didn't feel any pain, my love. Your embrace slackened, and those were my last moments of you, my last memories, my love; in losing you, I lost consciousness.

*

Hydra

I've been filling this notebook since my return to Hydra, sitting on the terrace, gazing out at the sea.

I regained consciousness in a hospital in Xi'an, five days after the accident. I was told that some fishermen had saved my life at the eleventh hour by pulling me out of the 4x4, which they'd seen plunge into the river. The car drifted; and Keira's body was never found. All that was three months ago. But not a day goes by without my thinking about her. And at night, when I close my eyes, she's always by my side. I've never experienced pain that comes even remotely close to the searing ache of missing her. My mother has given up worrying about things now; it's as if she's realised it was important not to add to the grief that had descended on our house. In the evenings, we eat supper together on the terrace where I'm writing at the moment. I write, because it's the only way I can bring Keira back to life. I write, because each time I describe her, there she is, like a faithful shadow. Never again will I smell the scent of her skin as she slept curled up next to me; never again will I hear her peals of laughter as she teased me; never again will I watch her digging the earth in search of treasure, or munching sweets as if they were about to be confiscated; but I've got a thousand memories of her and a thousand memories of us. All I have to do is close my eyes for her to reappear.

From time to time, Aunt Elena pays us a visit. But for the most part the house is empty, and the neighbours leave us alone. Occasionally, Kalibanos passes by the path that flanks our property; he claims it's to see his donkey. I don't know whether that's true or not. We sit on a bench together and look out to sea. He was desperately in love once too, a long time ago. It wasn't a river in China that took his wife away, but an illness; the pain we share is the same, and I can hear in his silences that he still loves her.

Walter is due to arrive from London tomorrow; he's called me every week since I got here. I just couldn't bring myself to go back. Walking down my street where Keira's footsteps still echo, pushing open the front door, the bedroom door where we both slept, would be more than I could bear. Keira was right when she was reminiscing over the death of her father: the tiniest details reawaken pain.

Keira was a dazzling woman, she was determined and stubborn too sometimes; but she had an appetite for life that knew no equal. She loved her career and respected those who worked with her. She had an unerring instinct and great humility. She was my friend, my lover, and the woman I worshipped. I've counted up the days we spent together and even if they were few in number, I know there were enough of them to fill the rest of my life. I just want the time to go quickly now.

When night comes, I look up at the sky and I see it differently. Perhaps a new star has been born in some faraway constellation. One day I'll set out again for the Atacama and I'll catch a glimpse of her through the lens of some gigantic telescope; wherever she might be in the vastness of the sky, I'll find her and I'll give that star her name.

I'll write you your list, my love, but later, because for that I need a lifetime.

Walter arrived on the midday ferry and I went down to the port to meet him. We fell into each other's arms and cried like a couple of kids. Aunt Elena was standing in her shop doorway and, when the cafe owner next door asked her what on earth was going on with the pair of us, she told him to go and mind his own customers, even though his terrace was empty.

Walter hadn't forgotten how to ride a donkey. He only fell off twice along the way, and the first time didn't count because it wasn't really his fault. When we got home, Mother welcomed him as if a second son were entering her house. She obviously thought I couldn't hear her when she whispered in his ear that he *could have said so earlier*. Walter asked her what she was talking about. She shrugged and whispered Keira's name.

Walter's always good value. Aunt Elena came to join us for dinner, and he made her laugh so much that even I ended up smiling a bit. That smile brought the life back to my mother's face too. She stood up, muttering about clearing the table and stroked my cheek as she passed me.

The next morning, and for the first time since my father had died, she spoke to me about bereavement. She hasn't finished drawing up her list yet either. And then she had this to say, and I'll never forget it: *It's terrible to lose someone you love, but even worse never to have met them.*

*

Night has fallen over Hydra. Aunt Elena is sleeping in the guest room, and mother has retired to her own room. I've made up a bed on the sofa for Walter. We're sipping a glass of ouzo out on the terrace.

He asks me how I'm doing and I tell him I'm coping as best I can. I'm alive. Walter says how happy he is to see me. He also tells me he's got something for me: a parcel that was delivered to the university, marked for my attention and sent from China.

It's a large cardboard box, posted from Lingbao, and it turns out to contain the belongings we left at the monastery: one of Keira's sweaters, a toothbrush, a few bits and bobs and two sets of photos.

"There were two disposable cameras," Walter says hesitantly. "I took the liberty of getting them developed for you. I don't know if I'm doing the right thing giving it all to you right now – perhaps it's a bit much?"

I opened the first photo wallet. Walter was sensitive enough to leave me alone and headed off to bed. I spent most of that night looking at those holiday souvenirs which Keira and I should have been flicking though on our return to London. They included the day we'd gone skinny-dipping in the Yellow River.

The next day, I took Walter down to the port. I'd brought the photos with me and, out on the cafe terrace, I showed them to him. I felt a need to tell him the story behind each one; the tale of Keira's and my experiences, and of everything we'd been through, from Beijing to the island of Narcondam.

"So you ended up finding the second fragment?"

"The third," I corrected him. "Keira's killers have one in their possession too."

"Although it might not have been them who caused the accident?"

I took the piece out of my pocket and showed it to him.

"What an extraordinary object," he murmured. "When you feel strong enough to return to London, you'll have to research it."

"No, that wouldn't do any good; there will always

be one missing, lying at the bottom of a river."

Walter picked up the photos again and looked at them carefully, one by one. He laid out two, side by side, on the table and asked me an odd question. Keira was swimming in both pictures, I recognised the spot. In one of the photographs, he pointed out, the shadow from the trees lining the river stretched to the right; in the other it lay to the left. In the first, Keira's face was normal; in the second, she had a long scar on her forehead. My heart stopped.

"You told me that the car had been swept away by the river and her body was never found, didn't you? Well, I don't want to arouse false hopes, but I think you ought to go back to China as soon as you can," Walter whispered.

I packed my suitcase the same morning. The ferry for Athens departed at midday and we caught it just in time. I managed to book myself onto a flight that left for Beijing in the late afternoon. So, I was headed for China and Walter was going back to London – our departure times were almost the same.

At the airport, he made me promise to call him as soon as I found out anything more.

As we were saying our goodbyes in the departure lounge, Walter started rummaging for his boarding card. He was going through his pockets and looking at me in a strange kind of way.

"Oh," he muttered, "I nearly forgot. A courier

dropped this off for you at the university. I seem to be playing at postman to the last here! Anyway, at least you'll have something to read on the flight, old chap."

He handed me a sealed envelope with my name on it and urged me to run if I didn't want to miss my plane.

*

Second Notebook

The captain had just switched off the fasten seat belts sign. The stewardess was pushing her trolley down the aisle and serving refreshments to those passengers in the first rows.

I took the envelope Walter had given me out of my pocket and opened it.

Dear Adrian,

I deeply regret the fact that we haven't really had an opportunity to get to know one another, just as I deeply regret the tragic events which you had to live through in China. I was lucky enough to become a little acquainted with Keira. She was an extraordinary woman and I know that your grief must be considerable. It was not fishermen who rescued you, but monks who were bathing in the river at the time your vehicle went crashing into it. You must be wondering how I know this. You will not remember, you were still unconscious, but I came to visit you in hospital. I took the necessary steps to ensure that you could be repatriated from China as soon as your health allowed. Why? Perhaps I feel in some way responsible for what happened to you. I am an old man who, like you, was once passionate about the sort of research that you two had undertaken. I helped Keira when I could, I convinced her not to give up, and I am guessing that without her you must want to abandon everything. I know that she would have wanted you to carry on. You must, Adrian. It would be so unfair if she had sacrificed her life for nothing. What you were in the process of discovering may well extend far beyond your own existence but I am convinced that it will, in the end, answer those questions you have been asking yourselves since the outset. During my many years of research, I came across another text which may not be unconnected with your quest. Few people have had access to it.

If I have not convinced you to change your mind, then please do not read the page I have appended to this letter. Familiarising yourself with its contents is not without risks. I am counting on your sense of honour, which I know to be impeccable. If, however, you wish to proceed, then please read it and I am sure that one day you will understand what it means.

Life has far more imagination than all of us put together. Sometimes it produces small miracles and everything is possible – you just have to believe with all your being.

I wish you good luck with your journey, Adrian.
With my endless devotion,
Ivory

I re-opened the wallet of photos to look once again at the print fuelling my crazy hope that Keira might still be alive.

Then I unfolded the second page of Ivory's letter.

"There is a legend which claims that a child in the womb knows the whole mystery of Creation, from the origins of the world to the end of time. When the child is born, a messenger passes over its cradle and puts his finger on its lips so that it will never reveal the secret that was entrusted to it – the secret of life. This finger, which erases the child's memory forever, leaves a mark. We all have this mark above our top lip, except for me. On the day I was born, the messenger forgot to pay me a visit, and I can remember everything."

As I folded Ivory's letter again, I recalled a conversation that I'd had with Keira one evening under the stars, on our drive to Cornwall, which we never reached in the end.

"Adrian, haven't you ever wondered where we come from? Haven't you ever dreamed of discovering whether life was the result of chance or the hand of God? What meaning can we give to our evolution? Are we just a stepping stone on the way to another civilisation?"

"And what about you, Keira, didn't you ever dream of finding out where the dawn begins?"

*

The London-bound flight from Athens was an hour

behind schedule. As the captain announced that take-off was imminent, a mobile phone rang. The stewardess had a word with the passenger sitting in first class who took the call, but he promised to be quick about it.

"How did he react when he saw the photos?"

"How would you have reacted in his place?"

"Did you give him my letter?"

"Yes, he should be reading it right now."

"From which I'll conclude that he's set off again. Thank you, Walter, you've done an excellent job."

"My pleasure, Ivory, it's a privilege working with you."

*

The Aegean Sea disappeared from view. In ten hours' time, I would be touching down in China.

*

Coming next:

The First Night

Thank you to

Pauline.
Louis.

Susanna Lea and Antoine Audouard.

Emmanuelle Hardouin.
Raymond, Daniele and Lorraine Levy.

Pauline Normand, Marie-Ève Provost.

Kim McArthur, Devon Pool, Kendra Martin, Ann Ledden, and the whole team at McArthur & Company.

Leonard Anthony, Romain Ruetsch, Danielle Melaconian, Katrin Hodapp, Marion Millet, Marie Garnero, Mark Kessler, Laura Mamelok, Lauren Wendelken, Kerry Glencorse.

Nicole Lattès, Leonello Brandolini, Antoine Caro, Elisabeth Villeneuve, Elisabeth Franck, Arie Sberro, Sylvie Bardeau, Tine Gerber, Lydie Leroy, Joël Renaudat, and the whole team at Editions Robert Laffont.

Brigitte and Sarah Forissier.
Kamel, Carmen Varela.
Frédéric Lenoir, whose *Petit traité d'histoire des religions* [*Little Treaty on the History of Religion*] (Plon) inspired Ivory's argument on pages 116–118.